Praise for *Still True*

"It's a rare experience to feel gratitude for a book's pleasures on nearly every page. But Maggie Ginsberg has written that book. I could stay in this story for years."—Luis Alberto Urrea, Pulitzer Prize finalist and best-selling author of *The Devil's Highway* and *The House of Broken Angels*

"What we assume about the past is that it is . . . past . . . and will stay past, that we have outlived, outlasted, or even outrun our former selves to become people we are satisfied, if not gratified, to be. Maggie Ginsberg's deeply felt and vivid new novel *Still True* underlines that home truth. Even as each of its characters curates a careful present, the shadows of the past creep up to confront them. When those realities collide, the result is troubling, affecting, and deeply true."—Jacquelyn Mitchard, author *The Deep End of the Ocean*

"*Still True* feels as intimate as eavesdropping, with characters so well drawn and so believable there is a sense that they are in the room with you as you read about their sometimes turbulent, sometimes mild lives. Ginsberg's prose is dreamy and rhapsodic and even as her characters make dreadful mistakes, she always treats them with profound decency and empathy. A wonderful, warm book about friendship, secrets, trauma, and love."—Nickolas Butler, author of *Shotgun Lovesongs* and *Little Faith*

"A wise and profound exploration of intimacy and privacy, marriage and family. In this story about a web of long-held secrets coming dangerously close to the surface, the novel asks how it might be possible to love someone fiercely but misunderstand them fundamentally. Maggie Ginsberg describes the complexity of human relationships with such honesty and compassion, it's hard not to recognize your own private truths in these pages. *Still True* is tender, moving, and so gorgeously written."—Hanna Halperin, author of *Something Wild*

"In *Still True*, Maggie Ginsberg explores not only the physical distances that separate her characters but also the charged emotional spaces between truth and lies, the present and the past, right and wrong. Not since Kent Haruf have I read an author so skilled at capturing the nuance and complexity of small-town life with empathy and respect."—Christina Clancy, author of *Shoulder Season* and *The Second Home*

"Big secrets, big mistakes, and an endearing collection of big, messy hearts fuel the wonder that is Maggie Ginsberg's *Still True.* This engrossing and emotional debut novel somehow manages to capture both the sobering grittiness and magical dreaminess of life, love, and long-told lies unfolding in a small pocket of rural Wisconsin." —Dean Bakopoulos, author of *Summerlong*

"*Still True* strikes a perfect balance: full of humane understanding of its characters' back-burnered shame and secrets, and rigorous honesty about the price. As soon as I dropped into the intimate, inevitably flawed small town of this novel, I wasn't going anywhere until it was done."—Michelle Wildgen, author of *You're Not You* and *Bread and Butter*

"Absorbing, lyrical, and revelatory! Maggie Ginsberg's astonishing debut is a deeply satisfying investigation of marriage, motherhood, and addiction. What secrets are justified? And what compromises? What do we keep from each other, and how much of ourselves do we really owe the people who love us? Can we have true intimacy while maintaining our independence? These flawed but captivating characters haven't left me since I finished reading this knockout of a novel, nor have I stopped asking myself: What would I do if their choices were mine to make? Book clubs, get ready!"—Susan Henderson, author of *The Flicker of Old Dreams*

"A generous ode to humanity's indefatigable longing for understanding, forgiveness, and love. Maggie Ginsberg's words sparkle on pages filled with hopeful characters and a story you won't soon forget."—Ann Garvin, *USA Today* best-selling author of *I Thought You Said This Would Work*

"A rich and unflinching study of the ways in which trauma and secrets can shape a person's life. The novel weaves together the narratives of a woman who long ago abandoned her young son, her husband with whom she shares a life but protects from her secrets, an alcoholic mother whose choices lead to near-fatal consequences, and the child who connects them all in a charged story of loss, grief, and renewal. This gorgeously written novel examines the darkest aspects of human relationships and offers an emotionally redeeming ending that suggests that we can overcome our worst in order to celebrate our best."—Chris Cander, author of *A Gracious Neighbor*

"An intricate, emotional exploration of the blessings and burdens of family bonds, and the ways in which the lies we can't let go of influence those we love the most. Full of original and multifaceted characters, this heartfelt story will captivate readers and encourage them to consider what it is that we owe our children, our spouses, and ourselves. A provocative and satisfying read that lingers long after the last page is turned."—Lynda Cohen Loigman, author of *The Two-Family House* and *The Wartime Sisters*

"Ginsberg has crafted a gripping, authentic portrait of small-town life, inhabited by meticulously drawn characters whose lives intersect in unexpected ways. In this memorable debut novel, Ginsberg does for the rural Midwest what Richard Russo did for New England in his Pulitzer Prize–winning *Empire Falls*. Graceful prose and a well-paced plot will draw readers into this heartrending, realistic tale of the many faces of love and redemption."—Susan Gloss, best-selling author of *Vintage* and *The Curiosities*

"A richly woven, big-hearted tapestry of characters so intensely alive they'll haunt you long after the last page is turned. Rendered in clear-eyed and heartbreakingly beautiful prose, it's a story about what makes us human and how we take care of each other, and serves as a testament to the power of love, grace, and family, in all its forms." —Erin Celello, author of *Miracle Beach* and *Learning to Stay*

"Reminds me of Robinson's *Gilead* for today's generation. *Still True* is a surprisingly plotted, deeply character-driven novel about the beautiful hope and struggle to heal what some think impossible. Beautiful writing. Flawed and wise and lovable characters. What a potent debut!"—Andrew J. Graff, author of *Raft of Stars*

Still True

Maggie Ginsberg

THE UNIVERSITY OF WISCONSIN PRESS

The University of Wisconsin Press
728 State Street, Suite 443
Madison, Wisconsin 53706
uwpress.wisc.edu

Gray's Inn House, 127 Clerkenwell Road
London EC1R 5DB, United Kingdom
eurospanbookstore.com

Printed in the United States of America
This book may be available in a digital edition.

Library of Congress Cataloging-in-Publication Data

Names: Ginsberg, Maggie, author.
Title: Still true / Maggie Ginsberg.
Description: Madison, Wisconsin : The University of Wisconsin Press, [2022]
Identifiers: LCCN 2021060199 | ISBN 9780299339340 (paperback)
Subjects: LCGFT: Fiction. | Novels.
Classification: LCC PS3607.I4586 S75 2022 | DDC 813/.6—dc23/eng/20220218
LC record available at https://lccn.loc.gov/2021060199

For

Mom and Dad, who read every draft.

For

Grace and Eva, always. Gib and Ruby too.

And for

Q, who told me so.

You hurt me long before you knew me
And I did the same thing to you
—Michael Perry, "Newfangled Cowboy Way"

Still True

Chapter 1

Lib Hanson could have made the walk to her husband's house by feel and sound alone, her eyes squeezed tight against the Wisconsin dusk. Three decades spent wearing a path between their separate homes made it all seem a part of her: The cool, slim trails of wet grass across her bare ankles as she cut across her yard. The dip of the ditch and the slipping pea gravel edging the county road. The chemical crunch of city-sprayed thistles already forcing themselves up through the cracked asphalt at the plastics factory where they'd worked for ages, until its sudden closing two years back. The way the air shifted, ever so subtly, once she hit town proper.

Jack preferred driving the two-mile stretch between their houses, but Lib almost always walked, regardless of weather. On rare occasions, they walked together. She'd asked Jack once if he could feel that change in climate on the trek between their houses, rising now like bated breath, cleaving her nightgown to her calves and thighs, her skin still sticky from the fear triggered by tonight's surprise visitor. *No*, Jack had answered. *I think that's something you made up in that glorious mind of yours.* Jack always told the truth, no matter if it stung.

Poisonous anxiety surged through her as she darted past the rows of warehouses at the edge of Anthem and the newer, jumbo cookie-cutter houses tacked onto this end of town like an afterthought, down to where the green ash and white oaks hovered over the older, more reasonably sized homes, tucked closer together. Her guard had been down. She hadn't seen it coming. But now she felt the recognition sink in sharp and deep, like a bone ache. As if the cancer she'd never had had come back.

Two hours earlier, she'd been in the back garden getting after the ruined tomatoes. No matter how she coaxed, those tomatoes did what they wanted, creating a gangly, sprawling, bloody mess. Year after year, the alleged annuals returned and insisted on their boneless tantrums, breaking free from their protective cages and hurling themselves, vine and fruit, to rot in the dirt. This spring, fed up, she'd winnowed them down to just two starter plants—one sandwich a day, the occasional dinner salad for Jack—but last year's stragglers had spread, and now they pocked the tidy garden anyway. She'd leaned back on her boot heels, considering. It was no longer in her to force them into compliance, and maybe that was the problem. Her days of wrestling things into place were over.

When the slow crunch of tires on gravel broke through her reverie, she couldn't quite place the sound. First she thought it must be the mail carrier bringing a package to the house that was too big for the mailbox at the end of the long, curved driveway. But her favorite old postman had retired last year, and these new kids never bothered. Anyway, it was practically supper time, the mail long done.

She pushed the rope of her silver braid over her shoulder and listened, caught a flash of a firefly in the shrub rose thicket on the periphery. A child on a bicycle wheeling by on the stretch of county road that bordered the sloped, eastern edge of her property. The faint smell of charcoal and grass clippings, the drone of a mower in the distance, the steady hum of the air-conditioning unit.

She brushed the dirt from her shins and rounded the back corner of the house, eyed where her driveway met the front porch. Saw the car first—a nondescript sedan—before she saw the man climbing the steps. Instinctively, she froze behind the ancient lilac. He could not see her, unless he knew just where to look.

He was shaggy-haired, clad in a long-sleeved T-shirt and faded jeans—*in this heat!* She eyed the forward slump to his shoulders as he faced her front door. There was something tweaked about the way he stood, as if his top half was clicked into place just slightly off from his hip sockets. She wasn't a good judge of age these days—they all looked like kids to her—but she guessed he was about forty, and, although she couldn't make out the details of his face, even at this distance she could feel his grimace. Steam rose in curls off the paper cup of coffee he held, and his other hand was raised as if to knock—but it didn't move, as though whatever had paralyzed her had gotten him too. He stood staring at her front door. Too hesitant to be a traveling salesman, too casual to be someone needing help.

She knew she should call out a greeting. Her resistance seemed more than the simple desire to avoid small talk with a stranger. Something older. Just as his knuckles grazed the door, his fist spread instead into a splayed, flat hand. He pressed it there for what felt like a full minute, an almost tender palming of the door at eye level. What was he doing?

Silly old girl, she thought, in Jack's motor-oil-and-molasses voice. *No such thing as a stranger when a man needs help.* She tucked her head into her shoulder to wipe the sweat from her lips and was about to take a tentative step forward when the man stepped back and pitched the coffee cup at her door, where it exploded in a dark spray. He hopped down the steps and strode to his car. Slammed the door, fired the engine, and swung the vehicle around, spinning out in a cloud of choking dirt.

Lib held her breath until he disappeared around the gravel elbow of her driveway, skidding down the hill and out onto the road. *Toward town then*, she thought, after she could no longer hear the angry squall of his motor. She waited there beside the lilacs a long time to come back into her body, not unlike she used to when things got bad. There was something in the way he'd thrown the cup. As if she were expected to pick it up. As a baby might, with his mother.

The awareness was already starting to tug at her: his familiar hips, his age, his fury.

She started again toward the house, slower this time, hesitant, keeping her head down as she shuffled through the ryegrass and clover she left long for the honeybees, dodging the ghosts that had begun to drift across her mind. She imagined Jack, instead: his blue eyes squeezing into a smile behind the pottery coffee mug he favored; the fine gray hairs that had begun to sprout along his freckled shoulders; the particular gold the maples had blazed twenty-eight years ago to match their rings on their wedding day. When the worn soles of her work boots hit the gravel marking the edge of the driveway, she let her gaze drift up the porch steps. She was hoping that she'd made the visitor up.

But it was all still there. Blood-rust coffee stained her screen door, pooled in the cracks of her porch planks. The crushed paper cup trembled in the evening breeze.

She sprang into action, hosing the coffee from the chipped blue door, from the faded brown planks. The prairie coughed up a wet wind, spraying seeds, blowing the porch swing, tickling the dampness at her hairline. Stooping to gulp from the cold, clean stream of water flowing from the hose, she braced as a fresh fear walloped her: if her visitor was who she thought he was, it was all over.

She wheeled off the spigot, wound the hose away, and went inside to scrub the dirt from the whorls of her fingerprints. Fixed a buttered turkey sandwich she left untouched, reheated a bowl of soup she forgot in the microwave. Put on her nightgown, went through her usual routine, but triple-checked the locks.

It was too early for sleep, but she tried anyway. Shut the blinds against the summer suppertime sky, climbed into bed, and pinched her eyes closed. Pressed her hands to her face, her breasts, her belly, curled her body into a fist.

But it was useless. And there was only one other thing she could think to do.

She rose, went back downstairs. Pulled her barn coat over her nightgown, slipped on her sandals, and set out for Jack's.

Maybe it's not him, she was still thinking, even now, as she turned into Jack's sweet little tree-lined neighborhood, spied his truck parked in the street next to the neighbor's crabapple. *Maybe none of this is true.*

Her husband's house clicked into focus. It sat practically atop the narrow sidewalk, separated only by a two-foot patch of tamped-down crabgrass and patchy fescue in what passed for his front yard. Unlike her own gravel driveway—a spindly outstretched limb that held the rest of the world at arm's length—Jack's was a patch of dirt just big enough for his pickup, which he rarely parked there anyway so as not to block the entrance to the garage. That garage was nearly bigger than the house, and fittingly so—he spent most of his time there, fixing everything on God's green earth and entertaining visitors. Its wooden doors were flung open as usual now but she saw no sign of him. The siding on both the house and garage was the color of cool milk, the shutters and trim painted golden honey. Lib's own private promised land.

Back when Lib and Jack first collided—in 1984, five years after she'd escaped back home here to Anthem to reclaim the farm after Mama's death—she'd suffered a relentless, disorienting infatuation. It wasn't just the swagger or the way he looked, strong-jawed and stone-eyed; it was his surprisingly gentle hand. She felt safe with him but also thrilled, two things she'd never felt with any man before, let alone the same one. For months, whenever Jack spoke to her, her head felt aflame. A slowly spreading tingle, as if he'd poured gasoline atop her hair and let it soak its way down, then lit a match with every grin. As he overexplained the mechanics of some clock or radio or engine, or belly-laughed his way through a story only he found funny, she placed a hand on top of her head to see if she could feel the heat from the outside. She always could.

Lib stood now on Jack's stoop, just as she had half the days of her life, sweating beneath the barn coat, feeling shakier than a fifty-eight-year-old woman should. She took a final fortifying glance through the open garage door at her favorite of all his possessions—the triangular truing stand clamped to his workbench. One of Jack's many trades was repairing bicycles for the neighborhood kids and their weekend warrior dads. And their suddenly divorced moms hoping to bike their bodies back into the saddle of new marriages—maybe even with Jack. He had always, as long as Lib had known him, reeked of some pheromone that clotted women to him. They'd sniff it out, especially those whose senses had grown sharp from years of marital dullness. Anthem was full of women wasting themselves.

Lib slipped through the screen door.

"Well, hullo there," she heard him say from the kitchen, sensing her the way he always could. She padded across the tiny living room to find him standing at the stove, stirring what smelled like one of his tangy tomato sauces. His pale eyes flashed at the sight of her, his etch-a-sketch whiskers more gray now than black, complementing her own vivid silver hair and the shadows cast by her carved cheekbones. This was how she had first understood she was beautiful—really understood it, years ago: these nanosecond flashes like heat lightning from Jack, too quick to be manufactured. Not that he could have faked anything if he tried. She trusted him beyond measure.

Jack reached up to grab a second plate from the shelf, his gold wedding band winking in the overhead fan light. She'd forgotten her own ring on the kitchen sill, the realization chilling her the way it wouldn't have on any other night. If he clocked the barn coat in summer or the nightgown beneath it, or thought either odd, he didn't say. She settled into her seat at his table, slipped free of her sandals and gripped the chair rung with her toes, pressed her knees up until the table's edge bit. Prayed that he couldn't see right through her, something she hadn't worried about in decades.

From the pocket of her barn coat she produced tonight's offering: a small bowl she'd spied at the flea market last weekend, a lifetime ago When she'd first spotted the swirl of glassy blue and pale pink, it had instantly transported her to one of their favorite Door County vacations, one they often returned to in laughter, or whispers, in bed. Jack in the kitchen of a rented vacation house, Lib sitting at the table, naked beneath a thin, pilled bedspread woven with pastel swirls of pink and blue, her cheeks sore from smiling.

Jack palmed the bowl, regarded it for a moment, then retrieved a bag of sugar. Gently poured the sweet silken sand into the bowl. "For the grapefruit," he said, as if he'd been waiting for this very thing, his voice the low gravelly relief of a lawnmower finally cranking to life. It was one of her favorite things about him, his voice. And that he saw usefulness in every beautiful object. He came around the table to kiss the top of her head, and she stiffened, just a little. But he didn't seem to notice, straightening and shuffling back to the stove. She stared hard at his back as he worked, the folds of his undershirt half-tucked into his fading Levi's. Thought, again, about the man on the porch.

Her porch. The one she'd paid for with her sweat and blood and tears after returning to Anthem, and with a darker currency before. She'd torn the old porch off, gutted the family house with her dead dad's sledgehammer. Pried up splintered boards and broke through crumbling plaster, demolished walls and flooring, wrestled reluctant appliances from their stubborn places. Battled with her childhood home for years until it relented, until it was unrecognizable, until it was hers and hers alone. Now it was like God himself had looked down at the life she'd reclaimed and smirked, given the whole thing a dismissive flick.

It had to be him—the baby she'd left with his dad four decades ago. Just one part of an entire life she'd deliberately kept from Jack. A reunion-in-the-making so old she'd nearly forgotten to dread its coming. And there would be no explaining any of this to Jack, the second husband who believed he was the first.

Now Jack slid a plate in front of her, settled in across the table.

"You don't seem like you ate yet," he said, taking a bite, as usual, without waiting for her. If there was more to the question, she was in no state to tell. Usually Jack said exactly what he meant, and he expected the same in return. He was a kind and generous man, but the responsibility was always yours—to eat if you were hungry, to say so if you felt some kind of way. His goodness seemed to sit with them in the room, a third presence at the table. Instead of its usual comfort, tonight it felt like an accusation. All that was wrong about her sitting next to all that was right about him.

"I had a big lunch," she lied. She had intended to eat some leftovers for lunch but hadn't gotten to them, on account of the tomatoes. Then the soup-and-sandwich supper she'd killed fifteen minutes making but ultimately couldn't stomach. Now, she dug in, in spite of her lack of appetite, filling her mouth with pasta, a perfectly reasonable excuse to not talk.

"You look dewy and pink," he said, smiling in a way that still slicked her between the legs without so much as a touch. "Been out in the garden?"

"Tomatoes again," she said, feeling herself unclench, just a little. "You?"

"Went by Lyle's wake."

"Oh." She set down her fork, feeling bad—not that she'd missed it but that she hadn't had the courtesy to ask, that she'd forgotten all about it in the midst of her own troubles. She hadn't known Lyle well, but Jack had coffee with him at least twice a week, and most folks in Anthem showed up to funerals for far less. "I'm sorry," she said.

"S'okay." Jack shrugged, and she knew he meant it. He had always spoken frankly of death, as if it was perfectly natural. Which of course it was, although it never had been in Lib's life. First Dad, pinned beneath the tractor. Then Mom, pickled in brandy and bitterness. Then the two men she'd wished death upon while God ignored her, up until the moment he decided to take her best friend, Carolina, instead, killing her with cancer and stealing whatever remained of Lib's faith in one fell swoop. Time had yet to do its alleged healing. Death was something she would never approach with Jack's matter-of-factness. Ten years ago she'd vowed Carolina's funeral would be her last, and so far it had been. Jack knew most of this. He let her be.

"Oh God," Jack suddenly said. "Oh God, at Lyle's wake . . ." He pressed a cloth napkin to his mouth. And as he began to silently tremble, his eyes gone pink and watery, she might have thought he was crying or even choking if she didn't know him better. She felt her own lips tugging into a smile, despite everything. Jack delighted in humanity while she found most people profoundly annoying. Except him, most of the time. She waited, forking a single penne noodle into her mouth, chewing as he struggled.

"Okay, okay," he said, huffing out a breath, dabbing at his eyes with the napkin, squaring his shoulders. "You know how I told you Clarence's kid has been at the village board meetings accusing the hardware store of causing a rat problem at the grocery but nobody else has seen these alleged rats as of yet?"

Lib nodded, though she didn't remember, not really.

"Well, long story short . . . long story short . . ." And then he was wheezing again, doubled over and clutching that napkin in silent laughter.

Lib pieced together the story, more or less, between Jack's fits—something having to do with a hidden camera and a stand-in ferret to stage a crime scene, a ruse ultimately revealed at the wake by a veterinary student dating the hardware store proprietor's son. She snorted as she listened, not at the story itself but because she delighted in her husband's easy and genuine glee, the warmth his presence created in this tiny house. Everything about this place was just so *him*, a fact that was every bit as sacred to her as her own house and the way she felt about it.

On another night she would have joined him in letting loose that laughter that fed off itself so that by the time they returned to their senses, they could no longer remember what had gotten them going in the first place. But now she focused on forcing only the necessary responses that would keep her hidden in plain sight, needing him so profoundly that he'd have rejected her if he'd known how much. Because as much as he loved people—and her especially—neediness made him uncomfortable. He celebrated independence, prized freedom. So did she. But oh how she ached in this moment to unburden all she could never confess to the one person left on this earth who could possibly make her feel better. She was in, as Jack would say, a genuine pickle.

Eventually, he recovered. They finished the rest of the meal in companionable silence, then washed and dried the dishes side by side. When the last pot was wiped dry and hung on its hook, Jack slid a hand from Lib's hip up her back and tugged the elastic band from the end of her braid. She let her eyes close as he fingered the silver strands free, expertly untangling the mane that had grown long and thick past her shoulders years ago.

In his sparse bedroom, they pushed the discarded undershirts and folded newspapers aside and made a place for themselves between the love-softened sheets. But as she took him inside her, the two uninvited men came along: the hired farmhand who had robbed her of whatever had remained of her childhood; then the first husband, who had repulsed her no matter how desperately she tried. Both men remained a secret to Jack, and goddamn it if she wasn't going to keep it that way. Besides, if she told Jack the truth after all this time, he'd never forgive her—not just because of what it revealed but because she'd lied. For Jack, there was no worse crime.

There, moving beneath him, she made a decision: whatever it took, she'd keep this third invader from him too. This baby that had fed off her from the inside, suckled her dry from the outside, made her feel like an utterly failed woman for the way she couldn't naturally connect with the poor creature, couldn't see him for what he was, a simple baby, a human being, instead of a thing that had been done to her, yet another choice that had been taken away. Even at seventeen and already a promised wife, she'd known she wasn't like other women. That something was broken in her, or missing completely. Still, she'd come so far, and it had been nobody's business, not even Jack's. It still wasn't.

She focused fiercely on her husband, this man she loved, this man she protected by protecting herself, this man who could always steady her. Visualized her oldest trick—the bicycle truing stand in the garage—and soon they were back in that rhythm won by decades of practiced trust.

Afterward, finally drifting off, she remembered something she used to say to Carolina, the only person who knew about parts of her old life and the one who'd helped her find her way into this new one. Several times over the years, Lib had bragged to Carolina that she didn't need Jack, certainly not to feel whole. But even as she'd said it, she'd known that when she started to wobble, only Jack could steady her. Just like the truing stand with a bicycle wheel, his subtle adjustments—a brush of his fingertips across her temple, a squeeze of his thumb against her knee—had a powerful stabilizing effect. So that, all those mornings, by the time she made her way back to her own house in the creeping dawn, her shimmy, if it was still there at all, was imperceptible to the naked eye.

Chapter 2

Lib was gone when Jack woke, but her scent was still there. He rolled into her pillow, still warm, breathed in lavender and dirt. Might've left twenty minutes ago, he calculated. Sometimes she was still around when he woke, which was fine. If she wasn't, well, that was all right too. Either way, lying there in the morning, he typically couldn't think of a thing missing from his life. Today, however, something felt a little off.

He hugged her pillow to him, gathered his bearings in pieces. He'd startled awake once during the night to the cat's angry meow at the screen door, let in a wired and haughty Tinker. The cat had retreated to the couch to lick off the night's adventure while Jack slipped back into bed, watched Lib sleep. Her back was to him, a tangle of silver on the pillow. One tanned-hide forearm, smooth and freckled, draped over her forehead. That rise of her rump beneath the soft faded sheet, looking like a harvest moon too full and lazy to haul itself up into the sky. He didn't remember fading out again.

Now he had to piss something fierce. His bladder woke him earlier and earlier these days. He swung his legs around and planted his bare feet on the smooth wooden floor. Slightly warm, temp probably low sixties already. Definitely humid. He'd put a small rug on Lib's side of the bed years ago, but not his. He liked to know first thing what the day might bring.

Jack pressed through an ache in his thighs up to standing. Put a hand on his back and arched out a tweak this way, a creak the other. He'd probably twisted it funny hauling Tim's mower into the truck. Everything hurt now. By midday he'd feel smoother and lighter, better greased. But these first few hours he felt all sixty-three of his years like a hangover.

He shuffled through the bedroom doorway, pivoted into the tiny bathroom, and set to draining himself. His mood started to lift in direct proportion to the lightening of his load. Humans really were pretty simple machines when it came down to it, thank Christ.

In these years since they'd lost their jobs at the plant—not nearly the hardship for them that it had been for so many others—whenever Lib left early, the first part of the day was reserved for unscheduled puttering. Go out to the garage, grease a chain, clamp a corner, glue a sole. If it got too quiet, he'd turn on the public radio station for company or put Ronnie Milsap on the tape deck until someone brought him a real problem. Few things satisfied him more than figuring out how a broken thing worked and then making it right again. Late morning, he might see what was going on at the café. Lyle wouldn't be there, of course. He supposed he'd have to get used to that.

He felt a pang, then chuckled. As much as he adored Lib, there were things he just couldn't get from her as much as he'd like. Banter for banter's sake and, funny as she was, a much lower bar for humor. She'd barely tolerated his hilarious retelling of the hardware store drama last night, failing to grasp how much Lyle would have appreciated such a spectacle at his own funeral. Lib avoided life's darker parts, but Jack, like Lyle, embraced absurdity to deal. Sometimes Lib found that dismissive, as was her right. He didn't need her to be different. But there would now be a Lyle-shaped hole in his life, no doubt about it.

A fat purple light pushed itself into the house, and he crossed the living room in three and a half steps to inspect the sky through the screen door. In the summertime he left the heavier inner door wide open to catch the breeze and to keep an ear out for Tinker. This morning the horizon glowed an unnatural hot rose, the trees poking through it like thorns. The weather was about to get weird. The charged air lifted the hair on his arms and sparked a shiver.

But when he stepped out onto the front stoop, he found it already wet from rain. Hot puddles breathed up from the sidewalk. A red-winged blackbird flitted in the paint bucket he kept as a rain gauge, flinging overflow onto the sopping grass. A storm had indeed come through, and quick. How had he slept through it?

"Tireder than I thought," he said to Tinker, then frowned. Had Lib made it home this morning before the storm got her? He went back in to start the coffee—though she usually started it for him on mornings she left before he woke, a thought he pushed away when he spotted the sugar bowl she'd brought him and remembered the sweet business that had followed. Aha! That's why he was extra tired and a little sore this morning—not Tim's motor, Lib's. Then he glimpsed her sandals peeking out from beneath the table. Odd she'd left them, but she did like to go barefoot sometimes—not typically on the long walk home, though. He tried not to add the sandals and coffee to the mental scorecard he seemed to be brewing against his will. No need to make trouble where there wasn't any, and no fair to put his off-ness on her. He was just feeling sad about Lyle. He slipped on his own shed shoes, pulled his summer cap from the hook. Poured coffee into his thermos, tucked the wooden block of knives under his arm, and left the house for the garage, sidestepping puddles.

His workshop garage was an immaculately maintained cement-floor shed bigger than his house, with three cottage windows running neatly along the side overlooking his fenced backyard. Its double doors almost always hung open, perpetually agape at the bounty inside: tools, ladders, jugs, oil cans, five-gallon buckets, license plates, radios, bicycles, wagons, wheelbarrows, garden spades, tent poles, spark plugs, you name it.

He propped himself on his stool and set to sharpening each knife blade, thinking of Lib's cheekbones. Her physicality. How pleasing it was to him and how it only seemed to improve as they aged together. The smooth pink of her earlobe against his roughened palm. The feathered lines that crinkled out when she smiled. The way she was always pushing on her own body as if she were made of clay and needed to press herself back into place now and again.

He especially loved that impossibly soft circle on the inside of her left thigh that fit his thumb perfectly, a space just below the warm cleft of her. That spot had no logical reason to be softer than the rest of her skin, but it was, and he fell asleep quicker when he slid his hand right there and settled. Had it not brought its usual comfort last night?

Jack peered at his reflection in the butcher knife, plucked a stray bit of lint from his stubbled chin. He wiped each side of the blade against his jeans and slid it back into place in the block. He was about to pull out another when a voice in the doorway startled him.

"Sir, I got a flat," said a kid, skipping the greeting.

Jack squinted at the slight boy pushing a bicycle through his open garage door, rain dripping from his helmet, fog creeping into his glasses. He was elementary-school aged, and appeared to be alone. Before Jack could speak, the kid said, "Your garage has all kinds of tools," and there was something about the kid's straightforward practicality that Jack liked, or at least respected.

"Boy, did you get caught in that storm? And what are you doing out riding so early? School hasn't started yet this year, has it?" Jack glanced at his bare wrist, where he'd forgotten to strap on his watch. Looked beyond the kid to check the trees. The late summer cicadas had died off, but the honey locust trees, always the first to go, had not yet turned their blazing yellow.

"I actually got the flat last night, but Dad said it would be rude to bother you so late."

Jack didn't reply. Although the kid was a stranger to him, this sort of request was not. Jack's place sat right in the middle of Anthem, so anyone who needed him for anything could find him straightaway. In addition to the odd jobs he picked up since the plant closed, Jack had made an informal business out of having just the right thing at just the right time. Folks borrowed his tools and equipment or dropped off fix-it projects. They left cash in his mailbox or bartered pay: hot baked bread, jarred preserves, spare parts. With the mortgage on the little house paid off long ago, he was managing. He even preferred this new life, to be honest. Point was, whatever you were looking for was likely here. No wonder the kid had come knocking, except he seemed a bit young for a solo task like this. How far had he walked his bike to get here? Did his parents really know where he was?

"I'm supposed to say sorry I woke you," the kid said.

"You didn't," said Jack.

"I know," said the kid.

Jack chuckled. "What's your name?"

"Charlie," he answered, pushing forward the bike again, with some effort. It was a sweet little blue-and-silver BMX, bowing slightly on its front wheel. "You think you got a tire in here for this bike? Google says a twenty-incher."

"Well, Charlie, as much as I appreciate the forethought of your research, the last thing you need is a new tire," said Jack, admiring the practical kickstand the boy had apparently added and the dirt caked to the bike's frame. The boy's face was similarly dusted with dirt—no, freckles, he realized, taking his measure. "Most anything in the world can be fixed 'stead of replaced. How big's your hurry?"

Charlie shrugged. "I guess I'm not really going anywhere specific," he said, the hint of a dimple denting one cheek, a fat raindrop clinging to his pointy chin. He hooked a finger inside his glasses and wiped the fog from each side with a practiced gesture, then swiped at his nose. "Just don't wanna be stuck," he sniffed.

"I hear that," said Jack, rising to the old dresser he'd mounted on castors, fashioning a mobile set of junk drawers. He pulled the top one open and dug around until he found the patch kit, pleased that the glue was still soft. He worked slower than he usually would have, conscious of Charlie's eyes tracking his every move. Jack pried the tire off, pulled the innertube loose, and overinflated it, listening for the telltale hiss. Once he found the hole, he scuffed the rubber around it smooth with a worn square of sandpaper, wiped the surface with alcohol, and carefully, expertly applied the glue before sliding the patch on.

"The waiting is the hardest part," said Jack, eyeing Charlie again. He was a slight boy, but sturdy, sinewy, as if he took in just enough food to keep his body running. Jack's own stomach grumbled, and that underlying current of anxiety rippled through again, too. He hadn't had any of his coffee yet. He didn't normally care one way or another for kids—

he'd never had any himself, and his sister's all seemed unnecessarily loud—but there was something about this boy that stuck to the ribs.

"Gotta let it cure, or the patch won't hold," he said, mentally scanning the contents of his refrigerator; unless he wanted penne for breakfast, he'd need to go to the café. The coffee was better there, too. It didn't seem right to leave the boy here alone, nor to send him away on foot. He still wasn't convinced the boy's parents knew their child's whereabouts—just what was Jack expected to do here?

"How long did you tell your folks you'd be gone? Do you happen to be hungry?"

Charlie looked over his shoulder out toward the street, his tongue poking just slightly at the corner of his lips, running some sort of math in his head. Then he turned back to look at Jack.

"I guess I am," Charlie finally said, ignoring, Jack noted with growing unease, the first part of the question.

~

Claire Taylor watched the silver haze of yet another hangover drift in and settle, pinning her to the mattress. Or maybe it was actual smoke, maybe Dan had tried and failed to light a damp pile of wood again—but no, she reminded herself, there was no fire. No cheerily painted ceramic wood stove in the master bedroom anymore. No tray ceiling set high above her allowing extra space to breathe; just your standard cap eight feet above her bearing down atop four walls, sealed with eggshell white bleeding into beige. Before they'd bought this new house last month, Claire had had no idea the world held so many shades of white.

Her skull felt packed with gauze, and her lips prickled. She needed balm, badly. A tissue to clear last night from her nose, and the lukewarm cup of water with lemon she drank on mornings she couldn't stomach coffee. Just barely out of reach, on her nightstand, she knew, was the Kleenex box; a small black-and-white tube of Chapstick rolling in the otherwise empty drawer below it. Half of yesterday's lemon waiting on the cutting board in the kitchen, the stainless steel squeezer beside it. But from where she lay, tucked straight and still like a harvested fish between the matted-down feather bed and the ocean-blue duvet, even this short list of simple tasks felt impossible.

"Are you sick?" asked Dan, from his side of the bed. She knew he hadn't looked away from his phone to pose the question.

"I think so," she said, the lie slipping quickly and easily from between her chapped lips. She was relieved for the excuse. She wasn't entirely sure it wasn't true anyway. She didn't know what she was these days.

"Charlie really loves that bike, huh?" he mused, and Claire remembered: she'd been awake already once this morning. She craned her neck to check the clock, expecting to see that a significant amount of time had passed—but no, it had only been fifteen minutes ago. Charlie had come in to ask if it was okay to find that fix-it guy for help with his flat tire yet, and Dan had of course said all the right things that always seemed to take longer to come to her: Stay off the sidewalks, and wear your helmet. Knock politely and apologize right away, let him know we're new. If he can't help, ask if has any recommendations in town. Do not, under any circumstances whatsoever, go inside his house.

But anytime now Dan would be headed in to his new job at the school district's administrative office, and it occurred to her she had no idea where her son was or who he was with. *Well, officers, yes, technically the man was a stranger to us, but Charlie said everybody knew him,* she imagined saying. *We did make him wear a helmet.*

"Hopefully he knows enough to come straight back after it's fixed," she said. Then, as if to prove she was operating on all cylinders, "How do you feel about red for this room? I know it's kind of bold, but hear me—"

Dan suddenly sprang from bed, yanked his phone from the charging cord, and scurried toward the bathroom, his shoulder bumping into the doorjamb as he made the corner. The latch clicked shut, and the fan began to whir.

"I think any color is fine," he hollered from his perch behind the bathroom door. "You should make this house your own, honey. Take some initiative."

Claire's eyes rolled to the top of their sockets, fluttered there a few times, and then closed. It was so like Dan to claim he had no opinion, but she knew there'd come a day—maybe next week, maybe next year—when he'd casually mention that he'd always hated red paint.

"Remind me, do we want flat or gloss in a master?" she called back, annoyed that she couldn't stop herself from seeking his approval, then cringed as the words rattled and clanged against her tender sinuses, a dull ache gripping her back teeth.

"If it were me, I'd skip the little hardware store downtown. They'll gouge you," he yelled, oblivious to her question over the hum of the fan. His morning dump was as predictable as his perpetual distraction. "I think I saw a Walmart a town or two down the highway on the way here." Claire wondered how many moments like this one had occurred in their twelve years of marriage. How many times Dan had unwittingly—but with apparent satisfaction—had a conversation with himself.

Swallowing back an urp of acid, she slid out of bed. Grabbed yesterday's shorts from atop a stack of boxes, pulled on the light zip-up hoodie she'd tossed on the chair. She really couldn't go without a bra anymore, but the hoodie at least hid that sad fact somewhat. She walked through the still-foreign great room, where the chianti bottle she'd stumbled upon in a box marked *Dining/Keepsakes* still squatted open on the coffee table. Claire sighed, corked the souvenir bottle, rewrapped it in a hand towel, and tucked it back into the box beneath a picture frame. In those better days she'd scrawled *Tuscany 2003* in pink Sharpie on its curved straw side, never intending to drink it. Now she couldn't even remember deciding to drink it last night.

In the kitchen, under the sink in the recycling bin, she found more evidence of her shame. The empty vodka bottle that had apparently given her the bright idea to break open the chianti, three or four bottles that had held the beer she'd chugged like water as they'd hauled more moving boxes up from the basement. She pulled the cans and bottles from the recycling and put them in the garbage can instead, beneath a banana peel and the wrapping from last night's frozen pizza. Tied the bag tightly shut, so Dan wouldn't see.

The room seemed to darken suddenly, as she worked. She dizzied herself standing up—and at the same time caught a spectacular flash outside the kitchen window, which gave a view of the street in front of the house. Lightning—and something else.

It was a woman. A beautiful woman. Older, running barefoot in only a white nightgown, her long silver hair whipping wild and loose against the rapidly blackening sky. Then the sky broke open, releasing bucketloads of rain that pelted her and darkened the pavement. The woman only ran faster, lifting a yellow coat straight-armed, capelike over her head, her full breasts swinging low against the thin soaked fabric. Lightning lit the sky again, and Claire jumped, watching the electric snakes slither across the sky as the woman raced down the middle of the street. And then she was gone.

Claire gaped over the sink. Was this a blackout? Had her drinking gotten so bad she had begun to hallucinate? She gulped against a sudden aching scrape in her throat. Maybe she had a cold after all, a fever? *Name the feeling,* Dan's voice whispered in her head, and so she whispered back through the window, to the street outside where the surprise rain was already letting up, the sharp sky fading into a duller peach, the entire scene resetting itself as if nothing unusual had happened there at all.

"Trapped," she breathed.

In her misery she had conjured a ghost of a woman who was everything Claire was not.

"Did you see that?" she called to Dan, who of course could not have seen, who of course did not respond. Only then did she remember Charlie. Had the unexpected storm soaked him too? Even though it had cleared up so quickly, even though she knew he was likely fine—even though she was starting to worry she'd imagined the storm in the first place—a deep unease settled into her. She crossed to what the realtor had ambitiously called a foyer, shoved her bare feet into her clogs. "I'm going to look for Charlie!" she yelled, knowing Dan could not hear her, that he never really did.

The drinking was a problem. She knew it, even as she immediately flexed against it: *This cannot possibly be true.* But if she was being honest, if it really was Charlie she was seeking, it would have made more sense to take the car. Instead, she set out on foot in the direction the woman—or apparition—had run.

Sidestepping the freshly beached earthworms on the sidewalk, she turned from the sugar maple–lined sanctuary of Adams Street to the still unfamiliar crossroads that looped and bound her to her new neighborhood. Not that Anthem was big enough for distinct neighborhoods, as far as she could tell. Each of the ranches, bungalows, stuccos, and Victorians looked different but complementary, a charming collection of mismatched china. She'd seen only one set of stoplights, and no obvious order to the streets; no grid system, not like Chicago. Even the angled one-way streets of Madison at least made sense, forking out from the Capitol Square, squeezed between lakes. But Anthem's so-called blocks were sometimes square and sometimes triangular; others curved like kidney beans, ending in sudden circles—and though she'd driven them a handful of times these past weeks, on foot she felt as lost as ever, a rat wandering a maze.

"So what," she said, kicking a wet walnut she might have turned an ankle on if she were still running. It's not like she was an alcoholic. She wasn't physically addicted. A little out of shape, maybe, but blessedly thin. Charlie was a wonderful, well-adjusted child. Dan was the best father she could have imagined for their son, even if she resented the ease with which he'd transitioned into parenthood or how it hadn't affected his career in the slightest. She hadn't lost a job or a house or a marriage; she didn't have a record full of drunk driving tickets. She knew plenty of people who drank more than she did, from book group to the old newsroom, and she'd gone long stretches without alcohol, including nine months of pregnancy. The new house, '90s ranch and boring as it was, was still nice, Dan's new luxury car tucked safely next to her stalwart Honda in the spacious, two-car garage. They had money in the bank. All of her Tupperware bottoms had their tops, as her mother might say. Which brought her back to the beginning—*The drinking is a problem. No it isn't.*—and round and round like this she went.

Claire was miserable—that she could allow. But she'd been miserable before and pulled herself out of it. For instance, those too-fat years, after Charlie was born. That was probably when things started to go downhill, if she had to pinpoint an exact moment. When Dan had stopped reaching for her, when the newspaper had moved on without her.

"Charlie is the best thing that's ever happened to me," she said aloud now, looking for him left, then right, in case a vengeful universe was listening—if anything ever happened to him, she would die—but there was no doubt she pined for who she had been. Mourned herself, Dan's hungry hands on her taut stomach, the freedom of those endless, easy hours that only seemed busy and hard because they were too young to know better. Now too many years and compromises had spit them out here in a town a fraction of the size of their last stop, Madison, and light years away from her hometown, Chicago.

"It's a step up," Dan had whispered into her back as they'd lain in bed, the night he'd broken the news about the job. But they'd both known he only meant for him.

At least Anthem was quiet, and certainly charming. Straight out of a movie set, really. The narrow sidewalk widened before spitting her onto Main Street. The perfect place for yet another one of Dan's fresh starts. If he was happier, she'd be happier. When her problem had been weight, she'd restrained herself—she could do the same with her wine and beer and vodka. She could even start now, if she wanted to. It was the easiest thing in the world to quit drinking when you were this hungover. She'd done it a thousand times.

A line of shops stretched to her left, but she headed right instead, beckoned by a picket fence in the distance that looked like a favorite place she'd forgotten. She smelled pancakes and honeysuckle and moved toward it, pocketing her ache for later, following her nose.

~

Jack took a thoughtful pull on his coffee, watching as Charlie swiveled right, left, right, left on the barstool, a steady, jagged move that came from the core. The boy's elbows dug into the countertop, a coffee creamer clutched in each small fist; leftovers from the pyramid he'd just finished stacking. Every once in a while, he pressed through his forearms to lift his butt into the air, then dropped back to resume his swiveling. Perpetual motion. It made Jack nervous, only because he recognized himself in the boy. What age was it that he'd learned to harness that uncomfortable motor? To gather all the things around him—tools, parts, ingredients, moods—and build them into use and good purpose?

"You know you haven't even asked me my name," he said, still feeling this strange mix of guilty, annoyed, and protective on the child's behalf. What if Jack had been one of those serial killers? Charlie shrugged, then stilled himself. Set the creamers down and looked up at him, waiting.

"It's Jack," he said, and Charlie nodded back once, as if that settled everything. It didn't, at least not for Jack.

"You boys doing all right here?" asked Frannie, breezing in behind the counter to unload her haul of spent silverware and sticky plates into the bus tubs tucked underneath. Jack loved Frannie, and her sister, Kit too, like they were his own. Good girls—though they were in their forties now. He frowned. Good women, then. They'd done the best they could with what their mom had given them, all of which could be contained within the walls of Café Carolina. Carolina had been Lib's best friend, and she was long gone now, of course, from the diabetes and cancer. Where did the years go?

"Maybe a little more coffee," said Jack, but Frannie was already pouring it. She winked and squeezed his arm once, in that nurturing, vaguely possessive way of women everywhere. Except Lib, thought Jack fondly. He'd known so many women over his six-plus decades, but only one had never tried to own him.

"And who's your friend?" The question was for Jack, but Frannie addressed the boy directly. Charlie looked up at the waitress. "Charlie," he answered.

"Well, hello, Charlie, and how do you know our Jack? Are you here to keep him in line?" Charlie looked apprehensive, as if it hadn't occurred to him that Jack might be someone who needed help staying out of trouble.

"Charlie's bike needed some attention," answered Jack. "He came to see me on his own this morning. He apparently takes care of business himself."

"Ah! So your parents must be at work?" Frannie fished, and Jack smiled into his mug to hide his nerves. She never felt bad about prying, neither of the girls did, which bugged him on other days but he appreciated just now. "What do they do?"

"Sleep," said Charlie. Was he being funny? Or had he misunderstood the question? Maybe Jack had misheard. Maybe Charlie had said, "asleep," as in, they were still sleeping. But you didn't see kids out on their own much anymore, bicycling around, dining with strange old men. In his day, sure, but not anymore. Parents these days hovered. Kids came up soft, which might even be a good thing, but also unable to think for themselves, which clearly wasn't.

The café door jangled then, cutting short Frannie's interrogation. Jack caught the quick flicker of her pupils widening ever so slightly, and turned to see what she saw: a man, about her age, maybe a little younger. Jeans, sunglasses, long sleeves. Overdressed for the heat and kind of messy-looking in the way women seemed to like nowadays. This was a small town, but strangers weren't unusual. Lots of folks took breaks from the nearby highway that bypassed the village on its way to bigger places. Frannie was reaching to grab a menu, but Kit was already greeting him at the door.

"Hang on," said Frannie, lunging to fill an ice water and then following the pair to a corner booth.

Jack smirked at the sudden two-to-one waitress-to-customer ratio. The stranger's charms, if he had any, would be wasted on Kit, who only took up with women. Not that either of them had much in the way of free time. Jack leaned back on his stool, crossed his arms, watched Frannie flirt.

"Kit and Frannie are sisters. They live in back. This used to be their mom's café," said Jack, thinking maybe the information would prompt the kid to share some of his. You had to give to get. "Carolina, their mom, was good friends with my wife. But she died."

"Your wife died?" asked Charlie then, interested.

"No, no, Carolina died. Back a few years now," said Jack.

"Oh. You have a wife, though?"

"I do."

"Where're your kids then?" said Charlie, looking around the café, as if he might find them there.

"Well, we don't have any," said Jack. "Never got around to it."

Charlie nodded, considering this, his leg kicking steadily against the wainscoting Jack had nailed on under the counter a couple of years back. One of his many projects, like the fence out front to keep the neighborhood dogs from spraying the petunias Kit pressed into place each season. As a result of all the years' labor—which continued into the present—Jack always dined on the house. He appreciated how much effort the girls put into Café Carolina's exterior, even though they had to spend most of their time inside. It was the right thing to do.

"I didn't think your house was big enough for kids," Charlie said, as if concluding something Jack hadn't known he was working out. Why was he sitting here with this kid, talking to him like he was a peer? He was just lonely, he remembered. Missing Lyle.

At this thought, Jack squirmed as Charlie had then steadied himself. Eyed the boy's plate, which still held a pancake and a half and one lone sausage link cooling in a pool of syrup. Jack was full, but he reached over to pluck the sausage anyway—he hated waste, and often helped Lib or Lyle finish—but the boy stopped him, gripping Jack's wrist with sticky surprisingly strong fingers.

"Ope, sorry," Jack said, a little wounded. Then the front doorbell clanged again—and before Jack had the chance to check who it was, he heard a gasp.

"Charlie!"

~

Claire blinked. As though she were coming awake, just now, here inside this restaurant, trying to remember the details of a dream she'd just had. There, at the counter, her nine-year-old son. And with a man she'd never seen before. My God.

"What on earth?"

"Mom," said Charlie, slipping off the stool and scuttling toward her, wrapping his skinny arms around her waist. "I saved you some pancakes and sausage," he said softly, into her belly.

The man stood from his stool. Though he appeared to be in his sixties, he was undeniably handsome; tall and lean, square-jawed. "Mrs. . . . Charlie's mom. There you are," he greeted her, his voice a low grumble, his grip strong and warm. "I'm Jack Hanson, and I'm sorry. We're waiting for Charlie's tire patch to set. I'm afraid we both got hungry. We shouldn't have left the garage without telling you, but to be honest I wasn't sure what to do with the boy."

Queasy, Claire appraised the situation: Charlie's hopeful but sheepish gaze. The half-finished plates, side by side. The steadiness of the man's roughened hand against the counter, tufts of gray hair peeking from beneath his light wool cap. Likely a perfectly innocent scene, but still. She let a breath out, slowly, through pursed lips. Tried to imagine what a capable mother would say in this moment.

"I'm Claire Taylor," she said, pulling Charlie tighter against her body. "I'm sorry my son has imposed himself like this. He's usually better mannered. Charlie, you don't just go wandering off to restaurants with strangers, begging for food. And you're wet!"

Charlie looked at his feet. "Sorry, Mom," he said in a practiced tone that only made her feel worse. Dan would have handled this differently. Dan never would have let it happen at all.

"My fault, Claire," said Jack. "I'm pretty set in my routines. You've got a good boy here. Good company."

Claire nodded, mortified. She needed to get Charlie to herself, throttle him, cover his sweet cheeks in kisses. She sensed curious eyes and perked ears trained on her from every direction, despite the boisterous clatter of the café.

"Well, I insist on paying," she said, releasing Charlie to reach for her purse against her hip, gripping only a handful of hoodie. Oh God, she hadn't grabbed it when she'd set off on this spontaneous walk to find a woman who probably didn't exist. What on earth was wrong with her?

"Nonsense, I've got a tab here," Jack said, watching her fumble. "In fact, why don't you have a bite as well. On me, for the trouble. Or I'm sure the girls will reheat Charlie's leftovers here. Please, sit a spell."

Claire could feel herself spinning out, and so she ran a quick mental tally of her emotions, just as Dan was always instructing. *Feelings aren't facts, Claire.* She felt shaky. Light-headed—no, tight-headed. Thirsty. Confused. Tired. Ashamed. What kind of mother loses her wallet and finds her son?

"No, thank you, that won't be necessary," she said, a coldness creeping into her voice she'd meant to sound parental, as if she'd gone looking for her missing son in the first place, and not some mystery stranger running barefoot through a storm.

"I really am sorry for the trouble, Claire."

"Mom, I'm okay."

Claire swallowed, felt her face grow hot—she couldn't think how to leave now without looking like even more of a fool.

"Jack's right, you should sit a spell," said a woman, a waitress, placing a hand on Claire's forearm, looking her straight in the eyes. "You can follow me. I'll take you right back."

Claire opened her mouth to protest but found her feet moving instead, letting the waitress's expert hand guide her. *Relieved*, she thought, still naming her feelings. *Baffled. Speechless. Lonely.* Charlie skipped ahead of them and hurtled himself into the bench seat, bumping the table as he landed, startling the water glasses already set there.

"I'm sorry, this is very kind, but I really just came looking for my son. I ran out of the house," said Claire, dropping her voice to a whisper. "Without my purse."

"You're fine," said the woman. "You look like you could use a moment and a good meal, and half this town is on a tab. We might as well start yours today. I'm Kit. Please, sit down." She gently pushed Claire into place across from Charlie, as if she were a friendly officer helping her into the back seat of a squad car. *Watch your head, ma'am.*

"Charlie, we need to tell that man we'll be back to pay for your bike," said Claire, loud enough for Kit's benefit, and Kit smiled at her again.

"You don't need to worry about Jack. I've known him my entire life; he's like family. I can tell you've had a little shock, but your son here was in good hands, I promise. You're a good mom. Would you like coffee?"

Claire swallowed, nodded, unnerved. *A good mom.* Why was this waitress being so nice to her? She watched the woman walk away, her hips rolling like she was pedaling a bicycle. Claire didn't want coffee; she half-heartedly scanned the menu for a mimosa then pushed the thought away, hard. She took a breath and pressed the paper placemat into submission before her, released the silverware from its tightly rolled paper cocoon. Squared the butter knife, fork, and spoon with her plate, smoothed the napkin into her lap. On the other side of the booth, Charlie was on his knees staring out the window. She followed his gaze to a vast park across the street that ran behind the restaurant: an empty play structure, a giant lion's head that appeared to be a drinking fountain, a lone but massive canopy tree with a bench beneath it. Beyond it all, a field of wildflowers all the way to a wall of pines. Like a bit of country right here in town.

"Charlie, do you have anything to say?"

"I wanted to let you sleep so you would feel better," Charlie mumbled against the windowpane, making her feel even worse. His breath allowed quick puffs of disappearing ink on the glass. He traced a C into one cloud before it faded.

He'd bested her with a single sentence. But there was no way Charlie knew about the chianti. She'd opened it after everyone else was in bed. Unless he'd seen it before he'd left the house this morning and somehow known that, somehow known . . . what? What was there to know, precisely?

"Have you decided?" said Kit, suddenly back, pouring coffee as she spoke, her voice a bit sharper this time, less friendly—no, this was a different woman, eerily similar.

"Scrambled eggs and toast," replied Claire, surprising herself. She'd intended to order a polite bowl of oatmeal, if anything. This new waitress—Frannie, according to her name tag—nodded without smiling, pulling the unopened menu with her as she floated away. Like the other waitress, she moved slowly—not lazily, but languidly. Fluid and steady, like a river that has no way of caring what time its passengers need to arrive downstream, yet always gets them there anyway. One of them spun the pie case to retrieve a small plate and set it before Jack with a wink. The other tapped a bell in the short order window, swirling away to top off water and coffee, using a hip to slide a high chair into place.

"Honey," Claire said, trying again. "I know I've been sleeping a little more lately, but you know how we get off our routines in the summer, even adults."

Charlie was stacking creamers now and did not look up. She felt that old familiar uncertainty, the one she'd long associated with motherhood: he was the one who'd technically done something wrong, but it was her fault.

"This move is wearing us all out, right?" she pressed.

"Not me." He shrugged, and Claire bristled. She couldn't tell if he was being sassy; he never used to be. But he was growing this year, changing. Had he meant it, that he was okay? Was this just his signature genuine no-nonsense goodness? She stared at him until her eyes stung. She loved this child so much it hurt. When she couldn't bear it a second longer, she turned her attention back up front to the older man, buying herself some time, some space from having to feel it all.

She couldn't help but notice the fuss everybody else made over Jack Hanson. Men clapped him between the shoulder blades or slapped his knee as they passed; kids pushed him and ran away, giggling; older folks hollered pleasantries about the weather. The women lingered the longest, brushing light fingers across his shoulders or squeezing his elbow while throwing back tinkling too-loud laughter. He seemed even more handsome the longer she looked, though a generation too old for her. But as Claire watched Jack deftly requarter a newspaper and tip his head back slightly to read the page, she felt something stir low in her body all the same.

It was probably the paper making him look so good to her. Journalism, specifically the act of calling herself a journalist, had given Claire an authority she no longer knew how to possess. When she'd lost that role, she'd also lost the shorthand that let people know she was smart; vetted, savvy, discerning, hard-working. Somewhere along the way, she'd become just an out-of-work mom, just a barely good enough wife. She tried to imagine what Dan would say to Charlie now.

"I know I've been distracted. And I know you must be missing your friends back in Madison. I miss my friends too," she said, although she couldn't bring a single face to mind. "But that doesn't mean you can go wandering off with strangers just because they're nice to you."

Frannie reappeared suddenly with a plate of steaming, trembling eggs—how did she do that? Claire swore she'd just seen the woman flicking crumbs into her palm with her pinky at a table all the way across the room. "Thank you," Claire sighed.

"Yep," Frannie said, slapping a bowl of jellies next to Claire's mug. "Can I get you anything else just yet?"

"No, I'm good," said Claire, though she wasn't. Claire took her napkin and pressed it atop the toast to soak up the butter, watched Charlie shred his own napkin into tiny commas.

"Jack seems nice," she said, trying to signal that his punishment was over. "The ladies sure seem to like him."

Charlie's eyes flicked up at her the way they did when she said something scandalous, and she wiggled her eyebrows. He giggled, returning his attention to the paper shreds he was sweeping into a sharp mound with the edges of his hands. "He doesn't have kids," he offered back.

"Ah, interesting," said Claire, and Charlie smiled. Sometimes they did this—gossiped, she supposed, except they made the stories up: offered each other's version of what was really going on between a family at the park or the actors on one of his TV shows when they'd mute the dialogue, invent their own. It was something they shared—curiosity, imagination, storytelling. Claire watched a woman wearing a visor leaning into Jack now, one leathery knee resting on the stool beside him, her tennis shoe twirling behind her as she said something into his shoulder. "I bet he's a womanizer, impossible to pin down despite decades of trying," Claire said. "Or no, he's a widower who never got over his first love, taken too soon." She imagined a younger version of Jack hunched over a gravestone, tenderly planting daffodil bulbs at its loamy base. A long line of women and casseroles waiting for him in a church basement.

"Actually," Charlie started to say, and then Frannie was back again—or, wait, it was the nicer one, Kit.

"How are those first few bites?" she asked.

"Is that bachelor ever going to give one of those women his rose? They're all acting like contestants," said Claire, still playing the game, regretting it instantly. She hated when she sounded like this to outsiders; rehearsed, a little mean. She'd never even seen that stupid show—and it dawned on her: she wanted this waitress to know she was smart, observant. She wanted her to ask who Claire used to be, before she'd become this person who couldn't keep track of her own son.

Kit puzzled, looking past the families to stare briefly at a good-looking man in the corner who'd caught Claire's eye when she'd first come in—then they landed on the woman leaning into Jack at the counter. "You mean Jack?" She blew out a laugh. "He's married, honey. Been married forever."

"That's what I was gonna say," Charlie said, triumphant.

Claire felt kicked in the gut again. It wasn't that Charlie knew it or that Kit had said it unkindly—she hadn't; and it wasn't that Jack had a wife, bully for him. It was the loss of her reporter's instincts, once razor sharp, that aggrieved her. She'd been mourning them steadily since Charlie had been born, and here she was, wrong yet again. Death by a thousand failed newspaper cuts.

"Today's on us. Take your time, no rush," said Kit, whirling away with the water pitcher, two menus expertly tucked under her other arm. Frannie and Kit exchanged a weighted look as they crossed paths, and Claire was sure of it now: Frannie didn't like Claire. It had taken only minutes for the woman to judge and dismiss her. And Claire couldn't blame her.

What little appetite Claire might've had had vanished. She rose, peeling the backs of her bare thighs from the sticky vinyl. There was no avoiding Jack at the counter as Claire met Kit at the register, who took down her name and address at Claire's insistence, though she suspected it was for show.

"Thank you again," Claire said to Jack. "I'll swing by for the bike this afternoon and pay you."

"No rush on my account," he answered, setting the newspaper down. "I really am sorry again for the trouble. I shouldn't have let it happen. No excuse." His hands flew up. They were nice hands; pleasantly scuffed palms, long, capable fingers.

"Charlie," he added, nodding his goodbye.

"Good to meet you, Jack," said Charlie, sounding like an old man himself. Claire felt her lips twitch into a smile. She nudged him toward the exit, then turned back.

"Which paper?" she asked, pointing with her chin. A peace offering.

"Does it matter?" He grinned, pressing the paper to his heart.

"No, I suppose it doesn't." She smiled back, following Charlie out into the gray morning.

Chapter 3

Lib ran. She ran and she ran, and when the storm swept through, she felt as if she were the one sweeping through it, a giantess spinning the globe beneath her feet, racing through seasons and decades and countries. She felt nothing—not the assaulting rain, not the gravel and wayward glass that should have shredded her bare feet, not the weight of her own front door as she slammed it behind her and collapsed against it, lungs heaving, heart clattering, her body melting into a pool on the linoleum floor. She did not know how long she lay there. It was a long time.

Finally, rolling from her back onto all fours, she lurched to standing and peeled the wet nightgown off, unbuttoning it at the neck and shimmying it down her body. She stepped naked through the kitchen, turned the corner, and began to climb the narrow stairs, using the paneled walls to push herself up each step. In the bathroom at the top, she cranked the shower as hot as it would go and stepped inside. Her night with Jack should have steadied her better than this.

But she'd barely slept, even with him there beside her, his hand tucked between her legs in the way that normally grounded her. She'd floated anyway, tortured by long-buried images: An overturned tractor in an eerily silent hay field. Her mother's wet laugh, the inextricable smells of tequila, vomit, and drugstore perfume. The telltale squeak of footfalls up the stairs, the precise pain of the buckle of a pair of bib overalls pressed against her tender collarbone. Then the milquetoast husband in his ill-fitting suit, the father of this new ghost, Matthew, who she couldn't stop seeing in her mind's eye, climbing her front porch steps, over and over and over again.

She hadn't thought about this in years but when she was little, when things got bad, she imagined a round house within her belly, her pink stomach lining forming wallpaper like the walls of a cave. Little Libby lived there inside herself with nothing more than a cozy bed, a recliner, a little television set with a V-shaped antenna, and a TV tray, the kind her mother set out with cocktails, cheese, and Ritz crackers at 4:00 p.m. every day to entertain her revolving door of gentleman callers after Dad died. In her real house, when Mom started to slur around 5:00, and dinner faded to nothing but a good intention, Lib stared at the TV as the rest of the room zoomed out, and she was that girl inside her own body, safe and fed, comforted by the canned laughter of happy strangers. Later in the night, upstairs in her room, she spent even more time inside her rose-colored house. Sometimes she wouldn't even remember getting there, putting herself to bed, tucking herself in tight against whatever was coming.

Now she kept a small basic TV and a DVD player on the hutch in her very own, very real living room. She had a recliner no one ever sat in but her, cornflower blue to complement the scarlet bee balm that grew in the summer outside the largest of the windows along the south-facing wall. The other three walls were lined with books, row upon row of paperbacks, every imaginable future and friend and trip she'd ever need. They formed a protective buttress, slim soldiers standing sentry like the tall thin pines that bordered her property. This room was nothing like her mother's living room but was wholly her own. She'd feverishly wiped out any trace of the woman—and her men—as she worked, rocked, watched, read, rebuilt her life, month after month, year after year.

Eventually, she let Carolina in. Later, inevitably, she let Carolina introduce her to Jack.

"He's been asking about you," Carolina had said. "He's seen you." And although Carolina meant Jack had seen her at work, and on those lunch hour picnics the women shared in the park across from the café, those words—"He's seen you"—would reverberate with Lib for years as she fell in love with Jack, as she'd walked home from his place feeling as if she'd been discovered anew every time, as if she was rediscovering herself through his eyes. After so many years of hiding, she couldn't fathom why she wanted this sensation, but she didn't care. "He's seen you," she'd whisper to the beat of her footfalls. "You are seen."

After the first few months of their courtship, her head no longer felt as if it would burst into flames whenever Jack spoke to her. And as that fiery heat faded, a new weight took its place, like a broken-in hat protecting her eyes from the sun or a pair of weather-softened work boots giving her a solid connection to the ground. The more she settled into herself, the more she liked Jack. He didn't push, didn't ask questions she couldn't answer. And she was never bored of him, despite his steadiness. She knew he had other options, and she liked that it was her he kept choosing. She never doubted he was hers for as long as she'd have him. And, somehow, their time together had stretched into thirty-three years.

Thirty-three years.

Lib turned the shower off, wrapped herself in a towel, and began the routine she usually reserved for bedtime, though it was still morning. The one she'd started and abandoned before going to Jack's last night. Nighttime was when she loved her house most, especially as she performed her sleep rituals, whether he was upstairs waiting for her or not. On good nights she'd slipper through each room, flipping off light switches, tugging fan strings, tightening window latches. Finger the rows of books, send a loving caress down shivering window sheers, stop in every doorway to appraise it all with fresh eyes, especially the kitchen with its sparkling counters. Freshly ground coffee awaiting the auto-timer; the egg pan massaged and seasoned and drying upside down in the sink. After brushing her teeth, washing her face, and swirling night cream into her skin, softened like old paper, she'd run her hands one last time under the hot water, pat them dry, and then press them to her belly. They gave off a flash of heat; a warmth that felt as if it were coming from some other source, a reassuring power she could absorb. She would close her eyes in these moments and press, feeling the heart-shaped comfort her own hands generated until it slowly dissipated, and she was recharged.

Now, she couldn't seem to warm up, couldn't feel her own heat against the fresh nightgown, and so she slipped beneath the covers of her bed and burrowed in deep. She squeezed her eyes shut yet again, willing sleep to take her, despite the midmorning light filtering into the room through the shades. She was exhausted. Her bed was the best comfort she'd ever found, next to Jack's. It was part of why she never could bear to move in with him—Carolina used to ask why she didn't give up this farmhouse with the extra bedroom she'd never need, and this property with its constant maintenance, to join him in his sensible, centrally located house with its sensible, beloved garage. But she couldn't articulate the way her own walls, despite their history, proved somehow foundational to keeping her together, nor could she afford to crumble, not after coming this far.

In Jack's bed, she would inhale the familiar mix of WD-40 and Ivory soap and slip off to sleep, his callused hand between her thighs. In her own queen-sized bed, she'd spread her arms and legs wide, picturing da Vinci's *Vitruvian Man* in her favorite old library book, before curling into herself, fading into nothingness in the dark.

But today, neither bed felt safe. There was no comfort to be found. The baby she'd insisted on forgetting had found her, bringing all the agony that preceded him right to her front door. Why now? It wasn't his fault, but no way would she ever put him above Jack, above this patchwork life she'd stitched together. This baby—*Matthew*, her brain whispered, despite her best efforts to block it out—he was innocent in all this, but he was also the thread. One tug, and she'd come undone.

~

Any lingering coolness from this morning's storm had burned off quick, and a thick mugginess hung in its place. Jack pulled a bandana from his back pocket, patted down his brow, the back of his neck. Come August in Wisconsin, you had to wipe the air itself off your face.

He was also likely still sweating out a bit of shame, he allowed, over what had transpired earlier with the boy. He didn't appreciate being taken for some creeper. He didn't know why he'd done what he'd done either. A couple hours after breakfast at the café, Claire Taylor had shown up at his house, alone, paid for the bike, and driven it away in her Honda. Her ongoing coolness had left him feeling misunderstood and unfinished, both of which he hated, and so he worked now to complete a task he knew he could master.

Specifically, Susie Hawk's new chainsaw, which sat balanced on his lap, light as a feather, nothing like the way they used to make them. When she'd dropped it off last week, she'd claimed she could only get the pull cord partway out, a malfunction he'd confirmed while she stood over him, just a little too close. Perfume made him nauseated on good days; in heat like the sort they'd been suffering, it was downright unbearable. Likely the two-stroke oil had gummed up inside the engine, the way it did on these new—or underused—machines. Stuff was meant to be used. He frowned, setting the chainsaw on the bench and standing to get the gas can.

"Hey Jack," called Charlie, swooping into view in a perfect skid-out on the street, and Jack felt his heart lurch clean against his chest—the boy was back!—followed quickly by a low swoop, a sinking feeling. Charlie stood and pedaled slowly up the dirt driveway like a man on stilts. "Bike's working really good."

"Well hey, Charlie, glad to hear it," Jack replied, looking past the boy for his mom. "You out alone again?"

"I'm allowed to be out alone," Charlie said pointedly, kicking the bike stand into place with perhaps more force than necessary. He freed his neck from the helmet's strap beneath his chin as he walked past Jack into the garage, running his hand along the workbench. "My dad is an expert in kids. He wouldn't just let me ride my bike around if it wasn't a good idea."

"Ah," Jack said, remembering the boy's soft fingers on his wrist, worried now about them snagging a sliver or a mower blade. "Watch yourself, please. Lot of sharp stuff there."

Charlie immediately drew back his hand. "Thank you," he said, surprising Jack. Not that he'd obeyed, but that he'd agreed so quickly, without the defensiveness Jack's direct style often triggered in children and adults alike.

"I'm glad you stopped by. I have to say," Jack ventured, "your mom didn't seem too happy with me, and I can't say as I blame her. I was wrong to take you from here and you were wrong to come with me. Can we agree?"

"We can agree," Charlie said, a parroting that also struck Jack as oddly adult. "But also, my mom doesn't always remember what she already decided was okay," Charlie added.

Jack let that hang there between them in the sawdust-filled sunlight.

"Anyway, I brought you something," Charlie said, digging into the backpack Jack hadn't noticed he was wearing and setting a small package on the workbench. Jack shuffled over to find a plastic baggy holding a sandwich. The bread was stained with clear, Charlie-sized dirt fingerprints and it smelled strongly of pickles. Jack peered inside—pickles and mayonnaise?

"I remembered you said it was your favorite thing to eat when you were my age," Charlie said.

Pimento, Jack had told him, as they'd looked over the café menu. Pimento and mayonnaise sandwiches had been his favorite.

"Thank you, Charlie," Jack said, hoping the boy didn't clock the throatiness in his voice.

"Now we're even," Charlie said. "So what are you working on today?"

Jack stole himself a moment, wiped at his face with his handkerchief, recalibrating.

"Well," he said, "this chainsaw doesn't want to start. I think the engine needs a little loosening up, even though she's new. I'm gonna pull the spark plug and pour a little fuel in, see if I can't get her cranking."

Charlie nodded, as if he were following, his little face solemn and alert. "Need any help?"

"You know what, I do," said Jack, thinking fast. "My eyes aren't quite what they used to be. Do you think you could aim the lantern while I pour?"

Charlie eagerly grabbed the lantern from Jack's hand, stood beside him at the bench. They worked, Jack adding narration to each move for Charlie's benefit. "Now I'm holding the throttle wide open as we turn her," he said. And then "Flipping her upside down to get rid of the excess fuel." When that didn't work, Jack pried off the starter mechanism and checked the spring-loaded coil, found a crack in the wheel the cord wrapped around. "Plastic," he hissed to Charlie, like a curse word. "Cheap." If it were him, he'd march this hunk of junk straight back to Walmart where she likely got it. Even if she had to drive those thirty miles, the refund was worth more than the gas. That is, if they'd take it back at all, the vultures.

"This here is exactly what's wrong with our consumer society," Jack started, and Charlie nodded like he'd seen it all before too. "People always think buying new stuff is better."

"We had a lot more stuff in our old house," Charlie said. "We gave it all to the kids who don't have enough stuff. And our new basement is still full of boxes!"

"Where'd you move from, anyway?" Jack said. "Not too many folks move to Anthem. It's usually the other way around."

"Madison," said Charlie. "My dad's a guidance dean, but he has to try administration now because the damn schools here are too small, and we need people to step up and do more at a time like this."

"Ah," said Jack, slightly mortified but impressed by the kid's casual use of the curse word. Anthem had recently joined with three other surrounding towns to form a consolidated school district, in an attempt to unburden the taxpayers and absorb cuts. He didn't follow it much, but the battle it created was hard to avoid in the paper or in the gossip at the café.

When Susie's chainsaw finally whizzed to life, its mosquito buzz was shamefully unsatisfying.

"Have you had the chance to make many friends yet?" Jack asked. Charlie's silence was the answer. If Charlie was anything like Jack had been—and the more time he spent with him, the more he sensed that he was—his straightforwardness and quirks likely set him apart, so it would be a long time before people his own age understood him, let alone appreciated him. It felt important, suddenly, to take him seriously. Rather, to make the boy feel as though he was being taken seriously. It was so easy to go down the wrong road these days.

"How long have you got before school starts?"

Charlie shrugged. "September," he said, glumly. "Fourth grade."

"Well, I was thinking," said Jack, surprised to hear himself speak the words. "I could use some help around here. I know it's only for a month, but this is my busy season, and I could get a whole lot more done if I had an apprentice. I can't pay much, so I get it if you're not interested. Do you think you've got time, with all your riding, to help me out officially?"

"I've got time!" he said.

"Well, here's the thing, before we get too ahead of ourselves—you need to talk to your parents," Jack tempered. "Let's not make that mistake twice. And tell them just a few hours a day—you should still have some free time to play with kids your own age too. But it can't hurt to earn a little pocket money, pick up a skill or two."

"I'll take care of it," Charlie said, lurching for his bike, then remembering himself, turning back. "Do you think I should go now and talk to them?"

"Whatever you think is best," Jack said, smiling as he watched the boy's narrow back as he rode away, his shoulders poking like blades through his blue T-shirt, a long shoestring hanging loose. The last several hours had passed like minutes.

All right, then, he thought. *Why not?* He felt lighter on his feet than he had since Lyle passed, maybe even since he had all summer.

He turned back to pick up his work, but he no longer felt like puzzling. He needed a nap—besides, it was Wednesday, the night he and Lib liked to join the girls at Carolina's for supper. He was even craving it, he realized: some family time. He peeled his damp T-shirt off and hung it over the sawhorse, draped his handkerchief similarly to dry. He'd sleep, then he'd shower, then he'd go get his wife and take her out to dinner. Tomorrow, he and the boy could start on the back fence. A month was plenty of time to get it sanded and restained, and he could teach him all kinds of things in between. Maybe help him ease into this new town, take the load off those parents of his, who, at the very least, were too busy for the boy. Not that he knew about parenting. He certainly couldn't judge. But he could clearly be of use.

~

After the morning's fiasco at the café and squaring with Jack Hanson for Charlie's bike, Claire went home to get herself together. Showered, brushed her teeth, put on a bra. Flashed to the apparition woman's rain-soaked breasts, pushed the odd vision away again. She cleaned the kitchen, including wiping up a sticky lake of pickle juice on the counter—she had no memory of buying pickles, nor whether she herself had made the mess in one of her late-night "states"—and made Charlie eat some lunch, even if it was only cereal. Applied her makeup, listening with one ear to the TV program he was watching, spoon clinking steadily against the bowl. They'd spent far too many hours this summer together in front of the TV, him with his meals, her with a mug of wine, and she'd grown surprisingly invested in the unlikely storylines. Where were these worlds where the kids weren't kids at all, more like tiny single adults living with their friends in bedrooms that resembled city lofts? Where were the parents? *Where is her mother?* Claire's own mom used to say whenever she disapproved of a girl Claire's age. It was typically snarky and judgmental, but it served its purpose. Claire had always kept her own mascara light, her pale skin tattoo-free.

She'd been on Claire's mind, lately, her mother, who now lived with her father in an Arizona golf course community where everyone drove carts instead of cars. Three times over the past month, the woman's musical voice had come jangling out of Claire's own mouth. What would she think to see her daughter now, hiding yet another night's recyclables, ignoring her only grandson, wandering around town searching for a silver-haired wild woman?

And what would she think of the way they were still living like squatters, a month after moving in? Claire knew she really should stay put today, unpack more things, finally make this house into a home as any other mother would. She had no valid excuses and all the time in the world. She knew exactly what she was supposed to do—she'd made list after list after list—but every day was starting to look the same: rise in the morning with pocketfuls of intentions, fall into bed each night with every one of them lost, as if they'd slipped right through a hole in the lining.

"Done!" Charlie said, skidding in to slam his bowl and spoon into the sink, wrap her in a quick hug. She bent to kiss the top of his soft hair, cracking her chin against his skull as he bolted for the door.

"Wear your helmet!" she'd called after him, watching through the kitchen window, envying his joy, his freedom, his passion as he pedaled away. As if it had been days since he'd had that bike beneath him, not mere hours of enduring a flat.

This time, she took the car, even texted Dan at work to let him know she was running a few errands. The sky was shot through with streaks of eraser-pink, rubbing out any trace of the morning storm, but the worms still baked in place on the driveway. She took the long way to the café, turning again in the direction the woman had disappeared, as if she might catch a glimpse of her, still running in some parallel universe. But of course she was gone, if she'd existed at all; no evidence of her among the ragged hedgerows and sneaky cul-de-sacs.

Claire pulled into the café parking lot, admiring again the picket fence, the tangle of brightly colored flowers growing through and against it. The chirpy striped awning, *Café Carolina* painted in swirled script above its scalloped edges. She put the Honda in park and twisted off the ignition. Held the keys in her lap, staring at her own hand, at her two white knees, her camel wedge shoe against the brake pedal. For a dizzying moment, she couldn't connect the body she was seeing with herself. She lifted her foot from the pedal, just to check. *Yes*, it responded, *I'm yours.*

She crossed the lot and entered the café, where a quick assessment of the gathered patrons came up short. The place was packed, much busier than it had been this morning, so busy in fact that no one was there to greet her at the door. She was about to give the bell on the counter a polite ding when Kit spun out of the kitchen, both arms raised, double plated, at the very moment a toddler broke free from his dad at the counter and careened directly into her.

"Shhhhhhhooger!" Kit hollered, grappling helplessly at the plates as they crashed spectacularly around her. "Sugar, sugar, sugar." Before Claire had the chance to think, she found herself squatting on the floor next to Kit, collecting shards and using the broken crockery to scoop coleslaw and ketchup splatter into the bus tub Claire had pulled from beneath the counter.

"Oh, stop, you'll cut yourself!" Kit whispered, but there was no force behind it, and so Claire kept working. By the time Frannie arrived with the mop and bucket, the floor was clear, and the father and son had already sheepishly taken their leave, cash tucked beneath the father's plate.

"Sorry if I overstepped. I didn't even think," Claire said, taking the wet rag Frannie offered and wiping her hands. She rose, smoothing her skirt, returned to her rightful place on the other side of the register.

"Careful, or she'll try to hire you," Frannie said, and Claire noted the slightly less chilly tone with immense satisfaction.

"I wish," Kit said. "That'd be fun, wouldn't it? But we can only afford teenagers, and only at night so that we can get the occasional break. And we're not usually this busy during the day, but we're getting a ton of traffic this week from the folks traveling to the Dairy Expo in Madison—and good grief, I don't know what I'm going on about, you obviously aren't here to apply for a job. Do you need a menu?"

"Actually I'm back to pay my tab," Claire said, reaching for her wallet inside the handbag, this time tucked neatly against her hip. This morning seemed like it had happened last week, this already turning out to be the world's longest day. She resisted the urge to check the date on her phone, make sure she wasn't losing it. "And I was going to ask for a muffin and coffee to go this time, but I can certainly skip it considering how swamped you are."

"Blueberry?" asked Kit, already eyeballing the pie case beneath the register. "Cranberry, at least?"

"Bran, please," said Claire, and Kit nodded as if she'd expected it. "Black coffee, no cream."

Claire took a closer look at the busy tables as Kit pulled a muffin from the pie case with a bakery tissue. There were only 1,628 residents in all of Anthem—it was one of the first things she'd Googled back in Madison, trying to get a bead on this town she'd never heard of, two hours to the north and west. The number instantly seared itself upon her memory—and she wondered how the sisters made a living when things like the Dairy Expo weren't happening. How sad it would be to work all the time—and yet, until she'd sprung into action just now, she hadn't realized how useless she'd been feeling. Would it be so absurd to work at a café? Would it somehow negate the master's degree she was still paying off, or erase the years she'd devoted to journalism? More likely it would worsen the sting of the sudden layoff she and the other highest-ranking reporters had suffered in one fell swoop, a blow she had yet to recover from, even without the excuse of motherhood. She watched as Kit used a second wax tissue as a makeshift glove, gently pressing the coffee top into place so her fingers wouldn't touch where Claire would sip. It was yet another unexpectedly thoughtful gesture from this woman, and Claire was horrified to feel tears stinging behind her nose again. Kit handed her a tissue then set to wiping down the already pristine counter that separated them, even though it clearly didn't need it, even though she clearly had other things to do.

"Thank you, I get these terrible allergies," Claire said, making a show of wiping her nose.

"They're awful this time of year," Kit agreed.

"Say, can I ask you kind of a weird question?" Claire said, surprising herself but unable to just shut up. "I'm looking for someone. A woman. Older. Long silver hair. Quite beautiful, actually. Does that sound familiar to you?"

"Actually, it does," Kit said. This, Claire hadn't expected. She blinked back at the waitress, whose brown eyes narrowed, not unkindly but in a way that definitely made her look older than Claire had first guessed. "Mind if I ask why you're asking?"

Claire had only meant to confirm that the woman was real. She peeled the cap off the coffee, blew on the steaming liquid to buy time.

"Oh it's nothing, really, I saw a woman like that run past my house and she . . . she dropped something," Claire said. "I wanted to get it back to her."

"Running?" Kit frowned. "Maybe we're not thinking of the same person. What did she drop?"

Claire flashed to the woman's bare feet, her soaked see-through nightgown. She obviously couldn't have been carrying anything.

"A jacket," Claire said. "A yellow coat. I'd like to get it back to her."

The lines between Kit's neatly shaped eyebrows deepened, and Claire wondered briefly when she'd last had her own brows done.

"She was running? And dropped her jacket and kept going?" Kit said. "That doesn't sound like Lib."

"Well, I think the storm was very sudden," Claire said, trying out the name in her head, *Lib*, deciding it could match its owner. "It must have caught her by surprise. There was quite a lot of lightning, actually."

"I'll tell you what, why don't you bring it by anyway," Kit said, glancing back over her shoulder at the tables she was now neglecting. "If it's Lib's, I'll likely see her soon. She might even be here tonight, actually, for family dinner."

"Family dinner?" Not only was the woman real, she was related to these waitresses? It didn't seem possible.

"Despite what you see here this afternoon, Wednesdays are our slowest nights. Most folks go to Mo's for bingo and meat paddles," Kit said. "Frannie and I like to make something different just for ourselves and whatever friends stop by. You know what? You should come."

Claire had no idea what a meat paddle was—and she had no idea if Kit's invitation was sincere or if she was just being polite. "Maybe I will," Claire said, which was as good as no in Midwestern-speak.

"I mean it," said Kit, who knew this too. "But I get it. Either way, feel free to bring the jacket by. I'm sure whoever it belongs to will stop in eventually."

"Will do," Claire said, suddenly in a rush to be anywhere but here. The whole idea of stopping back to pay her tab had essentially been to reclaim her dignity, and she couldn't figure out if she had succeeded. Paying her tab, helping in a crisis—these were pluses. Randomly crying, blurting some nonsense about a mystery woman, then lying—not so much. Was there really enough that was endearing about her that Kit genuinely wanted to befriend her? God, she needed a drink.

Claire drove away, making the corner past the café and the park, and driving along the county road she knew eventually met the highway.

On her left, a small, double-decker motel shared a parking lot with the gas station. Yet another good-looking man caught her attention, this one sitting outside his motel room door. As if pulled by a magnet, she yanked the wheel and turned into the station. She had half a tank but filled up anyway, sneaking sidelong glances across the parking lot to the spot where he smoked a cigarette.

When she had first entered the café, before spotting Charlie with Jack at the counter, her attention had been drawn to a guy about her age just sliding into a booth at the back. The man at the motel got her body's attention in the same way, a sort of subconscious longing she couldn't ignore. She straightened her spine, holstered the pump, and ducked inside the station, hyperaware of her body, her every movement.

Inside, she let go a little, softened her shoulders, caught her breath. At the end of the register, next to the lottery tickets and three browning bananas, a bin of travel-sized wine bottles lay like Easter eggs in a basket. She made a beeline and selected three—two red and a white—without looking at the labels. "Pump four," she said, sliding the bottles toward the clerk, who did not blink. "These are perfect for gifts," she said anyway, smiling as she pulled the paper bag into an embrace.

Back out in the diesel balm, she maneuvered the car and parked so that she was facing the motel, where the man was still sitting, a thin line of smoke rising from his hand. Claire considered the small white bakery bag, dwarfed next to the new brown sack. Mini bottles in the car. This was new territory.

She twisted open the bottle of white, lifted her skirt and clenched it there between her thighs. The perfect hiding spot until she could finish her coffee, though she'd lost all taste for it. She considered dumping it out the window and using the cup to disguise the wine but didn't have the heart—not after Kit's kindness, genuine or not. Did Kit ever have a glass of wine during the day? Not enough to impair and never to drive drunk, of course—just to regulate the bloodstream? Offset the damage of the previous night, privately bring herself back into balance? It wasn't like Claire was trying to get a buzz. She was just trying to get back to herself. There was a difference.

Claire took the muffin out of the white pastry bag and then smoothed the bag across her lap to form a paper plate of sorts. The muffin, she saw, was blueberry. She loved blueberry muffins, but she thought of them as a marketing trick, cake disguised as health food. Kit didn't seem the sort to make mistakes. Claire took the hint and bit into the sugary treat, her eyes fluttering closed in ecstasy.

When she opened them, the man was looking straight at her. Even from this distance, she felt the sear of his stare. She wondered what he was seeing.

A couple of months ago, when they still lived in Madison and she went to a yoga class—although less and less often as they prepared to move—she'd stretched strong and lean into downward dog, then made the mistake of twisting her neck to catch a glimpse of herself in the mirror. She'd been shocked to see her face hanging like a loose mask, her stomach sagging from her narrow hips, as if her skin was the only thing holding it to her abdomen. It had struck her then, as it was striking her now, that she had two selves. That what she looked like on the outside was nothing like who she felt like, who she believed herself to be, on the inside.

Claire pulled the bottle from between her thighs, pretended to reach for something below the dash and took a long swig, bent over. She dribbled then choked. When had the gap between who she was and who she wanted to be grown so wide? Where did the years go when they went? She wanted to go back. Rewind to the days before she resented Dan so much, before his easy relationship with Charlie could make her feel so small. Before, for their sake, she'd put off every trip or goal she'd imagined for herself. She would still choose to have Charlie, of course, just delay her pregnancy a bit. Go whitewater rafting, rock climbing, let herself turn tan and tight. Then she might have strutted back inside that gas station, taking her sweet time, letting him get a good long look. And she wouldn't have cared what he was seeing, because she wouldn't have needed so badly to be seen. Because Dan would still be crazy about her, desperately waiting for her, back home.

Dan. It was starting to feel too late. She'd always thought that they'd have more time to find their way back to each other. That the natural distance brought on by becoming distracted parents would close as Charlie grew up, became more independent. That as she became a better mom, Dan—such a naturally good dad—would admire her again. Now her husband felt like yet another part of herself to which she couldn't connect, some other piece that had broken off inside her, some other way she'd sagged away from her own bones.

She drained the last of the bottle and tucked the other two inside her glove box and the empty back in the bag. Walked as casually as she could to dispose of the evidence in a nearby garbage can, brushing the crumbs from her lap in long, slow strokes. She started the car, pulled slowly out of the parking spot and toward the man where he sat.

As she got closer and he came into focus, she saw that it was definitely him, the man from the café. Claire held his gaze as long as the maneuver would allow, and just as she turned the car to pull out of the parking lot, he stood, blew out a stream of smoke, and smiled. It was a delicious, wicked grin that spread from his mouth to her spine, tingling on impact. She whipped her head back to face the windshield and peeled away, forgetting to check her blind spot, getting lucky anyway.

Lib kicked the sweaty tangle of sheets to her feet and lay there, piecing the puzzle of the day together. Flimsy shreds of fitful dreams disappeared like wet tissue against her fingers, useless, escaping examination. A flock of barn swallows chattered excitedly from the mulberry, no doubt up to something. It was close to suppertime, then. Miraculously, sleep had found her, and her earlier torturous chill was gone; she now burned with the setting sun dripping down the open west window. Yanking her flannel nightgown up and off over her head, Lib fell back against the wet pillows, waiting to cool off.

It had been her second attempt at a nap. She'd given up on the first. Risen slick and stubborn to fight the day, bypassing breakfast, yanking every last weed from the south lawn berm, pulling punishing thistles with ungloved hands. She'd sanded the slivers from the garden shed as she should have done last summer, working straight through into lunch. Heaved and hauled and wrestled herself weak, but no relief came. *Another hot shower*, she'd thought. *Another try.* This time, it had worked. She'd slept like the dead, not a single ghost.

Her breath was just beginning to steady when she heard a car approaching up the driveway.

He was back!

Her heart seized, and a rushing sound roared from inside her ears. Her eyes darted to the door, the closet, the window, the ceiling. Nowhere to go.

She scrambled for her nightgown, but it fought her as she tried to wrestle it back on. He wasn't going away. She hadn't made him up. She'd have to face him, but not like this, not yet. She pulled the covers from the foot of the bed and burrowed in, waited for the knock.

Instead came the whoosh of the inner door and slap of the screen door behind it, then, "Lib?"

Jack! Happy disbelief dawned, followed by relief, but then a new sick fear swept through her. *Jack*. It was one thing, her going to his house. But his coming here was too risky. At least until she could sort this all out, figure out if the visitor had really been Matthew—who would surely come back if it was him. Figure out how not to lose Jack over this secret. She was still groping for a strategy.

The downstairs floor creaked as he took a few steps in and out of each room, searching for the wife he loved and thought he knew. She could imagine his expression so precisely. Could see his feet in the cold Door County sand, one hairy toe scaring up a digger crayfish at the shoreline. His bare back bent over the frigid waves as he dove against them. His gloved hand smoothing caulk into the cracks between the rental windows and their frames. She took slow, steadying breaths, timed to her husband's footfalls up the stairs. Pulling the blankets down to her neck, Lib smoothed the hair from her face and waited.

"Old girl, you're sick?" he said, sidling up to the bed and dropping a cool hand on her forehead. "I was gonna take you to Carolina's for dinner. It's Wednesday."

Lib closed her eyes against the pain the sound of her best friend's name spoken aloud still carried, even after ten years. Wednesday, when had that happened? Then she sat up into his chest, into the relief his scent brought her. "Nonsense," she said as he hugged her head. "I was just napping, and now I'm a little out of it."

"Oh, good," he said, though he didn't sound convinced. "Would you rather stay in? Watch a movie, eat cheesy noodles in the living room?"

He'd just described her favorite sort of night, but right now the idea of being alone together at home didn't feel as safe as it usually did. Even if Matthew didn't return, Jack would see into her, figure it out before she could tell him herself, and that would be worse. Not yet. She nuzzled further into his shirt. Not yet.

"Actually, family dinner's probably just what the doctor ordered," she said. "Let me just get myself together."

Lib felt Jack's eyes on her as she stood, crossed the room to her bureau, and pulled out a light pair of summer jeans and a soft lavender T-shirt. She grabbed a fresh set of underthings and padded to the bathroom, leaving the door slightly ajar. She brushed her teeth and collected her hair into its braid, ran several palmfuls of water over her flushed face. Staring back at her slightly bloodshot eyes, she flipped the faucet off, then pressed her damp hands against her abdomen. *Stay right here*, she telegraphed her reflection. *Don't spin out.*

Jack smiled at her when she emerged, then followed as she led the way down the stairs. Lib spotted her abandoned nightgown, still in a wet twist on the floor. She gave it a discreet kick beneath the kitchen table as she crossed the room, then plucked her wire-thin wedding band from the window sill above the sink. Lately it spent more time there than on her finger, but tonight she craved the cool tickle of it slipping into place. She pressed it there, closing her eyes once in quick silent prayer, then swiveled to face Jack at the door. She considered pulling her barn coat from where she'd apparently had the presence of mind to drape it over the kitchen chair to dry. Would she be running hot or cold? So hard to tell, these past twenty-four hours. She decided she'd rather be prepared, especially if the girls had the café's AC cranked. Threw it over her arm and walked through the door Jack held open for her.

Jack clasped her hand as they walked out together into the evening, then let her go as they split to their respective sides of his old two-tone Chevy pickup. He'd been so proud of it when he bought it, just a few years after they'd met, and she'd inherited his little blue '78 Toyota 4×4 now collecting dust in her shed. Lib got it out on occasion, for hauling mulch or when it was bitterly cold, but she preferred to walk most places if she could. She didn't mind riding with Jack, though, and she managed a smile as they clicked their seatbelts in unison. Jack popped the clutch, jostled the gearshift back and forth, and grinned back at her as they swung around and bounced down the driveway.

Chapter 4

"What's this family night thing again now?" Dan called from the bedroom as Claire pressed her flushed face against the kitchen door that led to the attached garage.

"It's just a café I found with decent food, just a short way from here," she yelled against the fiberglass door, her voice clattering up around her ears. She hadn't intended to accept Kit's invitation, nor had she intended to bring Dan and Charlie with her if she did—but escaping alone again seemed less doable over the dinner hour. She'd wracked her brain to think of an excuse to leave, then hated herself for it. What mother wouldn't want a nice dinner out with her family? They were new in town. They should accept a friendly overture from a local. Besides, maybe the woman Lib would be there, as Kit had said. Her curiosity burned almost as hot as the alcohol in her stomach. Which was another reason she needed Dan: she shouldn't be driving tonight.

"And it's family-style? Like an Italian joint?" he said, emerging from the bedroom. A tiny white tissue stuck to a spot he'd apparently nicked shaving, and a fresh red pimple glowed from the corner of his mouth. He often showered and shaved a second time between school days at work and his frequent evening meetings. She should appreciate that he was taking this outing as seriously—but, then, why did it feel like he was fighting her?

"No, not Italian," she said, staring at Dan's raw shorn face. Then, "Charlie! Let's go!"

Her son slid sock-footed into view, his head and shoulders hunched over the worn field guide to amphibians he'd asked for on his sixth birthday and still carried everywhere in that backpack of his. "Shoes," she said, and he disappeared again into the living room. "I guess the waitresses kind of make a special meal for themselves on Wednesday nights," she said. "Sort of take a break, even though they're still open."

"Why would they want to take their break in the same place where they work?" Dan frowned. "Doesn't seem healthy."

Charlie reappeared with shoes on, laces dangling.

"I don't know, Dan," said Claire, opening the door and pushing Charlie through first.

"Tie your shoes, Charlie," Dan said, inching the car out beneath the garage door that was slowly groaning open. Of course he'd backed in. Should she be backing her car in?

"Louie or Roger?" Dan asked.

"Turn right," Claire sighed, deliberately ignoring Dan's oldest joke.

"Roger, Roger," Dan grinned in the rearview mirror at Charlie, bent now over his shoes, who giggled. There was no good answer; had it been Louie, Louie, Dan would have broken into song. She used to laugh too, but the truth was Dan and Claire fundamentally disagreed over what was funny. She used to be more generous with his attempts at humor or at least fake it better. Now it seemed like a waste of precious energy.

Claire sighed, surprised to find her edges still sharp. She'd napped off the outing and the mini bottle earlier, then managed a glass of wine before Dan got home. She'd made a show of sipping from a can of Diet Coke after he'd arrived, waiting till he was in the shower to sneak a second glass. The two quick drinks should have been enough, but she still felt tense and jittery, inexplicably irritable, almost nervous.

She leaned back against the passenger seat, forcing herself to admire her sleepy new community. Several storefronts were vacant, but others creatively held their ground. An antique mall boasted squeaky cheese curds and local venison sausage. A brick facade with Savings & Loan carved across its front housed a funeral home instead. A sign tucked in the front window of the pharmacy advertised Fresh Bait, and a beautiful old cream city–brick Opera House looked to host both an insurance agency and a barber shop. Maybe they could make a go of it here. Maybe they could put a fresh face on this marriage, build off its good bones, make do with what was still there, for Charlie's sake.

"Here," motioned Claire, but Dan had already seen the Café Carolina awning and clicked the blinker on. Dan held the door for the family, and she noticed for the first time the thin elegant belt he'd strapped around the waist of his khakis, the leather shoes, and the dusty rose shirt that set off his olive-toned skin. He looked nice. Handsome, certainly, to anyone looking. He'd obviously made an effort, for her. For his family. He steered Charlie by the neck, whispered something into his ear. Charlie giggled and handed his dad the field guide he'd forgotten to leave in the car. All the world could see what a great dad he was, what a good husband. What on earth was wrong with her?

"Hey," said a gum-chewing teenage girl from a stool behind the register. Claire eyed the cell phone wedged between her thighs and thought of the remaining mini bottles in the glove box of her car. "You guys can sit wherever."

Claire scanned the café that was, indeed, nearly empty. She almost didn't recognize Kit and Frannie, who were sitting alone at a long row of center tables, pushed together for the occasion. Two open bottles of wine breathed between the women—oh thank Christ—and Frannie, who looked looser and happier than Claire remembered, was cutting wedges of cheese on a wooden board. She'd released her bun and removed her headband, revealing soft chestnut hair that skimmed her shoulders. She wore a flowing tunic—Claire never would have pegged the woman for a hippie—and Kit looked younger in a tank top that showed off the angles of her collarbone and silver earrings that dangled below her elfish dark pixie cut. Both had nice, open faces, friendly. They could have been any of Claire's Madison friends, the ones she could always call for drinks or a run but had yet to even think about since she'd moved. Not a single one of them had called, either, though they gushed supportive comments on her Facebook photos.

"Oh! You came!" Kit said, standing to greet the family. Frannie kept slicing cheese but nodded toward the chair across from her in invitation.

Claire moved toward it, strangely compelled to win this woman's favor. Dan hung back a few steps, his hand on Charlie's shoulder.

"You already know Charlie, and this is my husband, Dan," said Claire. "This is Kit and her sister, Frannie. They work here."

"They live here too," said Charlie. Claire registered a slight shock, both over the news and the fact that once again her son knew something she didn't. Dan shook each woman's hand, then automatically took the seat on Charlie's other side, as they'd done since Charlie had been in a high chair.

"So tell us, Dan," said Kit, standing to pour wine into two coffee mugs, "what is it that you do?" And Dan, who was always so good in social situations, began to sip and talk. Claire watched Kit's enthusiastic expressions as Dan droned on, admiring the ease with which the woman lobbed probing follow-up questions. She'd have made a great reporter. Frannie, on the other hand, stayed silent, watching Claire without apology. Something about the mug made Claire's wine go down fast, too fast.

"And how about you, Claire?" Frannie said, speaking for the first time. "What do you do?"

Before Claire could answer, the café bell jangled. Both waitresses' heads swiveled to the door in comic synchronicity. Claire looked too—and froze.

It was her! She had come! And there, at her side, was Jack Hanson. Her long silver hair was pulled back in a braid—and that coat! The same mustard-yellow cape the woman had held over her head in the storm. The one Claire had described to Kit. What was Claire's mystery woman doing with Jack?

"Auntie Lib!" said Kit, rising to envelope the older woman in a quick, tight hug.

"How are my girls?" Lib said, sending a smile down to Frannie.

"Charlie, are you following me?" said Jack, tousling the boy's hair.

"Hey, Jack," Charlie responded, flushing.

"You know each other?" said Dan, standing to shake Jack's hand. Claire felt the room move a little beneath her.

"Dad, this is Jack. He helped me with my bike this morning," Charlie said.

"Aha!" Dan said, softening. "Good man. Thanks much."

Jack followed Lib around the table to the chairs across from Claire's family. Claire tried not to gape as she scrambled to put it all together. So Lib was Jack's mystery wife and Claire's mystery hallucination—the two were one in the same. Claire watched as Jack took Lib's coat and nestled it on the back of her chair, then sat down beside her. He slid his arm around her and squeezed her shoulder, leaving it there as she talked with Frannie. He clearly adored her. Claire scanned the tabletop for a menu to hide behind, then realized they hadn't been given any. All she wanted was to freeze time, just long enough to catch up. To stare, undetected, at the woman before her.

"Well, is this her?" Kit said to Claire, nodding at Lib. "It must not be, unless you've already tracked her down?"

Claire blinked, caught in her earlier lie. Projected what she hoped was a blank expression.

"The woman you were looking for," Kit said. "The dropped jacket?"

"Oh, right, no!" Claire said, as lightly and cheerily as she could manage. "I've still got the jacket. Must be another woman—though she bears a strong resemblance!"

Both Kit and Lib smiled pleasantly back at her in a moment that seemed to stretch for minutes.

"Okay, I think everyone who's coming is here," Frannie said to the table. "Tonight, Timothy's making broasted chicken! Any vegetarians among us?"

Claire shook her head firmly, as if the notion was absurd, though she'd done several stints of vegetarianism throughout her life, the longest coinciding with the height of her eating disorder in her early twenties, when it had served as one of many excuses for her empty plate. She thankfully felt a gentler buzz settle in, restored by the table wine. If she could get a handle on her adrenaline, this was usually her favorite state; not hungover, not drunk, but pleasantly suspended between. Catching bits and pieces of conversations but not committed to any, relaxing into a protective wine bubble as she observed everyone else do their thing outside it. This would be a very good night after all. She was so glad she'd come.

"Did Charlie tell you about my job offer?" said Jack, glancing politely at Dan but turning toward Claire.

"He did!" said Claire, a little too brightly. Charlie had been going on and on all evening about how Jack needed a helper down at the garage and how his parents wouldn't have to do anything at all. He'd get himself there, and he'd be out of their hair every afternoon. He would spend the mornings getting some fresh air, and weren't they always telling him to get his nose out of a book and make friends and all that. Warning bells clanged in Claire's head, and so she'd ignored her son's monologue, hoping he'd get distracted and forget all about it. Clearly, that wouldn't be happening.

"I've got a fence that needs staining," said Jack. "It's a big job, and it'll take me twice as long alone, maybe longer."

"It's very kind of you," said Claire, glancing at Lib. And how would Jack's wife feel about a kid hanging around her house all day, tracking mud inside, asking nonstop questions and dirtying a different glass every time he got thirsty?

"Lib, how do you feel about having a young male visitor?" Claire asked her, and Lib's face sharpened, darkened—she'd offended the older woman somehow. "Charlie's a good boy," Claire added, quickly, "but he's definitely a boy. You know how messy they can be."

"Oh," said Lib. She took a sip of her wine, then set it carefully before her. "Jack's always got visitors at his place."

Now it was Claire's turn to startle. His place?

"Jack and Lib are married, but they don't live together," interjected Kit from the end of the table. "Isn't that delicious?"

"You're kidding," Claire blurted, feeling Dan's eyes swing her way.

"Well, isn't that interesting," said Dan, which she understood was for her benefit—he wasn't buying it. Didn't think it was *healthy*, she knew he'd tell her later, expecting her to agree.

"That's why you've got a whole garage just how you want it," said Charlie.

Everyone's laughter burbled up, and, looking at Lib, Claire felt a tad sick, the way she felt during the early days of a crush. Or, she realized, the way she'd felt when she noticed the man in the motel parking lot. Queasy. As if the joke was on her, somehow, though she couldn't imagine what the joke might be. She tallied up the things she now knew about the woman sitting across from her: Beautiful. Strong. Loved. Desired. Independent. Alone. Free. She went to take a swallow of wine and sucked air instead; apparently she'd drained her mug without realizing it. Jack's elbow rested on the back of Lib's chair. He held the feathered ends of her silver braid, circling it between his thumb and two fingers like an old habit.

"He's welcome any afternoon," said Jack, and Claire managed a nod. Truth was she craved alone time more than anything else, but only the guilt-free sort, when she knew Charlie was well cared for. They all so obviously loved and trusted this man, Charlie included, and it was already August. He could spend these last weeks before school rereading that ridiculous field guide or biking to God knows where—or, worse, in front of the TV with her—or she could take advantage of free babysitting while Charlie maybe even picked up a skill or two. Maybe this arrangement would give her access to Lib; maybe the woman's essence would shed like a virus that Claire could catch. And it could give her these last few days of summer to herself, before she made a real and honest effort at finding a job and making friends. Finally finish unpacking. Lose herself in a good novel. A vodka tonic or two in the hammock.

When the meal finally arrived, several bottles of wine later, Claire was starving as she hadn't been in years. She dug into the tender broasted chicken, helped herself to a second heaping spoonful of creamy mashed potatoes, shoveled forkfuls of buttery crisp green beans into her mouth. Lib hadn't said much, but Claire had greedily gobbled up every word she did let drop, and, by the end of the evening, a natural sense of companionship had settled upon the group. Claire even felt herself soften toward Dan. At one point while Dan was talking to her, she'd reached across Charlie and brushed that old cowlick from her husband's hairline, and she remembered the earnest, passionate social work student he'd been. She watched as Lib leaned into Jack's armpit and closed her eyes, Jack's head resting on hers and her body shaking with his as he laughed at something Dan said, and she'd caught herself laughing too, though she hadn't heard what was funny, gazing down the table at her own husband. She'd been so unhappy lately, but maybe she was making it all up. Maybe she was the problem, not Dan, not marriage itself, not the institution of motherhood. Maybe they looked to these people the way Jack and Lib looked to her: comfortable, in love, happy.

Maybe it would all be okay.

~

Lib had been extra quiet all night, so Jack wasn't surprised when she let him know she'd like to sleep alone.

"Maybe I am coming down with a little something," she said, jostling against the truck door as he drove her home after dinner, and he nodded back. Perfectly okay with him. Not everything meant something. Jack had long believed the main thing separating man from the rest of the animal kingdom was the former's compulsion to attach deeper meaning to everything that happened, which almost always resulted in manufactured drama and pain. Tired was usually just tired. Separate houses was just separate houses. Guessing at women only made for trouble.

After he kissed his wife twice and deposited her at the end of her driveway (where she often asked to be let off to "shuck the sea legs" on the walk up, a quirk he found particularly charming), Jack turned the pickup around toward town and headed home. Tomorrow he'd have the morning to himself, and then the boy would come. He smiled, realizing just how much he was looking forward to it, grateful life could still surprise him after all these years. He'd go through the garage first with his coffee; tidy up, do a little inventory. See what was missing, then buzz over to Mike's hardware store for supplies. He'd need fresh brushes. Probably sandpaper too.

He'd planned to finish reading the paper in bed, but he kept reading the same paragraph twice, Tinker pacing back and forth across his chest. His thoughts drifted to Charlie and his family. The Taylors. Claire had been a little more likable tonight. Maybe because she was warming to him or maybe because she was a little tipsy. She reminded him a bit of a woman he'd dated for a month or two in the '70s—Katie? Janie?—the one who had the photography studio uptown for a while. Reserved until you got her open. Either sad or sneaky, you couldn't quite tell with artist types. He hadn't caught what Claire did for a living, but he'd bet on something creative. Her husband, Dan, was a teacher or something? He had definitely talked too much. Talked down, even, to Charlie. Jack chuckled in appreciation now at the way the boy had respectfully but firmly rejected his dad's attempts to cut his meat, and felt a little less wounded about his reaction to Jack's attempted theft of his breakfast food. Kid was just setting boundaries, sticking up for himself.

With his tongue, Jack worried a chicken string still lodged in his teeth as he settled down to sleep. Had he acted too impulsively, committing himself to the rest of summer with this boy? What did he know about the energy that would take? Didn't he love his unstructured days for a reason?

Lib had been clear from the start that she didn't want kids. He was thirty when they met, still on the edge of possibility, should he find the right woman. She was only twenty-five, and, though she knew her own mind better than women twice her age, Jack still figured she'd change it eventually. The strength and depth of his feelings for Lib, pretty much right off the bat, had shocked him. He'd never felt anything like it before, and so what was to say she wouldn't keep right on surprising him and decide it was time for kids?

He flipped his pillow over, resettled his weary head, snorted as he recalled the general bafflement decades ago, not at the pairing itself—hell, he'd been on fire for her, which was clear to every last person in this town—but that they hadn't moved in together, not even after the wedding. The guys down at Mo's seemed particularly perplexed, barely waiting a respectable number of beers before asking, *So, you got a wife now, how's that work?*

The gals still came around for a while, maybe even more often, looking to test what a man meant when he made a commitment without a live-in witness to hold him to it. Jack supposed he could have gotten away with anything, but that was just it—there was nothing he felt like getting away with. He only wanted the woman he had, and that woman only wanted the man she had. So it added up; it made sense. And all these years, he'd been true.

What did irk him was the inevitable follow-up question: *Why'd you get married, then, if you're not gonna live together?* His response was always polite, but the premise stuck in his craw. Did he ever ask them why they had gotten married? Surely their reasons went beyond the opportunity to share a roof.

As time went on, having a larger family made less and less sense. The older he got, the more he appreciated his independence—that he could hop in his truck anytime he wanted and get his hands on anything he needed, including this good woman. After Carolina passed, he grew even closer to her daughters, and he knew Lib thought of them as her own too. Lib hadn't had the best home life growing up anyway—only child, dad dead in a farming accident, mom who drank herself to death—and she didn't like to talk about it.

Kids came up a few more times over the years, but only in response to nosy folks' inquisitions, the ones that started after they'd grown tired of obsessing over their unconventional living arrangement. Jack always checked for Lib's reaction first, then answered for her: *No plans. But you'll be the first to know, should something change*, he said with mock-seriousness to the grocer, the waitress, the gas station attendant.

And nothing had changed—but in the best possible way. Lib asked nothing of him that he didn't naturally offer, which only made him want to give her more. The forced spaces in their togetherness left him always missing her, yet his alone times felt all the sweeter for it—he was completely free of the bondage of expectations and resentments, those endless honey-do lists Lyle often complained about, the same old arguments on repeat. He never knew what she'd bring him—an idea, a token, a story. Onions plucked from her garden, dirt still clinging to their roots. Sometimes nothing at all, not a word, for days. He didn't care. He knew how lucky he was. Coming together with Lib hadn't felt like compromising or sacrificing, more like doubling himself in size. Expanding as though he'd swallowed some magic tonic. He waited, year after year, for its effects to wear off, but they never did. He was still drunk on her. Everything in his life was exponentially better for having Lib in it.

When they'd clearly left the childbearing years behind them, he couldn't say he really felt a loss. True, he'd never be a father, but it's not like he was lacking company or demands on his time. People would always need help: a ladder, a caulk gun, an opinion. Lyle was always free when Lib wasn't, and their camaraderie was easy, like that of his boyhood friends, even made him feel young. Jack relished his alone time because it was never guaranteed. He genuinely liked his so-called customers, and he liked that they went home. He didn't need to make some kind of claim on people to enjoy them. Loving Lib had taught him that.

Tinker finally settled onto his neck like a fur scarf, purring. Jack liked the way the creature disappeared, then showed up needing his company. It reminded him to enjoy his companionship while he had it.

~

Had her husband driven her all the way up instead of dropping her off at the end of the driveway, he'd have seen what Lib already suspected was there: an unremarkable four-door sedan. A man waiting on the front porch steps.

The fight drained out of her as she trudged up the gravel incline, memorizing everything around her. Saw her property like a dark wet Polaroid, slowly developing into a moment she'd return to for the rest of her life. Photographs had always unnerved her for what they captured of the past but kept hidden of the future for the poor subjects stuck in them. It spooked her, those innocent, frozen moments before it all went sideways. *Here is a happily married, childless woman walking up her driveway alone at night*, she thought, snapping a mental picture of herself. *Remember this, the moment before everything was lost.*

It was the man, though, who seemed taken aback as she crested the slight hill and came fully into view. He sat on the step wearing a leather vest over his long-sleeved shirt, his elbows propped on his knees, head hanging low. Jerked his head up at her footfalls on the gravel, squinting at her in the darkening night. She no longer doubted who he was.

"I thought you weren't home," he said, looking around as if he'd suddenly found himself dropped there from outer space. "I just needed a minute to think."

Lib stopped about ten feet away, waiting, resigned.

"Are you her?" he said, and Lib released a long breath she must have been holding. Her legs gave up, and she sank to the ground, a finisher at the end of a forty-year marathon. Arranged herself cross-legged on the sharp stones, folded her hands into a single fist in her lap and squeezed. She smelled sour milk suddenly, tinged with sweet baby shampoo, and vaguely wondered if she was having a stroke.

"I'm her," she said, her lips numb.

He nodded, looking past her, out and around, his jaw tightening and loosening in the porch light. She stole glances at him, but they burned, her eyes darting from him to the cloud of gnats swarming frantically in the bulb's artificial glow. So he'd gotten her facial structure, then. His father had a softer neckline, one he'd kept camouflaged beneath a trim beard. She recognized her former husband's compact body, those funny familial hips he tried to hide with his tailored banker's slacks.

"You know who I am?" he asked, still focused on the tree line beyond the yard.

"Of course I do." Young breasts swollen like coconuts, leaking sweet milk through her sour-smelling bathrobe. The faintly candylike smell of a plastic rattle wedged against her cheek. Lib crossed her arms, cleared her throat. "Matthew."

His eyes cut directly through her now. "It's Matt."

She nodded, forcing herself to hold his gaze. "Matt," she whispered.

They stared at each other for a long time.

"I'm sorry, this is bullshit." He laughed, stood abruptly, patted his chest hard through his silly leather vest. "It's not like I want to be here."

Why the hell was he here, then? Why hadn't he just left well enough alone? What could he possibly want now when she'd proven herself incapable of giving him anything?

He found the pack of cigarettes in his vest pocket, lit one, and took an impossibly long pull then blew out a quick, forceful huff of smoke. "In case you're wondering, I turned out a mess. Dad did his best, but I'm a fuckup. Like you." He kicked at the porch step, a childish gesture. "Believe me, I wouldn't be here if I had anyplace else to go."

Lib knew she deserved every ounce of his venom, but it seemed aimed at someone else, two other people captured in someone else's snapshot. She wanted Jack. She wanted to go to him now, take off running after his truck, flee this strange scene. She couldn't connect her present self to the pregnant girl-bride she'd been, couldn't reconcile this angry man with the giggling baby in the Johnny Jump Up, couldn't square his boots with the soft blue sleeper with the peeling white plastic on the bottoms of the feet. Couldn't bring his father's face to mind beyond the beard, couldn't place herself in either lifetime.

Matt was staring at her, and she thought she felt him soften then, just a little, though she couldn't guess why and didn't dare let her own guard down. She didn't look up as he exhaled another toxic puff and dropped the cigarette, grinding it beneath the toe of his boot on the porch step. She heard him take a cleaner breath, then felt him walk toward her, watched his boots come into view on the gravel. He smelled like stale smoke and too much cologne.

"Come on," he said, and she looked up to see his hand stretched down, palm up. She swallowed and took it without thinking. He pulled her to her feet, then abruptly let go so that she stumbled back a little before righting herself. "Come on," he said, again, quieter this time. "Jesus, what a pair we are."

Matt followed Lib into her house. She flipped on the kitchen light and looked at the refrigerator for a moment, then crossed instead to the little cabinet over the stove where she kept the guest liquor. Chose a bottle from the dusty bunch, then two juice glasses from the cupboard. Sat down at her kitchen table and began to pour as Matt leaned against the doorjamb between the kitchen and the living room, his arms crossed. It was only when she slid his glass toward him that he scoffed. "I don't drink." Lib shrugged, downed her pour in one swallow, let the foreign elixir spread, then pulled Matt's glass back toward her. For years, she'd imagined this day. And then, for even longer, she hadn't.

"Nice place," said Matt gravely, scanning the kitchen, squinting over his shoulder into the darkened living room. "Cozy. Bet the grandkids love it."

Lib sipped from her second drink. "It's just me here," she said around her thickening tongue. Another long silence followed. The wall clock ticked, loudly, and Lib felt her thumping heart sync up with it.

"No husband? Kids?" said Matt, the sentences lifting a little at their ends, unable to hide his surprise.

"Just me," she repeated, unwilling to explain herself just yet.

Matt pushed off the doorframe with his shoulder, stepped toward her, and slowly pulled out a chair, sank into it.

"You're just a sad, lonely old woman," he said. "Pathetic."

The fight reared up in Lib again at that, and she met his gaze directly. He hadn't shaved, and his eyes, she could see now, were threaded with streaks of pink.

"I'm not sad, I'm not lonely, and I'm hardly old," she said evenly. "I am surprised. I am sorry. I am confused." *And I am terrified*, she thought but kept that one to herself.

She watched his Adam's apple swim up his neck, bob back down again.

"I should go," he said, but he slouched back in his seat. The clock ticked. Lib took a breath.

"Why have you come?" she dared. *What do you need?*

Another too-long pause, then he slapped his hand against the table and pushed himself to standing.

"I'm at the Rodeway Inn, by the gas station, not far from here. I'm paid up through this week, then I don't know what," he said. "There's a café just up the road from my motel. Should we have lunch in the daylight? After you've had some sleep?"

Lib looked up at him, stunned. Then she imagined the two of them at Carolina's and nearly laughed.

"Why don't you come back here for lunch tomorrow instead," she said, unable to think of anything she wanted less, except to be seen in public with him. "I'll fix tomato sandwiches."

Matt nodded, as if he'd expected this. Why would she be anything but disappointing? And yet, he was here, wasn't he? So which one of them was the fool?

He swiveled to go and her breath caught—something about his mannerisms, the almost womanly curve to his father's crooked hips, was as jarring, intimate, and familiar as anything she'd ever seen in another person, and she felt nauseated, her skull crowded with ghosts.

"Are you gonna be okay?" he said then, pausing in the doorway. Less unkind than curious.

"I don't know," she said.

He left anyway.

Chapter 5

When they got home from dinner, Claire fell asleep drunk with a library thriller against her face, then woke after eleven to the assault of the bedside lamp, the blaze of the hall and kitchen lights, and Dan's open-mouthed snoring.

"Thanks for taking care of us, love of my life," she snarled, stumbling a little as she left the warmth of their bed to put the house in order. Locked the front door, flipped off the lights, and wobbled back to bed, then remembered the garage door. Her tight and aching head faintly ringing, she hauled herself up again, unlocked the interior door, and leaned out into the garage—sure enough, wide open to the stale, hot night. She stabbed the button with her thumb and surveyed the kitchen—the tangle of dishes in the sink, a wine glass stained with red dregs. Her heart was flutter-racing the way it did when she fell asleep loaded and woke shortly after, and she considered another quick drink—everyone was asleep, the glass already dirty, after all. *Jesus, Claire.* She propped herself against the sink and washed the glass, slipping it back inside the cabinet before she could change her mind, then stormed back to bed. Who would do these things, if not her? And worse, why did Dan and Charlie just expect that she would do them?

Claire lay in bed awake until after three. By morning, all the goodwill she'd felt toward Dan during the family dinner at Carolina's was fully gone. She had slept right through Dan leaving for work, even though she'd intended to rise early for once; maybe try going for her first run in ages, then check online for jobs.

On the ride home from dinner, still warm from the shared drinks and good company, she had allowed a conversation about work, specifically, her lack of a job. "We know you loved being a journalist, but we also know you're an all-or-nothing thinker," Dan had said from the driver's seat, and she'd let him say it, even though she hated his use of the plural pronoun. Who was the *we* he kept referring to, and who said they knew anything about who she was? She hated the way he "helped" when she hadn't asked.

"What if it didn't have to be a choice between the best job or no job?" he continued. "What if you just found a little part-timer? Something that got you out of the house, gave you a little spending money, engaged you in the community?"

Engaged you in the community. Claire had grown further annoyed by his relentless bastardization of verbs. If someone wasn't *engaging*, they were *dialoguing* or *circling back*. But Dan's words still lingered when Claire finally got up after ten. Charlie sat strangely arched on the couch, squirming obediently in front of the TV, where she instructed him to stay until it was time for his first "shift" at Jack's—he already had his backpack on, she realized. She had intended them to spend the morning together—but then she'd slept right through it. The coffee maker had shut itself off hours earlier, but the smell still nauseated her. She poured half down the drain so it would look as if she'd had her usual amount, then settled herself at the kitchen table in front of her laptop and her favorite yellow pad.

She thought about what she might like to do and who might be hiring. She'd seen the local paper, and there were no bylines beyond the lone editor. In a town this size, every story had already been told. What, then, keep freelancing for the city magazines from this distance? Cast a wider net and churn out "10 Ways to Please Your Man" pulp for *Cosmo* or *Redbook*? Most of her former colleagues that had been downsized along with Claire now fielded PR requests at hospitals or police stations, or wrote flashy copy for insurance websites or donor letters for universities. Back at the paper, ages ago, she'd accidentally received a memo not intended for her, in which an editor had listed the beat strengths for each reporter. *Serena: social justice and government; Raquel: women's health and education policy; Miguel: culture and lifestyle; Claire: can write anything.*

Claire groaned into her hands. Maybe if they were still back in Madison, she could pull off PR or build upon the weak stream of freelancing she'd managed for a while in between Charlie duties, but Dan's new administrative position for the surrounding rural schools had brought them more than a hundred miles away from anything anyone would want to read about. She knew no one. She'd be starting from nothing. Factor in the way that freelancing showed up as a ten-year gap in her resume, and she was patently unemployable. She took a deep breath, flipped to a fresh page in her yellow pad. Let her pen hover over it, listening for the voice that had always come. *Claire:* she finally scribbled. *Can't write anything.*

She could always go down and ask her new friends, Kit and Frannie, about possible jobs. They weren't hiring, but they'd surely know of any local opportunities. But yesterday's frenzy of socializing had left Claire feeling a little too exposed after weeks without really talking to anybody—months, if she counted the time spent packing and planning before the move. In Madison she'd stopped returning texts and RSVPing for Facebook events. What was the point? All that clanging camaraderie exhausted her. Admitting she was applying for entry-level jobs at age thirty-six was also, if she was being honest, more than a little embarrassing.

She flipped open her laptop, Googled *Anthem Wisconsin Jobs*. Whatever. It wasn't like anybody here knew who she used to be, and there was no shame in an honest day's work. She needed to get over herself.

What did Jack's wife do for a living? Lib looked young to be retired, and without kids to consider, she'd likely enjoyed a long, full career. Probably a lawyer, with a practice that essentially ran itself after all these years. Or a world-famous botanist, living in obscurity after the fame brought on by her discoveries proved too much a nuisance. A musician, perhaps—an orchestral bassist!—she imagined Lib straddling the towering instrument on a touring stage. She considered the way Jack touched his wife, the way he looked at her, and felt a deep, abiding sadness. Claire could be a lawyer, a botanist, a musician. A Pulitzer Prize–winning journalist. And Dan would still never look at her the way Jack looked at Lib.

She slapped the laptop shut, pushed back from the table. "I'm jumping in the shower," she yelled to Charlie. She would drive around again, look for something in person. Charlie would be off to Jack's in an hour—she intended to follow him there, make sure everything was on the up and up—but after that, it wasn't like she'd have anything else to do. She made it under the hot stream before the tears started. Let herself cry, but only briefly so as to avoid the puffy-eyed blotchy-faced aftermath. Bent in half to catch her breath, she whispered a flurry of soft, wet prayers to the drain: *Please forgive me these thoughts. Please help me love my life. Please don't let me turn into my mother.*

Claire straightened, suddenly remembering the handsome stranger from the motel. And just like that, like an answered prayer, she felt her breath slow, her grief lift, a tingling lightness take its place. He was nobody—just some random guy—but that was precisely the point. He had seen her, he had wanted her, and if he had, others still would. She wasn't trapped, not really. She couldn't go on hating herself like this; it just wasn't sustainable. If being a mother and a wife continued to let her down, she'd simply find a way to lift herself up. As Dan had said, it didn't have to be a choice between nothing and this thing, marriage or divorce. There was plenty of room in the middle.

When Claire got dressed, she chose the light and airy periwinkle A-line dress that brought out the blue of her eyes. She took extra care with the round brush as she smoothed her hair beneath the dryer. As she applied a second coat of mascara, she flashed to his eyes through the smoke, the slow grin, and she shivered. She'd go out today, and she'd get herself a job, any job. She could do most anything, why not? And if it turned out to be awful, she'd quit—simple as that. She was a free woman, after all, just like Lib.

~

Jack had been ready for nearly two hours by the time the boy finally arrived. It wasn't Charlie's fault—he'd pedaled up right on time, just after lunch, as instructed. It was Jack who'd been jumping the gun all morning. He'd woken even earlier than usual, anxious to assess his supplies. Decided against the power washer—it'd be quicker, but it'd take the old cedar a week to dry. Besides that, every boy should experience sanding a fence at least once before he'd earned the right to move on to the easier route. He considered asking Mike at the hardware store about the new chemical washes used to strip old stain from wood, but that, too, seemed like cheating. He then had to decide between several types of oil-based stain or a five-gallon bucket he could keep on hand. It'd be expensive, and it was more than he needed, but would he have use for it, down the road? *Sure*, he figured, sudsing his scalp in a quick shower.

He panicked when he'd arrived at Mike's and found it locked—then realized it was only 8:30, a full hour and a half before the hardware store opened. He swung by the grocery, so it wasn't an entirely wasted trip, then fixed himself a slice of peanut butter toast before heading back out to the garage, just in case the boy had misunderstood the plan. Jack was back again from the hardware store and munching on an old granola bar he'd found while reorganizing two junk drawers before Charlie finally wheeled into the garage a little after noon.

"There you are," said Jack, embarrassed at how happy he was to see the boy. Charlie wore a printed tee and cargo shorts, and his crisp white jogging shoes looked new. "Your clothes are gonna get dirty. Do you need to change into something you care less for?"

Charlie looked down at himself, pushed his glasses back into place, shrugged. "Mom won't mind," he said, and then, as if summoned, Claire appeared in the doorway; apparently she'd followed the boy in her car.

"Hi again," she said, looking around the garage as Jack moved toward her, wiping his hand on his pants before reaching out to shake hers.

"Claire!" She looked pretty in a bright-blue dress. He wasn't judging, but he was encouraged on Charlie's behalf to see his mother had gone to some trouble to take care of herself two nights in a row. Perhaps her scattered appearance and cold, distracted behavior on the day they'd met had been a fluke.

"You're sure this is all right?" she said, and he nodded, tucking a clean stack of rags into his armpit and smacking together two wood blocks to which he'd stapled squares of sandpaper. "Charlie, grab that wash bucket from the floor by the bench," he'd said, motioning with his chin, "and the wire brush next to it. Follow me." The trio headed out to the backyard, where Jack creaked the cedar gate open on its hinges and dumped the supplies at its base. He talked Claire and Charlie through what they'd be working on, and Claire gave the boy an affectionate hug before leaving them to it.

"Bye, Mom!" Charlie yelled at her back, and Jack smiled, feeling fond. The fact that Charlie liked his mom made Jack like her more too.

"I thought that woman would never leave," Charlie muttered as soon as Claire drove off.

"Excuse me?" Jack frowned, uncertain he'd heard the boy correctly.

"It's just a joke we say," Charlie said, but he had the good sense to look uncertain.

Jack wondered who *we* was in this case, but he decided to leave it.

"Well, I already dropped a spot of dish soap in there," he said, leading Charlie to the outdoor water spigot and showing him how to fill the bucket three-quarters full. "We start by making this old fence clean as a whistle. We'll wipe her down, sand her, scrape her, whatever it takes. You ready?"

Charlie jogged over to pick a rag from the stack, dunked it into the bucket, and ran to the far corner of the yard, water flying. "Don't wring it out till you get there," yelled Jack, following him with the bucket. "Squeeze it over four or five planks at a time, and then give each one a good rubdown." Jack thought he'd start at the other end, and perhaps they'd meet in the middle, then changed his mind. He'd trail the boy, at least at first. Keep an eye on his work and make any necessary corrections as they went.

"So tell me, Charlie, what do you like to do?" asked Jack, watching as the boy's tentative wiping grew stronger, more assured. "When you're not riding your bike, that is."

"I don't know," said Charlie, and Jack leapfrogged him to start with the wire brush on some rougher patches on the plank ahead. For a long time, the child said nothing. Then, seemingly out of the blue, he offered, "Dad gave me a science kit for my birthday, but it's kind of a trick. On the box it looks like you can do all this stuff, but really you can't. So I just make my own science."

"Aha." Jack nodded, understanding but not quite.

The duo worked as the fat sun squatted high above their heads and then crept infinitesimally into the late afternoon. They'd made it about halfway around the fence when Jack dipped inside for the package of frosted cookies and jug of lemonade he'd spontaneously picked up at the Save Rite that morning, carried it out in a pitcher on a tray with two clean mason jars, three ice cubes in each. "Pop a squat, take a load off," he said to the boy, who immediately dropped his rag in the bucket and sat. Jack groaned as he lowered himself down next to Charlie, who had already dug into the cookies. Jack dragged his handkerchief over his face and palmed it in Charlie's direction. "You'll need one of these," he said, eyeing Charlie's flushed cheeks, sweetly pink.

"I guess I like high places," said Charlie through a mouthful, twirling the handkerchief.

"How's that?"

"You asked what I like to do. I like to collect data from high places. I like to think about what birds and bugs see and then show my brain what flying might feel like and then it sees new things. I'm telling you, but you shouldn't tell my mom, because she wouldn't like it. Okay?"

"Okay," Jack said, almost certain that it was not.

"I have a thesis. Do you know what a thesis is?"

Jack nodded.

"One of my thesises is that everything in the whole entire world looks different if you get up high and look at it. The thing I don't yet know is why. But there must be a reason that some creatures have wings but we never did and then of course some dinosaurs had both so why didn't we evolve like that? That's why I got in trouble in third grade when Mr. Schmidt thought I was being disrespectful and doing vandalism, but I was just trying to see what the aquaponics tank looked like from up on his desk."

"I see," Jack said, afraid to say more.

"Madison had tons of high places and at first I thought it didn't but this town has high places too," Charlie continued. "Nothing like the Capitol observation deck of course but some of the buildings have two floors, and the Opera House has three. Do you happen to know how high the water tower is?"

"Charlie, please tell me you are not climbing the water tower," Jack said firmly, confident that this was the correct response no matter what the boy was talking about.

"Of course not," Charlie said, and Jack relaxed a bit. "But do you know how high it is?"

Jack laughed—he couldn't help himself—then made his face serious. "Too high for discussion."

"Why, are you afraid of heights?"

"No. Well, I don't know. I don't think so."

"Just afraid of blood? Like from falling? Because the higher it is, the less it will hurt actually. Did you know that if you fall from an airplane, you will probably die from the air before you even hit the ground?"

"Charlie, I don't think I like where this is going."

"Sorry," the boy said, too quickly, and Jack felt bad.

"I just don't want you to hurt yourself, that's all."

"I'm very safe," Charlie said, quieter now. "I'm just talking about thesises and facts. I'm not dumb."

"No, no, you most certainly are not," Jack said, gesturing to indicate Charlie should take another cookie, hoping to buy himself enough silence to get a bead on just what was happening here. Charlie obliged; they munched. Tinker emerged just then from behind the lilac, eliciting a tiny gasp from Charlie. Freshly alarmed, Tinker fled.

"My cat," Jack said, stating the obvious. "Tinker's shy, but he'll introduce himself one of these afternoons, if you're patient."

"Did you know that cats use their whiskers for balance and that's how they know if it's safe to jump from high places?" Charlie said.

"That so?" Jack replied.

"So they never needed wings," Charlie continued, in a whisper. Then added, almost apologetically, "Of course, who can explain flying squirrels?"

Jack waited. Then, "Look, Charlie, I'm not trying to shut you down or doubt your science or anything like that. I'm just not practiced in this stuff."

"What stuff?"

"You know, parent-type stuff. What's appropriate conversation with kids and what isn't, I guess."

"Because you don't like kids?"

"What? Of course I like kids."

"You just didn't want to have any?"

Now Jack was speechless. Even though it had been on his mind last night, he hadn't expected this line of questioning from the boy. He'd thought it might come up at dinner after Kit had announced his marital business to the table, but it hadn't. Jack considered giving one of his flippant responses, but something about Charlie made him want to match his earnestness. The kid seemed so literal; Jack wanted to be clear. He wanted to demonstrate that truth-telling and straightforwardness were important.

"I like kids," Jack said carefully. "I would have happily had some of my own, if that had been in the cards."

"But your wife doesn't like kids?"

Jack meant to laugh at this, tried to, in fact, but couldn't.

"My wife is a very independent woman. Do you know what I mean by that?" he said, and Charlie squinted, swallowing. "We figured out a long time ago what works best for us, and having kids never really fit into our lives."

"Because you would have to live with her?"

"Charlie, this is inappropriate," Jack snapped, immediately regretting it. Lord have mercy, this had gotten heavy. Jack had certainly put older people in their place for far less, but doing so just now had felt not unlike he imagined it might feel to kick a puppy. The boy's questions were innocent, after all. Charlie blushed, further breaking Jack's heart.

"Look, it's inappropriate, but I'm gonna go ahead and answer you anyway," Jack said, flustered. "Because I believe you are coming from a place of respect and good intentions, and that matters. Do you understand?"

Charlie nodded, and Jack hesitated. The truth was he never thought about whether he'd like to live with Lib anymore, but he knew that wouldn't sound right if he said it straight out. He loved Lib more than he'd ever been able to find words for. But he also knew that forcing a living situation would change who she was, thereby changing who he loved. Factor in kids, and those changes would not only be inevitable, they would be unquantifiable. How did you explain something like that to a child? Since when did kids needs to know everything anyway? And what, precisely, did any of this have to do with heights? Jack dug a finger in his left ear, stirred a sudden itch.

"I guess it's sort of like evolution. Everybody needs to figure out for themselves the best way to spend their days, and what most people don't realize is it doesn't have to be contingent on who they love," Jack finally said. "Damn, do you know what contingent means?"

Charlie drained his lemonade, his little brow furrowed beneath sweaty bangs. He flopped to lie flat on his back in the grass, his eyes behind his glasses even more magnified at this angle. Pointed up at a jet arcing across the pale blue bowl, traced its vapor trail with his finger. Jack felt the day's work sink deeper into his stiffening muscles and stifled a yawn, bracing himself for the next question.

"But you for sure don't know how tall the water tower is?"

"Can't say I do," Jack said, annoyed, relieved.

"Do you know much about frogs? Specifically, their organs?"

"No, no," Jack said, alarmed again but feeling himself smile. "Can't say I know that either."

"I'm an only child, you know."

"Is that so? I have a brother and a sister, but we don't talk much," said Jack, waiting to see if Charlie intended to connect any of these dots. But the boy offered nothing more, and Jack was grumpily grateful for what felt like forgiveness over their little dustup, if it had even been a dustup at all.

"I'd better go," Charlie said, sitting up suddenly, hopping to his feet. Jack wondered if he still had that old pogo stick lying around anymore, the one he'd found free on the curb on heavy pickup day, years back. Jack stood, too, though slower. Brushed the grass from his butt.

"I know I said mornings were off limits," Jack said, feeling weirdly self-conscious about Lib, about snapping, about all of it. "But we can start earlier tomorrow if you want. I'm seeing now that this fence is a pretty big job."

"I'll see," said Charlie over his shoulder, jogging away. He stopped suddenly, swiveled around and ran back to Jack, hugged him quick and tight around the hips. "Oho," breathed Jack, tipped slightly off balance, as Charlie ran off again, disappeared through the fence gate, leaving it hanging open.

Jack stood in his backyard for a long time, staring at the spot beyond the house where Charlie had disappeared. When he could move again, he cast his misty eyes about, assessing the progress they'd made. At this rate, the fence would take weeks, maybe longer. It wasn't an unpleasant thought either. Not in the least.

He was about to go in when he changed his mind, dragged the stepladder from the garage, steadied it in the grass. Climbed three rungs, then four. From his perch he assessed the yard where they'd just spent all afternoon, where he'd just spent four decades, and it was true; it did look different. Unfamiliar, somehow.

"How about that?" he said, climbing down as carefully as he could.

~

Lib was waiting for Matt on the porch swing when he came back Thursday afternoon, soothing herself by letting her bare feet graze the smooth planks as she rocked. Not a single cloud smudged the pale-blue horizon, and a gentle breeze pushed the humidity up and out of the rustling birch leaves. *You never know what Wisconsin is gonna bring you in August*, she could hear Jack say, as if this was an ordinary afternoon. She'd prepared tomato and mayonnaise sandwiches, but she could think of nothing to serve with them, save for a bag of pretzels she found at the back of the pantry. She hated pretzels but kept a bag on hand for Jack, who loved them. *Like chewing on wood chips*, she had teased when he'd spent that car ride to Door County sucking the salt off each twist.

Lib brought the sandwiches to the wire bistro table she kept on the side of the wraparound porch, laid the bag of pretzels on top of them in halfhearted protection against the flies, then returned to wait on the swing. She didn't like it that Matt had been inside her house last night, and it felt worse somehow in the light of day. They could talk well enough out here. She hoped the pleasant weather would serve as an effective excuse so she wouldn't have to actually say it.

When she saw him pull in, she realized that she hadn't thought of drinks. She jumped up, the swing smacking the backs of her legs as she hurried inside. Dug in the back of the cupboard and found two plastic cups, heard the car door slam as her trembling hands filled one and then the other from the faucet. Water sloshed onto the floor as she rushed—she'd deal with that later—used a toe to pry and a hip to prop the screen door open, letting herself through. She stopped when he stopped. They appraised each other from opposite ends of the porch steps. This time, she couldn't help but notice, she was the one on higher ground.

"Morning," he said, and she felt her right eyebrow shoot up. *Hardly.*

"Come on up," she said, carrying the glasses to the table. He took his time climbing the steps. She opened the bag of pretzels and held it out to him, but he looked away. "Can't stand pretzels," he said, and she wondered what she'd do with the bag now, why she'd opened it before asking, whether he'd ever take anything from her, whether disliking pretzels was hereditary. "How about tomato sandwiches, do you like those?"

"You're probably wondering about me, about my life," he said, ignoring her. And Lib, chagrined, noted that she wasn't, exactly. In the interval between the shock of his arrival and their confrontation last night, she hadn't yet let herself think of Matt as a person who had a life. But he was a grown man, it struck her now. Not just a thing that had happened to her. None of this was his fault. She understood precisely why he was so angry with her. What she had yet to get her head around was why she was so angry with him.

"Yes," she made herself say, her voice shaking. "Of course."

"Dad's dead," he said, and Lib felt it like a bee sting. A tiny prick of shock, a numbing awareness as the unexpected venom spread.

"But before that, I graduated with honors. All State Football. My stepmom moved back to Chicago after they got divorced. So, you know, she left me too." He paused to let his gaze shoot through her, reminding her she was his target. But she was distracted, running the math. Dead. Jon Marlow would have been eighty-four.

"I actually built a really successful financial services practice after college, you know, before everything collapsed in 2008. Moved back home with Dad temporarily, and I was getting back on my feet, but some bullshit happened, and basically my new boss screwed me. I got into some trouble, thanks to all the shit people in my life and the shit things I've been through. It got a little out of hand at the end, and I lost my new place. Kate dumped me, Dad's third wife got everything after he died, so I can't exactly go back home again, even though I'm totally clean and sober this time—so I figured it was finally your turn to help me out. God knows you've gotten out of it long enough."

She winced as he hawked and spit over her railing.

"Any questions?"

She had no questions for Matt, not yet. She felt stung and small. She was still thinking about Jon, trying to picture him as an elderly man. He'd already seemed ancient to her at forty-three, when she'd been just seventeen.

But Matt let out a long "Gahhhhh," throwing his head back to stare up at the porch ceiling, which Lib had repainted a soft sticky blue two summers before. "I can't even be mean to you the way I want to! I can't even do that!" And then, to her great astonishment, he began to cry. She leaned forward, looking for an escape hatch, then forced herself back into the chair. *Stay here, Libby.* Matt wiped furiously at his eyes.

"Matthew," she said. Then, "Matt."

At that, he began to sob harder, high, childlike hiccups, balled-up fists digging into his eye sockets, knuckles circling, he bent into himself, biting against his palms. She sat there while Matt keened and mewled, part of her appalled, part of her envious. She couldn't remember the last time she'd let go like that, let alone in front of another person. The sounds coming from him reminded her of the coyote pups she'd hear on the wind some nights, the fits that always started with a single low whine and culminated in a frenetic, harmonic cacophony. She, then and now, the lone silent witness. *Do not fall apart, Libby. You will not fall apart.*

In time, his breathing slowed, and the well of hot tears and snot dried up. Lib waited until she was sure he wouldn't take it as an affront, another abandonment, then stood and set a gentle hand on his shoulder as she passed him. She grabbed the tissue box from the living room and brought it back outside.

"You can stay here with me," she said, wishing she could take back the words as soon as they slipped out. It was the last thing she wanted. She couldn't hide him or explain his presence. She didn't know him at all, other than that he was apparently some sort of addict, possibly a criminal, and that no one else would take him in. And that he hated her guts. She couldn't imagine what she could possibly say to Jack to explain who he was, why she'd done what she'd done, who she'd been before she knew him. But she couldn't unsay it now, even if such a thing were possible. She couldn't leave this boy twice.

Matt squinted at the sandwiches before him, then picked up a half and tore into it. "That's a terrible idea, you know," he mumbled around the mouthful. Lib contemplated the platter, took a half for herself and then a too-tentative bite, leaning to catch a tomato slice that slipped free and slimed against her chin. "I know," she said, wiping, chewing, swallowing.

"Listen, I'm not here for some big reunion. I don't want to hear you making a bunch of excuses. I don't want you confessing stuff just to make yourself feel better. Your reasons stopped mattering to me a long time ago. Do you understand? If there's something I want to know, I'll ask."

Lib chewed slower, defensiveness rising like a tide in her, pulling. She waited for it to wash back out.

"I have a spare room. I'll need to get it ready," she said carefully. "And I understand that you are angry. But you are still a guest in my home, and it's been mine alone for nearly as long as you've been alive, and I'm the only one who makes the rules here."

Matt snorted, shoved the last of the sandwich in his mouth and shrugged, reaching for the cup of water, mumbling something inaudible into it.

"What's that?" she challenged, leaning forward. He set the cup down with a hollow plunk, swallowing.

"I said whatever you want, *Mom*." The word was not an endearment but a stone, hurled at her, a woman scorned. Matt leaned back in his chair, patted again at that vest.

"Listen, I'm going to have to explain who the hell you are, and I don't yet know how or when I'm going to be able to do that," she said. "So you can stay, but you need to be discreet, at least for now. And no goddamn smoking on this property."

Matt stood, lit the cigarette he'd pulled out, and took a long drag. If it had been a movie, Lib thought, he'd have blown the smoke right into her face, a sad cliché. But he turned and walked off the porch as he exhaled, then stopped to look back at her from the car.

"I'll think about it," he said, softer, and he climbed in and drove off. Lib watched his brake lights blink once at the curve of the driveway, then disappear down the hill, more gradually this time. Progress. She gathered the sandwiches, the cups, and the pretzel bag, hugging it all to her. Insanity, but progress.

She carried her load inside.

Chapter 6

After getting Charlie squared away at Jack's, Claire had driven around Anthem again, imagining where she might like to work. She'd tried the struggling little coffee shop first, but they had no need for employees. It was the same case at two combination floral/gift shops across the street from one another (Claire wondered if the town could handle this level of competition or if it was a rising-tide-lifts-all-boats kind of situation); the antique store, the hair and nail salon, even the gas station where she'd impulsively bought that crap wine. She was sheepishly disappointed to find no sign of the stranger outside the motel, though she lingered as long as she could, filling just a quarter of her tank again. She briefly considered applying at the motel as the gas glugged, then remembered a horrifying story on bed bugs from her newspaper days and shuddered, shelved the pump, got in her car, and drove back toward downtown. She made a stop at one liquor store for a fine bottle each of red and white, then stopped at a second liquor store for two six-packs of microbrew and a bottle of high-end vodka. She was far too proud to purchase two weeks' worth of alcohol at the same place.

"Having a cookout?" said the skinny goateed man working the register, and she laughed to cover her embarrassment.

"You bet!" she said, scurrying ratlike back to the car to resume her search.

When the chirpy woman at a sewing notions store informed her that she hadn't had an employee in decades and that the only place she knew in town that regularly hired was the grocery store across the street ("Everybody works there at some point, honey"), Claire pulled into the grocery parking lot, twisted open the last mini bottle from the glove box, and stared at the store. The parking lot was strangely full for midday, a cross section of townsfolk pushing carts in and out the automatic doors. So this was where everyone went when they weren't at the café. The *v* in Save Rite was smashed out, and some birds had made a nest in the hollow where it had been. *Sa e Rite*, it commanded, and she answered, "Right." She was tired, annoyed, and craving a real glass of any of what she'd just bought, but the time on her phone read only 2:04. She'd make this her last stop, ask inside, even take an application home, where she'd consider—and likely reject—it from the comfort of her couch.

But the manager, Ben, insisted she fill out the application in the store. Caught off guard and too exhausted and depressed to resist, it occurred to her that there might even be an employee discount on alcohol sales. Dutifully, she took the clipboard and pen in slightly shaking hands.

"You have no retail experience whatsoever?" he said as he looked, balefully, over the application, apparently unimpressed by her degrees.

"No," she answered, distracted by the way the fluorescent lights ricocheted off the impossibly bright circle of his bald crown each time he bent over his clipboard.

"And no criminal record?"

"Nope, don't have that either." Jaunty elevator Muzak burbled overhead, interrupted by interludes of the same prerecorded plea—she recognized Ben's voice, the long drawn-out *o* in *boneless*—promising savings on skinless chicken breasts. She felt caught in another one of her dazes, disembodied from the woman handing the ballpoint pen back to Ben. But it was her palm that displayed the evidence, an accidental slash of blue ink indicating this new curve in her lifeline.

"What's your availability?" he asked, and Claire murmured, with more than a little sarcasm, that she was pretty much wide open forever. But then Ben reached into a cardboard box behind his desk. "Ladies small?" he said, looking her up and down as he handed her what turned out to be a standard-issue red polo shirt. "Can you train right now?" And just like that, Claire was a Save Rite employee.

She thought her new boss was kidding when he asked her to pull the shirt over her dress, but she was beginning to suspect that Ben wasn't much of a jokester.

"I've got three dozen high school kids working here," he said, digging in his desk drawer, "and at least two dozen make it in maybe three hours a week, if I'm lucky. And I'm a guy who never gets lucky, you know what I'm saying?" Claire knew exactly what he was saying.

He handed her a pin that spelled TRAINEE for those who couldn't already guess by the way she soon stood in the checkout line, shadowing a woman named Pat, who kept sighing and removing her glasses to clean them right in the middle of every third customer's purchasing experience. Pat was Save Rite's longest-running employee, Ben said, now that his dad, Clarence, was gone.

"I'm so sorry," she said, thinking Ben meant his father was dead.

"Don't be," he said over his shoulder as he walked away. "He's got a condo down in Boca. The ladies love him. It's like four to one down there. Did you know that?"

Even now, two hours into her first shift, Claire figured she'd go home and laugh with Dan and Charlie about the whole thing. But she couldn't seem to snap out of it. She couldn't even blame her strange state on the mini bottle, now entirely worn off. She shifted from one already sore foot to the other, tugging at the collar of the polo scratching against her neck.

"I'm on break in three minutes," Pat the cashier growled, and Claire jumped. It was the first time the woman had spoken to her. "We'll have to shut the register down. You're not ready, of course."

"Of course." Claire nodded. Pat sat hunched on a stool—a concession that must come after a certain number of loyal years, Claire figured, glancing at the three other clerks standing behind their registers. Pat wheezed heavily through her nose. Every shift on her ample bottom seemed an effort, as if she were insulted by her body's instinct to move. Claire was staring at the frenzy of whiskers on Pat's soft chin, calculating again when her own last wax had been—God, not since

Madison—when she was startled by the smack of a package of hot dogs slapped onto the conveyor belt before her; a bag of buns, a bag of chips, a small bottle of ketchup, and a bright green Mountain Dew.

"Take two packs of Marlboros too, please," said a low voice, and Claire looked up to see the man—him!—from the motel smirking back at her.

Claire went rigid. Pat didn't bother to stifle a groan as she slid from her stool. She flipped off the switch on the light that glowed 3 above the register and trudged off, apparently to wherever the cigarettes were kept.

"How's the training going?" he asked, eyes lingering a little too long on the pin on her chest. He was even more handsome up close, and he smelled delicious, despite the smoke; his cologne or aftershave had a masculine and sweetly raw scent. His presence in front of her was unbelievable, as if she'd conjured him, much like she had Lib that first day. Claire felt her legs go numb.

"I don't really know what's happening." She smiled at him, finding her voice. "I wandered in for a loaf of bread and, the next thing you know . . ." She trailed off. He stepped a hair closer, the front of his jeans grazing the counter between them, as if it were suddenly magnetized. She felt its pull and pushed herself back slightly, nudging Pat's stool.

"Must pay well," he said. He looked around, then he began to dance to the piped-in music in a mock '80s toe-step, fingers snapping, head bobbing. "Or are you just here for the rad tunes?"

Claire laughed, nodding her head in time. "Nice," she said. "With moves like that, you could work here too. Save Rite needs men with your skills."

It was mortifying, the kind of thing Claire could only imagine saying in a weird dream or in one of her and Charlie's games. But he stopped his silly dance, his stare intensifying. Maybe he was as surprised as she was that she'd said something so forward, goofy as it was. She could see now that his eyes were red. Tired, or high?

"What's your name?"

"Claire," she said, steadily returning his gaze, as if this were a challenge she regularly accepted, as if she wasn't a lost and lonely housewife who'd wandered into some parallel universe of avocados and tabloids and flirtations with good-looking, cigarette- (or whatever) smoking strangers.

"Claire," he said, as if tasting it. "I'm Matt. Do you work tomorrow?"

Claire hadn't any intention of coming back here—not tomorrow, not next week, not ever again.

"I think so," she said, and he nodded slowly.

"Maybe I'll see you then," he said. "Man's gotta eat, after all."

"After all," she replied, unable to think of anything else to say.

Pat returned then, setting the cigarettes on the belt and then leaning hard on them, smashing them, to gain enough leverage to climb back onto her stool.

"You didn't even ring these things up?" she wheezed, exasperated.

"I'm sorry, I didn't realize I was supposed to," Claire said, widening her eyes in warning at Matt, who'd begun to laugh.

Pat finished Matt's transaction, moving with a swiftness Claire hadn't witnessed in the woman before now. Then she talked through the procedure for temporarily shutting down a register, but Claire had a hard time following as she kept an eye on Matt through the front windows, ambling to his car, the plastic bag swinging from two fingers, already smoking. God, he was good-looking. She hadn't talked to a man that way in years.

"You'll have to check with Ben," said Pat, and Claire nodded, though she hadn't heard what she'd just agreed to. Pat shuffled off, and Claire walked toward Ben's office, ready to receive her next instructions. The music overhead had shifted to an orchestral version of "Stayin' Alive," and she found herself whistling along. Poked her head into the office, resisting the urge to announce herself with jazz hands. *A checkout girl*, she thought. There were worse things.

~

It was probably nothing, Lib's distance. He was so distracted anyway, the next three weeks whizzing by with a consuming swiftness Jack hadn't experienced in years. Charlie came nearly every day, and if they weren't taking breaks from the fence to tackle any one of a half-dozen projects, or making supply runs to Mike's, they were having backyard picnics—Charlie often brought pickle and mayo sandwiches, which Jack had decided to learn to love—or riding bicycles, as they were today.

"It's . . . up here, past . . . barn!" Charlie shouted over his shoulder, the rushing wind in Jack's ears swallowing the bulk of his words.

Remarkably, Charlie had gotten Jack back on his old bicycle, the yellow Schwinn Varsity he'd picked up in the early '70s (hanging from his garage ceiling since at least the '90s)—"vintage" now, he shuddered to think. What started as a mechanics lesson had morphed into several rides with the boy, who had seemingly boundless energy. Charlie had been awestruck watching Jack pluck and pry the pedals, brakes, crankset, and derailleurs from the bike frame, creating a pile of greasy bones on the floor, then reassembling the bicycle from a skeleton before his very eyes.

"Like a dinosaur excavation!" Charlie exclaimed. "Do you ride it, though?"

The second question revealed to Jack the true source of the boy's excitement. Before long, Charlie had talked him into accompanying him on his explorations, and Jack found himself enjoying the view of his familiar town through fresh eyes and tired legs. He'd even taken the old Schwinn out for a spin by himself a time or two, when Lib was too busy or tired to visit, which seemed more frequent lately. But maybe it was just that he had less free time himself, so imposing his schedule on her was causing more hit-or-miss opportunities than in the past. Besides, he was enjoying himself immensely—she'd never begrudge him that, especially given the recent loss of Lyle. In fact, he found he could go hours without thinking about Lyle now. He felt guilt over that, tinged, admittedly, with relief.

He still couldn't quite get a bead on the boy. Sometimes he said something smarter than half the adults Jack regularly spoke with, and other times he sounded so ridiculously young that Jack would wonder what on earth he was doing with this kid. He could be a real motormouth, going on and on about his "experiments," which as far as Jack could tell mostly involved either climbing up on everything within sight, or collecting the corpses of dead bugs or small critters flattened into road kill and scribbling his findings in the notebook he always carried in his backpack. Then some days he clammed right up, and, to be honest, Jack would have enjoyed the silent spells if he hadn't started to worry about the boy. Was he okay? Had he made any friends his own age? Was it weird that he wanted to hang out with an old man so much? Were his obsessive scientific pursuits unnatural? Jack wished, for the first time in his adult life, that he had some context for the relationship. Some other kid to compare Charlie to. But of course he didn't (other than Carolina's girls, but they'd been so different from this boy, and his sister's kids, who might as well live on another planet) and so he had no choice but to go with his gut, following Charlie's whims, accepting his invitations when they came.

They crested the hill past Sutter's farm, and Charlie stopped to let Jack catch up. Both were breathing hard, though Jack knew he'd take far longer to recover, and Charlie was gesturing wildly toward the bridge down in the shallow valley a half mile away.

"Did you even know this was here?" Charlie hollered.

"Psht, sure did," Jack panted. "Pretty great, huh?" As a boy, this had been one of his favorite vistas. It looked like something out of a painting: a rolling expanse of prairie and farmland for miles, save for the meandering creek carving an equator of sorts through the middle. And there, at the center of the portrait, a green metallic bridge. A miniature version of bridges Jack, at the time, had only seen in photographs of cities. He used to think of it as a green alligator, crouching in wait for a hapless boy to wander into its steely maw.

"This bridge is my favorite because it attracts frogs. Wanna go down there? There's a bunch of bad words carved on it," Charlie said, and Jack assessed the oppressive heat of the day, the deceptively gradual downward slope of the hill. He remembered how long the hill really was and dreaded the endless climb back up. He also recalled the view was best enjoyed from afar, that it lost a bit of its magic up close.

"I don't think these old legs can take that just yet," said Jack. "Don't you need to be getting back soon? That thing at the school tonight?"

Charlie sighed, muscled his BMX around to turn back. That was a key difference with kids compared to adults, Jack was finding: the boy rarely argued or pushed back. If Jack said a thing was so, it was so. Jack turned his own bike back toward town and let Charlie pedal ahead—but the boy soon braked.

"Wait! Here's a good one!"

Jack rolled to a stop next to Charlie, who was leaning over his handlebars and peering down at a dead frog next to his front tire. Almost in slow motion, as in a horror movie, Charlie rolled his tire over the frog's belly.

"Charlie!" Jack said, alarmed.

"Shhhh, watch," Charlie said as the poor frog's innards slowly emerged from its mouth. "That," he said, "is one of my very favorite experiments."

Charlie got down to examine his work up close. Jack continued to straddle over his bike, afraid he wouldn't be able to stand back up if he joined him.

"It doesn't hurt them," Charlie said. "It's the same as in a lab but more like recycling. And if you don't get to them in time, the sun dries them up, and then the experiment won't work."

Jack was at a loss. What did parents and teachers say when a kid did something disturbing? Did the automatic authority his age engendered with Charlie require a sort of responsibility too? He'd rather it didn't. He'd rather continue to treat the boy as a peer. If Lyle or Lib had done such a thing, what would he say to them? "Charlie," he finally said, checking his watch to hide his distaste, "you are a very interesting person."

They were a couple of miles outside town, on a quiet stretch of road outside Anthem, on the opposite end of the four-lane, where Wisconsin's famed Driftless Region really started to show off. Jack loved telling Charlie about how the glaciers had skipped this special area during the last ice age. How their homeland was gorgeous, remarkable, and more or less taken for granted by the humans that lived here now, who were as used to postcard vistas as they were to finding world-class cheese at the gas station. He knew he repeated himself a bit, but he didn't think the boy was humoring him. He seemed genuinely curious, seemed to like hanging out together as much as Jack did.

It was a Thursday afternoon, and they had the road to themselves; anybody out this way either lived in one of the sprawling valley farms or was headed to the isolated bars that marked so many country corners, usually a convenient stone's throw from at least one church. This was, in fact, the road to Jack's old family farm, now run by his siblings and their families, who'd built brand-new ranch houses on the back forty to keep up with the duties his folks no longer performed. Jack could have done the same, but he'd broken tradition early on, preferring his hard work went to tasks of his choosing instead of the regimented, relentless demands of farming. He visited of course for Sunday luncheon and holidays, or performed odd handyman tasks when needed, but mostly he thought of his family as a friendly but foreign group into which he had accidentally been born but never quite fit. He'd mentioned bits and pieces of his family life to Charlie but didn't dare share how close they were to the farm now, for fear he'd want to bike the fifteen miles to Cranville. Jack was hardly feeling up for a trip like that, not today or any day. He made a mental note to show Charlie the crushed limestone bike trail that most locals stuck to and that ran parallel to the highway, one of many former railroad tracks the state began converting in the '60s. Probably too boring for him, but at least on the trail he could pedal his little legs off without adult supervision or the risk of getting lost with a wrong turn. Then Jack wouldn't have to worry so much when he was out of sight.

Apparently satisfied, Charlie began pedaling again, yelling back over his shoulder, "You're right! I'd better get home before Mom does so I can tell her I already took a shower!"

Jack lingered behind at a safe distance—you never knew when the boy was going to brake abruptly to conduct yet another "experiment" or swerve suddenly into Jack's path to share some revelation. It was like he rode that bike so often that sometimes he forgot he was on it. At the corner of Pine and Fir, just past the fabled water tower on the edge of town, they waved goodbye as their paths split, and as Jack rode home, he imagined Charlie riding along his own route. He thought about it until enough time had passed that the boy had surely arrived safely.

Charlie had told Jack that his mother had taken a job at the Save Rite. How anyone could stand Clarence's kid as a boss, Jack had no idea—but he was hardly one to judge a woman for wanting an honest day's work. Did she bear Jack any ill will for occupying so much of her son's time? Jack was perfectly happy, even thrilled, but he couldn't help but wonder yet again what Charlie would have been doing this summer if they hadn't stumbled upon this arrangement.

Back home, Jack collapsed into the camp chair he'd set beside the garage door. He didn't want to sit too long, for fear he'd stiffen up. "I'll just rest my eyes for a minute," he said out loud (in case the cat was listening somewhere), knowing full well he'd nod off, just as he had multiple times since Hurricane Charlie had hit. He'd never had trouble sleeping, but now he found himself dozing pretty near anyplace he held still for too long—the back step, the café stool, even the john once last week. He'd been climbing into bed with the sunset and sleeping through its rise, and though his body ached all over, it was the good kind of hurt. Proof of a day well spent. A life well earned.

If Lib was bothered by this turn of events, she hadn't said as much. It occurred to him then that he hadn't been by her place at all since Charlie started coming around. He'd been lazy, letting her come to him, instead of keeping it even. Was she mad about this, and not saying? She had seemed a little off the handful of times she'd visited recently, he allowed. Extra quiet, overly sensitive, maybe stuck up in her head over something. Maybe his friendship with Charlie really was bothering her more than she wanted to admit—but as long as she wasn't telling him that, he wasn't going to assume it. Who was he to say she didn't like a break from him once in a while?

They'd learned through some dicey trial and error early on that most arguments could be avoided if you just trusted the other to speak up when troubled, and otherwise you shut up. *Speak up or shut up*, he thought fondly, and he missed her something fierce just then. He'd let himself doze a bit and then clean up, head over to see her. Maybe stop by the grocery and pick up fixings, cook her something over at her place.

Or maybe not, depending on how the sleep did him. All that worried him could wait. If there was one thing he could count on, it was that life would still be there for him in the morning, if he was lucky.

~

August was nearly gone now, and Lib had spent most of it walking on eggshells around Matt. Ever since he'd moved into the guest room—the childhood bedroom she'd closed off from the rest of the house, now breathing open like a tomb—she'd faced his sudden attacks. They'd be having an innocent conversation about Matt's new workplace, the Save Rite, and its cast of characters—especially that Claire Taylor, Lib couldn't help but notice—and then she'd move to snap the beans or wipe down the stove, and he'd suddenly lash out. But she was already learning that if she suppressed her pride and addressed his concerns as honestly as she could, his vitriol would evaporate, and their precarious equilibrium would return. It was exhausting, but she stayed. She, Lib, who had never stayed before.

Don't get too excited, Libby, she scolded herself. This so-called staying was just another way of running, as far as Jack was concerned.

The fact that Matt had taken a job in town made hiding him in her house that much more real—he was here, he was staying—and yet she still had no intention of telling Jack. The more time that passed, the less possible it seemed that she could find any way out of this mess.

There'd been a couple of close calls. Last week she'd stopped into the Save Rite, as usual, Thursday midmorning—a time she favored both because it was relatively slow and because the weekly produce delivery was fresh off the truck. Although Matt was working, he'd told her he mostly stocked shelves and manned the loading docks, plus they'd agreed they'd never let on that they knew each other; still, she tiptoed through the aisles like a shoplifter—until she stumbled upon a real one. She rounded the condiments aisle just in time to see that boy, Charlie, who Jack had been spending all his time with, slip a jar of pickles into the enormous leg pocket of his knee-length shorts. She was sure it was him.

Rattled, she skipped the aisle entirely and made a beeline for the cash registers, only to find Matt there helping that ridiculous Pat woman bag up groceries—the other cashiers just did this for themselves. But he'd pretended he didn't know her, and they'd made it through.

But on today's visit—chosen purposely because it was not her usual time—she rolled up to the registers and was relieved to find Matt nowhere in sight. She found she had only two choices—Pat's lane, or Claire Taylor's, the boy's mother and the subject of so many of Matt's daily rundowns. The latter looked out of place in her tomato-red collared shirt and matching lipstick, vivid against her lovely pale skin.

"Well, hello there," said Lib, pushing her mini-cart into place, hoping to get it all over with quickly. "What a pleasant surprise."

"Lib, hello!" chirped Claire, and Lib instinctively decided not to mention seeing Charlie the other day as if, in turn, Claire would find no reason to mention Matt. Though why would she? Claire had no idea of Matt's connection to Lib, she reminded herself. To Claire, Matt was just another coworker. Lib's lies were dulling her senses, mixing her up. She pressed a discreet hand to her belly, repressed the urge to look wildly about for signs of either boy, hers or Claire's.

"Do you ever just know you're about to say something weird, but you can't stop yourself?" Claire said, and Lib was certain the woman's hands were shaking as she dragged each item across the scanner. There was a speck of glitter at the top of Claire's cheekbone, near her eye. Had she done something different with her hair? Her perfume was pungent, the scent almost like something fermented, and she chewed furiously at a minty gum. Claire tapped in the code for broccoli, then pushed the wet green bunch to the side. "Because I saw you that day, out in the rain."

"How's that?" said Lib, a sudden trickle of sweat tickling down her lower back.

"I saw you before we officially met, earlier that morning. I'm sorry, but I can't not tell you this for a minute longer. You ran past my house in that crazy storm in your nightgown, barefoot and soaking wet, and

I thought you were the most beautiful thing I'd ever seen, and after that I tried to find out who you were, if you were even real."

Sweet Jesus. What was this now? To her credit, Claire looked surprised herself. Lib kept her face plain as she struggled to remember the details of that terrifying morning and that dinner, weeks ago.

"I couldn't believe my luck when you walked into the café with Jack," Claire pressed. "Before that, I was honestly worried I'd made you up."

"Well, I'm certainly real," Lib said, thinking of Matt lurking in the aisles, the impending doom waiting for her with Jack. She let herself glance around, but the atrium was quiet, and Pat appeared to have nodded off at her register.

"Is it that you love storms?" Claire asked, grabbing an errant peach that had begun to roll away, then pushing the lot of them together on the scanner bed as though she were racking a game of pool. "You just looked so . . . free."

If she only knew. But she could feel the sadness beneath the woman's questions, which, though deeply intimate, didn't strike Lib as nosy, just weird. She couldn't help but feel sorry for her, even as she was desperate to escape her company.

"You have a beautiful family," Lib redirected, trying not to think about what she'd seen the boy doing last week. Maybe she'd been mistaken. "Jack is really so fond of Charlie. I hear he's a smart and helpful worker. You've raised him well."

"Oh, yes, thank you," said Claire, and her eyes, to Lib's horror, suddenly flooded with tears. "That's good to hear. It was a little weird for me at first, letting him go off with a stranger like that. No offense," she added quickly.

"None taken." Lib smiled, wildly uncomfortable.

"It's just I haven't seen Charlie this happy in . . . years. Jack seems great. And he's obviously crazy about you." Claire wrapped Lib's package of chicken in a second layer of plastic. "What's your secret to such a long and happy marriage?"

"Privacy," Lib said, smiling to soften the hint but hoping that the younger woman got it. She seemed to, wisely keeping her mouth shut as she took the cloth bag Lib held out, tucked in the plastic-wrapped chicken and asparagus spears with the expert care of a mother. Lib felt a wave of something unfamiliar roll through her, envisioning a place setting of three at a backyard patio table, Claire's husband at the grill, little Charlie giggling as Claire chased him through the freshly cut grass. Pickles for dessert. Jack stopping by to say hello to the perfect little family.

"You're not by chance an orchestral bassist, are you?" asked Claire, who apparently hadn't gotten the message after all. Lib accepted her change and receipt from Claire's hand, turned to hustle out of the store—and ran smack dab into her husband.

"Lib!" Jack cried, his face opening up with his arms. She leaned into him—but it was, of course, awkward with the bags. He tried to slip one free to relieve her, but she pulled it away from him, leading to their most awkward interaction in memory. "Everything okay?" said this man with whom she had always been so effortlessly in sync.

Thinking quickly, she said, "I don't want to get you sick." The lines across his sweet brow deepened beneath his cap. She was acutely aware that Claire was watching all of this. She had somehow become a liar. A terrible, horrible person. At least she wasn't stealing pickles. She wondered if she should tell him what she'd seen Charlie do. He'd certainly disapprove, but she didn't want to hurt him.

"How did I not know you were sick?" he said, though they both knew how absurd the question sounded. "I'd been thinking I might come over tonight, cook you something in your kitchen."

She cleared her throat, managed a cough.

"I'm on the tail end of it," she said, holding up the bag she hadn't let him take. "I've got provisions. One last pot of chicken soup ought to do it, and then I'll be paying you a visit."

"Promise?" he said, looking both skeptical and deeply concerned.

"I promise. I miss you," she said, meaning it. "If we're both lucky, I might even be by tonight. I appreciate your offer but it'll be good to get out of my place. I've been cooped up."

"Okay," he said. "But if you're not, I'm coming to find you. I don't care if I catch a little cold."

"Deal," she said, leaning to offer her forehead. He kissed it, long and soft, and she stood there siphoning that energy from him, pretending she'd finally found a way to freeze time.

"Love you," they said, and she slipped out the automatic doors.

She walked home, carrying her groceries, sweating out the close call, astonished that this deception of hers was quickly reaching the one-month mark. How was that possible? Would it be different if Jack had bothered to pay closer attention? Had she really tried that hard to hide Matt's arrival from Jack? It was no longer that clench-jawed, bull-headed intention she'd set that first night. And nothing like a lifetime ago, when she'd gotten the news about her mother and decided it was finally safe to come back; left Jon and Matthew, tore her mother's house into pieces.

She'd never lied to Jack. Not in thirty-three years. He wasn't going to see it that way, but it was true. All she'd done was start over at the age of twenty—a full five years before she even knew him. How was that a crime? Everything that happened before that was nobody's business but her own, and everything that had ever happened since they'd met shortly after her twenty-fifth birthday was the truest living she'd ever known. Jack was her partner in that new freedom and joy, often the very source and the reason for these things, and whenever he asked her about her upbringing, she only told him true things. They were five years apart in age, and she'd kept to herself another five after coming back—so it had been easy, even in her small hometown he'd adopted, to sketch in vague details without revealing the whole awful picture.

She'd never told anyone but Carolina how bad it really was; even then, not the worst of it. What she left out was meant to erase more than deceive. That girl simply wasn't her, so there was no reason to share her story. Eventually the numb detachment of those early years evolved into what felt like a genuine rebirth. At some point, she was no longer outrunning trauma or a foolish young woman's mistakes; she literally no longer recognized the person she'd been.

She crested the hill, rounded the driveway, felt the extraordinary relief her front steps always brought. Put the groceries away, headed out to her favorite spot among the prairie field, settled in to lay on her back. Not long after, she heard Matt's car roll in. She knew it was him by the speed with which he took her driveway, unbothered by the way he disturbed the gravel, and the lack of care with which he always let the screen door slam behind him on his way in. The bottlebrush and June grass formed an itchy mattress beneath her back, not quite enough padding to block the wedge of limestone poking into her pelvis from behind. She shifted to better fit herself against the cool earth.

She'd been coming out here a lot since Matt's arrival, always telling him she needed to pull the weeds—but if he'd bothered to explore the property even once these past weeks, he'd know there was nothing to pull. This was prairie, native to the area but absent throughout the farm years, when the plow had favored alfalfa and corn. In the early '80s, Lib had begun to coax the native plants along, with the help of a natural seed saleswoman down from Westfield. Lib had carefully selected bluestem, vivid purple asters, fuchsia milkweed, and golden coreopsis as though she were mixing colors from a palette, painting a new landscape for a new life. It had taken a decade for the muted blooms to take hold, then flourish. To this day, she'd never seen the sky look so blue as it did against a floral fortress, viewed from the dirt. She badly needed the break. Matt's brooding and her lies, their stilted conversations and his sudden flares of anger: it all left her utterly drained. Overhead, a trio of vultures churned the late afternoon sky. She watched them circle, thinking, not for the first time, that self-preservation took a special kind of patience. Before long, she drifted off.

When she woke, she had the distinct sensation she'd been dreaming about Jack, though she could bring no concrete images to mind. Perhaps she was missing him all the more for having run into him at the grocery, felt his lips on her forehead, inhaled his signature musk. She'd go to him tonight after all—especially to keep him from coming here—but also because when she was with him, she was still most herself.

~

Claire thought every school seemed gloomier at night, but Anthem Elementary might have been the worst yet. Additions and renovations across different decades gave the institution a mazelike feel. Tonight's back-to-school open house was exclusively for fourth graders; next year, Charlie would graduate to a building that housed fifth through twelfth grades. She felt a surge of panic, imagining Charlie stuck in one place for the rest of his school career. They'd finished their tour and Dan had already introduced her to Charlie's teacher—now it was a matter of pleasantries and waiting for Dan to make his administrative rounds so they could leave. She dreaded meeting the other moms. She needed another drink. She wanted to be home or at the Save Rite, with her new friend, Matt.

"Enjoy it while you can, buddy. Next year it's the bottom of the dog pile again," said a dad in a neon-green sleeveless T-shirt, clapping Charlie's shoulder so he staggered into Claire. She hugged her son to her, noting the man's nose, which was grotesquely red under the fluorescent lights. An antiseptic cocktail of booze and mouthwash seeped from his pores. She, naturally, had fortified herself beforehand as well—but she had enough sense not to reek of it like this guy. She and Dan each had a glass of white wine with the salmon she'd cooked. She'd splashed a little into the pan as she worked, and then she'd done something she'd never done before, while he was seated with his back to her at the table—splashed a glug or two of vodka into her wine. The mixture didn't taste as bad as she expected, and she felt a proud thrill at the double-strength potion she'd concocted. In this way, she'd appeared to have a single glass of wine at dinner, just like Dan, just like normal moms.

"I'm Keith. My boy's gonna be in fourth grade too," the ruddy-nosed man said, pointing across the room to a bored-looking heavyset child standing next to a smartly dressed couple. "You'll like him. Hey, Kevin! Kevin!"

Kevin looked wide-eyed at Keith, then back to the woman at his side, who shook her head no. She steered him away, poor Kevin stumbling ahead, his eyes volleying back and forth between Keith and Charlie.

"Must not a heard me," said Keith, looking down at his boots and kicking at the crumbles of caked mud he'd tracked in on the pistachio-colored floor. "This is asbestos tile, you know," he said then, stepping closer, another whisky-waft coming forthwith. Claire took a step back, tried breathing through her mouth instead of her nose. "People get all freaked out about asbestos, whooooo," he said, wringing his hands in the air, "but it's not a big deal until you make it one. It'd cost taxpayers thousands to tear up this perfectly good floor. Don't even get me started on the expense of 'safety protocol.' And the damn thing's not even a problem!"

"Crazy," said Claire politely, scanning the room for Dan. She spotted him near the glass trophy case, holding court amid a crowd of parents and teachers. A bespectacled woman to Dan's left with surprisingly muscular calves above her sharp heels stood with arms crossed, warily eyeballing a small pack of boys running wild through the commons, stepping up onto the benches of the cafeteria tables and then hurtling themselves off them. Claire watched, fascinated, as a gaggle of girls giggled into their cell phones, holding their screens stiff-armed out before them, twisting their faces into grotesque poses and clicking selfies. She couldn't imagine Charlie with a phone, although maybe that was irresponsible of her, now that she was working and he was spending so much time out of eyeshot. But he'd never even asked for one. Should he have by now?

"I'd better find my husband. It was really great meeting you."

"Welcome to Anthem!" Keith said as they walked away to join Dan.

He was laughing, gesturing grandly.

"But this district never shied away from a challenge," Dan said, as if he'd been at the helm for years. "Heeey, there they are! This is my son, Charlie. He'll be in fourth grade. And this is my wife, Claire. She was a fearless journalist before she gave it all up to become a devoted stay-at-home mom, the most important job in the world."

Folks murmured around them, and Claire withered. That wasn't exactly how it had gone. She was used to the hyperbole that accompanied events like this, but tonight in particular his condescension irked her. Hadn't it been his idea that she pick up part-time work? Was he not going to mention her job at the Save Rite, then?

"I'm Dale Magnuson. I'm the principal here at Anthem Elementary," said the woman with the glasses and killer calves, thrusting her arm forward toward Claire. She was prettier up close, green eyes startling behind the lenses. Dan had spoken quite a bit about Dale these past weeks, but Claire had pictured a man.

"So nice to finally meet you, um, Mrs. Magnuson," said Claire, shaking her hand.

"Please, call me Dale," she said. "I was just telling the group that your hubby has been a godsend. A terrific asset to the district. He just gets it, you know what I mean?"

"I sure do," said Claire, distracted by the woman's use of the word *hubby*, her manicured hand at Dan's elbow. Had he mentioned his new colleague was a woman? Truth was, anytime Dan had filled Claire in on his days at the office, she'd found herself zoning out to her own new job and, more and more frequently, Matt.

Incredibly, Matt had followed through on her absurd challenge to join her in working at the Save Rite, and they'd spent an inordinate amount of time together lately in a strange suspended reality. When customers were spare, Claire was expected to leave her cash register and help out where needed in the rest of the store, and Matt, hired to organize deliveries on the docks in back of the store and stock shelves, claimed to always need her help badly whenever their shifts overlapped.

Behind stacked boxes of canned beans, Matt told her he appreciated both the extra money and the distraction, that he was going through something—a recovering alcoholic, he'd confessed—in town because he'd had to leave Chicago in a hurry. Other than that, he seemed wicked smart, and she related to how out of place he felt, a fellow former Chicagoan. A professional, something to do with finance, temporarily unemployed—a couple of drunk driving mistakes on the public record, there for anyone with an Internet connection to see, made getting a real job nearly impossible. "They've all done the same thing. They just haven't been caught," he said as they stacked boxes on a flatbed cart in the back room. Matt's dad had just died, and he'd just been through a big breakup. She told him things, too, mostly about her old life in the newsroom. She never mentioned her marriage and he never brought it up, but it wasn't like she hid her wedding ring. It was all innocent, and she found him fascinating, especially when he talked about his drinking problem, which was obviously so much worse than she herself could ever imagine, the poor thing. More and more often, she caught him staring at her in the aisles, and there were times that being on the receiving end of that look felt the same as taking a shot herself. She started to pay attention to her appearance again, finally scheduling that wax and opting for highlights with her fresh angled cut. It might only be the Save Rite, but she'd let far too many years slip by in sweats. Just two days ago, she'd finally thrown out her favorite maternity leggings.

Several school lockers slammed in rapid-fire succession, tearing Claire from thoughts of Matt. She saw that the crowd at the open house was thinning out. She couldn't wait to leave. Then Dale was speaking to her again.

"Claire Taylor, this is Marcy Johnson, Tracy Rowling, and Beth Sutter," she said. "We've got a great group of school moms here. I just know you're going to fit right in. Isn't that right, Charlie?"

Charlie squinted up at Claire from behind his glasses. The trio of moms responded with pleasantries, eyeing Claire up and down, and Claire smiled brightly in return. She'd never fit in with moms anywhere, frankly, and she suspected they could sense that tendency in her already.

"Are you excited for the new year, Charlie? Fourth grade's a big one," said Marcy or Tracy or Beth.

"I guess yes," he said. "Miss Alfering is nice."

"It's Mrs. Alfering," corrected Dale in her principal's voice, and Claire bristled.

"Charlie's been working hard at a summer job," Dan announced, and the women crowed their approval as he asked Charlie pointed questions about the garage, the fence—then answered himself before Charlie could reply. Claire sighed heavily. She felt bone-weary, completely, utterly wiped out. She wanted nothing more than to be home with a bottle of wine. She wondered what Jack and Lib were up to tonight, if they were snuggled together watching a classic movie or enjoying the full moon from a patchwork quilt in the yard. She pictured Matt lying atop a motel bedspread, pay-per-view flickering across the TV at the foot of the bed.

Her flirtation with Matt still didn't feel real, but she was admittedly no longer leaving it at work. In fact, that sensation of harboring split, parallel selves had only deepened. Each weekday, once Charlie was out of the house, she drove over to the grocery store and punched in for a four- or five-hour shift. At night, even as she cooked dinner and sorted laundry, she distracted herself by replaying all her interactions with Matt over again in her mind. It was especially useful when it was too late for any self-respecting mother to open another bottle—she'd just think about him instead, and, strangely, the moment would pass. It had become almost compulsive, and although she knew she would never act on this harmless flirtation between them, Claire still felt thrown off guard by the power and frequency of these fantasies. She'd save up each scene with Matt as though she were making a movie, then go home and watch it play out across her brain each night. She'd started looking forward to bedtime with a new, heightened anticipation, knowing she could finally enjoy these homemade films in peace, Dan fast asleep, she on the pillow beside him, a world away.

"Well, we should probably get Charlie home to bed," Dan said to Dale, eyeing Claire, and she nearly swooned with relief. Soon, they'd be out in the car, then into the house, then making their way through a rushed bedtime routine and then, finally, sweet, dark utopia.

Perfectly harmless, she repeated to herself, ignoring the shiver that ran through her.

Chapter 7

Jack had been surprised to run into Lib when he'd popped into the Save Rite, and as promised he'd returned home to wait for her to show up. But as dinnertime crept closer, he changed his mind—so what if she was sick? All the more reason to take care of the cooking.

Jack was halfway to Lib's place when he saw her there on the road, walking toward him to town. She'd been coming to see him after all and she looked fully, gloriously recovered. He pulled over onto the gravel shoulder, cut the engine, and cranked the window down, watched her walk. Woman might be nearing sixty now, but man, she still had it. She wore loose-fitting jeans, worn thin enough to hint at the strong muscles working underneath the denim, and she had on one of the tank tops she liked to layer beneath gardening button-ups. Her long swinging arms had grown the golden shade of a smoked marshmallow, his favorite way to cook them on the stick, cured by heat instead of flame. He'd like to taste her.

A gentle sandy breeze blew across the dash, fluttering some auto parts receipts that lay there. It was coming up on September, and a faint coolness had crept into the air, just enough to make you wonder if it was all in your head.

"I'm a lucky man," he shouted out to her, and she seemed to startle. How had she not noticed him yet? Was it not him she'd been coming to see? But then her face broke open into a wide smile, and she picked up her pace, looking once behind her before jogging across the road to meet him. She leaned in for a quick kiss, and he grabbed the back of her head to make it last.

"Well, hello," she said, once he'd finally let her go. "I missed you too."

"Where're we off to?" he asked as she came around and climbed in beside him, buckling herself in place.

"Anywhere you want to take me," she said, leaning back against the headrest and closing her eyes. He took the opportunity to examine his wife's unguarded profile. She looked tanned but tired. She'd left her long hair loose, the way he liked it, confirming that she'd been on her way to see him, but there was still something different about her that he couldn't quite put his finger on. He'd always loved coming together after a few days apart, but today he felt like he hadn't seen her in a month.

"I bought groceries, but I don't know—do you feel like Carolina's?" he said, and he could have sworn she winced. She opened her eyes and looked straight out over the dash.

"Sure, why not," she said, finally. "Good to see the girls."

Jack started up the truck again, whipped a U-turn, and drove toward town. He left the window down, and she wheeled hers open too, slapping her hand against the flurry of papers before tucking them beneath her rump. They pulled slowly into a mostly empty parking lot, Jack eyeballing the fence to see how it was holding up. "Folks must already be out of town for the Labor Day weekend, one last hurrah. Funny," he said, leaving off the rest as he realized it for the first time: all these years, he and Lib had synced their rhythm with Anthem's, even though it followed the schedules of the children they'd never had.

They took a booth in back, waving off Frannie and Kit as they passed. The girls dropped what they were doing anyway, ran over with ice waters and greetings. He thought Lib hugged them each a little too long. Sure, they'd skipped a couple of Wednesday night dinners, but he'd assumed Lib was still stopping by to say hello here and there. But maybe she hadn't been? What *had* she been up to? He felt a little guilty, probably had been taking her for granted. But wasn't she doing that too?

He was just so goddamn pleasantly occupied. He'd been thinking, on the drive over, of sneaking in a quick solo ride before breakfast tomorrow. Take the old Schwinn for a spin out past Sutter's, and even beyond what he'd now come to think of as Charlie's Bridge. Funny how you could know a thing your whole life and suddenly see it so differently.

Everything would go back to normal next week anyway, which is why he hadn't been too worried about spending less time with Lib. Charlie was already coming around for shorter periods. Just yesterday, Claire had taken the boy all day for back-to-school clothes shopping, securing notebooks and folders and the like. Jack had actually fought back a pout when Charlie told him his mother wanted to get the family back in their routine: earlier supper times, baths, and other ministrations that left him with less time to visit. It was just as well, Jack supposed now. They'd finished the fence, and he was behind on the work that paid the few bills he had. He'd seen Marta Taft in town yesterday and went so far as to pretend he hadn't, just so she wouldn't ask about her rototiller. It astounded him that he'd known Charlie for less than a month, but it felt like a lifetime. It would probably be good for Jack to get back into his routine too.

"You've got a bad light," he said now to Frannie, frowning up at the ceiling where the darned thing flickered in and out.

"Yeah, we just haven't had the chance," she said, pulling a pen loose from the bun atop her head, scribbling a little something on her order pad.

"I'll try to stop back sometime this week and take care of it," he said.

"What, in all your spare time?" spit Lib, and Jack froze. It was uncharacteristic of Lib to speak that way—coldly, unkindly. There was obviously more going on between them than he'd realized.

Frannie looked up and grinned at Lib, thinking it was a joke, but her smile quickly faded. Lib wasn't looking at either of them, staring fixedly out the window instead. Jack swallowed.

"Frannie, I'm feeling like pie," he said carefully, keeping his eyes on Lib. "So I think I'll just have a cup of soup first, and call it a meal. Honey?"

Lib sighed, still looking out at the snarl of box elders and volunteer oaks beyond the back side of the parking lot.

"I'll have the same," she said. "Wait, no, I'll take half a club sandwich, please. No fries."

"What's wrong?" Jack said as soon as Frannie scooted off.

"Nothing. I'm sorry," said Lib. "I'm just tired. And I guess I feel like I haven't been much of a priority to you."

A tinny ringing sounded in Jack's ears just then, high-pitched and whining. It was true, sure, but he didn't think she had ever said such a thing to him. It just didn't sound like her. He couldn't even muster up a mad feeling, he was so surprised. Of course he'd had these thoughts himself, but he hadn't actually believed them. He didn't want to defend his time with Charlie; he just felt . . . scared. His brain was rapidly paddling under the surface of smooth water like a duck's feet, and he hoped he sounded calm as a lake's surface when he spoke.

"Hey," he said. "Hey." He reached out to press his hand atop hers on the table, but she pulled it away. He puffed his cheeks, and a low whistle escaped through his pursed lips. "I'm sorry. I didn't know."

Lib shook her head quickly, like shaking something out of her hair. "No, no, don't listen to me, it's nothing. Like I say, I'm just tired," she repeated. "It's fine."

Jack endured his soup in an awkward silence he couldn't remember ever feeling with his wife. Lib's sandwich sat untouched, and, when Frannie arrived with the pie, Jack asked her to box both items up. "Sorry kid, change of plans," he said, and Frannie brushed off his apology, floating off to wrap the would-be dinner and setting the bag discreetly on the front counter near the register.

"Jack," said Lib, but then she said nothing more, and he felt the hair on the back of his neck stand on end. He was far too savvy to have ever admitted it to her, but he'd tracked her menstrual cycle for years before the change, and this mood reminded him of those days when, exactly one week before her period, he'd smarten up and stop making any jokes at her expense. But that was a long time ago, and this was different, though he couldn't say how. He just knew.

"Jack, let's go home," she said, surprising him again. He'd thought for sure she'd run back to her place after this.

"Good," he said, pushing himself gingerly out of the booth and offering her his hand, which she took. Maybe that was all they needed, a quiet night at home to remember who they were. He would have liked to say he left his growing unease behind them at the café, but Jack Hanson was no liar.

~

Two nights later, from the kitchen table where he was shuffling and reshuffling cards as Lib stood over the sink, peeling carrots, Matt said, "Why didn't you just get an abortion?" She exhaled. She should have seen it coming. He found it easiest to voice the painful questions when her back was turned.

She pressed two wet fingers to the tight space between her eyes, prayed for patience. This was the pattern since he'd arrived, yet it still caught her off guard. And she'd almost blown it with Jack the other night at the café. Picked a fight for no good reason, put everything at risk. *Maybe I'm finally losing it*, she thought, the growing pile of orange tatters tinged red from where she'd sliced her thumb-knuckle. She scraped through the sting, raw with remembering.

She was exhausted, not just from all this talk-talk-talking with Matt but from constantly corralling her own emotions. But she was afraid if she didn't allow Matt to confront her whenever he needed, he'd lose it completely and blow their cover, and she'd be forced to face Jack. That still seemed far worse, and yet now she'd gone and provoked her husband anyway. Maybe it wasn't Matt who would blow everything before she was ready; maybe it was her.

"Well?" he said.

She wasn't about to give him a history lesson on Roe versus Wade. That even if she could have stomached going that route, it's not as if there was a clinic in every town back then. She didn't have it in her tonight to explain to him that in those days, in rural parts like these, generations of girls who got pregnant out of wedlock either got sent to the Salvation Army Home for Unwed Mothers in Milwaukee, or they had a wedding. Lib hadn't even thought to terminate her pregnancy, not because she'd been particularly liberated in 1977 but because she'd already been married a year. Because it hadn't felt real until the pregnancy became a baby. Because the idea that she had any choice at all in anything hadn't occurred to her yet. Because she'd been hardly more than a child herself.

"If you knew you couldn't handle another baby, why even have me at all?" he pressed. "Why not just leave Dad before you brought me into it?"

Lib flipped the dial to preheat the oven. Gave her hands a quick rinse, dried them on a towel she kept tied to the cabinet handle, and pressed them into herself, harvesting her heat again.

"If you knew," he repeated.

"I guess I didn't," she said to the window. "Until it was too late."

"So when did you know?" he fired back, and she thought of that night in the bathtub. The night they brought the baby home, ten months before she would get the news about her mother's death and leave. When they first handed him to her in the hospital nursery—"Baby Marlow" according to his tag—she thought they'd made a mistake. She still wasn't used to her new last name. The last thing she remembered was the gas mask, then she woke up a mother. It seemed like a trick they were all playing on her.

Worse, through four days in the hospital, he'd refused to latch on. Home again in the new house that still felt like someone else's, away from the nurses' icy touch and their manhandling of her swollen breasts, she'd refused him right back. Dropped the squalling newborn into Jon's arms and walked straight into the bathroom and locked the door. Filled the tub to sloshing and sank into the water as she wept and bled, each sputtering gasp releasing a gush from between her legs, where she'd been torn open and gutted against her will, just like all those other things that happened between her legs without her permission. *This is a mistake, this is a mistake, this is a mistake*, she'd whimpered, forehead pressed against the porcelain, watching the water grow pink and cold. Had that been the moment?

"I was so young," she said.

"Yeah, and on your second baby," he muttered.

"Wait, what?" she said, remembering only just then what he'd said moments before. *If you knew you couldn't handle another baby.* "What do you mean, on my second baby?"

"I know about the baby that died, the one you had before you met my dad."

Lib set the peeler down, turned to face him.

"Matt, you are the only baby I have ever had," she said. "I don't know what you're talking about or what your dad told you, but I was never pregnant before you. I never had a baby who died."

"You don't have to lie," he said. "I have a photo of you holding him!"

"That's impossible," she said, already beginning to wonder if she was going crazy. Had she blocked out an entire child? She leaned against the counter to steady herself as Matt fumbled through his phone, stabbing and swiping.

"Here!" he said, rising from the table, triumphantly shoving the screen in her face. It was a picture—a picture of a picture, actually, a framed photo. She looked blankly at it, the impossibly young woman standing in a button-up dress and pumps, holding a burrito-wrapped baby. It was absolutely her; she knew the photo well.

"Matt," she said, shaken, "this is you. This is me, holding you."

"What?" he said, snatching back his phone, sinking to the table again. "No it isn't."

"It is, I assure you," she said, remembering the very moment the photo had been snapped, the frame she'd found at Goodwill, the spot on the mantel where it lived, the last glance she'd taken at it before walking out for good.

"You are crazy-young in this photo," he said. "It was taken before dad met you. Teen pregnancy, runaway father. When this baby died, it nearly destroyed you, and your family had already rejected you. When Dad met you all those years later, he tried to give you a good life, but you were never the same. You had me, and it was too much for you, and you left us. Why are you denying this now? What do you possibly have to lose in being straight with me? I've heard this story a thousand times. Everybody I grew up with has heard it."

Lib placed the carrots next to the chicken and potatoes in the pan and joined him at the table.

"I don't know why he told you that," she finally said, though she indeed was starting to know why, and it hurt deeply. "I suspect he was trying to protect you from knowing how young I really was when he married me."

A long silence followed. Lib waited, letting him run the math, so many things coming together in her own mind.

"Wait," Matt finally said. "How old are you?"

"I'm fifty-eight."

"Only fifty-eight!"

"You really thought I was older?" she said, crossing her arms, trying not to feel insulted.

"I just thought . . . I mean sometimes women age . . ." His voice trailed off. "Dad was eighty-four," he said, finally.

"Yep," Lib said, sinking even lower in her chair.

"I'm thirty-nine. That makes you . . . that makes you, what, nineteen when you had me? Jesus Christ. Dad was forty-five."

"And I was seventeen when we got engaged," she said.

"What the fuck. Is that even legal?"

"Not really, but parents have to report such things," Lib said darkly, remembering. Then, "I don't understand. He really told you I was older? That I'd had some other baby, that it died?"

She watched Matt swallow.

"He just said that you were broken and he tried to fix you and then you were gone and that we were both better off for it."

Lib blew out a breath. Funny that this story stung as much it did, all these decades later. And yet she'd thought the same thing, hadn't she? That they wouldn't miss her? That she couldn't possibly give them what they needed? And, as absurd as the story was, weren't the parts that didn't exonerate Jon Marlow essentially true? Hadn't she been broken? Hadn't she left without a backward glance? Even the absurd suggestion that she'd had a prior pregnancy wasn't technically out of the realm of possibility, not after what the farmhand had done to her. She'd been lucky, in that sense. How much did this unexpected betrayal really matter in the long run, however twisted, if it had given Matt some peace, if only temporarily?

Matt began to shuffle the cards again, as if to shut her out—though she thought there was something gentler in it. She stood, turned her back again for both their sakes, returned to the sink to wait.

"How did you and Dad meet?" he asked, as she'd known he would. She wiped the carrot peels from the cutting board Jack had carved for her so many years ago. It was somehow smoother than the day he'd finished it, when she'd told him it was so perfect she hated to use it. *Nonsense*, he'd said. *If God hadn't intended beautiful things to work, you wouldn't exist at all.* She pushed back tears.

"My mother always liked her cocktails, but we didn't mind it before Dad passed," said Lib, so quietly that Matt again ceased his shuffling. "We liked her better that way. The drinks smoothed her hard edges, and that woman had more edges than anyone I've met since. Dad never said as much to me when I was little, but we needed her drunk."

She had a sudden memory of her mother leaning against the old Formica counter, sweating off the thick foundation she'd begun to apply for dates. Thin rivulets of mascara ran down her flushed cheeks, and goopy clumps of sable black pooled in her inner eyes. *Her face is melting*, Lib remembered thinking, just before her mother swiveled to vomit into the kitchen sink. But not this sink, Lib assured herself. It was one of the first things she'd replaced.

"After he died, the drinking didn't work the same anymore," she continued, picking up the pan, considering those cold, gelatinous chicken breasts. "She drank more, earlier, later, more often, but the magic effect was gone. It only made her mean or knocked her out. Dad was gone. The farm needed farming. I had to do more to take care of us."

"How old were you?" Matt asked. "When your dad died?"

"Thirteen," said Lib, sliding the tray in and slamming the oven door shut on the chicken, on the sudden image of the overturned tractor. "Nineteen seventy-two."

"Just a kid," he said, and Lib let the silence sit for a bit.

"I guess so," she said. "I never felt like a kid, though."

Lib tidied up the counter, then rejoined Matt at the table. Took a deep breath and steeled herself, trying to release what remained of her words.

"Mama couldn't run the farm by herself, so she hired farmhands. I remember lots of men around during that time, some who worked, some who didn't. Some were nice, and some . . . weren't. One of them . . ." Her voice disappeared suddenly, her throat seized shut. She squeezed her eyes closed and waited for it to relax again. "One of them liked girls better than women," she croaked. It was the first time in nearly forty years that she'd said this aloud.

Matt exhaled through his nose, sat back in his chair. She didn't dare look at him. She didn't dare stop now.

"Even with the hired help, we struggled. Mama was a mess. She couldn't keep up with the note. We started getting visits from the bank," she said, her voice cracking. She stared at the freckles on the back of her hand, the skin that had become thinner, bluer, like someone's grandmother's.

Even now, she felt guilty. Bad. Jon Marlow was Matt's father, after all. He had been a kind man, considering. He'd rescued her, in a sense, even if he'd lied about the circumstances to Matt. *It's not as bad as it sounds*, she wanted to reassure his son, but she was starting to understand that that wasn't quite right. These things that happened to her in the dark—these things she'd kept from everyone, including herself—were starting to look different in the dawning light as she spoke them aloud for only the second time ever.

"Your dad was the banker," she said, finally meeting his eye.

The rest, she could not tell him. She'd barely told herself, she reckoned, as she lay in bed that night. She had never told anyone except Carolina about the farmhand, and she had helped Lib to see it for what it was, then agreed to help her keep it from Jack.

"Are you going to tell me where you went?" Carolina had said as they slapped the third coat of paint on the porch planks, pleasantly drunk. The morning had started off chilly, and Carolina wore bibs that did not flatter the rolls at her stomach when she sat cross-legged like this, but the sight of her made Lib want to snuggle into her all the more—not that she ever would.

"I told you, that stupid brush was driving me crazy," Lib slurred. "I needed a new one."

"I meant for those three years you moved away," Carolina said, forgetting her own brush as she pushed a fat cinnamon curl out of one eye, leaving a splatter of brown paint on her forehead. Her girls, Frannie and Kit, were safely squared away with one of the regulars from the café, and Lib liked Carolina even more this way; looser, free.

"It's not like you were missing me," Lib said, buying time. They hadn't known each other well before she'd left town, really just in passing—Carolina was closer to Jack's age, not hers. And although they swiftly became close upon Lib's return—in a manner Lib had never experienced with anyone else in all of her short life— she still refused to speak of anything that had come before. Carolina, only twenty-four, had recently been widowed: three months earlier, Frannie and Kit's trucker father had fallen asleep at the wheel, veered off the road, and died in a head-on collision with a limestone wall. He'd been a funny man, a boisterous, blowsy, good-timing charmer. He'd also been a womanizing shit, and in a few years Carolina would decide to forget that part, his untimely departure absolving him of his sins. Their dusty wedding photo still hung in the café, next to the short-order window. But on this day in 1980, she was both still grieving and sick to death of mourners; she'd begged to help Lib on the house project she'd been protecting so territorially and undertaking so vigorously for the past year. Lib hadn't wanted to share her healing before that day; suddenly, she did.

They'd chosen a Monday. Lib had called in sick to the plant and Carolina had closed the café, and the two of them had gotten good and drunk. Lib had decided painting the porch was an important but relatively risk-free job, as far as sobriety went, and Carolina's tragedy had brought them even closer, made Lib trust her more for reasons she couldn't articulate. Now they sat side by side, sloshing away, trading stories.

"Did you run away from home?" Carolina asked.

"It was more like I was kidnapped," Lib confessed.

"Are you joking?"

"I'm too old to make jokes," Lib said. "I feel like I'm a hundred years old."

"Neither of us looks a day over ninety-five," Carolina said.

"There was a man," Lib said.

"There always is," Carolina said.

Then all of a sudden it was like a fever dream—before she knew what was happening, she was telling Carolina not about Jon Marlow but about what Mama's hired man had done to her all those nights, years ago.

"Wait, wait," Carolina said when she was finished, crawling over to Lib, holding her face in her hands. "I want to say something to you."

Lib giggled through tears, uncomfortable with the intimacy, dizzy with the cheap wine, incredulous that she'd actually told another living soul her most sickening secret.

"Thank you for telling me," Carolina said, her blue eyes grave, working to annunciate. "I am so, so sorry you were raped."

"Oh, no," Lib said, squirming away. "It wasn't like that. It's not like he had a knife or anything. I mean, I knew him."

She hadn't struggled, hadn't even screamed. Not that it would have woken Mama, who was passed out again downstairs. And besides, she hadn't fought back the next time or the next time either. She had simply lain there as still as she could and tried not to die. She was fourteen.

"Libby," Carolina said, stern in a way she so rarely was, years older since becoming a widow, even though it had happened only months earlier. "You were a child. He was an adult. Violence doesn't require a knife. I am so, so sorry you were raped."

"Stop," Lib said after Carolina repeated it for the fifth time.

"Okay," Carolina said, and Lib pressed herself into her best friend's arms after all.

Now Lib lay in bed, thirty-seven years older, thinking again about the words she hadn't attached to her experience until Carolina said them: *You were a child. He was an adult.* Carolina had been talking about the farmhand, but Lib returned to Matt's revelation in the kitchen. She had never looked at what happened with Jon Marlow as anything resembling what had happened with the farmhand—but now she wondered if that was because she hadn't let herself think about it at all.

She remembered Mama and Jon Marlow whispering together in the kitchen. Years later she would understand that they were negotiating a trade: Lib's engagement and subsequent leaving with the older man—they'd have to wait a year to be legally married—in exchange for a sum of money large enough to bring her free and clear with the bank. At seventeen, she had no name for what was happening. She only knew that this was required of her, and that life with Mama was already unbearable, and that Jon Marlow didn't raise her hackles the way the farmhand had. Sure, she felt the extra weight of his stare from the doorway each time he visited, but his attention somehow flattered her. She didn't fear him as she had the others that were always coming through the house. He looked sad, and impossibly old, but safe.

They would leave Anthem and start a new life together, he told her, in a town he'd chosen, Elmhurst, Illinois, where neither of them knew a soul. On the long slow ride in Jon's Buick, he told her about the money, how easily her mother had made such a dark deal. He said it nicely, but she sensed a threat in it all the same. If she had any doubts, if she changed her mind, there'd be nowhere for her to go. No one to want her but him.

Still, he seemed ashamed in their new bed, where he kept apologizing. *For what*, she thought, *for what*, soothing herself in rhythm with the bedsprings. This was the man who would be her husband. He wasn't hurting her, not like that other man had. In fact, she felt nothing at all.

For what, for what, for what.

The following year, on her eighteenth birthday, they married in a courthouse on the other side of the county. The clerk side-eyed them both but there was nothing she could do about the union that would have been illegal the day before, even with her mother's consent, due to their age gap. Lib was now a wife. Something about the change in title made her wonder, who else was she?

She started to search for herself in library books and magazines, television shows and movies. She sought out stories that felt familiar, determined to find out if there were others, girls born with a scent that only the wrong men can smell.

By the time she discovered *Ms.* magazine, she was already pregnant, and it was only then that she started learning about the things that happened to so many women and the ways in which they'd started to fight back. It was almost 1978, and women all across the country had spent the decade awakening to their power. Snatching off their own bras before some man could, throwing them in barrels, burning what bound them. They went to college, started careers, had copies of house keys made for their children, and won the right not to have any more. These women frightened her, then they emboldened her. She wondered what might have happened if only their collective mighty roar had reached tiny Anthem just a few years earlier, when fourteen-year-old Libby had lain frozen in her bed.

In Elmhurst she began to feel a new repulsion for Jon, though she couldn't articulate it. Found herself weeping, suddenly, in public. When a woman in Lamaze class cornered her afterward to ask if she needed help, she'd run from the building, blazing with shame—and something else. She was starting to burn from a source all her own.

She found herself returning to what had happened with the man before Jon—even if she still didn't call it what Carolina would in a few years—and the more she thought about it, the harder she found it was to face Jon. Poor Jon, who let her turn her back on him night after night, who bought vitamins and blamed prenatal hormones. Who didn't say a word as she retreated further into herself, even after the baby was born.

And by the time the letter from the bank found her, alerting her to mom's death and the sudden inheritance of the farm, she'd detached so completely from Jon and from the baby he'd put in her, mixed both of them up so thoroughly with the rest of her earlier trauma—*trauma*, another word she picked up in magazines and books—it was almost easy to slip away. To just go and not look back. She knew he didn't have the courage to come after her or to fight her on the property she'd earned with her own body. In just three years, she'd lived an entire life.

Some people fall apart and land in the arms of others. Lib fell into her own arms, collapsed like the plaster walls she demolished with her dad's sledgehammer.

Then she rose.

But what she hadn't learned from books back then or in the decades of destroying and rebuilding and forgetting, since—but was starting to understand now, as the cricket song raged through her bedroom window screen—is that what old Jon Marlow had done was rape too. Although she'd confessed to Carolina about the farmhand that day, she was never able to bring herself to share the truth about Jon's age in future conversations, and she certainly couldn't tell her about Matt. Carolina was so proud to be a mother—she never would have accepted that Lib had abandoned her baby. She might have even forced her to try to reconnect with him, maybe even fight for custody—no. She couldn't bear the thought of losing Carolina's respect, or of being pushed into a reunion. Couldn't think of that time at all without feeling as though she couldn't breathe. There were moments she came close to telling Carolina, then swallowed it all back. She told her just enough—that she'd run off with a man and gotten married, a young, stupid impulse. That it had all gone sideways and she didn't want to talk about it and didn't want Jack to know—that was truth enough. If she wanted to tell her more later, there would always be time. But that turned out not to be true either.

Now she saw that she'd been operating from a place of trauma all along, making decisions with a young, warped mind. What Jon had done had also been rape. Of course it had been that. And of course he had known it, too, as evidenced by the story he'd constructed for their son about a photograph of her. How he'd let her go when she'd left, never came after her. He'd known he was wrong.

Here she was, fifty-eight years old, learning something new, feeling as foolish as she had back then, worn out from explaining herself to the man-child sleeping soundly across the hall despite his own truckload of problems. And though she hadn't had Jack to help her through it back then, she'd had him in the years since, and he *had* helped her, he just didn't know it.

And he still couldn't know it. It would have been bad enough before, telling him all of this—he'd have pitied her, lost all respect for her, even if he'd tried not to. Now time and ignorance and Matt's uninvited appearance had made her a liar—the one thing Jack didn't tolerate. And yet. She felt as though this, too, had happened against her will. That she'd somehow managed to betray Jack before she even met him, broke promises years before they'd utter them to each other aloud.

Chapter 8

Claire spun the cans face-forward and tucked packages neatly in line, carefully constructing the facade. Manager Ben had showed them how to pull the cans and Rice-a-Roni boxes forward, then press them flush against the shelf to make the rows look full and stocked. "Eliminates most of the dusting too!" Ben added, and Matt had barely waited for him to round the corner before parroting the line in a perfect Ben impression. He'd gotten very good at his Ben voice in their time together. They'd both gotten good at spending time together.

"Hey, hot stuff," said Matt from behind her, letting a stack of boxes fall from his arms and land with a satisfying thwack. So cheesy, but Claire found herself living for these moments all the same.

"Hey," she said, tucking a strand of hair behind her ear, then discreetly running a finger against her nostrils, a tongue over her teeth, just in case. He'd been more and more forward with her, and she'd let him be, only because it was still so impossible to imagine anything ever happening between them. It was also damn good to hear the things he said, and she thought about what might come out of his mouth as she dressed each morning. She charged several new items to her credit card, working creatively around the required uniform shirt: New earrings, skinny jeans, wedge boots that lifted her butt just so. Bras and lacy panties Matt would of course never see but that gave her a certain swagger just the same. Her recent spending flurry had triggered a fraud alert to Dan's phone; the card had lain dormant so long in her wallet. When she showed her husband the new lingerie with a breathless excuse about reconnecting, they finally had sex after a three-week dry spell, Claire's eyes shut tightly against Dan's shoulder. She endured the routine in a semi-clenched silence he misread for ecstasy, terrified of saying aloud the word that was now constantly at the back of her mind, at the back of her throat: *Matt*.

"When you finish up here, come find me in the liquor section," Matt said, stepping forward to brush something from the collar of her shirt, a paper-thin flake of cardboard that fluttered to the floor between them. She felt the warm puff of his breath hit her cheek. "Ben said to keep you busy."

"I can come now." Claire swallowed, eyeing the register to make sure the place was still dead. "Pretty much done here."

Matt stepped to the side and waited for her to lead the way. She felt his eyes roving over her, the heat of their searching, and the entire back half of her body began to tingle head to heel. It felt so strange to be aware of her body again, after all these months of disconnect. She'd had no idea just how numb she'd really been until she felt herself coming back to life.

Claire walked, acutely aware of her gait, acutely aware that the only reason she was continuing to work at this ridiculous job was because of this ridiculous crush. She knew this because she'd woken from a panicked dream last night, one in which Matt had left town without a word. *If he goes, I go*, she'd screamed at a flustered dream-Ben, and she'd gasped awake, sweaty, embarrassed, and scared. There in the dark, wondering if she'd actually cried out (though Dan looked undisturbed on his back, mouth agape), Claire talked herself down. Nothing had happened between her and Matt. Nothing ever would. It was perfectly okay to bask in his attentions, his free and borderline-lewd compliments; she deserved to be appreciated that way. She decided to characterize her flirtation with Matt as creative problem-solving. If she could fill up her gas tank here, she'd have the fuel she needed to get through those dull dinners at home. She was feeling a little happier, even drinking less.

In that regard, she could argue Matt was actually making her a better wife. Besides, they weren't hurting anybody. And she would never, ever hurt Charlie that way.

Charlie had been back to school a full week now, a momentous occasion that should have passed with more fanfare. On the first day, Claire had been unable to shake the feeling she was forgetting something. But they'd made two trips for new clothes and school supplies, even visited the cellular store to pick out a phone for Charlie, to both of their surprise. They'd taken the obligatory backpack and lunchbox photo on the front step. She'd covered all the usual motherly bases, but she felt no angst, no nostalgia. Here they were in a new town, a new school, armed with devilish new technology—but the only feelings she could name were impatience and relief.

"So, this doesn't bother you? Working around all this alcohol?" Claire asked Matt. The Save Rite liquor section was bigger than the produce, dairy, and bakery departments combined, and this had become one of her favorite conversations: Matt would catalog his past bad behavior, and she would mentally tick off the ways her drinking wasn't anything like his. It had been three days, in fact, since she'd had anything to drink at all.

"No big deal," said Matt, pulling a box cutter from his back pocket and tearing into one side of the shrink wrap that held the boxes in place on the pallet. "Alcohol was never really my problem anyway. I could take or leave the stuff. I mean, before."

"Before?"

"Pills," he said, "I tore my rotator cuff at the gym. I guess all those years of high school football finally caught up with me. Doc prescribed opiates, and less than a year later, I'm shooting up at 7:30 every morning in the Walmart parking lot."

Claire hoped she didn't look as shocked as she felt at this unexpected turn, this heretofore unmentioned sin. Was he seriously talking about heroin? "Oh, yikes!" She managed to laugh, bending to lift a case of beer before he could see her face.

"It happens more than you think," he said, watching her. "You wouldn't believe some of the addicts I met in rehab. Guarantee you they're the same people you ring up here every day. Best part is that the same doctor who prescribed them to me ended up a patient in my group."

Did he mean a support group? Like, a detox or AA meeting? Claire felt prudish and silly, absurdly unworldly. They'd covered a meth epidemic back at the paper years ago and published the occasional mug shots of wild-eyed down-and-outer's on their seventh OWIs, but she'd done so at a professional distance, feeling no personal connection to any of it. She dropped the case of beer into place, picked up another, and followed suit.

"I'm sorry, I thought you said that you're a recovering alcoholic. Your words," she said, watching as he set a tent card atop the pyramid of beer they'd made. *All the smoothness, none of the calories.*

"Well, yeah, that's just because it's easier to explain. I was addicted to opiates. Not alcohol. All that was just bad decisions, bad situations, shitty timing. I always had my drinking under control, but you never wanna say that out loud in rehab," he chortled.

"Got it," said Claire, uncertain that she did. "Well, you're good now, right?"

"Better than I've ever been." He grinned at her, then suddenly grabbed her forearm. She felt held there more by his gaze than his grip, unable to move, though she couldn't really tell if she was trying to free herself or not. *Is this real?* she thought, wine and whisky logos swimming in and out of focus, Kenny Rogers gambling on the radio overhead, disconnected from her body again. *Whose arm is that?*

And she watched, dizzy, as Matt unwrapped his fingers from her pale pink skin, leaving four perfect white ovals, fading.

~

Jack pedaled through the crest, closed his eyes, and let the bicycle coast down the long smooth hill. The county had repaved it last summer, and the Varsity quickly gobbled up road. He gave in and gently squeezed the brakes, just a little, peeking through his left eye to keep his balance. It was much smoother than it had been when he and his buddies had had their sailing contests on this same stretch, counted who could ride blind the longest despite the buckles, pea gravel, and potholes. That was back even before the Varsity. *The Typhoon!* he suddenly remembered. He'd let his legs fly out to prove his feet weren't touching the brakes, then tuck them in for streamlining purposes. Eyes glued shut beneath his dad's Sunday necktie, Jack would jiggle and jaw—*"That's twenty-three seconds, candyasses!"*—trusting the machine to stay true, as long as he did his part and his path stayed lucky.

Now, even without the hazards of those days, he had a hard time holding steady unless he kept an eye on the horizon. His strength wasn't the same either, though it was improving as he rode more. All the riding these past weeks had loosened him up tremendously, once the initial soreness faded. He'd also lost his childhood thirst for speed, and it was just as well. If he had a spectacular crash cruising way out here, no one would find him for hours. He wondered, not for the first time, if he should scope out the flea market for a bicycle for Lib. Would she join him out here? He wasn't sure. But he hadn't seen her in nearly a week again, not since that awkward botched night at Carolina's, and he didn't like how he was feeling. It was almost like he was . . . suspicious. Of what, he couldn't say. Suspicious of her suspicion? And with Charlie off at school making new friends, Jack suddenly had all the time in the world again. And not in the way he liked.

It was crazy how much he already missed having Charlie around. Here it was, a week of September already gone, which meant he'd only known the boy a little more than a month. A measly month! "I'm sixty-three years old!" Jack yelled into the wind, and the bike swerved. How the hell had that happened? Six or seven weeks, in sixty-three years, was a mere hiccup. The tiniest of wrinkles in a long swath of time. How had this kid become such a big part of Jack's life so quickly? How could life pass so damnably slow and lightning quick at the same time? How could he go days at a time now without thinking about Lyle, this man he'd had coffee with most weeks for the better of his adult life?

How could each of us live an entire life—all those heartbreaks, sorrows, passions, all the worrying over things that seemed critical at the time—and then simply disappear from the earth, as if we'd never been here at all?

Jack had harbored a childhood fear of flying off the face of the earth. He'd recently relayed to Charlie the story of how freaked out he'd been when his third-grade science teacher had told the class, "It might feel like we're all standing still, but we're actually spinning a thousand miles an hour, hurtling on a rock through space." Jack hadn't bought it. The evidence around him directly contradicted the lesson. He'd asked so many follow-up questions Mr. Johnsrud had threatened him with the ruler, and despite his stubborn refusal to believe it, he began to have nightmares of floating aimlessly in space. After that, it became even more important to Jack to know what was real. If you couldn't trust what you felt beneath your own two feet, what could you trust?

Jack coasted, pedaling backward, drinking in the rushing cool fall air against his unprotected scalp. He probably should have worn a helmet, but he didn't own one, and he'd outright gasped at the sticker price shopping at the hardware store a couple weeks back, after both Charlie and Lib had mentioned it. He promised her he'd keep his eye out for a used one, but, truth be told, he wasn't gonna look that hard. *This old brain's not worth $48.99 on one to a million odds, that's for sure*, he thought, letting the bike finally come to a slow wobbling stop at the base of Charlie's bridge. Besides, he'd made it this far without one. They hadn't even had seatbelts in cars when the two of them had come up. Had she forgotten that? Jack dismounted, walking rubber-legged to assess the burbling creek below.

Thick clumps of sickly white foam bottlenecked against the wet rocks, slick with moss. They used to climb down beneath this bridge with stolen *Playboys* and Camel butts that still had life left in them, swiped from someone's mother's ashtray. Argue for hours about what a good place it'd be for a gangster to hide a body, and the rumors they'd heard about Al Capone's hidden cabin up north. Only God and the cottonwoods knew what secrets Scarface's four-hundred-acre woods held.

"My wife has a secret," Jack whispered to the water. The rush of the stream garbled up the truth he'd kept in, and so he tried again, louder this time: "My wife has a secret!" His voice came back to him, ringing through the open country, ricocheting off the metal beams, slicing him with its aural shrapnel. Wounded, he limped back onto the saddle and began the long climb back up to town.

A man could do a lot of thinking from the seat of a bicycle, and Jack had been over and over his interactions with Lib. He sifted through every scene in recent memory, searching for any clues he'd missed in the blissful ignorance of old habits. It seemed things had been different ever since Charlie had arrived, and she had accused him of not paying enough attention to her, but that didn't add up. He didn't believe she would be that jealous of the time he spent with the boy. They'd always had spaces in their love, as those poets in her books liked to say. Did having a child around, especially one that took up so much of Jack's attention, make her regret not having kids? Did she resent him for it, all of a sudden? Well, if so, she sure had that twisted. Jack grunted, downshifting to the second-lowest gear, saving the easiest as long as he could.

He pedaled on, slow and steady, churning through the past month's scenes. Maybe things had been off since before Charlie. Maybe since Lyle's death? He thought about the morning of the storm, her sandals beneath the table, how distant she'd seemed, the underlying anxiety he'd struggled to shake. After family dinner at the café, the night he'd introduced her to Charlie and his folks, she'd said she wanted to sleep alone, even though they usually spent the night together after a dinner date. Had she been lying? Why? Was there someone else? It was highly unlikely. Not after all these years, and most especially not Lib. *No*, he thought, certain. *Lib doesn't sneak.*

Jack recalled the day he'd found her in bed in the afternoon, how out of sorts she'd been acting. Plus, at the grocery, although it was weeks later, she said she'd been under the weather. A tiny wave of panic rolled in, and he flipped it into granny gear, so close now to the top of the hill. Pain gripped and released his quads, cramping his calves with each forward push. What if she was really sick and keeping the diagnosis from him? That, he could actually see happening. It wasn't that he thought Lib didn't or shouldn't have harmless secrets; everyone was entitled to a bit of privacy. But if Lib was dying, he could see her putting off the day she'd have to tell him, especially so soon after Lyle. That was just the sort of lie she'd tell. She loved him more than anything. He knew it in his bones. That's why none of this made sense.

"Enough," Jack yelled, picking up speed again as he finally bested the hill, cranked the gears back up, and raced into town. He wanted to skip the shower, but he knew that would leave him chilled to the bone, once the sweat turned to salt. He nearly spilled the bike taking the last corner on his block too fast, didn't even brake as he rounded up the dirt patch and into the garage. Enough guessing. He had to see her. Whatever it was, he could take it. They could face it, together. What could be worse than not knowing?

~

Lib went outside to wait for Jack, though he hadn't called, and it had been almost a week since they'd even spoken. She couldn't say how she knew he was coming. Maybe she felt it on the wind, the mournful shift whispering to both of them that it was time. Maybe it had carried his scent to her somehow, from wherever he was, the same way she felt the air change whenever she walked to his house. They'd been Jack and Lib nearly twice as long as she'd been Libby alone, and he was no doubt a part of her in ways she had yet to comprehend. Now, the reckoning.

More like rending, she thought, memorizing his face as he pulled up, the way his hands gripped the wheel, the big square knuckles. She wondered then what it felt like to have a limb torn off.

Jack didn't get out of the truck, and they stared at each other for a time through the windshield. *He knows something, but he's going to need me to say it.* His forehead was pinched, but his jaw looked relaxed. So he wasn't mad, then, she marveled. Worried, more like. She drank in the tenderness pooling in his eyes, and her own eyes stung as she held his stare. *Stay with me, Jack*, she telegraphed. *I'm still me.*

Lib walked around to her side of the truck and climbed in.

"We're going by the Save Rite to pick up a few things," said Jack, still looking out the front of the truck toward where she'd stood just moments earlier. "I'm going to cook us a meal, we're going to sit down together, and you're going to tell me everything."

Lib said nothing as they rumbled away. She could smell his shower soap, tinged with something metallic. Knew, without looking, the precise pattern of his combed gray hair as it lay drying. They rolled past patchwork fields stitched of soybeans and lush, bold sweet corn, grown taller now than the farmer who had planted it, green arms stretched up to the evening heavens with no apparent fear of the reaping. Lib envied the confidence.

Onward, past the bloated carcass of a barn that had simply given up. Past the old plastics factory and the VFW park. Past Carolina's, which somehow went on without its namesake, though Lib still couldn't see how. On down Main Street and around the corner to the Save Rite, where Ben already had the hanging baskets of fall mums set out for purchase. They sat clustered next to the lingering bags of dirt and mulch, their white plastic hooks forming rows of question marks. Lib sat forward, in case Jack would ask her to follow him in, but he didn't. Simply slid out, pocketed the keys, and marched inside. *Thank God*, she thought, sinking back into the cloth seat. The only thing that could possibly make this confrontation worse would be to have it in front of Matt.

Matt. What if that's why they were here? What if Jack had gone in to get him? What if this was Jack's way of showing her that he'd known all along? A wave of adrenaline rushed her ears. She gripped the armrest, listening to it wash back out again. No, that couldn't be it. An ambush wasn't Jack's style. If he somehow already knew about Matt's existence, he would have said exactly that.

Suddenly sedated, she took in a scene she'd viewed hundreds of times before: Berta's outline through the sewing notions window, watching the world go by on the sidewalk. A plastic bag caught up against one of the wheelbarrows secured with bike locks outside Mike's Hardware, whipping in the breeze. The top half of the peeling water tower peeking over the old Opera House, and the Main Street shopfronts, the ones Lib always thought resembled a wild west movie set with their facades connected to create an Etch-a-Sketch roofline. Just then, she thought she saw a little ghostly face at the window of the Opera House, but she blinked, and it was gone. There'd always been stories that these old buildings were haunted. Finally, Lib tipped her head until it hit the passenger window, and she let it rest there, her eyelids sinking shut, lulled by the clanging of a rope against a flagpole and a chorus of mowers rumbling, somewhere far off.

Two car doors slammed in the space next to her, startling her awake. The occupants tumbled out and then into each other, laughing as they walked into the grocery store, clasped hands swinging between them. Just as the automatic doors swallowed that couple, they spit out a different one. No, not a couple—it was Matt, Lib saw now. And Claire Taylor.

What fresh hell?

They looked like demented Doublemint twins, laughing together in those ridiculous red Save Rite shirts. Matt's leather vest hung from a curled finger over one shoulder, and he had a six-pack and a plastic shopping bag dangling from the other. What, so he was drinking now? He was saying something to Claire, who was walking backward in front of him, and the intimacy between them was undeniable. *You fucking fools*, Lib seethed. She was so intent on watching them that she didn't see Jack reappear at his door, jostling the truck as he dropped two paper bags in the bed, then climbing in beside her.

"Is that Claire Taylor?" said Jack, following Lib's glare to determine what had her so fixated. "And who the hell is that guy?"

Lib said nothing as she watched, letting Jack catch up, at least as much as he could without knowing the half of it, the worst of it. Matt's hand rested on the beer he'd set atop Claire's car. Claire was leaning against the open driver's-side door but not showing signs of leaving anytime soon.

Jack whistled low, shaking his head slowly back and forth.

"Damn," he whispered into the steering wheel. "Poor Charlie."

Lib felt the rage shake her body. The man couldn't stay on the wagon, even after everything that had resulted from his drinking? Couldn't go a month without trying to get in some poor housewife's pants? No thought for the woman's husband, her child? No thought for what that level of exposure could mean for Lib? That a scandal in a town of this size would out his presence to Jack? Was this his definition of lying low?

"What are they thinking?" shrieked Lib, and Jack put a firm hand on her knee.

"Hey, hey, hey," he said. "Easy."

Lib reeled, fumbling to get her footing. She'd blown it, she'd just blown it. "She's married," she tried, hoping to salvage what was left of the charade, though she was no longer sure what good it would do her.

"I know, I know. It's terrible. But why . . ." Jack's voice evaporated as he searched her face. She felt him look and look and look, and she wanted to shrink, she wanted to die, she wanted a sinkhole to open and swallow the truck right now. Her heart pounded so hard it pained her, and she pressed against her chest to hold it in.

"Lib?" said Jack quietly. She'd never heard him sound so timid.

She couldn't survive this moment one millisecond longer.

"Lib?" he said again.

Finally, she began to cry.

Chapter 9

Up until the moment Claire got into Matt's car, she would have sworn on her life that it would never happen.

It reminded her very much of when she'd lost her virginity. The frequency of her mother's increasingly desperate lectures on abstinence had escalated in direct correlation with the number of months she'd been dating Steve. Sophomores, they'd just celebrated their six-month anniversary—eons, in high school years—and she meant it, every single time, when she insisted to her mother that sex was not even on her radar. That they weren't even talking about it, that she had no intention of doing it, that no, he wasn't pressuring her, and that God no, she was not that kind of girl. And she believed herself, right up until the instant it happened, at her request, after twenty minutes of messing around on her best friend's trampoline the night of the regional soccer championships. Her virginity truly did feel like something she'd lost, like a single flattened glove in a parking lot.

"What a view, huh?" said Matt, crushing the empty Miller Genuine Draft can in his fist and tossing it into the river below. They sat side by side on the hood of his car, parked near a huge bridge they'd found just outside town. It was his third beer already, and she was halfway through her second. Claire rarely drank this sort of cheap stuff, and she was already surprisingly, deliciously buzzed, especially after abstaining for a few days.

"It sure is," she replied, mesmerized by the crispness of the green leaves dangling from a tree that was bent over the water, as if to drink too. She couldn't remember the last time she had felt this oxygenated.

Claire had used her employee discount to buy the six-pack of cheap beer in which to boil the brats for dinner, thinking Dan and Charlie might appreciate one last cookout this season. She'd also bought a box of wine, not to drink, she told herself, just something she could keep in the pantry to have on hand for cooking. Matt had clocked out at the same time she had, then offered to help carry her groceries to her car. She was just about to close her driver's-side door when she got the text from Charlie on his new phone: *can i go too kyles house his parents r home.* She'd been typing out her reply about dinner, one leg in and one still dangling toward the parking lot, when she was interrupted by a second text—this time Dan letting her know he had to stay late for a meeting. *You two eat without me*, she'd read, then sat a full minute, considering the plastic bag of brats, buns, and potato salad beside her, the carton of strawberry ice cream, Charlie's favorite. Then she'd looked up at Matt, who was leaning against his own car now, smoking, staring unapologetically at her leg. "Such a nice night," she'd said, and he grinned.

Now here they were, just far enough outside town that they probably wouldn't be spotted together but close enough to pretend nothing untoward was happening. Just two friends hanging out by the river on a gorgeous Wisconsin evening, having a beer. *Or four*, she thought, watching Matt crack the last can.

"God, I forgot how good beer tastes," he said.

"Yeah, I don't drink it very often myself," she said, which wasn't entirely true. She drank the cheap stuff once she no longer cared; after the richer beer, which came after the wine, which came after a cocktail or two. For reasons she wasn't about to say out loud, having just a glass or two of many different drinks didn't add up in her estimation to the same thing as if she'd had, say, six of the same. She shivered, shoving the fuzzy math from her mind for now. "How's motel living?" she asked instead, conjuring the matching queen beds and flickering TV of her imaginary nighttime travels.

"Welp," said Matt, sucking beer through his teeth into a sort of grimace and squinting out at the valley. "Funny thing, that." Claire snuck a side-peek at his haunches flattened against the hood, battled a powerful urge to straddle his lap. She pulled her right knee up to her chest, forming a slight barrier between them. Her jeans, which kept her warm in the Save Rite's frigid AC, felt stiff and hot out here as the sun began to set. She took another swig, waiting.

"I checked out of the motel a month ago."

"Oh! You're kidding. You found a place?" But this couldn't be true. He'd made regular cracks about his lonely, transient nights. The dozens of channels with nothing on, the endless takeout dinners.

"You could say that," he said, taking a long pull on the can, then stifling a burp. "I've actually been staying with my mom."

"Your mom." Claire swallowed. What mom? She felt dizzy, as much from the quick beers as his intoxicating nearness, the blurring of her nightly fantasies with this in-the-flesh moment, and she sensed she wasn't processing her surroundings accurately. She was certain he'd said he had no family in the area, that he was estranged and alone, that he'd sort of chosen this place like throwing a dart at a map. But she also had a protective perfectionism that reliably kicked in in moments like these. Whenever Claire suspected she was growing drunk, she made herself quiet so as not to say stupid things she'd regret the next day, so there would be less evidence of her indulgences. The tool had served her well over the years, and she employed it now, pressing three fingers to her pursed lips.

"Yeah, I'd never met her before this summer. My mom walked out on me when I was a baby," said Matt, draining the can. He twisted his wrist to palm it, gently curling and uncurling his fingers around the can as if practicing the impending crunch.

"Holy shit," Claire whispered against her fingertips, unable to help herself.

"I wasn't ready to talk about it, but she lives here. I came to Anthem to find her, to make her . . ." Matt shook his head. "Truth is I don't know why I came here." He finally crumpled the can, tossed it to join the others below. "But right about now," he said, turning toward her, "I'm sure as fuck glad I did."

Claire felt as if all that extra oxygen was suddenly sucked away. Her heel slipped from beneath her, its yellow sandal dangling from her big toe, then dropping to the ground. She was staring at it lying there when her own right hand, out of the corner of her eye, caught her attention. She watched it drift out, tentatively, then float down to rest on Matt's knee.

He gripped it, caught her eyes, and leaned in close. She watched him watch her as he slid her hand ever so slowly up his leg, leaving it to rest just inside his thigh. She felt her pinky creep, just barely graze the rise of him. His lips were just inches from hers now, and she flashed to the high school trampoline. Bare ass against stretched canvas. Crickets furiously strumming in tune. Claire's entire body crackled and ached like coming alive from a novocaine shot. *If he kisses me right now*, she thought, *I will never recover*. But she did not back away. She closed her eyes. *So be it*.

Instead, he said, "Wanna get a real drink?"

~

Inside the truck in the Save Rite parking lot, Jack waited. When she finally spoke through her tears, it came out all in a rush.

"I was married before I met you. I had a baby and that's him, there with Claire. His name is Matt."

Jack blinked. "What?"

"I had a baby but I left him and I've never known him, never spoken to him in forty years, but he came to find me and he's been staying with me and I had to deal with him before I could deal with you and I'm so sorry. I'm so sorry, Jack."

"What? Staying with you?" He was sure he wasn't hearing her correctly, that this was some trick of age or overexertion or spoiled meat—did he have a fever? His anger hadn't quite caught up with the information yet, like how he could always bike the first twenty seconds or so up a hill before his heart caught on.

"Staying with me," she repeated.

"Like, in your house?" he asked dumbly. "Where? For how long?"

She mumbled an answer he didn't catch. He made her repeat herself.

"A month or so," she whispered.

He sat there sifting the words but they slipped all the way through and his mind went white except for one.

"Out."

Lib did not move.

"Out!" he wheezed, and Lib exited the truck as he was already peeling away.

Jack was shattered. Brutalized from the inside, as though he'd swallowed a horse and it was bucking its way out. His intestines twisted and churned dangerously low in his gut. He raced home, barely making it to the toilet before the bottom dropped out of him. *I can finally feel it spinning*, he thought as the planet hurtled him through burnt-black space. He couldn't hang on. He wouldn't survive the void.

Lib had a kid. Lib was a mother. And he, Jack, would never, ever be a father.

Another wave of violent cramps reared up and had its way with him. When he was finally empty and buckling his jeans back onto wobbling hips, scrubbing his hands raw, another wave came at him, this time released as tears. He held himself up against the sink, nearly chipping a tooth against the faucet as he sobbed. Grief wracked his body.

He crawled to the couch, elbowed his way up to it. Somehow, he dozed. Sun sliced through the blinds, setting fire to lower and lower slats each time he opened his eyes. How many times had she looked him in the eye over the past month, over the past thirty-three years, and lied?

He could hardly hold it all in his head. What was worse? That she'd lied? That she'd denied him kids? That she'd so easily left a child out there in the world to flounder, even once she was old enough to know better? That she'd for some reason come around all these years later—and still decided lying was the best policy? Who *was* this woman?

He bent suddenly at the waist like a mouse trap, sprung. What if she came here? He couldn't bear the thought of seeing her. Wouldn't survive more of her explanations, her fumbling attempts at amends.

He couldn't take the truck, because she'd see it, she'd find him, and so he climbed back on the Schwinn. Reflected, absurdly, how grateful he was that it wasn't a horse, that it needed no rest from its earlier ride.

Wheeled out into the fragile blue dusk, wondering if he could outrun his own body, his own life.

There is no fixing this, he thought, pedaling faster and faster.

~

The roadside bar was nearly empty when Claire and Matt tumbled in, blinded now by the daylight outside. Claire blinked, rapid-fire, willing any shapes to reveal themselves against the penetrating darkness. Only four shadows materialized: A flanneled old man wiping glasses behind the bar. A fat couple intently focused on flashing poker machines. A lone skinny lump hunched over a stool at the corner. And so they beelined to the opposite end of the bar, ordered shots. Fed dollars into the jukebox, blindly poked at selections. Matt demanded the barkeep turn it up as loud as it would go. He obliged.

They whipped darts at the board, Claire growing dizzy each time she swooped down to retrieve one she'd dropped. More dropped darts, more shots, this time with salt and lime, and Matt checked over his shoulder once before licking from her hand instead of his. Her body grew extra nerves. She numbed them, grew some more.

Two rounds later, he unfastened all three buttons at the neck of her red polo, sprinkled salt, and dragged his tongue, quick and hard across her collarbone, to taste her. They were at a corner table now, and she inched her vinyl chair closer, opened her legs to allow one of his between, and clamped her thighs around his knee as though it were one of her mini bottles.

"It's too bad you checked out of that motel," she said in someone else's raspy voice, tongue thick, ears ringing. Just a girl in a bar. Just a bad idea of the best kind.

"Funny, I was just thinking," he replied, fingering the hem of her shirt, sliding a hand under to tickle the bare skin at her waistline, "about checking back in."

~

Lib didn't become aware that she was walking home until she slipped on the pea gravel in the same spot as always, there in that ditch where the county and village roads crossed. She'd made the walk to and from the Save Rite a thousand times before, but she usually cut past Carolina's and down Main. Now she found herself near the plastics plant and realized she must have gone the longer way so as to walk through Jack's neighborhood. She'd likely trudged right past his place without noticing. Apparently the body stayed magnetized by what it knew, even when the compass came loose.

She was spinning. At the intersection, she blinked and mustered up the presence of mind to check for cars as she crossed over to walk against traffic, then she closed her eyes. She walked as far as she could blind, and when she felt the cool transition to farmland and her own prairie fields, she opened them. Behind her, Anthem stretched out like a quilt, the water tower a pin stuck through. Before her, the back of her precious house and its neat outbuildings looked unchanged against the wide-open skyline, there atop the gentle rise. Sometimes she came up on her property like this, and she still couldn't believe it was hers, like a page she'd flipped to in a picture book about someone else.

When she came to her yard, she cut straight across to the garden. She would finally dispatch those useless tomatoes, come hell or high water. She considered the tarp and the wheelbarrow, chose the tarp. Dragged it around back and laid it carefully next to the tomato bed, then yanked the bent silver cage from its prison of tangles and tossed it behind her. Dropped to her knees and began to pull each plant; first the big three or four that were supposed to be just one, then the tiny volunteers, of which there must have been a thousand. One by one, pointer finger and thumb, she plucked. Placed the tiny little chlorophyll bodies side by side on the tarp, slick with dirt. How she loved plants, even these stubborn, annoying supposed annuals, because they created themselves out of thin air, year after year after year. A plant was not a plant until it decided to be. That magic was so beautiful it made her ache.

But they can't do it alone, Lib, Carolina said to her once, after an early dustup with Jack. Although she could point to only a handful of real arguments in their marriage, those early disagreements terrified Lib. She couldn't stand being challenged by him; it felt like a direct assault on the independence she'd cobbled together brick by brick, plank by plank. Each time they fought, she'd fled to her house, her dirt, thinking, *This is why, this is why, this is why.*

But it was true, she realized now, as she pulled. The plant doesn't know how much help it needs to stand alone. The seed has never heard of the sun when it's magically converting that light energy into a whole new alchemy. The sun surely knows nothing of the seed, or any other life it makes possible simply by sitting up there, radiating away. The rain has no idea where it comes from, where it's going when it flows. How could so many seemingly sovereign things need one another so much? Lib wanted nothing more in this world than to stand, alone, with Jack.

She was thirsty. More tired than she remembered ever feeling before. Dusk had to be a good hour or two off, but she could already feel it like a blanket, pressing down on the day, a woolen weight on her back, and she gave in. Let it pull her down to rest beside her green seedlings on the tarp.

Lib slept.

She was crying in her dream, and so she thought, before she was fully awake, that the sound was her, keening. That the strange, mournful moan she heard was coming from inside her, before she finally understood that she was hearing sirens.

It was not quite dark but close, closing in on dinner time. The jack pines blurred into a solid wall as the car raced past them, past the rolling hay fields and the pastures dotted with dairy cows, back through the jaws of that glorious bridge where they'd first sucked those beers, then crossed that moral center line. But had they crossed it yet, really? Was it too late? She had maybe an hour, she guessed, before Charlie would be home, or Dan, or both. *This is so fucking crazy*, she thought, reaching for her phone. But her purse wasn't there at her feet, and it dawned on her that it was still in her car, that she'd left her whole life back in the Save Rite parking lot.

"Oh God," she moaned, feeling sick as the car hit a dip, caught air. What if they were trying to reach her? What if Dan for some reason couldn't pick Charlie up? Shit, how was she supposed to pick him up? What kind of monster was she?

"I think this isn't . . . I'm sorry," she breathed. "I don't think this is a good idea."

Matt turned the radio up.

"Seriously, I'm not feeling well," she yelled. "Let's just go back to my car."

He nodded, then shook his head in time to the stilted beat, threw her a look. "Let's just drive," he hollered back. "Decide when we hit town."

Claire relented, hung her head between her knees, and closed her eyes. She tried to quell the nausea by yawning, then holding her breath—tricks from the perpetually carsick haze of her childhood—praying for the feeling to pass. She could smell the empty Folgers coffee can her mother used to keep in the backseat.

"Oh God," she said again, cheeks smashed against her knees, darkening her jeans with drool as the car jostled her back and forth. She imagined her mom side-eying her daughter, this drunken, adulterous mess in the passenger seat, imagined her voice: *Where is her mother?*

"Hey." He palmed her shoulder, pulled her to sitting. The world spun into white streaks as he pressed her back against her seat. He grinned, slid a hand down to cup her breast. She stared at it there on her body, the awkward angle of his wrist, the corn yellow of his chewed-up nails. "Keep an eye on the horizon, girl. You can't—"

She heard it as a thump. That's the only sound she remembered when she looked back later, trying to piece together the details. Had there been anything else? There must have been a screeching of tires as Matt righted the wheel, came to stop fifty yards up. Shouting, at least—hers, maybe his? Or a scraping of metal against paint? There had to be something more after that single drum beat that shook the car, shook her to her core, like a heart beating only one time and never again. Then they were stopped, engine barely humming, everything eerily, deadly quiet.

"A deer," said Matt, finally. "I think we hit a deer. We must have hit a deer. Did you see the deer?"

Claire's mouth had dried up. No air reached her lips. She couldn't breathe, couldn't move. She'd seen nothing. Then the bile rose, her stomach revolted, and she pushed open the passenger door to vomit on the gravel shoulder.

"Wait," Matt hissed, gripping her forearm as she heaved, choked, emptied herself. He yanked her arm, hard, tearing against the socket. "Wait."

He was squinting into the rearview mirror. Claire squeezed her eyes shut, pulled the door to her like a blanket. She would not move again. She would not look. *Just tell me tell me tell me tell me tell me—*

"It's moving!" Matt shouted, clamping her arm even tighter. "It's okay. He's okay."

"He?" Claire squeaked.

"He's moving. He's okay. Listen, Claire," and he turned in his seat, grabbed her face with both hands. "Claire, look at me."

Hot spittle showered her face. How could she feel her face, but not her lungs? Were all her parts attached?

"Claire," he said, like banging a pot, and she ripped her eyes open.

"Claire, listen to me. We've had a tiny accident. We just barely grazed someone. He came out of nowhere, swerved into us. Believe me, it's his fault. He's moving around, and he's going to be just fine, but we have got to go. Now."

Go? The words floated free, shifted course, settled all around her in the wrong order, nonsensical. Go where? Was he still talking about the motel?

Matt released her face and gunned the gas pedal, barreling toward town. Claire was suddenly, horrifyingly sober.

"Wait, what the fuck, Matt? Wait wait wait. We've got to go back."

"I know, and I get it, but you are not thinking straight, and you need to trust me now." He slowed as they neared the village limits. "I've got two drunk driving arrests. A third, especially with an accident, means I go to prison. That is not going to happen, not when I'm finally clean and sober. Do you hear me?"

"But someone could be really, really hurt," she pressed, thinking, *Clean and sober?* "He could need help!"

"Listen, I saw him with my own eyes, and he is fine. It wasn't a hit so much as a bump, believe me," said Matt, talking faster as the vehicle slowed. "I just know it in my gut, and I need you to trust me now."

"Matt, no," she said. "No."

His jaw tightened.

"And what about you?" he said through gritted teeth. "How are you going to explain why you were in this car, Claire?"

A fresh wave of fear rippled through her, followed by the rest of it, in a rush: a breathalyzer and jail bars for Matt, town gossip and a scarlet letter for her, middle school bullies for Charlie. He was right. Of course, he was right. Something horrible had just happened, but it could have been so much worse. And Matt going to jail, Claire losing everything, Dan and Charlie saddled with her shame—that was unthinkably worse. If they left, if whomever they'd hit was indeed okay, it could almost be like none of it ever happened, couldn't it?

"But, surely he'll call the police," said Claire. "What if he saw us? He had to have at least seen the car."

Matt nodded. "I know some property. I think I can hide the car there. And even if they do somehow track me down, I'll say it was a deer. Nobody even knows I'm living here. My mom has a vehicle she never drives. I bet she'll let me use it."

Claire couldn't fathom how he was already able to think this through, as if he'd frozen time to plan his defense without her, as if he'd already seen this coming and thought through all possible outcomes. She could barely follow what he was saying. She wanted to resist, but she couldn't form words.

"Get your keys out," said Matt, pulling into the Save Rite. When had they gotten here? "Put your shoes on. Come on, come on!" She pushed into the sandals as he reached across her and opened her door. "Follow me to the motel. Don't argue. We need to move fast. Follow me, Claire."

And she did, somehow. Climbed behind the wheel of her own car, though it no longer felt like hers, but there it was, her purse on the floor next to the boxed wine, the rest of the groceries on the passenger seat, a pool of pink oozing from the carton of melting ice cream, now tipped on its side. By some horrifying miracle, she was no longer drunk—she was certain of this—though she wished she was as they drove their sick little parade down Main Street, out past the café and to the motel. Matt parked his car on the other side of the building in one of the furthest corner guest spaces and hopped into hers, motioning her to drive back the way they'd come, through town again and out the other side, out to an old farm. Out of habit, even in this state, she dug out a stick of gum from her purse and the tiny bottle of mouthwash she kept zipped in its inner pocket.

"I will see you tomorrow at work," he said, stepping out at the end of a long driveway. "Claire, say nothing, no matter what. Do you understand? We will talk soon. I will find you when it's safe."

She nodded, and he slammed the door, jogged up the gravel driveway, waving her away. She slowly turned the car around and retraced her steps back into town, wide eyed and fear-struck, hands at ten and two on the wheel. *Get it together, get it together, get it together.* She rounded the corner and approached her house, waited as the garage door yawned open and sucked her inside. She'd beaten Dan home, thank God, and she reached to gather the grocery bags, considered the melted ice cream on the seat, lifted her purse from the passenger floor, and tucked the strap over her shoulder. Stood, and the strap slingshotted her back into the driver's seat, hooked as it was on the gear shift. She sat a minute, took a breath, tried again.

She was just about to climb the garage steps into the house when the patrol car pulled into the driveway.

The groceries slipped from her arms, the ice cream splattering at her feet. How had they already found her? How had they already tracked her down? Was she operating in some sort of fugue state, some kind of blackout? How much time had she lost? Had somebody witnessed the whole thing?

"Mrs. Taylor?" said the officer as he climbed out of his car. He sounded kind. Why was he being so nice if he was here to arrest her?

"Mrs. Taylor, please don't worry. Everything is okay," he said, putting out a cautioning hand meant to comfort, eyeing the mess at her feet. Was this some sort of cruel trick?

"Everything is all right, Mrs. Taylor, but I'm going to need you to come with me."

Chapter 10

When Jack took off on the Schwinn, he wanted nothing to do with anything or anyone he knew, and so he avoided the county road down to the bridge. He sure as hell wasn't going to go Lib's way, so he made for north instead, pedaling out past the motel toward the four-lane highway, then hopping on the bike trail headed east, getting as far away from her as he could get. No one would ever think to look for him on this straight endless path to nowhere, and the crushed limestone would likely cushion, at least somewhat, any potential fall. He knew he wasn't right. He knew he needed truing. But he was an object in motion, and he didn't know how to stop himself, so it seemed wisest to clear the barriers. At least he was still thinking that straight.

The harder Jack pedaled, the less resistance the bike gave him. The trail was a completely different beast from the road, particularly at this speed, and he felt as though he caught some kind of orbit as he flew. So Lib had been married before. But how? When? She was twenty-five the first time he laid eyes on her at the plant, a baby herself. Granted, she'd always behaved so much older, but that was just on account of her unusual depth and smarts. *She's an old soul*, Carolina had told him, waiting for her to arrive for family dinner that first night they were officially introduced, which had turned out to be a setup. *One of the good ones.*

Now he knew she'd had a whole other life before him. Had Carolina known? Had she betrayed him too? The two were thick as thieves, and Carolina always took Lib's side, no matter how irrational the debate.

She had a blind spot when it came to Lib, but maybe it was more deliberate than he'd realized. Maybe they were coconspirators, covering up a crime all along.

Jack felt weak again, and lost; ceased his pedaling, let gravity bring the bicycle to a natural rest. He was panting hard over the handlebars when he heard it.

He didn't recognize the sound at first, rumbling against his wallet from the buttoned chest pocket of his flannel. He used his phone so infrequently, and his body still vibrated from the ride, so the first round of rings went unanswered. But when they started up again, he realized what it was, fumbled to unfasten the pocket, flip open the phone and poke at the buttons, put it up to his ear.

"What's this now?" he said instead of hello.

"Jack?" a tiny voice at the other end, sounding miles and miles away. "Jack?"

"Charlie?" he said incredulously. "How did you find me out here?"

"Jack, I need help. With my bike. I'm scared it's broken."

"Broken how, son?" He turned his bike around, checked his watch: quarter 'til seven.

"I don't know, bent and stuff. Can you fix it? I can't reach it."

Everything inside Jack slowed.

"Why can't you reach it?" he said, already pedaling. "Where are you, Charlie?"

"On the way back from the bridge. It's down in the ditch. I think the car that hit me bent it."

Jack was back in orbit, rocketing toward town, hanging onto one handlebar for his very life, yelling into the phone.

"Charlie, I'm coming, but I need to hang up. I need to call for help. But I'm coming, okay? Can you stay right there and wait for me?"

Charlie said something in response, but Jack could no longer hear him for the rushing of the wind.

"Charlie, I'm sorry, I have to hang up, but I'm coming," he said, flipping the phone shut, pausing for what felt like an eternity, flipping it back open. The numbers jiggled before his eyes, but he somehow found them, 9, 1, 1, pedaled on. Dispatch was maddeningly thorough, achingly slow, but somehow, although Jack made it back through town and out the other side in record time, the EMTs still beat him to the scene. The ambulance was just pulling up next to a navy-blue Suburban with a flashing light on its dash. The truck belonged to Tim, the cook at Carolina's, who was also a volunteer firefighter. He was squatting next to the boy, who was lying flat on his back in the ditch, his head turned to the side, gesturing toward something. Charlie was trying to sit up, and Tim was holding him back against the grass as the medics hopped from the cab of the ambulance, pulled a stretcher from the back, and jogged down the incline toward them. Jack came to a skid on the shoulder and dumped the Varsity, skittered down into the ditch, lost his balance, and fell into a roll at Charlie's side.

"Jack!" Charlie said, and Tim said, "Good, Charlie. You know this old fool?"

Jack recognized Barbara from the antique mall as the EMT stabilizing the boy's head, holding up two fingers and moving them back and forth in front of Charlie's eyes.

"How about me?" Tim said. "Do you remember my name?"

"It's Tim. You just told me that," Charlie said, then, "Jack, Jack, do you see it over there? Can you fix it?"

"Shhhh, of course we can fix it. Listen to Tim now, Charlie," he said, unable to bring himself to look directly at the tangle of silver and blue ten yards up the road and in the ditch, not yet ready to know just how bad this was. "His glasses are missing," Jack said. "Has anyone seen the boy's glasses?"

As Jack searched the scene for the glasses, a flash of white caught his eye: a single, pristine bone poked through the lower part of Charlie's jeans. Jack swallowed back his lunch.

A patrol officer lumbered up—Nicky Pete, a classmate's cousin's youngest brother with two first names, all the more ridiculous now for his advancing age.

"Tim, Barb, Jack," he said, nodding. "And who've we got here?"

Charlie repeated his name, and Nicky Pete introduced himself as Officer Nick. Charlie yammered on about the bike. He wiggled all around despite his injuries, one arm bent like a little broken wing. Jack was as relieved as he was terrified.

"Charlie, listen, it's a BMX, okay? It's built for smashups. We'll fix it," said Jack as Barb and a younger girl in a white uniform loaded the scoop stretcher into the ambulance and closed the doors. Jack watched helplessly as the bus wheeled away, sirens blaring. What now?

"Do you know the boy's parents, Jack?" said Nicky Pete, and Jack nodded, swallowed, raked a shaking hand through his sweaty hair.

"Come on back to my squad, help me track them down," he said, and Jack stepped to follow, but his legs wobbled and gave out beneath him.

"Whoa, whoa, whoa," said Nicky Pete, and Tim rushed over to his side, and the two men supported Jack on either side to the police car, deposited him with care in the back seat. Tim jogged back to his suburban, then reappeared with a bottle of orange juice and a granola bar. Jack couldn't stomach the bar, but he chugged the sweet juice down as though his life depended on it.

"Why don't I give you a lift back to town, Jack?" said Nicky Pete, and Tim was already loading the Varsity into the back of his truck. Another squad car pulled up, and Jack watched as the officers had a brief conference, pointing down into the ditch and out toward the road, pausing to mutter things into the radios at their shoulders. Finally, Nicky Pete ambled back, climbed in behind the wheel, and with one finger typed something slowly onto a screen.

"Can we bring the BMX?" asked Jack as Nicky Pete checked his blind spot, pulled away from the shoulder, and silently rolled into town, no sirens, to the Taylor home.

"You know it's gotta stay till the boys are done out there," he answered, and Jack cranked his neck to get a look at the lone handlebar reaching up from the ditch. He might as well have been leaving his own body behind.

~

Lib's left side was numb as she hoofed it into the house, every other footfall a tingling stab of rippling prickles as it woke. How long had she slept there on the tarp? Not quite dark yet. She twirled her left wrist as she climbed the porch, squeezing and unfurling her hand, forcing it back to life. Sirens, though somewhat unusual out here, were not entirely uncommon due to the proximity of the highway. *Still*, she thought, then, *Still what?*

All of this—the sleeping in the garden, the worry about a possible fire or accident—she was trying to avoid facing her new reality. Jack knew. Jack hated her. She entered the kitchen, startling when she heard the shower running upstairs. She checked the window over the sink, looking for Matt's car in the driveway, but it wasn't there. Was it possible? Could it be Jack up there?

She took the stairs two at a time, rapped on the closed door.

"Jack?" she called hopefully.

"What?" came the hollered reply, and she slumped against the doorjamb, let it help her hold the weight of her disappointment at hearing Matt's voice.

Lib couldn't muster up the energy to respond. She eyed his bed through the door he usually kept shut tight, saw the heaps of clothes on her Turkish rug, her antique pale-green coverlet in a disrespected pile on the floor, tramped beneath a pair of dirty boots. Empty soda bottles everywhere, one of her delicate plates and a silver fork on the nightstand. She sighed, retrieved the dishes, and wistfully eyeballed her own neatly made bed as she turned to descend the stairs. Sleep had always been a sort of therapy, but if she gave in now, she'd be wide awake at 3:00 a.m.

Downstairs, Lib gently set the plate and fork in the sink and shuffled into the living room. This was the time of night she liked to flip on each of her lamps in succession, enjoying the warm glow it cast on the books as she chose one to read. But tonight she went straight to the blue recliner in the dark, gingerly settled herself in, and swiveled to face the big picture window. The deep red ages-old hollyhocks were in full effect this year against the split-rail fence she'd built just for them along the back of the south garden. They formed a soft sweet wall, and the books around her on three sides made her feel she was sitting in an enormous throne. She let her eyelids slide shut again, absorbing the support of this place of safety and healing.

She woke to the scratchy feeling of her crocheted afghan sliding across her shoulder and cheek, Matt at her side pulling it from the back of the recliner and covering her with it.

"Whoop, sorry. Didn't mean to wake you," he said, tucking it into place around her.

"You didn't," she snapped, licking her dry lips, then softening. "But thank you. That's sweet."

"It's dark in here," he said, and she thought he seemed different than when she'd last seen him. Smaller, somehow. Younger with the wet hair, baby-faced with flushed cheeks from the shower. Maybe it was the night. Maybe it was her.

Matt made to leave the room but hesitated in the doorway, then turned and sat down on the davenport at her left.

"Not feeling well?" They both said it to each other in unison, then laughed.

"I guess not," she said, answering for both of them.

The silence stretched, and she thought she might nod off again when it came back to her all at once, the scene in the Save Rite parking lot. In the madness with Jack, she'd nearly forgotten what had started it all in the first place.

"I saw you," she said, hearing in her own words an echo of Claire Taylor, who had said the same thing to Lib that day at the cash register at Save Rite. And though the room was dark, she felt Matt's whole body stiffen on the couch.

"You saw me," he said, his voice low, almost a growl.

"With the Taylor woman," she said, not backing down. "In the Save Rite parking lot this afternoon."

Matt stood abruptly, walked out to the kitchen. She heard him pace back and forth across the room, open the refrigerator door, shut it again. He came back into the living room, sat down heavily on the couch, and rubbed his hands up and down the thighs of his jeans. *Here is a guilty man*, she thought.

"I also saw the beer," she continued, feeling brave or maybe reckless, she wasn't entirely sure. She was past the point of caring.

Matt stopped his rubbing and rocking, cocked his head. Then let a slow breath push him back into his seat.

"You saw me," he said, slower, lighter. "This afternoon."

"She's married, you know," said Lib. "She's got a little boy, a sweet one, though he is possibly a thief. He's become Jack's best friend this summer. She's got a whole family, Matt. Did you know that?"

Matt nodded, stepped one toe atop the other, pinning it, then pulling against the white cotton sock. Releasing himself, repinning himself, repeating.

"I know," he mumbled. "It's not like that. There's nothing going on."

"Well, that's sure as hell not how it looked to me. And probably to half the town," said Lib. "It's not like it matters anymore anyway."

Matt jerked his head toward her. "Why's that?"

Lib felt her lower lip start to tremble. One of her eyelids was seizing, little rapid flickers beyond her control. She pressed at it with two fingers, then palmed her face.

"I told Jack about you," she said into the heels of her hands, her chin pulled in and tucked against her chest. "He knows."

Matt whistled, long and low. Neither said anything for a time.

"Well, shit," he said, finally. "What now?"

Lib shook her head, hard. "Now he's never speaking to me again, what else?" She leaned over suddenly to turn on the lamp, saw his pale face, tinged with green. "Matt, I'm just gonna say it. Are you drinking again?"

He looked as if he might cry, as he so often had these past weeks. But there was something else there beneath the sickly pallor, something more than the usual pain. He was scared.

"What is it, Matt? Are you in love with her?" She rocked, waiting for him to speak the words.

"Lib," he said, swallowing. "Mom."

Lib froze in her chair. It was the first time she'd ever heard him use the word, save for sarcastically.

"Mom," he said again, whispering this time. "I think I need some help."

~

When the police officer escorted Claire to the backseat of his squad car and opened the door, Claire received a second shock: Jack, in the backseat, curled against the opposite door. What was he doing here?

"Please, Mrs. Taylor, have a seat. I believe you know Jack, right?" But Claire couldn't move, couldn't remember how to bend her knee just right to lower herself into the car without collapsing. She stared at the seat that awaited her in the car that would take her to jail. *It was a deer we hit. Maybe a dog. Matt was wrong. Matt was wrong.*

"Mrs. Taylor, please," said the officer, giving up on pressing her to sit, taking her by the shoulders instead and swiveling her around to face him. "There's been an accident. Your son, Charlie, has been the victim of a hit-and-run on his bicycle out near Highway Q. He's banged up pretty good, but he's moving and talking."

Charlie—

"He's being transported to the hospital in Richland Center, and I've come to take you there. Jack here was one of the first on the scene, and he's the one who identified your son and led me to your house. Would you like me to take you to the hospital now? It's about a twenty-minute drive."

Charlie. Charlie? Claire's legs finally buckled as she felt the officer tuck her into place next to Jack, his hand gentle on her head.

Jack immediately slid his arm around her shoulder, pulled her to him, and embraced her in a strong sideways hug. "I'm sorry I wasn't with him, but he's gonna be okay, Claire, I can tell," he said, squeezing her shoulder once more before retracting his arm.

Charlie? She felt herself shrink, become small and brittle, pressed into the plexiglass-and-wire cage that separated back from front, bad from good. Her knee knocked against Jack's. Both of their knees were wedged against the front seat.

"Not a lot of leg room in these things, huh?" said Jack. "I've never sat back in one of these before."

"Charlie?" said Claire, aloud this time, the only word she could seem to form. She was already losing track of everything. Why was Jack here again? Why were they in the back of a police car together?

Jack was opening his mouth to answer when the officer interrupted, turning to look over his shoulder as he backed down the driveway. "Mrs. Taylor, would you like me to put those groceries into the refrigerator before we go?"

Claire couldn't think what he meant. She shook her head, and the car began to move along the street.

"Claire, listen," Jack said. "I saw him, and I think he's going to be just fine. Looks like a bad break to his leg, maybe his arm, but he was moving and talking, and all he really cared about was how his bike was faring." He chuckled.

What was so funny? Had he done something to Charlie? Were they arresting Jack together? Why did the police need her help?

Claire closed her eyes against the dizzying motion of the car, the outside world tilting and careening in slow motion through the windows, the horizon nowhere in sight. Then they had stopped, and Jack was gone. Were they just going to let him go? Claire's cheek pressed against the vinyl seat, a lone, petrified french fry visible on the floor under the passenger seat.

"Mrs. Taylor?" she heard, as if from another room, and then she was sitting somewhere with a strange loud blanket wrapped around her. She was drinking from a water fountain. He'd brought her to school, then, and that was good, because she'd waited a long time to drink; she was parched,

parched, parched,

in line for the bubbler,

bubbler, bubbler,

on the nurse's cot again, counting the square tiles on the ceiling, waiting for her mom to come.

"Mrs. Taylor, I believe you're in shock," said the principal. "We can wait here a minute. We don't have to go just yet." Was she in trouble? Where was the nurse? On the playground? Was recess over?

"Mrs. Taylor, do you mind if I take a look through your purse? I'd like to use your phone. I'd like us to call your husband. Can we do that?"

She closed her eyes. She wanted to be helpful, but she didn't know how. The water was helpful. She drank more. She was a good person. She'd thought Jack was a good person, but he wasn't. He'd been arrested. Or maybe she'd dreamt the arrest. Maybe she was dreaming, still. She wasn't ready to stop dreaming. She stopped anyway.

It was Charlie, on the nurse's cot.

Her mom was not coming. She was the mom.

Claire was not hurt; Charlie was hurt.

Jack was not the criminal in the back of the police car.

Claire was.

Chapter 11

"I was thirteen the first time I got drunk," Matt said from the couch in the living room, and Lib tried to envision a teenaged version of his face—acne-pocked or smooth. "You wouldn't believe how easy it was for a kid to get weed," he said, and she thought of her gardens, her thistles.

Then it all came pouring out of him, more than he'd ever shared, more than she'd ever asked. He told her that Jon Marlow had actually had three wives—there'd been a second, right after Lib. A woman drawn to a sad man raising a baby alone but less interested in parenting an increasingly sullen adolescent. She was long gone by high school, when football kept Matt more or less in line—though he and his teammates always figured out how to get smashed every weekend. College in Chicago was a glossy brochure brought to life; ivy-covered, untethered freedom. Poet professors and philosopher bartenders. Matt sowed his drunken oats and everyone drank as much as he did. After graduation, he returned to Elmhurst and started a loan-making business inside a strip mall.

Matt described how he kept the party going until his friends and colleagues began begging off for quiet nights at home with new wives and babies, and soon he was the only one in the bar on Tuesday nights. Then came the first drunk-driving arrest.

"I don't know," he said, after a silence so long Lib thought he might be finished. "I think that might be when I started to become an alcoholic."

She scoffed aloud then, couldn't help herself—that *was when he'd realized?*—but she didn't have the energy for outrage, and she was certainly in no position to pass judgment. Lib knew a drunk when she saw one: she'd been raised by the best of them. But Mama had never possessed the self-awareness or humility to use the word *alcoholic*, so she'd give him that.

As Matt spooled out his story, the night seemed endless, the edges of Lib's living room windows darkening from sapphire to onyx. They were exposed, lit up in a display case; anyone could have come along and seen them there from the outside. When Matt talked about the loan-making days, how he had followed in his father's footsteps, she let herself wonder just a little bit more about Jon. Whether he'd gone on with his life as though he'd never married a little girl, if she was the only one who'd had to recover and rebuild. If he'd found even more freedom without the shame of her. Anyone he met later wouldn't have known how young his first bride had been, only that she was the kind of woman who left. That had been the point of the lies he had told Matt about her, after all.

Matt detailed the second drunk-driving ticket, the court-ordered AA meetings. He always left them feeling worse thinking more about drinking than when he'd arrived. His problems were different from theirs, more pressing: the market had crashed, Jon's third wife had turned him against Matt, and the best girlfriend he'd had to date had dumped him. All he needed was for somebody to give him a break.

"Besides, in those meetings they all talked about their parents. How terrible they were, how they'd inherited their problems from them. And I didn't know what I'd inherited. I didn't know who you were at all."

She ducked the jab out of habit, and it didn't land, and she could see that, for once, he hadn't intended it to.

"And then, you know, that was before the pills. I went to the doctor to get help, and walked out with a new problem, the worst I've ever had."

His quick and slippery slide from prescription painkillers into heroin addiction shocked her. He pushed up a sleeve just then and with a swift, sinking blow she realized why he always wore them long. Red scars dotted his arms, reminding her, bizarrely, of her tomatoes.

Then Jon died. His death shook Matt into getting cleaned up. The withdrawal was worse than the using, and he'd gone willingly this time to AA to avoid having to go through it again. He had forty-six days sober when he'd come looking for Lib, thinking maybe he could make a fresh start. If he couldn't, there was nothing left for him anymore. He'd lost everything else.

How ironic, Lib thought, that she would be anyone's fresh start, let alone his.

"It feels good to say it all out loud, all at once. I don't think I've ever done that before," he said, sliding the sleeve back into place at his wrist. "Not to anyone. Not even in group."

And she surprised herself by standing then, moving toward him, and squatting at his knees, placing both her hands on his face, waiting.

"I honestly didn't mean to drink again," he said, and he sounded so much like a child, a child she'd never known, a child she'd maybe always known, that she couldn't think of anything to say back except *shhhhh*, and so she'd said it again, *shhhhhh*, and he began to quietly weep. They stayed that way, foreheads pressed together, even though she could smell it on him then, tequila, just like Mama. And it nibbled at her for the first time: Had she passed this ugly thing on to him? But she didn't let the new guilt swallow her whole.

She helped him upstairs to bed. "Mom?" he said, right before falling asleep. "Could you help me find an AA group in the morning?" Less than a minute later, he was lightly snoring.

Lib tucked the coverlet around Matt's shoulders, resisting the urge to hover a palm over his mouth and check his breathing again. *Long night*, she thought, surveying the chaos of her old bedroom. She hadn't yet told him it had been hers. How much it had pained her to be in here again, readying it after he'd first arrived. How this was the one room in the house she hadn't gutted, for reasons she'd never examined. In the half-light, it didn't look so bad, messy as it was. Perhaps his chaos had given it a new sort of order.

Then she started with the empty soda bottles and spent wrappers, gathering them into a pile near the door after the decorative wastebasket proved too small for the job. She worked by lamplight, pulling wet towels from the floor to hang from the closet hook, straightening magazines and squishy packs of cigarettes, corralling the spilled contents of a canvas toiletry bag on the dresser. When she had the room mostly under control, she plucked the top shirt from a heaping laundry basket and held it to her face, then pulled the basket over to the rocker and settled herself there. One by one, she folded Matt's soft things, tucking one sock into another, making a gift of each pair.

As she straightened seams and buttoned collars, hanging his work shirts in the childhood closet she used to hide in, she felt something different for him as she moved about the space, squaring it all away as he slept, rearranging for both of them, making everything new.

She felt like a mom.

Matt slept late, and Lib let him. Distracted herself by dragging the heap of spent tomato plants to the compost pile. Matt often slept in, but for some reason she'd thought today would be different, given the rock-bottom feel of last night.

And maybe it still could be. Maybe his body needed to sleep it off, to recover from the twin tolls of drinking and hiding it, from the exhaustion of carrying the secret and confessing it, and he'd gradually rise earlier as his days grew more fruitful, with her help. She tossed the plants atop the compost pile and gave the tarp a shake, the breeze lifting and carrying the last of the dried dirt and tiny stragglers to float to the side of the pile. She used the rake she kept propped there, wrestled the rotting mulch into organized decay.

The pain of what she'd done to Jack ate away at her, but work had always been the most effective distraction. She knew Jack was the same way and pictured him now, tinkering in his shed. He'd probably have one of his most productive days ever, thanks to her. She ached to go to him, to make this all right, but she just couldn't see how. And she knew well enough that pushing would only alienate him further. She needed to be patient, and selfless. It was critical that the next move be his.

Eventually he'd need to know more, she thought, a little selfishly. She'd bet her life that, at some point, if she could wait it out without making it worse, Jack's need to solve the puzzle would compel him to come there, whether he wanted to or not. So she'd wait, and she'd work.

She felt less patient with Matt, however, when the sun hit noon. She crossed the yard to the house, washed at the kitchen sink, jogged up the stairs. She pushed his door open, found him lying there, facing the wall, the coverlet pulled tight up to his ears. She crossed to sit in the rocker as she had the previous night, but this time she let the floorboards squeak and groan as she whooshed back and forth, hoping to rouse him. She'd done the same as a kid in this same rocker when it had sat downstairs in the living room, attempting liftoff as Mama slept it off. Thinking that maybe if she got up to speed, she could fly right out of there.

Finally, Matt stirred, and Lib pounced. "Morning, sunshine," she chirped, and he moaned. Writhed and stretched, coming to terms with his surroundings, then froze. Lib stopped her rocking, waiting. When she saw him close his eyes and put his hands to his face, she knew it had all come back to him.

"I thought you might sleep all day. It's practically lunch time," she said kindly, hoping her lightness would let him know she was on his side, that he didn't need to be ashamed. That he'd asked for help and she was here to give it. Matt rolled to sitting, surveyed the room.

"Whoa," he said. "Someone's been busy."

"Well, someone's been a slob," she teased.

"I'm sorry. I really need a smoke."

She pointed to the cigarettes she'd organized next to the still-wrapped two-pack of deodorant and the half-empty bottle of cologne. Then, when he didn't move from the bed, she realized he wanted her to leave.

"I'll fix you some eggs," she said, rising. "But as soon as you come back inside, we're going to find you an AA meeting."

Lib started on the simple dish she knew best: sunny-side up eggs with a sprinkle of lemon pepper, served on top of toast. She heard him use the bathroom, then stumble down the stairs and out the front door. She peeled an orange at the sink, watching as he smoked and paced in the driveway, kicking rocks. Splitting the sweet bulb of the orange in two, she set half on his plate and half on hers, waiting for the sizzle from the pan, the ding from the toaster. *We can do this thing*, she thought. *This moment is survivable.* That's what life was, she knew by now: a series of survivable moments.

"Where is your car?" she remembered to ask when he pushed back inside and made to run upstairs, smoke still curling from his hair and shoulders.

"Oh," he said, stopping at the foot of the stairs. "I left it parked at work. Truth is . . ."

Lib plucked the hot whole-grain toast from the toaster between her thumb and forefinger, flicked it onto the plates, then slid the eggs into place. She brought the dishes over to the table and set them there next to the butter crock, turning back to grab a couple of forks from the drawer, tear two paper towels from the roll. She looked up at him, expectantly.

"Truth is I drank that six-pack in the parking lot and didn't think I should be driving, so I caught a ride home," he said, all at once. He was getting pretty good at confessing, though her tired brain must have imagined the tequila smell that had really been beer.

"With Claire?" she said, making a warning of her voice.

"No, no, no," he said, slapping the door frame. "A friend from work. But, listen, Mom, I was thinking. That car is actually a rental, because I didn't know what I was getting into when I came up here, and it is costing me a fortune to keep it so long. I should probably return it, but I'm not in a position to buy something yet. Did I see a truck out there in the barn? Is it drivable?"

Lib nodded, pleased that he was thinking responsibly, that he'd woken focused on solutions, just as she had.

"Sure, that's my truck, and I hardly use it," she said. "That's a good idea, Matt."

He grinned, sauntering over to the table and dropping into the chair across from her. Lib picked up her fork and considered her egg. For nearly two months, Matt had been an aneurism waiting to burst, and, once it did, she'd thought it was entirely possible she wouldn't make it. Now the worst had happened, and it was all done. The bleed was out, and there was nothing left to do but repair the damage and heal.

"You're the best, Mom," he said, leaning forward, hovering his fork over Lib's plate instead of his own. She watched, wordless, as he lowered the tines and popped the yolk of her egg and its golden insides oozed over the edges of her toast.

Chapter 12

Jack etched his name into the side of his Styrofoam cup with the half-bitten edge of his thumbnail, letters jagged like sticks laid end to end. He used to write his name that way, with twigs, on the creek bed, as a kid. *Jack*—a strong name, efficient and solid, built to hold up other heavier things. He'd always felt Lib's name suited her too; unique and pretty, but no-nonsense. Straight to the point, no longer than necessary. He wondered if she'd heard about the accident yet, who would possibly tell her. A row of multicolored cartoon faces stared back at him, ranked by number, happy to sad: *How is your pain today?*

Jack didn't know what he had a right to feel in this situation. He surreptitiously surveyed the folks around him, triaging his own place among the people with sprained limbs, the mucus-clogged hackers, and the feverish slumpers. How could he gauge his particular pain on this spectrum of trauma? How did compound emotional fractures figure in? Who was he, Jack, but a tired old man waiting for news of someone else's boy?

Waiting alone, to boot. He sulked, eyeing a couple wrapped in each other's arms. No wife beside him or waiting for him at home either. Not allowed behind the massive swinging doors, because he was nobody's family, as the young lady at admissions proffered with a little too much glee for his taste. He wasn't even sure anyone knew he was here until Nicky Pete spotted him on his way out and filled him in. After they'd picked up Claire, called Dan on Claire's phone, and gone by Jack's house so that he could get his truck, Jack had watched Nicky Pete nurture an incoherent Claire with an emergency blanket and a bottle of water from the emergency kit in his trunk. Impressed by the way he'd tenderly held that bottle to her trembling lips, Jack decided that from here on out, it was Officer Nick after all. Nick pulled away in the squad car for the twenty-minute drive to the county hospital, and Jack followed closely, like a shadow, tense and dark, floating.

Now, an hour later, Jack observed that hospitals were noisy, quiet places. All shushing hustle and constant hum. Jack overheard things he didn't want to know, agonized over the things he had done—and couldn't do. All that beeping and dinging, coming and going. So jarring, the way nurses joked mere moments after consoling some bellowing patient or family member. Unnerving, how the toddlers kept tugging on pant legs and purse straps, the way siblings kept up their rivalries and couples their cold routines. Unfathomable, the way the world kept spinning for some of them.

There was something else gnawing at him too, and he wasn't sure what to make of it. It could have been the shock of Charlie's accident, but he could have sworn Claire Taylor was drunk when they'd picked her up. At half past seven in the evening and on a weeknight and just getting home from the grocery store—long after she'd spent God knows how long chatting it up with that man in the parking lot. Lib's *son*. He crushed the cup, refocused his concern. Not that it was any of his business. But if anyone asked, he'd have to tell the truth: that her eyes had been a little unfocused, her footing unsteady. He was sure he'd smelled liquor when he'd hugged her, something darker and more antiseptic beneath the plastic and leather of the squad car.

"Jack?" said a man's voice, and he looked up to see Charlie's dad standing there.

"It's so good of you to come," Dan said, as if Jack would have been anywhere else. Dan nodded at what remained of Jack's coffee cup. "Any good?"

"Not bad at all," Jack replied, though he'd wasted several overwhelmed minutes at the machine, sorting through all those flavors and creams, desperate for a simple cup of black coffee. "How's he doing?"

"He's amazing. Luckiest kid on earth. You wouldn't even know anything happened, if not for the cast on his arm and the wires and everything. The docs are talking about surgery on his leg. All he's talking about is his bike—and you."

"Well, that's terrific," said Jack, exhaling, unable to suppress his grin. "Not about the surgery, but—unbelievable." He thought of the sunken spot where the boy's temple met his hairline, always shining and damp. The tender cord that pulled his heel into his lower calf. The human body was simultaneously both the hardiest and most fragile of all machines. Jack had never felt so vulnerable in all his life.

"That was his principal earlier, by the way. The woman you might have seen me with," Dan said, and Jack didn't know what he meant, couldn't have cared less; he hadn't seen any woman. "We were in a meeting when I got the call. I told her not to come, but she insisted."

Jack said nothing, confounded by Dan's words.

"She cares deeply about the children," Dan added.

"Good of her to come," Jack said finally. He nodded, looking away from Dan's persistent eye contact. He was uncomfortable, wanted to quit this small talk, get his eyes on Charlie.

"Anyway, he's asking about you. You can go on in. All the way to the back."

Jack jumped up, nodding to the admitting clerk whose permission he no longer required. Her long face charted about a seven or eight on the pain scale as he passed her desk. Jack smiled, tossed his cup into the garbage can next to her, and pushed through the doors to find his boy.

The last thing Claire remembered was climbing into Charlie's hospital bed. But she woke now on a sticky vinyl couch, blinking into the liquid doe eyes of a towering young woman in scrubs covered in frolicking kittens.

"It's okay, honey. He's okay," said Nurse Ami. *Ami with an* i, Claire remembered after a quick glance at the name scribbled on the whiteboard, the *i* dotted with a heart. Ami smelled like shampoo and the fruity gum she snapped. "You're okay. I'm here to help."

Claire stood too quickly and stumbled forward, moving to Charlie's bedside to lean over her son. He was asleep, his face restful and smooth against the starched linen pillow, the rough, heavy plaster of his casted arm. He slept heavily with his good knee bent, a tiny sedated inchworm in a gown, propped in a white sterile sea of blankets, tubes, and wires. At least they'd removed the neck brace after the CT scan had come back clean.

"I can't believe I fell asleep," she said to Nurse Ami, who was sidestepping her way out of the cramped corridor between the couch and Charlie's bed. They'd set both of his broken bones in the ER earlier, after analyzing the results of the images taken by a big portable X-ray machine; the staff flitting around Charlie like capable birds, the ER physician consulting with the orthopedic surgeon, Dr. Pearson. Charlie was eerily quiet, heavily sedated, maybe, finally, in shock.

Dan had come rushing in then with Principal Dale, straight from a meeting, and they'd all been shooed from the room by the X-ray tech. Dr. Pearson went with them into the hallway, explaining that there was a high volume of OR cases but that Charlie, given his age, was a priority, and he'd likely have surgery on his leg by morning. There wasn't much to do except wait for the surgery that would repair his badly broken tibia, the worst—miraculously—of his injuries.

"Honey, don't beat yourself up. You're not the first to pass out in front of me," said Ami, squeezing the hanging IV bags as though she were checking cutlets at the market. "There's only so much a person can take sometimes."

Claire ran a light finger over the taped portal on the back of Charlie's hand. His fingers flickered in sleepy response, and she cringed, remembering the needle sliding into the plastic contraption. The automated blood pressure cuff spluttered and wheezed to life, making her jump. A spiderweb of wires spread from Charlie's chest to a steadily beeping heart monitor.

"It's funny, I've seen parents as strong as you can imagine power through some pretty ugly stuff, then that same mom or dad will faint or puke over the tiniest thing." Ami grinned, dimpling. "I think our brains protect us when things are bad. And then, when they know everything's gonna be okay, they let go."

They'd all been so nice to her. So much nicer than she deserved. The doctors, Ami, even the police officer that had brought her to the hospital, the kind way he had questioned her and Charlie. Claire could stomach no more kindness from strangers.

"Where's my husband?"

"He and Grandpa went to grab a bite to eat." Ami fussed with another of the machines, and Claire had no desire to correct her. Jack, that poor sweet man. He'd been in the police car, the ER, the waiting room, this private room, everywhere she'd turned. "Pulse ox looks good, and his pain is under control. Don't you worry, Mom."

Claire nodded, running her fingers through Charlie's sweaty cowlick before kissing his forehead. She began to pull at his pillow, but Ami set a gentle hand on her arm to stop her.

"I just flipped it to the cool side about ten minutes ago." Ami smiled. "Let's take care of you now, honey. Can I get you a Coke? I even have ice."

"Diet, please," Claire said, nodding to be rid of her, her head swimming with medical terminology, beeps and thuds, hisses and screams. Ami squirted antibacterial gel onto one fleshy palm and disappeared, rubbing her hands together.

Finally alone, Claire dissolved as it all slammed into her, everything she'd held at bay—the wretched awareness, the self-loathing, the vile regret, the terror. *God, if you exist, if you can hear me, please let me start over.* She squeezed her hands in prayer between her thighs, rocking, rocking. *I get it. I get it. I get it. And I won't fuck it up. I promise.* She was sharp as a thousand needles now, fully present in her body in a way she hadn't been in months, years.

Obviously, she'd quit the Save Rite. That was easy. God, what a joke. Charlie would be missing some school. He'd need to stay off the leg, and who knew how much emotional caretaking he'd require. She'd look into getting a therapist for him. There would be insurance to deal with, follow-up doctor visits, more from the police, of course. How long would it take them to put it all together and arrest Matt? And in that desperate moment, what would he tell them about her?

Seeing Charlie moving and talking, after the miracle of his test results indicated no internal bleeding, head injury, or spinal damage, she'd been so flooded with gratitude and intoxicating relief, she'd almost forgotten she'd had anything to do with his condition. She'd steeled herself as he answered Officer Nick's questions, ready to take whatever punishment the universe had in store for her. She certainly had it coming. But, incredibly, Charlie had seen nothing, not even the color of the car. His glasses had been knocked off his face, an image that made her shudder still. Even as she'd watched the officer collect the plastic bag of clothes they'd cut from her son's body and the helmet with its sickening cracks, even as he'd asked if he could chat with her again tomorrow, she had the sense she was getting away with something terrible, at least for now, and that in return she would need to punish herself.

And I will, she vowed. She would atone in every way possible, make herself 100 percent available to her son, to her husband, become the mother and wife of their dreams, goddamn it. Because this was the truth: even though she hadn't technically been the one to hit Charlie, she easily could have been.

God oh God oh God, please. She rocked, casting a frantic look at the door, then again at Charlie, who was still out cold. She reminded herself of her husband's steadiness. His good job, his stupid jokes, even his belted khakis and boring, predictable reliability. She was so grateful for it all now, watching as he drilled the police officers and hospital staff, asking all the right questions, holding all of it effortlessly in his mind. She'd gotten so sloppy. Eliminating alcohol would be nothing; the least of her penance. First, they'd get through this part: surgery, then recovery. Next she'd nourish her family, put food on their table, nurse them all back into a healthy unit. Devote herself every day to forgetting that what's-his-name ever existed, that this horrible night had ever happened at all, because the universe, for whatever reason, seemed to be on her side, or at least on Charlie's. They'd been spared true devastation, and though she didn't deserve it, she was going to live up to her part of the bargain. If there was a God, He clearly wanted this family together. He clearly felt she could handle the massive weight of this terrible lie. So she would.

She would take this secret to her grave, because Charlie had been spared his.

Chapter 13

They had to wait nearly two days for an AA meeting. Matt arranged to have someone from work help him return the rental car to save Lib the long drive to wherever their nearest office was, and Lib rolled out the truck. It sputtered to life, but just barely. Matt would be gone all day, so she'd taken it around to Oimoen's Service to ready it for him. This morning, while Matt was at work, Chet Oimoen called to say it was running like a top. Matt was off at 4:00 and the AA meeting was at 4:30, so she'd picked him up from his shift and driven him over.

"Do you need to register somewhere?" Lib asked, using the steering wheel to pull herself forward so she could better examine the little eggshell house with navy trim, but it gave away nothing. She was still surprised that Anthem had an Alcoholics Anonymous group, that it even met three times a week, here next to the Grace Lutheran Church. She must have passed it a thousand times without seeing it. She pulled into a parking spot, cut the engine. "Do you want me to wait until you're done with the meeting?"

"No, I've told you this," he spit out, back to being annoyed with her. He'd allowed himself to be so vulnerable with her the night before last when he had confessed everything to her, but since then, even in their brief interactions, his mood swings were back. In fact, they had become even more pronounced, and she felt as if she was smothering him simply by existing. For all her experience with a drunk, she'd never really watched someone get sober, and she already felt useless and foolish, in the way.

Matt pushed the passenger door open, then hesitated, pulling it back with him.

"I really appreciate you driving me, but I think I'm ready to do it on my own, if you don't mind."

Lib instinctively gripped the keys tighter, squeezed until the little teeth left bite marks on her palm, then relaxed. Offered the keys to her son.

"Well, I didn't mean right this second," he said, but he looked relieved, pleased.

"Nope, you're right. I told you, you could use the truck, and I meant it. I trust you," she said, though more out of duty than belief. She was trying so hard. Wanted so badly for this cure to stick, for both their sakes. These past weeks since Matt arrived had aged her, these past days even more so.

"Thanks, Mom." He grinned, and she marveled yet again at how quickly his energy could shift, how charming he could be when it suited him. They both exited the truck, Matt disappearing inside the little house with her keys, which had once been Jack's keys.

She walked away from the truck, thinking about the handful of times she'd had reason to rent a vehicle. She and Jack had traveled to some pretty spectacular places early on in their marriage, but they hadn't done that for a long time. He always said they'd built the sort of life he didn't need a vacation from, and she never could argue with that.

Until now. She'd give anything to escape Anthem for a while, she thought, turning to hoof it home—but to where? Her own house was different, changed, no longer hers alone. As much as she genuinely wanted to help her son get himself straight, she no longer felt any support herself, not from her home and not from Jack. "Or Carolina," she whispered, and she knew then where she would go.

She loped across the street just as another truck rounded the corner, and she found herself eye to eye with Mike from the hardware store. They nodded to one another, a polite greeting, and then she picked up the pace to a jog to give him clearance and privacy as he swung into the church parking lot. She held this new information about Mike in as she strode, fast and powerful, feeling for just a second like her old self—as though she had a prop motor on her butt, Jack liked to say. When she finally made it to the stone bench etched with Carolina's nameplate, she let it tumble out: "Would you believe old Mike goes to those alcoholic meetings? How has he kept that secret all these years?" The willow overhead gathered itself, shook its limbs.

Carolina had claimed this tree, which grew at the center of the VFW park across from her café, as her own long before she died. For years they'd met here for lunch when Lib still worked at the plastics plant or for picnics with Frannie and Kit when the girls were little. Carolina was the sort of mom Lib had never known, and even though she knew she'd never be a mother herself again, she'd watched Carolina closely just the same. She trusted Carolina—that was why she'd allowed Carolina to set her up with Jack—and it felt natural to attach herself to that family tree from a slight but safe distance; she became the girls' beloved if somewhat reluctant auntie. Even after Carolina was in the chair, post-amputation, the girls would wheel their mother over to talk to the elegant solitary peachleaf willow whose rain-gray limbs foretold the coming fall with furry clumps of miniature orange fruit. Carolina's Tree, that's what they all called it, and now there was a wooden sign in front of it that said as much, and a stone bench they'd installed with the funeral gifts, instead of a gravestone.

After Carolina's death, Lib had brought seeds she'd harvested from her own prairie and surreptitiously began a project on the far edges of the park, near the tree line. She'd never been questioned or caught—she liked to think Carolina had something to do with that—and year by year, her private prairie had flourished there.

Now, Lib settled on Carolina's bench beneath the shady willow, surveyed the prairie in its full early fall bloom. Wondered if it would be awkward when next she went for nails or mulch. "Mike always seemed so together," she murmured, closing her eyes. When she felt the breeze tickle the dampness at the arch her back made against the stone bench, she could almost believe her old friend was sitting there beside her, that it was her whispering when the leaves rustled just right.

"God help me, Carolina," she said, unwilling or unable to say Jack's name aloud just yet. "That mess of a kid might be all I have left."

But I thought you didn't need anybody, Libby. There it was, her best friend's voice. Her tone teasing in the manner reserved for pushing Lib when she needed it, back before she gave up insisting that Lib make a better effort to show Jack how much he was appreciated. It was true: there was a time Lib would have loved feeling this solitary. "You never know what you've got 'til it's gone," Carolina would warn, already wearing out Lib's nerves with the authority widowhood had granted.

"Jack knows I appreciate him," Lib had countered, adding, "He loves me this way." *What way?* Carolina had pushed, and Lib had said, simply, "My way."

And she'd meant it. Lib not only believed she was the most independent woman she knew; she believed Jack required it of her. He'd never say so, but it was clear. She'd spent years gossiping with Carolina, railing against the neediness and codependence they witnessed in nearly every other couple in town, who stayed miserable together much more often than they split up to seek happiness elsewhere. That would never be her, not after what she'd already been through. Of course it was wrong, the way she'd left Matt—but she'd been right to leave Jon. And she believed she was right to keep Jack at a bit of a distance so she wouldn't meet the fate of all those other women. "Oh, please," Carolina had said. "Fight all you want, but you're just pretending."

"I'm not!" Lib would laugh, ignoring the low-level anxiety that always hummed when Carolina said things like that. Of course her friend didn't know the half of it, but not telling Jack what had happened before she'd known him—that was a different kind of pretending. It didn't count, and even Carolina eventually agreed as the years went by and Jack seemed happy to just let her be. And Lib loved Jack as truly and deeply as was humanly possible. But she didn't need him, never had.

"What if you were right all along?" she said now.

"Right about what?" Carolina said from behind her.

"Christ, Frannie!" Lib yelped. "You nearly scared me to death!"

"Oh, nuts. I'm so sorry," Frannie said, settling in next to Lib on the bench and scratching her back, squeezing her shoulders. "I didn't mean to sneak up on you like that. I saw you sitting over here and wanted to pop over and see if you've gotten any word from Jack and if either of you need anything."

"You sound exactly like your mother," Lib said, wiping at her nose, catching her breath. What was this now, had the girls already heard about their fight? Was Lib big news at the café? "What do you mean word from Jack?"

"About the accident. Charlie, the Taylor boy."

Lib went cold, turned to Frannie.

"What happened to the Taylor boy?"

"Oh, goodness, I'm sorry. I just assumed . . . Well, aren't they giving Jack any details? He must be beside himself. Is he okay?"

"Frannie, so help me, spit it out, please. I'm clearly not up to speed."

"Well, his name hasn't been released, but I've got it on good authority—Tim was at the scene," she said, lowering her voice in deference to the confidentiality she was clearly breaking. "A car hit Charlie on his bicycle the night before last and drove off. They haven't caught whoever it was. Jack was there, I know he was. Tim said so. I realize he's not actual family, but for all the time he's been spending with that boy, it's really wrong of the Taylors to not to keep you two in the loop. I knew something wasn't right with that woman. Kit loves her, but I haven't trusted her from the jump."

"My word," Lib whispered, remembering the sirens two nights earlier. To think that Jack was so angry with her that he hadn't even reached out during something like this.

"Auntie Lib, are you okay? You don't look so good. Can I get you to come across the street? I've got to get back anyway, but I don't want to leave you like this. I didn't mean to upset you."

"No, no, I'm fine," Lib managed, though she most certainly was not. She needed to get home, where it was safe. There would be no falling apart in public.

"I don't know," Frannie said, clearly anxious to get back. "Are you sure? Maybe just a muffin, perk your blood sugar up a tad?"

"I've actually got dinner in the oven. I need to get back," Lib lied, mustering up an ancient, stubborn firmness. *Hang on*, she thought. *Hang on*.

Frannie clucked a time or two more, then reluctantly hugged Lib goodbye. Lib watched until she was safely across the street and inside the building before she let loose the sobs—three short bursts, just enough to make room for breath. Then she stood, pointed her body toward her place, and walked home as fast as her legs would allow.

~

Claire was grateful for once that she'd never finished unpacking the clutter that would only be in the way now. Besides the backpack he still kept ridiculously near, the coffee table was stacked with word puzzles, mechanical pencils, stacks of library chapter books. Boxes of chewable pain reliever in three different flavors and two prescription bottles, one for pain, the other to prevent infection. A pitcher of ice water sweating next to a plastic Spiderman cup and a sleeve of Saltines. Charlie's handheld video game, his new phone, her old iPad.

"Do you think we should grab a third pillow?" she said to Dan, who was tapping something into his phone. "For under his leg?"

"It just needs to be up above my heart," said Charlie from the couch, where he was hanging on to the wrist of his broken arm so it wouldn't flop over the edge of the sofa. Shit. This setup wasn't going to work, not with Charlie having to constantly fight gravity, his casts on opposing limbs.

"You guys, I think he's going to have to be in bed after all. I'm sorry," Claire said.

"No, this is fine! It works great, see?" panicked Charlie, pulling his plaster wing to his chest, but it slipped out of his grip again, and he let out a yelp of pain this time.

"It's got to be the bedroom. I'm sorry, kiddo. It's only temporary, right?"

She was disappointed too. She had envisioned the spacious living room as command central for the next week or two, with its proximity to the bathroom and kitchen—not to mention Charlie's beloved TV.

"Dan, what if we move the television into Charlie's room for the time being?"

"Yes!" Charlie responded, before Dan had the chance. "Please, Dad, can we?"

Dan looked at his son, pocketed his phone, and smiled. "Charlie, if I were you, I'd ask me for a Lamborghini right about now," he said, and Claire smiled too. As her husband worked to untether the flatscreen from its tangle of wires and cables, she practiced feeling something more for him. *I can do this*, she coached herself, watching his back muscles through his dress shirt. *What a strong, capable man. What a loving father and husband.*

After two nights at the hospital with Nurse Ami managing her every need, Claire had been terrified to go it alone at home. It reminded her of when she'd given birth, then balked when they said she could actually take the baby home. What was she supposed to do with him? But now she had Jack, who'd hardly left Charlie's side at the hospital, and who'd promised to help out every day now that they were back home. It was clear he'd come to love her son deeply, and it was equally clear that Charlie wanted him close. And as fearful and self-conscious as Claire was feeling—particularly without a drink—around Dan, who might sense something more in her and become suspicious, Jack's presence was both a distraction and a comfort.

When the doorbell rang, Claire looked to Dan, puzzled. She had never actually heard the chime before, as they had yet to have visitors at the new place, and they weren't expecting Jack until after lunch.

"That'll be Marcy, Kyle's mom," said Dan over his shoulder, hustling off toward the front door, and Claire frowned. Was that who he'd been texting all afternoon?

"No, no, no, I refuse to intrude, I'll just drop this with you and leave," sang Marcy through the open front door, waving off Dan's attempts to usher her in. Dan took the casserole Marcy offered into both hands and cradled it. She'd first met Marcy at the open house, but Dan had handled most of the interactions when Charlie had befriended Kyle. It occurred to Claire, not for the first time, that her husband was far better acquainted with the parents of Charlie's classmates than she would ever be.

"Charlie you poor sweet thing. How're you holding up, my dear?" said Marcy in a sugary voice as she squinted at the couch from the front stoop.

Claire stepped forward, placed her right hand on Charlie's head, and waved quickly before tucking her hand into her armpit. "Marcy, this is so kind of you. Thank you," she said. "You didn't have to do this."

"Oh Claire, I just feel so terrible," she said. "Jim should have stayed with him to make sure you were home. I'm just furious with that man."

They'd pieced it all together at the hospital: Kyle's dad had given Charlie a ride home, dropped him off at the door, unaware that his parents weren't there. When Charlie had found himself in an empty house, he'd decided to squeeze in a bike ride before dark.

"Nonsense, it's nobody's fault," said Claire, pushing through a fresh wave of guilt. If they only knew.

"Well, a bunch of us have started a meal train," Marcy continued. "We'll be dropping off food, but we won't bother you, believe me. We'll just have the kiddos leave it on the doorstep. Pretend we were never here."

Claire swallowed, touched by the unexpected gesture, particularly from a group of women she couldn't have picked out of a lineup. Maybe Dan was right to embed himself the way he always did. Maybe she could try harder, do better, with this part of her life too.

"You ladies are the best. Thank you so much," said Dan, and Claire was grateful, once again, that he knew just what to say. "This is the most welcoming, supportive community we've ever lived in."

Marcy smiled, stepped backward down the cement step, and then stopped. "Oh, gosh, I almost forgot!" she said, pulling a bottle out of her bag and handing it to Dan. "Some grown-up medicine for the adults," she said, winking at Charlie, then waving as she trotted away. "If you need anything at all, you know where to find us!"

Dan closed the door with his back, balancing the casserole in one hand, the bottle of wine in his other. Claire recognized the label from a distance, Santa Margherita pinot grigio, one of her favorites. She blinked back tears as she scooped several items from the coffee table and headed to Charlie's room. She didn't know how she'd beg out of it if Dan decided to open the bottle now, but she wouldn't be having any wine. She hadn't had a drink in three days.

Dan took the gifts to the kitchen, and when Claire returned for a second haul, they nearly collided at the living room entrance. Flooded with sudden tenderness, or at least a desire to feel it, she embraced her husband impulsively in a quick, tight hug.

"She's right, you know," Dan whispered, his breath hot against her ear. "You should have been here."

Chapter 14

Since the accident eight days ago and Lib's bombshell in the Save Rite parking lot that preceded it, Jack had been tortured. Desperate to unload it all to a wife he didn't care to speak to, obsessed with finding whatever scoundrel had done this to a boy that felt like his own but wasn't. He'd barely slept, lying awake at night pushing horrific images from his head. He'd missed countless calls from Lib and ignored her knocks at the door on the two occasions she'd shown up when he was home. For the first time in more than three decades, that door was locked to her.

When he wasn't over at the Taylors' running errands for Claire or fussing over Charlie, he was driving the village roads off Highway Q, retracing Charlie's path, looking for clues. He stared down every car that passed, looking for telltale damage. Suspected every person whose path crossed his, even those he'd known all his life. Pete still politely took his daily calls asking for updates, although the officer's tone was becoming shorter, more curt, every time he was forced to break the news that no, there was no news to share. How could there just be nothing? Likely someone just passing through, he feared.

On a day the Taylors would be returning to Richland Center for a follow-up visit with the orthopedic surgeon, leaving Jack with too many empty hours before him, he finally slid onto his usual stool at the café. Only then did he fully realize how long he'd been away from his routines, how out of sorts and crazed he'd been.

The girls acted as if he were just back from war, fussing and clucking and hovering. And then Frannie sat down—Frannie never sat down—and asked if he was feeling all right. She leaned into his left elbow, and then Kit flanked him on his right, and the whole thing caught Jack so off guard—and Kit looked so much like her mother in that moment—that to keep himself from sobbing into the slice of cherry pie they'd placed before him, he started rattling off everything he knew about the accident and how he'd passed the time since he'd seen them last. As for Lib, well, he was keeping that to himself. Had he opened his mouth about that, he'd have crumbled on the spot.

"Dear God in Heaven," Kit gasped. "We heard about the hit-and-run, but no details."

"Tim didn't give any?" Jack thought of how quickly the cook had arrived on the scene. It must have been his night off, or he must have been on his way to work. Funny how in a small town everyone knew everything, and nothing at all.

"No, he certainly did not," said Frannie, sounding annoyed, then leaning behind him to whisper something to Kit. "He wouldn't do that. He only confided in us that it was Charlie, because you'd been there and he was worried about you. But so many people have come through talking about it. A lot of people heard it on the scanner, but nobody really knows anything. It's been on the news, but they never say Charlie's name."

"Yeah, he's a minor, and he didn't . . ." The word *die* evaporated in Jack's throat. He cleared it, tried again. "In an ongoing investigation into a non-fatality accident involving a minor, standard procedure is not to release names," Jack said, parroting Officer Nick's words. Jack realized he'd been so engrossed in the story from the inside, he hadn't thought what it might look like from the outside. In fact, you couldn't get much closer than Jack had been all week, and yet he still felt like an intruder, from the moment he had seen Claire's shocked face from the back of the squad car.

"How long was he in the hospital?"

"Not long. A couple of days. It wouldn't have even been that long, modern wonders and all, but his mother was afraid to take him home, so they got an extra night."

"Poor Claire," moaned Kit. "How long will he have the cast on his leg?"

"This one, two months, then maybe a lighter one after that, depending. It's already driving him crazy. Claire says bathing has been a nightmare, like trying to get a plastic-wrapped alley cat in the tub."

He actually chuckled at that, remembering how Charlie had been unable to sit still the first time he'd brought him here to the café. To have come so close to having all that frenetic energy snuffed out for good . . .

"Do they need food? Tim could send home-cooked meals with you anytime."

"Oh no, they're swimming in casseroles. School moms and such."

Both women nodded. If there was anything folks around here knew how to do well, it was feed the convalescing and bereaved.

"Sounds like you've really been there for him, not that I'm surprised," said Frannie. "I'm glad that Taylor woman is giving you the respect you deserve."

"I like Claire," said Kit. "She kind of reminds me of Mom."

Jack could see it, now that she mentioned it. Every time he had seen Carolina, she was that same mix of tired and busy, and she had a sort of distracted but fierce love for her girls. Course Carolina had been a single mom most of her life, and Claire wasn't that. Not technically.

"I keep hoping she'll come around more, that we can get to know each other a bit better," said Kit. "Before all this, I mean. I can't imagine what she's going through."

"Well, you've always been the trusting one," Frannie said, though not as unkindly as she might have a few minutes before.

"I like her too," said Jack, meaning it, feeling newly protective. Thinking of the handful of moments he'd witnessed in the Taylor household that he'd just as soon not have seen: Dan appearing warm in front of visitors, then snipping at Claire in private. When the man was even home, which was not all that often, he just tap tap tapped away at that fancy phone like a bird pecking against glass. Not that Jack should judge. What if he hadn't carried his own portable phone that horrible day? What if Claire hadn't bought one for Charlie and thought to program Jack's number in?

Now he checked his watch: probably an hour or so before Claire would be calling with an update from the doctor's visit. She called every morning to let him know how the boy had fared the night, and to give him the day's order. It was the most use he'd ever gotten out of this portable phone, and he found he looked forward to hearing her voice. It felt good to be of service, to provide help in a concrete way.

She was still afraid to leave Charlie alone, even for a minute. But she did want to tackle some projects she'd been putting off around the house, and so Jack would stay at his own place in the mornings, working in the garage and taking care of business until the anxiety drove him to his truck for his daily sweep of the ditches, and then she'd call him, just before the noon hour, with a list of the day's requests. Relieved for the reprieve from the burning mandate, he'd bring the candy bars, ointments, or toys they wanted from the drug store and whatever supplies Claire needed to make her house a home: paint, shelving, wall hanging kits, and the like. Then Jack would hang out in Charlie's room while she worked, and he'd stay until Dan came home at dinnertime. Initially he'd been afraid of overstepping, but they'd fallen into a nice routine.

Both Dan and Claire claimed they were grateful for Jack's presence, but he still couldn't shake the feeling he was inserting himself somewhere he didn't belong. "Don't be silly," Claire had said. "It's you he called that day, isn't it? It's you he wants," and that was true. He was probably oversensitive, watching too closely, especially for signs of drinking—but he hadn't seen any, not from either parent. Mostly they seemed as though they lived separate lives under the same roof. The opposite of what he had with Lib.

Rather, what he'd had.

Jack bid the girls farewell, ambling out to his pickup as the first few drops of a cool rain hit the brim of his hat. Wouldn't be long now before Tim switched from Door County cherries to apples, Jack's favorite pie of all. He'd already begun to see the paper bags of Cortlands and Honeycrisps at the Save Rite, knew the Macouns the cook favored couldn't be far behind. Jack didn't have a favorite season; rather, it was the transition he loved most. The excitement of change to keep things interesting, tempered with the promise that things would always return to what had been, year after year after year.

He pulled out, avoiding looking over, as he usually did, at Carolina's tree and Lib's flower beds across the way at the park. Sometimes it was hard to say what Jack found worse, obsessing over Charlie's accident or revisiting the surreal afternoon he'd learned about Lib's betrayal. Those awful moments in the truck with his wife were among the darkest in his life, but the life-shattering episode was also strangely truncated by the accident: her face as she confessed, his visceral response—all of it had been eclipsed the moment he first saw Charlie broken on the side of the road, his twisted bicycle in the ditch. He had seemed so tiny on that hospital gurney, swarmed by nurses, orderlies, and machines. And here was Jack, big and helpless, then and now. And his wife likely knew nothing about any of it. Rather, she had to know about the accident—she wouldn't be trying this hard to reach him if it was just about their fight, he was certain of that—but she couldn't possibly know the details, or how tortured he'd been.

What he really wanted, more than anything, was to get Lib's take on all of it—the accident, Claire's drinking that night, Claire and Dan's marriage, the fact that she'd seemed so friendly with Lib's son in the parking lot—but of course he couldn't. He'd spent a good part of these eight days distracting himself from the painful truth about his own marriage, which is that it wasn't one; at least not the one he'd thought it was. Worse than the betrayal itself, though—yes, he was certain this part was worse—was that he hadn't seen it coming. That she'd not only so effortlessly kept a secret of this magnitude for thirty-three years but that she'd harbored a man in her home for a full month, and he hadn't had a clue. It wasn't just her he couldn't trust, it was himself. His own judgment.

Do you take this woman, Jack remembered, pulling into his dirt drive for once to ward off visitors and softly shutting the truck door behind him. They'd chosen to get married in the fall because Lib did have a favorite season. She loved the shifting watercolor of the trees, the don't-blink-or-you'll-miss-it magic of the leaves transforming, gasping, falling. They hadn't chosen a wedding date; instead, they'd waited for just the right moment. *Today!* she'd shouted with glee, and they'd tumbled into the old Toyota—you could do this back then—and hightailed it to the courthouse in a blur of bronze, copper, and garnet. *Do you take this woman, from this day forward? Will you protect her independence as your own?* the clerk read from the slip of paper Jack had presented with a trembling hand.

I do, he'd said. *I will.*

"I did," he said now, stepping into his little living room to wait for Claire's call, thinking how Lib had essentially broken every vow in one fell swoop. "She didn't."

~

Claire balanced on the stepladder in her bedroom, red brush dripping, covering up the old paint. She was thirteen days sober. Thirteen excruciating days.

When she could stomach looking in the mirror—only when necessary and never meeting her own eyes—she thought maybe she looked a little different. She'd always thought she had good skin, but now her face seemed smoother and clearer, less puffy when she hadn't even known it had been puffy. And although she'd developed unspeakable nightmares, she still woke feeling more rested than she was used to. The coffee had never tasted better, despite the fear and self-loathing ever-present at the back of her throat. That, she couldn't wash down for anything.

She scratched an itch on her forehead, blinking dumbly when her fingers came away red, then realized she'd just smeared paint across her face. She looked around the master, now two-thirds finished, and admitted it: she hated the new color. She'd taken a break earlier, walked away to wipe down the space above the kitchen cabinets, thinking maybe it would help to let the pigment develop; but time had only served to give it a duller, browner hue, like dried blood. Red was supposed to inspire "amorous intention," according to an article she'd torn from *House Beautiful* magazine at the dentist last year. "What Your House Tells the World About You" or something like that, and she'd decided red was the right compromise between the creative riskiness of orange and the romantic promise of pink. But without the aid of the glossy magazine paper—not to mention these low ceilings and the lack of contrast between the walls and the brown wood trim—the creepily reddening room was closing in on her.

Claire descended the ladder, dropped the brush into the tray, and stumbled out of the bedroom, taking an extra moment to gulp fume-free oxygen from the hallway. What had she been thinking? Now she would need to describe some new shade for Jack to pick up on his errands, unless she wanted to do it herself, which would mean finally leaving the house, which she hadn't done since they'd come home from the hospital, with the exception of Charlie's follow-up visits. She just didn't know what to do out there in the world, how to behave, what might happen, whether she'd be caught out.

Under the circumstances, no one pushed. The shock of Charlie's accident was more than enough to excuse the erratic behavior of his mother, even without them knowing her unspeakable involvement or the private bargain she'd made with an unfamiliar God to never, ever drink again.

In the garage, she had a trunkful of alcohol. That was the best she could do, at the time—gather all the wine, beer, and vodka in the house and sneak out after Dan and Charlie were asleep, lock it away in her car. (She left Dan's special-occasion whiskey as a decoy; she'd never had a taste for it anyway.) One of these days, as soon as she could gather her nerves, she planned to drive over and hurl it all into the Save Rite dumpster.

Meanwhile, inside, she had more than enough to keep herself distracted. Charlie's accident . . . well, she could barely hold its happening in her head. It was too much; she was too raw, the whole thing like waking from one of her nightmares but never quite. She relived it every time the lights went out—the thud, the screech, the vomiting—but by day she busied herself with caring for him and, when Jack was visiting, finally getting the house in order. He was there now, in Charlie's bedroom, playing yet another game of Pass the Pen, during which they took turns drawing on the same sheet of paper, creating the collaborative works of art now pinned all over Charlie's walls.

She moved toward their voices, leaned against the doorjamb.

"I think I might make a quick run to the hardware store," she said, surprising them all. Jack stood up from the kitchen chair they'd placed next to Charlie's bunk beds then, reading her, sat back down.

"We're fine here. I mean, I'm happy to run out for you, but we're okay."

"I hate the red." Claire nodded, sheepish. "It's not your fault. I don't think any shade would do. I'm gonna start over, and there's no sense putting you through that. I won't be long, just there and back. It'll be good for me."

"We're perfectly fine," Jack repeated, smiling, and it seemed true; they had such a natural, easy connection. Claire often eavesdropped on their conversations as she cleaned windows or rearranged furniture, though Charlie did most of the talking, and Jack seemed genuinely interested in his stories, in the homework that arrived at 3:25 p.m. sharp each day alongside yet another casserole; one mom or another, curbside in an idling car, waiting for Kaden or Jaden or Braden to return from delivering these items to the Taylors' front stoop.

"Take all the time you need. Fresh air always does the trick."

Claire nodded, ducking out to her bedroom to change before either of them caught her face registering their kindness, the guilt it laid bare. Fresh air was a logical cure, but Claire was terrified of all that waited just outside that door, where anything could happen.

She backed the Honda out of the garage and drove downtown, blinking in the shrieking daylight. Everything looked as she'd left it, though the car seemed empty without Charlie, and the wheel felt foreign in her hands, as if she hadn't driven in years.

She hadn't heard from the police since Officer Nick had called last Friday, a follow-up to the visit he and his partner paid the family at home, where they'd asked Charlie almost word for word the same things as before in the hospital, and his answers remained consistent: He saw nothing that night. Heard nothing. Remembered nothing.

"I promise we won't let this go, Mrs. Taylor, but you need to prepare yourself for the possibility that we might not ever find out who did this," Nick had said on the phone. "I'm sorry to say that 80 to 90 percent of hit-and-runs involving bicycles are never prosecuted. Without any witnesses and so few clues at the scene, it's a needle in a hayfield situation at this point. Even Charlie's bike isn't offering us much in the way of clues. But we'll keep trying."

He'd hung up then, and Claire had sunk to the floor, curled into herself and sweating. Craving a drink more than ever.

She'd been over this a thousand times in her mind: Even if they somehow managed to connect Matt with the accident, there was no reason they'd put her there with him—unless he put her there himself. But why would he? And yes, they'd made a ridiculous scene at that stupid roadside bar, but if the police had asked around, no one had mentioned it, or she'd have heard something by now. That was the twisted beauty of places like that—most of the people out drinking in a rural Wisconsin tavern on a weekday either found nothing unusual about it or didn't care to be seen themselves. They minded their business, a sort of unwritten code. She wasn't known enough in her new town to be recognized, and her and Matt's behavior hadn't been strange enough to be remembered.

Still, she scoured the Internet eight or nine times a day, but there was surprisingly little out there besides the well-intentioned but unnecessary online fundraiser one of the school moms was holding on their behalf, which Dan had approved without Claire's knowledge. Their first names were mentioned on that page, but not in any news stories. Each of the local affiliates had run brief clips asking for the public's help solving the mystery of the hit-and-run, but they only showed the ditch, stock footage of cars driving on a different, busier highway, and a close-up on a bicycle helmet that wasn't Charlie's. Not a single reporter had called, as Charlie's name hadn't been released; he was a minor with non-life-threatening injuries. The state paper Jack brought every day said nothing, and the local weekly only ran the police department's sparse press release seeking witnesses. Claire had assumed small-town living meant the absence of privacy, and yet here she and Matt were, criminals hiding in plain sight. That they'd possibly gotten away with something so abominable felt surreal—and if she hadn't been so stupidly sober, she might have wondered if someone else had hit Charlie after all, that she'd had nothing to do with it.

Now she pulled up to the hardware store across from the Save Rite, intending to choose new paint, then dump the booze. She wondered how Matt had passed these weeks. Did he even know it was her son they'd hit, considering their name wasn't in the papers? He did if he was still working at Save Rite. She'd told Ben about it when she called to quit, and word would have spread throughout the store and beyond. Likely he'd gone back to work, business as usual; it would have looked suspicious if they'd both left at the same time. And what about this mother of his, the woman he said he was staying with, whoever she was? Did she ask questions about his need to suddenly borrow a vehicle? Was he able to keep it together somehow? Was he going on as if the world hadn't ended when it was all she could do most days to keep breathing?

Just as she was about to get out of her car, as if he'd been waiting for her there, as if he'd never left at all, Matt materialized in the Save Rite parking lot, getting out of an old blue truck. Claire sank low in her seat, waiting for him to go into the store. His crooked amble looked so natural and relaxed it enraged her. He looked shorter than she remembered, pudgier. His torso sat strangely on his hips. From this distance, his silhouette seemed melted, leaving less definition than she'd thought between his jawline and neck. He leaned against the brick corner of the building to light a cigarette, as though he hadn't nearly killed her only child.

"That's the guy, Claire, really?" she whimpered, wiping at her nose. "That's the guy?"

She waited for him to disappear inside and then blew her nose and forced herself to go into the hardware store. Pushed weakly against the glass door and slid down the aisle to the back, fingered the paint samples under the bright florescent glow, searching for something as far away from red as possible. She finally settled on a sort of pistachio green and a two-in-one base that promised to cover dark colors, no primer coat needed.

"How hard is it to paint wood trim white?" she asked the aproned woman watching the machine jiggle the paint.

"Not hard." The woman shrugged but offered no more.

Claire pulled out her phone to Google the question and found she was shaking; thought better of it and slipped the phone back into her purse. Jack would know what to do. She'd had enough adventure for one day.

As she'd hoped, the loading docks were quiet as she rounded the backside of the Save Rite; the shipments usually arrived earlier in the morning and midafternoon, so they'd already been hauled inside. God help Matt if he popped out the back door right now. She might kill him. But she had to do this now in case she never worked up the nerve to leave the house again. She pulled the Honda up flush to the bins and tossed in bottle after bottle, holding up the heavy plastic cover with the other hand. It was painful—there had to be hundreds of dollars in booze there, from the Two-Buck Chuck she'd dragged from Madison to the pinot grigio Marcy had dropped off to the high-end vodka, smooth as a silk scarf going down (and coming up).

She hesitated, growing more doubtful as she worked. Maybe this was overkill. Maybe she could at least keep the best of it, perhaps for gifts? This was ridiculous. If she was a real alcoholic, could she have so easily quit cold turkey like this? What if she was conflating a logical assessment of her drinking habits with these staggering circumstances, the unbearable guilt over her near-infidelity, the near-miss of the accident that could have claimed Charlie's life?

Maybe, she thought, looking around. There was still no sign of any employees or passersby. She surveyed her nearly empty trunk, the treasure trove of booze awaiting some lucky dumpster diver, if Anthem had such a thing. Then, *No.*

She unloaded the last of it, allowed the cover to slap shut. *See how easy that was?* She drove away before she could change her mind.

Chapter 15

Time crept.

The oven ticked.

Claire squeezed every last drop out of the lemon wedge. Held the honey bear over the tea, waited for the drip. Got up, ran it under scalding water, sat back down, tried again. Eventually the crystals loosened their molecules, the heat worked its magic. She blew. Sipped.

The oak seat of her kitchen chair creaked beneath her. She bit at a hangnail. Swiped a finger down the glass screen of her phone, refreshing nothing. The furnace kicked on, blowing from the table a sheet of paper that fluttered to the tile and settled there, a blank, flat feather. The furnace ceased its blowing.

She squinted; the register vents had grown fuzzy. Too tired to pull the vacuum cleaner out again and deal with its myriad attachments, she knelt before the grates. Slid a finger across each slat, one by one, wiped the dust across her pant leg. By the time she finished, the evening had turned just dark enough to warrant electricity. She looked up at the light switch from her haunches, miles away across the kitchen.

Down the hall, in Charlie's bedroom, high laughter mingled with low. What would she do without Jack?

What did normal people do with their afternoons?

There were four hours to suffer through before bedtime.

Four hours until it would become fourteen days since she'd had a drink.

And somehow it became fifteen. Then sixteen, seventeen, eighteen.

And then it had been twenty-one days, each passing almost exactly like the one before. A mixture of scatterbrained house projects and the business of Charlie's healing and avoiding Dan and the horrible, ugly truth, and this terrifyingly quiet nothingness, this void that sucked into it all time and noise and purpose and in which she sat, all alone, not drinking, waiting.

~

Jack was puzzling a little too hard over a fourth-grade math problem when Dan suddenly opened Charlie's bedroom door and stood in the doorway. Without a greeting or a preamble, he said, "I think it's important that we get Charlie out of the house. I think we could all use some good normalizing social time around here. Family time."

He looked pointedly at Jack, who stood abruptly from his spot in the chair next to Charlie's bed. He'd let his guard down, grown so comfortable with the routine that he'd stopped searching for clues that he was in the way—but this was a big one. Dan must have just come from work; he still wore a sport coat and necktie, though he was tugging the tie loose as he stood in the doorway.

"Claire, can you bring me a beer?" he hollered over his shoulder, then turned back to face Jack. "You've got to help me talk her into it, old pal. You know as well as any of us how badly we need a normal night on the town. Enough is enough."

Jack smoothed his pants, looking down at Charlie, who'd sat up so fast when his dad opened the door that he'd nearly cracked his head on the top bunk.

"Can we go to the restaurant?" he shouted, and both men smiled.

Jack was sure the boy was feeling ornery and restless in captivity, but he didn't show it much. He didn't seem consumed by the same outrage that still burned within Jack most days, and for that, Jack was grateful, even if he didn't fully understand it. He was just one of those kids who seemed to take things in stride. Now it hit home just how sad and contained Charlie must really feel, as Jack watched this fresh flicker of glee ripple through him. "Can we all go, Jack too? Please, Dad?"

"Of course, Jack too. I said family, didn't I?" Dan winked at Jack, who smiled down at his feet.

"Yes!" said Charlie, flopping back onto his pillow. "Yes!"

Claire didn't seem as thrilled.

"Wait now, what's happening?" she said, appearing in the doorway empty-handed. Dan threw an arm around his wife, gripping her shoulder, pulling her in. Jack was surprised, and Claire appeared to be too. Jack hadn't seen any tenderness between the two of them at all while visiting their home since Charlie's accident. He hadn't seen much of Dan, period. He supposed the busy schedule as a school administrator went on, regardless of what was happening at home. And he knew from his calls to Officer Nick that Dan was making regular calls of his own. Still, he seemed . . . absent, somehow. Not eager as he was now.

"We're going to the café," Dan said to Claire. "It's Wednesday night, isn't it? You're going to see those waitress friends of yours. Jack, you'd better call your wife. Charlie goes back to school on Monday, and we might as well get a practice run in. We're gonna get dressed up like normal human beings, and we're gonna traipse our pathetic selves down there and feast like it's a holiday. Do you hear me? Let's get healthy!"

The man seemed fizzy, as though he'd already had at least one of the beers he'd requested.

"I don't think so, Dan," said Claire.

"Yeah, I don't think Lib can make it," said Jack, wincing at his wife's name on his own lips. "I'm not sure what she's—"

"Oh, come on, guys! Don't be so damn silly!" said Charlie, and Jack barked a laugh. The boy had been a lot of things lately—bored, pained, restless—but never rude.

"Charlie!" gasped Claire, but Dan laughed too.

As good as it felt to watch Charlie revel in this light fun, Jack still wasn't ready to deal with Lib, and this whole situation was rapidly spiraling out of his hands. Could he put aside the growing pit in his stomach and finally return Lib's calls, for the boy's sake? He wanted to be that man. But he wasn't, not yet.

"Yeah, guys, come on," said Dan. "Don't be so damn silly! Jack, call your wife. Honey, go get yourself hot. And bring me that beer!" he said, slapping her on the bottom. "I thought that damn woman would never leave," Dan said, winking at Charlie, who giggled, then disappearing down the hallway.

Claire lingered in the doorway, looking lost.

"I'm sorry, I don't know what's gotten into him," said Claire. "I don't think I . . . And Dan never . . . Oh, Charlie, wait!"

Claire lunged at Charlie, who was already swinging his legs over the side of his bed. Jack grabbed his elbow, then waited until Claire had him in a bear hug before opening the wheelchair they'd propped against the wall in the hallway, flattening the seat and locking the bottom safety hinge into place.

Claire set him in the chair and propped up his leg on the adjustable support while Jack waited in the hall.

Charlie stared at his feet. "Do I need to wear shoes? Or, like, a shoe? Do I need to wear shoe, Mom?" Charlie giggled, though it was a fair question, momentarily stumping his mother, who finally sighed.

"Okay, hang on, let me get some things together for you," she said. "Please just wait here. Don't move."

"Jack, call Mrs. Jack!" shouted Charlie from the bedroom, and Jack leaned against the wall, closing his eyes. He and Lib would eventually have a confrontation, but no way was this going to be the night. He wasn't ready. He couldn't trust himself. But he couldn't fathom denying this boy anything either.

"I'm gonna run home," said Jack, unable to think what else to say, or do. "What time are you thinking?"

"Six sharp!" Dan hollered back from the bedroom.

"Be there or be hexagonal!" added Charlie in his father's voice, hopelessly giddy now.

Jack made the short trip home through the foggy night, a gentle spittle of rain coating the windshield. He easily could have walked to Charlie's each day, but he almost always had a truckful of sundries for Claire, and he needed to be ready for most anything. This was the same excuse he gave himself for why he didn't ride his bike there, or out to the scene, or anywhere, but truth was he hadn't been on it since the night of the accident, and he couldn't imagine climbing on it ever again.

"I'm not ready for this, though, Tinker," he said, entering the house, crossing through the living room into the kitchen and kicking at the empty food bowl as he flipped on the lights. Tinker sat atop the kitchen table, blinking expectantly. Jack looked around the house. It was starting to feel like someone else's. The cat meowed a warning, and Jack was pleased for the reminder, hustling to fill a dish and top off his water bowl, which was low and stagnant. "Sorry, old boy," he said, meaning it.

Since the day he'd met her, he'd never gone this long without seeing or talking to Lib. Truth be told, he ached for her. But he also felt as if he were in a state of shock, as if she'd died. As if he'd lost the woman he'd married, and there was nothing left to do but grieve. But Lib was very much alive. He could hear the cat purring as he crunched away at the dry food, a sound like little rocks being pulverized. Jack wondered briefly about the cat's system, what allowed it to breathe and purr separately from swallowing.

"I guess I haven't been thinking about it like something I could fix," he said to the cat, who did not look up from his task.

It wasn't that Jack had somehow deluded himself into believing the woman carried no secrets; it's that he knew her to be an inherently honest woman. Honest with herself. Honest with him. And of everything he'd ever valued, ever believed about his own life, this had been most important: that Lib, the love of his life, was exactly who she was.

"It hurts, too, about the kid," he said. The kid who was now a grown man, this Matt. Did she have to let him live with her? Never, in all these years, had she indicated that she'd be open to her own husband living in that house with her, and here she'd let a stranger in overnight. How the hell did he reconcile that?

"I do want to know, Tinker," he said, realizing it was true. He wanted to know who she'd been and who she'd been married to before him. He wanted to know how she'd ever left a child; he couldn't fathom doing something like that to Charlie, and that boy wasn't even his. He wanted to know what she'd been thinking when she met him and exactly what had gone into the decision to hide this all from him, back then, and in the years since, and in these months now. How could she think so little of him, of what they had? How did she even view their marriage? It had to be different than the way he had viewed it all these years.

"I just want to know what's real," he said, sinking onto the couch, and Tinker padded in and hopped up to join him. Rubbed his body back and forth across Jack's lowered face, mixing his fur with Jack's tears.

Jack thought of the ruined pink ice cream he'd cleaned from the Taylors' garage floor the morning after Charlie's accident. Thought of the joy radiating from Charlie's whole body as he flew down the hill in front him on his bike. Lib, lying in a bed of leaves, shirtless and belly laughing into the sun.

Tinker abruptly jumped to the floor, piercing Jack's thighs with his back claws. Jack stared for a long time at the lap the cat had vacated, then unbuttoned the chest pocket of his shirt and pulled out his phone.

~

Lib and Matt were sipping tea together at the kitchen table when the telephone rang. Matt jumped and Lib's breath caught; it had been so long since she'd heard it. The old mustard-yellow rotary phone hung next to the stove near the doorway. Mama used to pull the receiver with her into the broom closet around the corner and shut Lib out, and although Lib had gotten a profound satisfaction out of taking a sledgehammer to that closet, she could still instantly call up the loneliness of a stretched phone cord. Who had her mother been talking to, voice high and unnatural, a world away behind that door? It didn't matter.

The phone itself was one of the few things that Lib had chosen to keep intact. She'd even kept the telephone table with the attached chair that sat beneath it for the phone book that grew smaller and thinner each year, now swimming in the deep shelf. Still ran a lint brush over the chair every now and then, its vacant needlepoint seat perpetually waiting for a guest who wasn't coming. Lib could have replaced the phone but with what? She'd never bothered with a cellular—just one more thing to keep track of—and she'd never cared for computers. There was something else too, about this light anchor to the past that Lib needed. Every once in a while, she wanted proof she hadn't invented her own trauma. That she had her reasons for being the way she was.

"I had no idea that thing worked!" said Matt between long jangles, the phone a live thing, pausing only briefly between rings to take a rattling breath. Lib rose and crossed the room in two paces to silence it, let her hand rest a moment at its neck, then cleared her own throat.

"Hello?" she said softly.

A deep exhale at the other end. Then a muffled shifting, followed by a man clearing his throat too. *Jack.*

Lib sank into the telephone chair she hadn't sat in since she was a child. It creaked and groaned beneath her sudden weight, wobbling a bit.

"I didn't call to talk," he said.

Okay, she thought, in case he could hear inside her mind, with hope that her polite reverence made even the slightest bit of difference. *Whatever you need.*

"Charlie was in a pretty bad accident."

"Oh!" She gasped genuinely, despite knowing it. "Oh, Jack, I'm so sorry. Is he okay?"

"It was three weeks ago," said Jack, and though she already knew that too, it stung as it sank in. It had taken her husband three weeks to make this call. To return any of her desperate entreaties.

"Oh," she repeated, a whisper this time.

"Anyway, the Taylors want us to go with them to family dinner. I don't feel like I can say no. I want to do right by the boy."

"I see," said Lib, scrambling to keep up. It was Wednesday evening. Jack was inviting her to dinner at the café. The Taylors would be there, and obviously Frannie and Kit and the rest of the world she'd kept at bay from her bubble these past weeks. Lib looked at the back of Matt's head, the fine curls at the nape of his neck. She'd never seen him from this angle before, at least not this up close. Not at this age. She was suddenly certain that if she pressed her nose there now, she'd smell spit-up, sweetly souring.

"You can bring him," said Jack, as if he could indeed read her mind. Why wouldn't he be able to by now?

"Oh," she said, but nothing else came.

"Six o'clock," said Jack, and he hung up. Lib held the phone to her ear for a long time, until the honking pulse shook her back into the present. She stood, carefully placing the receiver into the cradle, then drifting back to take her seat at the table.

"Everything okay?"

"Jack has invited us to dinner with the Taylors at the café," she said. "I think he wants to meet you."

"You're kidding," he blurted.

"I am not," she said, adrenaline lifting her from the lungs out. She felt lightheaded and weak, but airy; thrilled. She saw that Matt had blanched a bit. *Right*, she remembered, *the flirtation with Claire.* Well, this would be sufficiently awkward all around. "And we are going. He still sounds angry, but it's something. He asked, and there's no way I'm denying him this."

"Well, I'm sure he doesn't actually want to see me," said Matt, looking at the door.

"No, he specifically mentioned you. It will likely be strange and maybe even a little awful, but we're going."

She watched Matt swallow, tried to catch his eyes, but they shifted back and forth between the tea and the table, the space behind her.

"Are you nervous? Don't be. It's not you he's mad at. At the very least, he's the polite, friendly, old-fashioned sort. He won't mistreat you. This is good. We've got to face this. I honestly didn't know if we'd ever get the chance. If I would, I mean."

Matt looked down into his lap. He opened his mouth to say something, then shut it again.

"Oh, and I don't know if you heard about that hit-and-run a couple weeks back," she said, running back over Jack's words in her mind, running a hand to smooth her hair. She hadn't wanted to bother Matt with her own troubles as he navigated this delicate walk through early sobriety, so she hadn't told him any of what she'd learned from Frannie. "Apparently the child that was hit was Charlie. The little boy Jack has been spending so much time with. The one—well, you know, Claire Taylor's boy. I gather they'll all be at dinner, though, so he must be okay."

Matt rubbed his hands against the tabletop in a circular pattern, pressing them apart from each other in opposite rotating swirls. His head was bent and his gaze fixed, and Lib was drawn into the motion, temporarily hypnotized. For a few moments, that's all there was; the steady swooshing movement and the metronome tick of the clock.

"You know," he said finally, "there's this guy at my meetings, Mike. I guess he's kind of my sponsor."

Lib had heard of sponsors, of course. But it surprised her to hear that Matt's was Mike from the hardware store. No matter, she wouldn't judge either of them, she was just relieved he was taking the whole thing so seriously. But what this had to do with anything, she had no clue.

"He's got forty-three years sober. And he still makes that meeting three times a week. Never misses a day. Can you believe that?"

"Wow," said Lib, registering that this meant Mike had been struggling in secret for as long as she'd known him. We lived entire lives in front of each other, yet behind each other's backs. But why was Matt bringing this up now?

"I'll go change," said Matt, getting up from the table, and Lib calculated whether she should do the same. She'd raked leaves again today for the mulch pile, and bits and shreds still clung to her hair. She rose, following Matt up the stairs to get herself straight. The air was crisp enough now that she could wear that sweater Jack loved, the sage-green one that brought out the flecks in her blue eyes, like that old bedspread, like the bowl she'd bought him. She brushed her braid out, leaving the locks long and loose. Reapplied her deodorant through the neck of her shirt. Considered lip gloss, then decided against it, sensing the effort would ring false and repel him. She felt dizzy and unsure, twenty-five years old again. And at the same time, she felt twice her age, brittle and tentative.

Lib's disorientation continued as she climbed into the passenger seat of her own truck, just as she had when it used to be Jack's, but her grown son was now at the wheel. Whether they were driving toward reconciliation or ruin, she had no idea. But, incredibly, she was going anyway.

Matt was sweating, though the long sleeves and ever-present leather vest that held his cigarettes were finally appropriate for the weather. They were like two people on their way to the same blind date.

"Don't be nervous," she said. "Putting these things off makes it worse."

"You know, it's funny," he said, his expression unreadable. "That's exactly what I've been talking about with Mike."

~

There was no beer in the house to bring to Dan, of course. Claire covered for its absence by pulling down his whiskey, rooting around in the refrigerator for a Diet Coke, and mixing up his favorite drink. She wasn't really thinking—it was almost mechanical, really—when she slurped a bit off the top, just to test the ratio. It was just a sip, a sip of something she didn't even like, but she felt its warmth immediately spread, coating the creases of her brain like honey.

"You about ready, Claire?" Dan was humming to himself in their bedroom. She crossed the room, handed him the cocktail. "Oooh, even better!" he said. "Now you're talking. Make one for yourself too," and she smiled, nodded, even kissed his neck.

"Give me a minute," she said, floating out into the hallway, drifting back into the kitchen. She didn't bother with the Coke when she poured her own whiskey into Charlie's plastic Spiderman cup and took it like a shot of cough medicine. Poured another, tipped her neck back again, a smooth, automated motion. It burned in the most delicious way. Like ending a fight with an old lover, one she couldn't remember why she was mad at in the first place.

She tucked the bottle back into place, rinsed the cup, and headed for the bathroom to brush her teeth, freshen her face. As she was returning the mouthwash to the medicine cabinet, she took a shot of that, too, and then another, swallowing instead of spitting. It burned fiercer than the whisky had, clawing savagely at her stomach as it landed, and the pain strangely thrilled her even more. She slammed the mirrored door shut, grimaced at her reflection, and they were off.

Café Carolina felt like a live pulsing thing; a beating heart with its clanging pots and tinkling laughter. A warm and bright island in the dark, nearly empty parking lot, friendly and familiar and true. Claire struggled to maneuver Charlie's wheelchair through the inner doorway that Dan held open as she propped the outer door open with her foot stretched behind her. The door slipped and bit into her Achilles tendon, but she was feeling no pain. The ensuing scuffle was just enough to draw the sisters' attention from the back of the restaurant.

"Well, hot damn!" squealed Kit, rushing forward to embrace Claire, pulling her in and holding her tight. "We didn't even push the tables together! What a wonderful surprise!" Claire watched as if from outside herself as Kit fussed over Charlie in his chair, taking over the pushing, leading the group to the back.

"Charlie you poor thing, how have you been? We heard all about it," said Frannie, rearranging the tables, clearing the head spot for the boy's chair. Kit leaned into Claire, whispered, "We got the details from Jack. Do they have any suspects?"

Claire only shook her head, not daring to open her mouth.

"My God, honey, what a thing."

"Come right on up, young man!" said Frannie with a flourish, guiding Charlie into his place of honor. His broken leg stuck straight out in front of him, so the women angled the chair to accommodate it, Claire sinking into the seat immediately to his left, the side with the broken arm. Dan headed straight for the open wine bottle, pouring himself a healthy mug before taking the seat across from Claire, to Charlie's right. Frannie poured Claire a mug, prepped the table for two more place settings.

"How are you holding up?" asked Frannie, pulling another chair close to Claire's and leaning in to study Claire's face.

Claire absorbed this new treatment from the woman who'd always held her at arm's length. *I don't think I can do this*, she thought, though she wasn't sure exactly what it was she couldn't do, her mind drawing a white-hot blank. Frannie smelled delicious, like cinnamon and vanilla, and Claire wanted so badly to nestle her nose in the woman's neck, to lay her head there and rest for days, bask in the grace Frannie had suddenly felt compelled to show. She heard a soft jingling at the back of her brain, but it turned out to be Jack at the door.

He was alone, and he was moving slowly. He appeared shrunken, missing his usual commanding presence. She watched him cross the room without saying hello to anyone, and she wondered if it was her buzz softening him only in her eyes or if something had actually changed during his brief trip back to his house to change.

"Jaaaaack," said Kit, taffy-stretching his name as she stood to hug him, then moving aside to let Frannie do the same. Claire felt the coolness of Frannie's sudden absence. The sisters' quick movements clashed with Claire's insides, where everything felt deliciously slow.

"Hello, everybody," said Jack, sinking into the chair next to Dan's.

"You don't mind if I sit next to Charlie tonight, do you?" Dan asked Jack, who looked immediately taken aback. "I'm kidding! Relax!" said Dan, knocking his shoulder into Jack's.

Jack looked to Claire. *I don't know. I'm sorry*, she thought, sending him more apologies, losing track of what for. Dan was always the reliable one. The charmer. She was in no state herself to take up that role, not tonight.

"Do you guys have hot chocolate and whipped cream from a can?" said Charlie to the young waitress, a girl Kit introduced as Lacey. She stood blinking back at him, holding the tray full of water glasses. Claire hadn't seen her approach, and she couldn't find the words to protest Charlie's request. Kit sprang from the table to jog back to the kitchen again, apparently deciding it was easier to grab the drink herself. Sure enough, by the time Kit returned with the hot chocolate—an unnaturally red cherry perched atop a towering spiral of cream—Lacey was just setting the last of the water glasses into place.

Claire reached for Charlie's wrapped silverware, unrolling to release the spoon, the knife slipping through to the floor. She left it at her feet, pushed the mug within his reach. "Let it cool," she warned through thick lips, but he was already digging gleefully into the sugary buried treasure.

"Ravioli and garlic bread tonight," said Lacey with clear indifference, ambling away. Claire followed her movement, wondering if it was unique to older teenage girls. Would Charlie age into the same apathetic attitude? She couldn't imagine it. Claire considered her son and suppressed the urge to ask him how he was *really* doing. He'd taken this whole thing remarkably in stride, but maybe he was in some sort of prolonged shock. She wondered if his cheerful resilience had anything to do with his in-between age: old enough to grasp adult-sized constructs, young enough to underestimate their long-lasting impact. But Charlie had always been different, special somehow. She knew she wasn't the only one who thought so. She knew she didn't deserve him.

All around her, they performed. Claire felt as if she was watching dinner from backstage. She felt relaxed, peaceful, more like herself than she had in weeks. She didn't feel drunk so much as *dosed*. Clearly alcohol wasn't a problem for her but more like a medicine. Couldn't she take it to feel and act like everyone else? How was it any different than an antidepressant, really? A little something to connect the wonky synapses, a bridge to connect her to the world around her, with just enough distance from its people. She was facing the front of the restaurant, zoning out, when the door opened. Lib, looking stunning in a green sweater and jeans and, behind her, of all people—*God, no*—Matt.

"Shit!" Claire fumbled after her mug of wine that now tipped onto its side and rolled, releasing a bitter merlot bloodstain across the table that soaked her white paper placemat and her own silverware roll and spilled into the lap of her skirt. "Shit, shit, shit," she said, everything speeding up, bleeding out, falling apart. What the fuck was he doing here? And why on earth was he here with Lib?

"It's okay, honey, relax. It happens! I've got it," said Kit, expertly staunching the flow and sweeping the contents of Claire's place setting into her own dry paper mat, temporarily containing the disaster long enough for Frannie to swoop in with clean rags. Claire fell back in her seat, let the women care for her amid the chaos. *Christ fucking almighty*, she thought as the sisters placed a fresh place setting before her, patted a stack of napkins into her lap. Frannie somehow had a can of sparkling water and was telling her how to use it to get the stain out of her skirt. Claire watched her lips move, not hearing a word.

As the odd couple approached the table, stopping behind Charlie's wheelchair, Claire's face flamed hot. She wanted to disappear almost as badly as she wanted to gauge the others' reactions. Charlie scooped away at the hot chocolate, skimming the last of the whipped cream off with his spoon.

"Hello, everyone. There's someone I'd like you all to meet," said Lib, sounding shaky, and Claire stared at her neck. She'd never noticed before how thin it was, how translucent the skin. *Do not look at Matt*, she told herself, choosing a tiny freckle on Lib's throat and zoning in on it.

"This is Matthew. Matt. He's been visiting me. He's . . ." She looked at him—Claire caught the swivel of Lib's head, the movement of Matt nodding in her peripheral vision—and then turned back to the table. "He's my son."

Kit sank into the seat next to Claire's. No one said a word. Charlie picked up his mug and slurped. The freckle on Lib's neck blurred in Claire's vision. The mom who had abandoned Matt. The mom he'd been staying with. It was Lib. All this time, it was fucking Lib.

"Well, how about that!" said Dan, standing up to shake Matt's hand, clapping him on the back. "I'm Dan Taylor. It's great to meet you! My wife, Claire, and my boy, Charlie."

Charlie said something into his mug. Claire tried to stand but couldn't. "Hello," she said, maybe. Maybe she said it.

Charlie drained the drink, setting it back down precariously close to the edge of the table. Claire's instinct was to push it toward the center, but she could no longer feel her arms.

"Jack!" said Charlie, craning his neck to try to look at Matt and Lib behind his wheelchair, then turning back to look at Jack. "You said you didn't have any kids!"

~

Jack froze. Or maybe it was that he suddenly became aware that he'd been frozen for weeks, and he only knew it now because he felt himself beginning to thaw. A hissing crack, deep inside him, followed by a meandering, glacially slow fissure. And then what could only be described as a melting.

He blinked back at Charlie, whose chocolate-stained lips stretched in a broad smile.

"Oh, he's not my . . . My dad isn't . . ." Matt's voice trailed off.

Jack watched him shift back and forth on his feet, the fingers of his right hand drumming a beat against his jeans. He caught a faint whiff of cigarette smoke mingling with the diner smell of pepper and grease, cut with the unmistakable scent of his wife, who he still couldn't bring himself to look at. Staring from Matt to Charlie and back again, Jack felt himself slipping away from the table, a lone man clinging to a floating chunk of ice. He had no idea why it hadn't occurred to him until Charlie had said it: If Lib had a son, then, in a manner of speaking, so did he. A stepson. Huh.

Jack pushed himself slowly to his feet, using the table to steady himself. Then he squared his shoulders, cleared his throat, and reached out his hand.

"Jack Hanson," he said, waiting until a hesitant Matt took his hand. The younger man's grip was soft and clammy, though that could have been Jack's own nervous sweat; he couldn't tell. He felt a shudder ripple through Lib as she sighed, then the collective exhale of the group behind him.

"Well, Matt, my goodness, what an incredible surprise," said Kit, and Frannie echoed a welcome.

Jack finally met Lib's eyes, the wet glass of her blue-green irises rimmed with pink, and he thought of the sugar bowl she'd brought him—when, last month? Last decade? Time could be so brutal. He wanted to touch his wife's face. Wanted to wring her neck too.

"Later," he said, finally. Not a warning but a gift.

"Thank you," she whispered, circling past him to take the seat next to his, across from Matt.

"So," said Kit brightly, taking a deep breath in. She reached to pour Matt a mug of wine, but he held up his hand.

"I don't drink," he said, and Jack frowned, thinking of the six-pack swinging from the man's hand in the parking lot on that horrible day when he'd first laid eyes on him. Since when was everybody a liar? And had these chairs always been this hard? He shifted uncomfortably in his seat, pushing through a dull ache in his lower back that got sharper when he sat. He thought of Carolina and grew even more suspicious. If she had known about Matt all along, had she ever told the girls? Had they known all this time too? He couldn't keep track of what he himself knew anymore and what he didn't. He felt like a fool.

"So, Matt!" Dan chirped from Jack's left. "What brings you to town, business or pleasure?"

Matt could barely hide the look of disgust that took hold of his face as Dan spoke, and Jack, sitting kitty-corner from him across the table, liked him for it, despite himself. Jack studied him—he looked disheveled—and suddenly remembered him as the unfamiliar customer in the café the morning he'd first met Charlie and Claire. One and the same! Had they come in together that day? Is that why they were together in the Save Rite parking lot later on? Did Matt and Claire know each other before? Was Claire in on it somehow? Lib reached out then and pressed his right hand, and Jack flinched; she pulled away just as quickly, placing it next to his instead, palming the table.

"The thing is, Dan," said Lib, leaning forward to catch his eye, "I've only just met Matt myself. And Jack here hasn't had the chance to get to know him yet. This has been quite a thing for all of us."

Jack recognized Lib's "check yourself" voice, her tone steady and pointed. Anyone with a passing grasp of social cues would have easily picked up on her warning and let it go.

"You're kidding!" Dan laughed. "Well, how about that! Jack, you should have said something! We see you every day."

It could have been his imagination, but Jack thought he saw Lib's hand inch just a hair's width closer to his. He thought he could hear the clicking and spinning of the gears in her brain and her body, the wonderful way she whirred. He missed her. He also wanted to smash her springs and coils. Coming here tonight was a mistake.

"Mom and Matt are friends, though," said Charlie, and the table got real quiet. Jack felt a prickle at the back of his head. He thought of the scene they'd made in the Save Rite parking lot. Surely Claire hadn't been stupid enough to have Matt visit her at home? Charlie was looking right at Jack, and for the first time, he couldn't read the boy's expression, just that whatever Charlie was doing seemed intended for him. There was something light about the way he said it, but there was nothing light about what he said. Jack knew the boy well enough now to know that something was not quite right.

"You don't say," said Dan, sounding uneasy too. Claire was smiling brightly at Charlie, but her forehead was contorted, her face strangely blotched. Jack had that sense again that she was drunk, but there'd barely been any time for that to be true. He'd only just left her house. He looked at the table wine.

"I picked up some hours at the Save Rite when I got here," said Matt loudly, grinning. "I didn't want to take advantage of my mom."

Jack blinked at the word—mom—in reference to his wife.

"Ah, so you worked together," said Dan.

Claire nodded. "Yes, not all the time," she said, looking at Charlie, then back at Dan. "But I had no idea that Matt from the loading docks was Lib's son. What a small world!" Her voice was high and tight, and that grotesque smile was still pasted onto her face. "Jack, I'm surprised you didn't tell us."

Jack's head swam.

"That's my fault," said Lib before Jack could say anything. He stared at her hand next to his. "It's a long story. I promise I'll tell it another night."

"Well, we were all so sorry to hear about Charlie's accident," said Frannie, from the head of the table. "How are you Taylors all holding up?"

"We've got tremendous community support," said Dan. "Really tremendous. Charlie's amazing. And Jack has been really great too. Really stepped up to take my place while I have to work. We couldn't do this without him."

Jack smiled politely and nodded into his lap. He was struggling, but whenever Dan spoke, he was reminded that he wasn't the one with the biggest problems at this table.

"How long do you have to have the casts on?" Matt asked Charlie, and Claire looked over at him sharply.

Kit, between them, said, "So, Charlie, will you get a new bike?"

Charlie, ignoring Matt's question, said, "Well, Kit, the last thing I need's a new bike." He was clearly imitating Jack, which touched him deeply. He recalled the first day Charlie had arrived at his garage, how there was no way he could have understood just how profoundly this boy would change his life. "Most anything in the world can be fixed steada replaced, right, Jack?"

"Is that right, Jack?" asked Kit. "Are you fixing Charlie's bike?"

"The police haven't released it yet, but when they do, I'm sure old Jack is up for the job," Dan answered for him, raising his mug in salute.

Jack and Charlie had of course had multiple conversations about the bike, but it was all speculation at this point. Jack had no idea what shape the bike was in, and he'd hoped maybe he could talk Charlie into swapping it for another, but the thought so upset the boy that he hadn't brought it up again. He had gone down to the flea market just this past Saturday, though, searching for a suitable replacement. But he wasn't ready to tell Charlie that just yet.

"I'm gonna do what I can," said Jack, wishing Dan would let it lie. He was acting so strangely toward Jack tonight, almost like a jealous lover. *Resents my time with his son after all*, thought Jack. He felt flooded with shame as he looked around the table, stealing another long stare at Matt, who himself was staring at Charlie. Lib's son. In the flesh.

It was almost more than he could bear. Nothing felt as though it was put together or running the way it was supposed to. Technically, by the law of marriage, even by custom, this strange man who'd completely upended Jack's life was his stepson. And that sweet, remarkable boy at the head of the table? The one he'd come to love in a way he had no comparable experience with?

Jack had no claim to him at all.

~

Jack smelled like pine needles. She'd never realized it before. As when she walked into her house after a day or two away and caught a glimpse of how it smelled, a scent you got so used to that it became undetectable. Lib noticed it more with other people: once you got the scent of them inside your nose, you could pick them out blindfolded; smell it on their hair and clothes whenever they drew near. But it was harder to sniff out your own scent—and, Lib realized now, Jack's. She knew the fragrances that lingered on him—motor grease, paint thinner, aftershave—but she'd never before noticed this woodsy undertone that she clearly recognized now as cellular-level deep: carbon and glucose and sunshine. Even with their built-in distances, she'd gotten too close to distinguish his smell from her own. Being next to him now felt like coming home, like coming back to herself, like fresh green growth.

Even more thrilling—or terrifying, she wasn't yet sure which—she could feel the sizzle again. The charge that had always crackled between them, despite his clear discomfort and the trembling anger burbling barely below the surface. She wanted so badly to signal him that whatever happened here tonight, she had his back. That she took full responsibility for this mess. *Then why'd you invite us to this godawful awkward reunion*, she thought meanly, then closed her eyes in penance. *No, Lib. None of this is his fault.*

Lib let the conversation float like smoke around her. Like it was happening to someone else, somewhere else. Considering the accident, Charlie seemed to be doing just fine. Down there at the end of the table, animated and warm. What a wonderful child. She reflected on the ailing adults she'd known, the way they never let you forget what they'd been through, even Carolina, God forgive her. Not Charlie. He seemed exactly like himself, making no extra claim to drama, though he deserved to. Was that a kid thing? Or a uniquely Charlie thing? Either way, she could see why Jack liked him. What he recognized in him. The pickle stealing, she decided, only made him more interesting.

Claire, on the other hand, looked a mess—appropriately so; she obviously had a lot on her plate. Dan was as daft and tone deaf as Lib remembered, and, if she wasn't mistaken, both were already a little drunk. The couple said little to each other, and she might not have guessed they were married if she didn't know them. But at least they were still a family, she thought. At least they got to go home to each other tonight.

Every pleasantry felt forced, manufactured. Lib longed to escape, to get her husband to herself and finally hash this thing out. Give voice to the defense she'd been practicing on an endless loop in her head.

I was protecting you, she'd start. *I know you like fixing problems, but I wasn't your problem to fix.* Matt was shaking his leg, jittering the entire table; Lib kicked his ankle with her toe, and he stopped. She tried to telepath him some comfort, but he was fixated on Claire. *Leave that be, son*, she warned. Her boy clearly had a self-destructive streak.

"Charlie, I bet you're real mad at whoever did this," said Matt, and Claire looked stricken. Dear God, this was mortifying. Lib aimed to kick her son again, but he'd moved his leg, and she only swiped air. She'd grown used to his rudeness, knew how to forgive the pain beneath it, but he was a stranger to these poor folks. It'd been just the two of them for so long. Without the protective context of her house tonight, his behavior seemed particularly brash and edgy. She knew he was nervous about meeting Jack, and he was also probably jonesing for a smoke, but the least he could do was muster up a modicum of etiquette, considering. Lib felt responsible for him, as though his behavior reflected on her somehow. Maybe it was the wine, she realized, ashamed she hadn't thought of it sooner. It had to be difficult for him to be around all this drinking.

"I'm sure the police will find him," Matt pressed. "Should we beat him up when they do?"

"Matt," Lib hissed. Beside her, Jack simmered.

Charlie, who was spinning his mug like a top on the table, regarded Matt at the other end of the table, his little brow knitted together.

"I'm fine." He shrugged, though his voice sounded impossibly small. He pushed himself back from the table and then pulled himself to it again. "It doesn't even hurt anymore. I just want my bike."

"Enough," Jack warned, his low voice almost a growl.

"Claire, didn't you put the brakes on this thing?" said Dan, frowning at the ground below the child, and Claire slowly rose to fiddle with Charlie's chair.

"I like it rolly," protested Charlie, and Claire dumbly sat back down again, as if drugged. Lib considered making up an excuse to take her to the ladies' room, to ask in private if she was okay. Behind her, Lacey pushed through the swinging double doors, arms laden with a gigantic bowl of salad. The teenager dropped it into the center of the group, leaving it slightly askew at the crack where the two tables met, and sauntered off. Lib had absolutely no appetite.

"I'm starving," she said anyway, digging in, hoping to trigger them all to eat quickly. Get this show on the road so they could get of here, get Matt out of proper company, get Jack alone. Despite the hurdles, she felt hopeful. He was here, wasn't he? Maybe she could make this thing right, put her life back where it belonged.

I never lied to you, Jack, she thought, forking a trembling pile of greens into her mouth. *I left things out, things that would hurt you, things that had nothing to do with you. There's a difference.*

Besides, wasn't her independence the part of her Jack prized most? How many times had he said as much? Bragged about their easy, uncomplicated love? Who else would keep a wife across town all these years, go days without seeing her, ask nothing of her? And how many couples over her lifetime had Lib watched destroy each other for sport? Woke up bored and unfulfilled by their domestic state and blamed each other for it? She had never once done that to Jack. And Matt was a grown man now. He needed nothing from her, and there'd obviously be no interference from Jon, dead as he was. *We're talking ancient history here, Jack. None of it matters now. None of this drama is real.*

Lacey brought two baskets of crisp, buttery garlic bread and a heaping platter of ravioli, the meat-filled pockets quivering in creamy white sauce. Lib chewed without tasting, watched Dan and Claire fuss over Charlie, felt another sharp longing for the boring simplicity of their little life, even in the face of Charlie's accident. *Look at the way they take care of each other. That's what marriage is really for*, she thought, and realized she was mad. When had she gotten mad?

Jack wouldn't have wanted her if she'd insisted on the more traditional road. She'd given that up for him, even if it had seemed like her choice at the time. Maybe she hadn't known herself as well as she thought—but if he really loved her for her, if he were truly a partner, wouldn't he have sensed the gaping hole of the years she'd hidden from him? Couldn't he have pushed harder to learn her secrets?

The motley crew had quieted for the most part, blissfully feasting on Tim's dinner—well, save for Claire, who picked and pushed at her food. She seemed even thinner than when Lib had last seen her, come to think of it. Just as they were finishing up, Tim appeared from the kitchen, holding a cake ablaze with candles.

"For he's a jolly good fellow," he sang as he approached, and Dan quickly joined him in an off-key baritone, Frannie and Kit chiming in on harmony. Lib tried to breathe out the refrain, but her mouth wouldn't open. Jack sat silently beside her, his eyes gone glassy. "For he's a jolly good fellooooow. Which nobody can deny," they sang as Tim slid the cake before Charlie, whose face lit up with joy and the flickering glow of the candles.

"Charlie, you probably don't remember me," Tim said, "but I was there when you had your accident." Tim hunched over the boy. "It's so good to see you're doing so well. You gave us all quite a scare."

"It's not even my birthday!" yelled Charlie with delight, and Tim laughed.

"You can make a wish anyway, kid," he said, grinning. "You've earned it."

Lib watched Charlie take a deep breath and close his eyes. While everyone else was distracted looking at him, she took a breath too. Closed her eyes and made a wish of her own.

~

Jack sat in the truck, waiting as the group broke up under the café awning. He'd told Charlie he'd see him tomorrow afternoon, announced to the table that he wasn't feeling well, and gone outside to wait for Lib. He hadn't told her as much—didn't need to—and he watched her now from his safe distance as she hugged the girls, who'd walked her out before going back inside the café. Jack could see them now, fussing over the cleanup with Lacey; the lit windows made the restaurant a diorama. Lib called something and waved goodbye to the Taylors as they wheeled Charlie to Dan's car, and now she was speaking with Matt, who was smoking against the side of the building. Such a filthy habit. Why smokers thought it made a whit of difference to step only five feet from any public entrance, Jack had no idea.

This is too soon, he thought, tamping back the licking flames of his anger as he watched her slowly approach.

Lib opened the passenger door, then hesitated.

"It's okay," he said, and she climbed up.

They drove in the dark, the short ride stretching out in an agonizing trick of time. Neither spoke. Jack had the windows shut tight, but that made it ungodly quiet, so he cracked his to fill in sound, despite the chill, and she followed suit. He'd be on stronger ground at his place, he thought, but then he decided it was better to go to hers, so he could leave in a hurry if he needed to. Lib said nothing when he jerked the wheel right instead of left at the plant, spun her out past the sleepy soybeans and fields of shadowed hay rolls lurking in the dark. Turning into her driveway, he let the wheel spin itself back into place against his palm, allowed the muscle memory to pull the truck forward the rest of the way up the long gravel path, park itself beneath the hickory tree. He cut the engine, waiting. Neither of them moved.

"I keep thinking about all those trips to Door County," Jack started, quietly. He did not look at his wife, but he felt her turn toward him. "The first time we set eyes on Lake Michigan, how it looked like an honest-to-God ocean. Coming up on that field of sunflowers in full glory. Climbing every last one of those damn lighthouses."

Lib nodded slowly. She slid a hand out toward him against the seat.

"And I keep thinking," said Jack. "I keep asking myself, 'Was she thinking about him?'"

Lib quickly pulled her hand away.

"When we talked to that sweet little family selling cherry wine in the parking lot of that farm stand, the one with the baby in the backpack, was she thinking about her other husband, her own baby? About that other life? Because if she was . . ."

Lib had started shaking her head, and Jack began to rock in time to the motion. The truck swayed with their rhythm.

"Because if she was, then she was looking me right in the eye and lying to me every damn time. Every damn day."

"No," said Lib.

"She was making that choice over and over and over again," he pressed, a choking sob rising up and out of him before he could push it back down. His heart was beating too quickly now. "That's what I keep coming back to. That everyday choice."

"It wasn't like that, Jack. All those times in Door County, and all those times back here in the homes we made, all I was thinking was: *Finally.* All I was thinking was, *Here I stand, the luckiest woman alive.* That's it, Jack. I swear."

Lib was the one breathing hard now, wiping her nose with the sleeve of her sage sweater. Jack caught himself looking at her and looked away.

"The first part of my life . . . I've told you some, but I left a whole lot out. It was terrible for me, Jack. You don't know what went on. When I came back here, all I wanted was to start over, clean. I put everything I had into fixing this place up and forgetting every awful thing that had ever been done to me. And later, after we met, I honestly didn't remember being that other person. All I cared about was this new Lib and this life and you."

"But we talked about it! Your mom was a drunk, your poor daddy's accident. We talked about having kids! You don't think any of this should have come up then?"

Lib only shook her head, which infuriated him.

"There came a point, you're right, when I could have told you about Matt and his dad. I get that that sounds rational," she said. "But put yourself in my shoes for a second. Could I, really? Too much time had gone by. Even a year, five years, whatever it was, that was way too long to keep something like this."

"Something like what, though?" he spluttered.

"Jack," she said, "if I'd have told you, I'd have lost you."

"Now that's not fair," he said, his voice shaking. "What kind of cretin do you take me for? You don't think I could have handled knowing you'd had an earlier marriage? That you had a baby?"

"No, no, no," she said. "It was too late. Too much time had gone by that I hadn't told you the truth. I'd have lost you. And I'd already lost too much. So you're right, I decided."

"Well, which is it?" Jack spluttered. "Did you forget? Or did you decide? Which type of liar are you?"

Lib nodded, shook her head, twisted her hands together in her lap.

"I'd have lost you," she repeated, a whisper now.

"And what about these last two months? He's here, you're caught out, why didn't you have the integrity to face me? Why didn't you pay me the respect I deserve and tell me the truth? You're not a messed-up kid anymore, Lib, you're a grown-ass woman!"

Jack smacked the dashboard, and Lib jumped beside him.

"You had the same choice to make as an adult woman, and you made it again!" he yelled.

"I'd have lost you!" she screamed, her glorious eyes shot through with defiance and blood, cords straining from her neck.

"Maybe so!" he hollered back, looking right at her now. "But that was my decision to make, not yours! You stole that from me! Twice! A thousand times!"

Jack's words echoed in the cab of the truck. He watched Lib deflate in front of him. He was right. They both knew it. He could see she hadn't thought of that.

"You should have told me the truth," he said, quieter now. "I don't know what would have happened. I can't say. But now it's too late to know how it was supposed to go. It already went like this."

Lib swallowed, raked her fingers through her hair. Slowly stretched the strands until it looked as though they were coming from her fingertips, a spider spinning herself out of glistening gossamer magic. He was caught up in her, despite what he had said. He thought, *I love this woman more than I have ever loved anything or anyone in my entire life.*

"It already went like this," he repeated. He wanted to touch her. He didn't.

She whispered something then, and he clenched his teeth so hard he thought they might shatter.

"If you have something more to say," he said slowly, measured, "speak up."

Lib opened the truck door, slid down, and quietly pressed it shut. Jack watched her climb the porch steps and disappear into her house. He wanted her to stop. Wanted her to go. Wanted her to look back.

She didn't.

Chapter 16

Exhausted, pickled in self-loathing and now only half drunk, Claire locked herself in the master bath and fumbled with her third negligee. The package from Amazon had arrived two days earlier, but she'd tossed it in her sock drawer until she could deal with it properly. Now she ripped into thin plastic bags, finding each more disappointing than the last. The problem, she'd decided, was her breasts. They'd once been her pride; high and tight, small—the perfect palmful, Dan always said. Just enough to give her a solid curve but never in the way for sports or running. But after the glorious, swollen era of pregnancy and nursing, followed by another ten years of aging and weight loss, they'd deflated and sunk, and now they hung like two tiny spent balloons pinned to her breastbone, days after the party had ended. She'd learned to disguise the problem with the right bra, but this lingerie was having the opposite effect.

"Jesus," she said to her reflection, pulling at the drawstring seam meant to sit beneath her breasts that instead cut straight across the top of them, about four inches too high. "You look like a lamp in a whorehouse."

She loosened the drawstring, yanked the negligee over her head, and threw it into the discarded pile in Dan's sink. It was late, and she was sweaty now, her staticky hair on end. She smelled ripe, but there was no time for a second shower. Matt's ambush at the café had completely blindsided her, and she was spent, the whiskey and wine and mouthwash souring in her stomach. But she was also bound and determined to make love to her husband, the way she imagined good wives were doing all across town this very instant. As Lib and Jack probably were this very moment. She blushed at the thought.

She could hear Dan readying tomorrow's coffee in the kitchen, and he'd also offered to get Charlie to bed, signals that he wanted to have sex. He hadn't been initiating lately, and maybe she was paranoid, maybe it was her miserable pre-hangover and the self-reckoning she'd face in the morning, but connecting with him tonight felt critical. *He still wants me*, she thought, as she pulled the fourth negligee down over her body. *He still sees me. I'm still here.*

The material was only slightly less scratchy than a potato sack, but this one was all right—clingy, but a forgiving solid black; with an actual bra fastener in the back. She adjusted the thin straps to give her breasts the illusion of cleavage, then bounced three quick times in the mirror. They slipped but not too badly—if she moved just right and got the lights off right away, this could work.

She heard her husband enter the bedroom. Quickly gathered the packages and shoved them into the wastebasket under the sink, then ran another layer of deodorant under each arm and a wet comb through her straight hair. Went for a gargle of mouthwash, then thought better of it—settled instead for a last-minute spritz of perfume to her neck. Ready for battle. She closed her eyes. She was shaking, just a little. Why hadn't she had a protein bar? She had a third of one left still in her purse, neatly folded inside its wrapper so the greasy crumbs wouldn't stain the lining. She hadn't been able to stomach all that rich food at dinner; there was no way she could have—or would have—kept that down.

Claire opened her eyes again, and for the briefest moment, she saw herself as she was. Shrinking, trembling, scared shitless. Drunk.

Matt wanted to meet. He'd whispered it to her in the chaos as they were leaving, Dan caught up in conversation with Kit as they pushed through the tables, Jack already gone. *That bridge tomorrow, one o'clock.* He'd said it like a drive-by shooting, right at the point in the evening she actually thought she might make it out alive, though barely. What was it that Charlie had said about her and Matt being friends? What the fuck did that even mean? She needed time and a sober head to think this through. At some point over these last weeks, had she inadvertently mentioned Matt to Charlie? Or had he seen them together, somehow, maybe at work? Had he been at the Save Rite? There had to be an innocent explanation on Charlie's part, at least—but there was no time to be had. The last thing she could risk was Dan's suspicion, and she certainly wasn't going to blow an opportunity to sleep with him. *The Taylors are a happy family*, she thought, gritting her teeth at her reflection. *Charlie is okay. I am okay. Things with Dan will be okay.* Matt would be okay too. Nobody suspected anything. They all just needed to get through this.

Claire took a last breath and opened the bathroom door, flipped off the lights behind her. Dan was waiting in bed on his phone, but he immediately shelved it when he saw her standing there.

"Whoa, look out!" he said, heavily inchworming himself into place. Claire cringed as the oak headboard scraped the fresh paint, now the lovely pale pistachio, worlds better than the red. It would really pop once she finished painting the trim white. Dan had lost weight, she realized, maybe even put on some muscle. There was a time she'd wanted him desperately. A time he'd wanted her even more than that. She made a mental note to pull the bed slightly away from the wall tomorrow.

She had to meet Matt, of course. It was risky, but she could think of no way out of it. Maybe he needed reassurance that she hadn't said anything. Maybe he wanted to know what the police knew. Maybe by baiting Charlie at the table, he'd been signaling her that she was still on the hook. Maybe he just wanted to make sure they were on the same page. He deserved that, she supposed. *It's still reckless*, she thought, sidling up to the bed, Dan's eyes on her as she gave him her best smile, then flipped off the lamp. Talking on the phone wasn't a good idea, phone records and such—the journalist in her wouldn't shut up—but neither was talking in person. Better to not speak of it, ever. *You will never know this awful thing*, she thought, sliding into place next to her husband. *I can carry this for all of us.*

"Mmmm," said Dan, pulling her to him, immediately thrusting a hand between her legs. She stiffened, which he of course mistook for pleasure, because no matter how many times she'd told him how much she liked the anticipation of the buildup, he proved unwilling to consider her needs. He began rubbing away at her as though he were a cat, she, the scratching post. She flipped around so her back was to him, pressed her ass into his hips, buying herself some time. Truth was, her anxiety was justified. Matt was behaving foolishly at dinner. She hadn't imagined that, even in her altered state.

Dan tugged at her ridiculous thong now, which actually brought relief; if she could just hang in there, it would all be over soon. *Come on, Claire, don't fuck this up.*

She turned over to face her husband, who took this gesture as an invitation to stop working. He moaned, leaning back against the pillow, eyes closed, let his arms flop down in surrender. In the shadows, she could just make out his expression, and he looked a world away. She knew she needed to seduce him, that she was the one with the most to lose; but in that moment, all she wanted was for this man—this man she couldn't remember how to want—to want her terribly. For just a split second, she couldn't move at all. She'd never felt so small, so alone, so hopeless, so invisible in all her life.

Dan opened one eye halfway. She'd waited too long. Covering for the lapse, she quickly straddled him, and his eyes squeezed shut again. She leaned down to kiss him, fumbling at the same time to direct him back inside her. His breath was garlicky from dinner, and his mouth felt stiff on hers, as though it had changed size or shape somehow and she couldn't get it to fit against her own. They were completely out of sync. She couldn't reach him. She couldn't even reach herself. In the old house, she'd kept a bottle of lube in the nightstand drawer. Now she wondered where it was, realizing she hadn't come across it while unpacking. *This needs to end as much as it needs to happen,* she thought.

"I love you," she tried, but the words caught in her throat. "I love you," she said again.

"Love you too," he said, bucking his hips, eyes squeezed shut.

Claire nuzzled into her husband's neck. She took his hands in hers, brought them to her lower back, remembering the way he used to press one there when guiding her through a crowd, how safe she used to feel every time he did it. How long had it been since he'd touched her like that? Hot tears sprang from her eyes and pooled against Dan's sweaty cheek. She wiped her face against the pillow beneath him, waited to feel him caress her back and hold her, but he gripped her butt instead, ramming her up and down on him as if she were a tool he'd been looking for and found, her bottom half separate from her top. She heard his breath catch and quicken and knew he was close. Her own body hadn't even bothered to show up, but she felt immense relief just the same.

"Oh yeah," she breathed into his ear, and that was all it took—he arched into her, digging his fingers so hard into her hips she thought she'd likely bruise, and she was glad for it. To feel something, at least. She matched her breathing to his, resting atop him as it slowed, waiting.

Dan, still miles away, patted her ass twice, her cue to dismount.

"You good?" he said, twisting out of bed to pad into the bathroom. She heard the sink come on as he started to brush his teeth. *You couldn't have done that before?* she thought, pulling the negligee back into place, feeling around with her foot beneath the covers for the thong, waiting her turn for the bathroom.

"I'm good," she said.

~

Lib stretched out in the center of her bed, as she'd done a thousand nights before this one. She'd left the bedside lamp on, but she did not read. She spread her arms and legs wide, da Vinci's *Vitruvian Man* come alive, though just barely. Tonight had left her gutted.

She didn't know why she hadn't told Jack everything. Why she still couldn't say the word out loud—the word Carolina had helped her understand—why she couldn't have that same kind of frank conversation with Jack after all these years, not even when it mattered most. She'd had her shot at repairing their relationship, and she'd blown it. He'd just been too mad. She'd just been too afraid.

In seventh grade, the year her daddy had died, she'd found a brown book at the village library filled with da Vinci's "anatomical, physiological, and embryological" drawings. In it, the first vagina she'd ever seen, both horrifying and captivating. One sketch revealed a baby crouched inside his mother's womb, which was popped open like a locket; there on the thinly carpeted floor, she'd found herself crouching in precisely the same way, curled into herself, chin resting on her knee. She'd checked the book out, brought it home, and pored over every page.

That baby haunted her the most, seeming more a hunched older child than a fetus. Da Vinci was a master of the human form—later she learned that he'd dissected more than two dozen cadavers in his lifetime—and so she knew the drawing of the baby was accurate. But it reminded her of the part of herself camped out deep in her own belly, safe from her mother's world. She could even see space for the baby's belongings in da Vinci's sketch, like a TV, perhaps. A cheese-and-cracker tray.

The book was now downstairs on a shelf in her living room, wrapped in its original library plastic. She'd tucked it between her mattresses, swearing she lost it at school. Mama, drunk and grieving her husband's death, overdue fine notice trembling in her hand, had slapped her for the first and last time. Libby hadn't fought back and then had followed Mama to her bottom dresser drawer, where she had unrolled the cash to pay the steep replacement fee from a plastic hosiery egg. Lib instinctively understood that her mother felt immediately guilty for hitting her and that she ponied up the money as a result of that guilt. The pain of being slapped was easily worth the price of the book, which she carried with her to Elmhurst and looked at in secret for years. When she returned home to Anthem at the age of twenty, her first act was to place the book on the old built-in shelf in the living room, right out in the open.

In the thirty-eight years since, Lib had never once minded being in this bed alone. On the contrary, she'd relished it, going through the motions each night first of the Vitruvian man, then of the child, tucked into the bed like a fetus, on her side. The da Vinci fetus hadn't been safe, his walnut womb cracked open, but Lib was. She was in total and complete control. No one was coming to reveal or dissect her. She was her own parent, had grown into her own partner. But tonight she felt more like a child than she ever had.

It was my decision to make, Jack had screamed, spittle flying against the dashboard, and Lib wondered, *When exactly had it become Jack's decision to make about how to react to her past?* She just couldn't figure out when they'd crossed that line. When her self-protective secrets had turned into lies that hurt him. When her life had become his just as much as it was hers. Because it had. It was.

Maybe that was why she hadn't told him. Maybe she was pulling something back to herself, even now, like a reflex.

Lib heard Matt pull in, the old truck door slam. She knew it would be a few minutes yet before he entered the house, enough time to have a cigarette first. She'd grown used to his rhythms, though she hadn't thought before now about where he'd been since dinner. She wondered if she'd have to give him a lecture about his behavior. He'd been acting oddly at the café, but odd was as much a part of his natural state as the smoking, she supposed. And besides, everything was odd. She and Jack and Matt had all been operating in a suspended sort of reality since Matt had come to town, though that had ended tonight, Lib suspected. Jack was done with her. This was her new normal, and she'd better get used to it.

The screen door finally creaked open, and she heard Matt come in, climb the stairs a little more slowly than he usually did. Then, a gentle knock on her door.

"Yes?" she said, startled, propping herself up on her elbows, then pulling the quilt against her chest. Not one time in the past two months had her son approached her in her bedroom.

"Can I come in?" he said, sounding old and far off.

"Of course," she said, waiting.

Lib always left the door cracked, and now Matt pushed it open and entered the room, then looked around as if taking it in for the first time. She supposed he was; no reason for him to have ever been in her room before.

"Nice," he said finally. "It looks like you in here."

Lib kept a small tufted chair in the corner next to her vanity, but Matt sat instead at the foot of her bed. He looked worn out. She remembered again her thought about all that wine at the table. How much tougher it must have been for him to meet Jack under those circumstances.

"Are you okay?" she asked softly. "Tonight was kind of a big night, and I just sort of threw you into it."

Matt shrugged. "They seem like a really nice family," he said.

Lib frowned. She hadn't been talking about the Taylors. "And, Jack? He wasn't too hard on you, was he?"

Matt shook his head, his lips curved downward. "Nope," he said. "He was nice."

"Nice," said Lib carefully. "Was it hard, having all that wine around? I didn't even think about it."

"No," he said, sounding surprised, his eyes shifting past her head to the wall and fixing there. Then he smiled. "Not at all, actually. I didn't even think about it either."

"Well, that's good," said Lib, surprised. What was all this about then?

"Mom, did you ever second-guess your decision not to tell Jack about me and Dad over the years? What was the big deal? I mean, why not just tell him? You didn't even do anything wrong, at least not to him. You weren't with Dad when you met Jack. It's not like you'd done anything . . . criminal."

"Sure, when you put it like that, it wasn't that bad," she said quietly. "But it was, to me, at least at first. You know I couldn't bear to think about any of it for a long, long time. And then, later . . ."

"But you've been married for like thirty years," said Matt. "It had to be safe to tell him at some point. Especially after I came here. I mean, how long did you think this would go on? What did you think was going to happen?"

"When I came back here from Elmhurst, I wished that everything that happened to me as a kid had never happened. And I wished for it harder than I'd ever wished for anything in my life," said Lib, finding the words she'd groped for in Jack's truck. "At some point, the wish started to come true. It's like I'd wanted it bad enough, and then I made it real. All these years, it was real. I was me. That time was . . . never. What could I have said to him? When would it have made sense?

What would he have thought of me? When you showed up, when you were . . . real . . . I guess it's becoming clear—to me as well as to Jack—that I've actually been lying. But before that . . ."

Matt nodded, still looking at the patterned wallpaper behind her head.

"If I hadn't come here, would you have ever told him the truth?"

"No," said Lib. She knew how true it was as soon as she said it. "No, I don't think I would have."

"And it wouldn't have bothered you, you don't think? Continuing to live with that big secret between you? Not just that you . . . abandoned me . . . but that you didn't tell him? Didn't that . . . hurt?"

Lib thought a moment.

"It did hurt. And I was—am—so very sorry, to both of you. I guess that's the thing: I didn't feel like I had a right to spread the pain, so I just sort of . . . absorbed it. That was just the price of leaving, you know? Of doing something so terrible?" She shuddered, imagining what Jack would think of her if he really knew how ruined she'd been. "I thought I should carry it alone, not put it on him. And I guess I felt like I could."

"But . . . now that it's out, now that he knows, do you wish you'd told the truth?"

Lib stilled, contemplating this. Did she? Knowing everything she knew now? Having lost Jack, possibly for good? *Yes*, she thought, though she didn't say it. *Yes, I want to go back*. But the world certainly didn't owe her a second do-over, not after the miraculous first.

"You know about the twelve steps, right, from my meetings? The big obvious one most people are familiar with is the ninth, where you make amends. I skipped over it at first because I feel like a whole lot more people owe me apologies, more than what I owe."

Lib nodded. The boy still had a chip on his crooked shoulder.

"Well, now I've got something I feel very sorry for. Something I don't know if I can live with," he said, his eyes pleading, but she had no idea what he could be asking of her. How could she help? What could be so terrible? Suddenly, she knew.

"Matt, are you having an affair with Claire Taylor?" she said, trying to clear her voice of judgment. No sense beating around the bush anymore.

"What? No," he said, then looked down in his lap. "I mean, not really. I probably could have, but no. This is bigger than that."

Lib felt a numbing chill like a spinal tap, dread dripping down her spine.

"Here's what's confusing," he said, gazing back again at the wall. "Mike tells me I can never be truly sober without rigorous honesty. That my pathway to recovery is through owning every mistake out loud. But they also tell me that I'm not supposed to make amends if doing so would make it worse for someone else. Like, that's exactly how the step is written: 'Except when to do so would injure them or others.'"

"And this would? Telling would bring you relief and someone else harm?"

"Actually, I think it would bring me the most harm. And the most relief. So which is it?"

Lib swallowed, afraid to think through what he was talking about, further shaken by the way his question echoed Jack's from earlier in the night, *Which type of liar are you?* She couldn't imagine what Matt's *it* might be, and she didn't want to know. Whatever it was, it couldn't be as bad as what she was still hiding from Jack. Matt was the least of it. Couldn't her son just erase whatever this was? Carry it for thirty years? Was that really so absurd an idea? Couldn't everybody just stop thinking so hard about everything and get on with it?

"Which is what?" she said, finally.

"Do I tell the truth so I can stay sober," he said, "or do I lie and let other people recover?"

Chapter 17

In thirty-three years, Jack and Lib had never had a fight like that, and he hadn't been able to shake it. Not last night and not now, in the basement of the Anthem Police Department. They should have found resolution, but somehow things had only gotten worse. *Focus on Charlie*, he thought as Officer Nick opened the door to the so-called property room. It looked more like an overstuffed junk pile, and he and Nicky Pete were like kids again, picking scraps out at old Ikester's farm.

"Easy, right on top, like I thought," said Nick. "Elaine just sort of throws things in here, but you try telling her otherwise."

"You sure this is okay?" said Jack. He'd known he was overstepping when he made the request for Charlie's bike, cashing in on a personal favor—but Nick had surprised him by not putting up a fight at all.

"It will just sit down here and rot otherwise," Nick said again, as he had on the phone. "They've got what they need off it, and, between you and me, even if we do find the guy that did this—and that's a big if—the bike itself won't matter much to the case. The paint scrapings and photos will be evidence enough."

Jack whistled low, shook his head.

"I feel terrible about it," said Nick, pulling a knife from his pocket and tearing into the plastic wrapped around the bike to protect the evidence that didn't seem to exist. Jack had been astonished to learn that there had been some initial confusion between who had jurisdiction, Richland County or Anthem PD. In the end, it was the latter, or that was still somewhat up in the air, and it further infuriated Jack that if the accident had happened on Highway Q itself, there might have been more resources in hunting down Charlie's assailant. He couldn't believe that departments didn't work together more efficiently, but that apparently wasn't unusual, according to Nick. And since Charlie was making a full recovery and his parents weren't pressing the authorities harder by going to the press, the county sheriffs had gone back to pursuing worse crimes. Nick personally canvassed homes asking about banged-up cars or suspicious activity, but his efforts so far had come up empty. Why didn't Charlie's parents press harder? Why didn't this whole thing eat them alive the way it did Jack? Now if Charlie had died, Nick had confided to Jack over a couple of beers two weeks back, there would have been more public outcry, and maybe the county would have pushed harder to join forces. Could all of that be true? Jack no longer knew what to think or whether it even mattered at all anymore.

"You would not believe how often this kind of thing happens—cars hitting bicyclists, I mean. Besides that, I'm two months from retirement." Nick grinned, pocketed the knife, glanced at his watch. "After a few decades on the job, you start to keep your own score. And I'll tell you what, I'm not about to add to the kid's injustice by keeping his bike from him on top of it all."

"Thanks, Nick," Jack said, swallowing back the resentment that was always so quick to rise lately. "I can't tell you how much I appreciate this."

"Feels good to do something." Nick shrugged, lifting Charlie's BMX from the plastic tatters and carrying it out past Jack, up the stairs. Jack followed, squinting into the bright morning sunlight as he held the door open for Nick, then helped him load the bike into his truck.

Last Saturday, Jack had gone down to the county flea market again to pick through bicycles. His secret mission was to buy something good enough to make Charlie happy, should it come to that, but ideally he would find a bike he could strip for parts after getting Charlie's bike back. They actually had an excellent selection. Jack could have gotten a Huffy or Murray for five bucks, but he'd bypassed them for a pretty decent fifty-dollar Redline, circa 1984, according to the sweet little Wisconsin license plate screwed beneath the saddle.

"Hot dog!" he'd said, straddling the bike and walk-gliding it down the long aisle toward the checkout table. As he slowly rounded the corner at the end of the aisle, something caught his eye—a hazy mish-mash stack of pastel dishes—and he stopped in his tracks. This had to have been where Lib had found the sugar bowl she'd brought him this summer. Jack rolled back and forth in place on the Redline, mulling it all over for a while, then scooped up the identical bowl and wheeled away to pay for his booty.

"I don't know yet," he'd said, back home, setting the bowl gently next to its twin on his kitchen counter, attracting Tinker's attention. "I don't know what I'm gonna do with you." And then, of course, that awful dinner last night and the fight with Lib, after which he'd had half a mind to run inside the house and smash both bowls to the floor.

But here, in the garage with Charlie's BMX, Jack felt thrilled again. Giddy, as though he were getting away with something. Heart racing like Christmas Eve, he Santa's elf or, he supposed, the Big Man himself. Charlie's bike wasn't in bad shape at all. The worst of it appeared to be the front wheel, which was folded like a taco, along with a bent fork and one terribly shredded saddle. He'd pull all three parts from the Redline, and he'd transfer the plate too; Charlie would love that bonus. And the red seat would give the blue and silver a sort of patriotic shine.

Jack began whistling "God Bless America" as he went to work on both bikes, dismantling the front end of each. Charlie was gonna be so excited. It would be a while before he could ride it, but knowing his bike was waiting for him would surely help speed his healing. In no time at all, Jack had the new fork and front wheel on Charlie's frame. The twenty-inch wheel fit perfectly, just as he'd hoped; Jack gave it a good spin and caught a pretty serious wobble, but he could work that out on the truing stand, no problem.

He pulled the wheel off again and set to truing it, spinning again and watching the rim for tells. He wasn't a bike mechanic per se, but he'd always had a deep and abiding love for bicycles as machines—a truly genius invention. Truing was his favorite part, a slow give-and-take finesse that combined knowledge and intuition, and couldn't be rushed.

Jack spun, made adjustments, spun again. Checked for humps and hops, tweaked the spokes each time around, tightening and loosening, making it right. He only wished Charlie were there to watch and learn.

Did Matt have any mechanical skills? He realized he knew nothing about the man. Or the man's dad, for that matter. Had they spent time together in their own garage, a father teaching his son the basics? How to fix a flat, change the oil, things like that? Had there ever been a woman around to replace Lib? A stepmom?

Try as he might, Jack just couldn't picture his wife as someone else's. Couldn't envision her in that domesticated scene, baby in the high chair, CorningWare casserole on the table, like at his sister's place. And the husband, what, in a suit and tie? Did he look like Matt?

Maybe he couldn't picture Lib there because she never really was. Because that was never her, as she'd said.

He felt the truth of that in his gut, knew it was right, and it softened him again. If he let himself think through her words—*I honestly didn't remember being that person. All I cared about was this Lib, and this life, and you*—they made sense. He knew they were real. That she was real.

But goddamn it, why'd she have to lie about it again now? Hide a grown man in her house? He threw the spoke wrench to the floor and took a few steps back. It was one thing to lie to him before he knew her, quite another to double down on it today. Hands on his hips, head shaking, Jack began to pace the garage. He was stuck on that part. He could forgive a scared little girl. But how was he supposed to forgive his fully grown wife?

And that was the other piece too, something that really hadn't hit him until dinner last night, when Charlie had said as much—all these years, he'd had a stepson. And sure, that son had his own father, but who knows what Jack and Matt's relationship might have been like? Wouldn't Lib have had some sort of shared custody? What sorts of things might they have gotten up to, how might the weekends and holidays have gone, what might they look back on fondly together now? All this time, he'd been at most a day's car drive away, and Jack had had no idea.

So, what now? He stared out at the street through his wide-open garage door, hands still on his hips. It was midmorning, and there was only an hour or two left before Jack was due to go see Charlie—enough time, the way things were going, to finish the bike. Problem was, Charlie would probably have all kinds of questions about Matt. Questions Jack didn't know how to answer, because he had no idea himself. Was Matt here to stay? And what did that mean for Jack, if he was? If there was no Lib, was Jack still a stepdad?

And was there really no Lib?

Jack scooped the spoke wrench from the floor, scraping his fingernails on cement. He let himself be buoyed by his excitement for the boy, the impending surprise. Got back to work.

Half past noon, half awake and fully sick, Claire sat straight-backed at the kitchen table. She'd dug her old GPS watch out from one of the last boxes and strapped it on, found her running shoes and laced them. She'd thrown up twice, sick over the unholy sex she'd participated in and suffused with shame for getting drunk last night—particularly the manner in which she'd gotten drunk last night—and especially when it was the last thing she'd intended or ever expected. She still had no idea how it had happened. She felt a vise gripping her temples, and she was as baffled as she was scared. But dealing with Matt, who was at this point clearly unpredictable, was the most pressing issue, and so, as soon as Jack arrived and Charlie was settled, she'd head out for her first run in ages. She figured it was two miles or so to the bridge, and she didn't want to chance her car being spotted.

Ten minutes early, Jack bounded through the front door.

"Oh!" he said, seeing her there. "I didn't even knock! Guess I'm getting a little too familiar. Sorry!"

But he didn't sound sorry; he sounded delighted. His blue eyes crackled, and there was a fine sheen of sweat at the edges of his salt-and-pepper hairline. Claire had forgotten lately how handsome he was. What a lady-killer he must have been in his prime. She had another flash of him and Lib together in bed and blushed again.

"You don't have to knock, Jack. Our home is your home," she said, hoping her voice sounded lighter than she felt—although his effervescence was contagious. The comparison made her wish for an Alka-Seltzer.

"Is Charlie in his—"

"Jack!" said Charlie from the doorway. He was standing there on his crutches, a bold new move he'd been practicing all morning, especially tricky with the broken arm. "Jack, look what I can do!"

"Whoa-ho!" said Jack, taking a comical skip back, as though he'd suffered a cartoonish blow. "Look at you!"

Claire grinned despite herself. All morning, although preoccupied with the impending confrontation with Matt, she'd helped Charlie practice. The boy was bound and determined to master the move, though she'd not yet let him try it alone.

"Charlie, you know you're supposed to wait for me," said Claire. "We talked about this."

"I wanted to surprise Jack!" said Charlie, and she nodded to let him know he wasn't in trouble, but he wasn't even looking at her. His little apple cheeks were flushed from effort, his eyes twinkling to match the older man's.

"Well," said Jack, approaching the boy and tousling his hair. "Great minds think alike, because I've got a surprise for you too."

Claire looked back and forth between the two, who seemed to only have eyes for each other. There was so much warmth in the room, as though she were sitting too close to a campfire but had no desire to back away. This is love, she thought, watching from the outside. She wondered if she'd ever really felt such a thing for anyone besides Charlie—and, more specifically, if anyone had ever really felt such a thing for her.

"Do you think you can crutch those things outside?" said Jack, looking at Claire now. "Or is that too much?"

"Well," Claire started, shaking her head, but Charlie was already hobbling forward.

"Easy!" he shouted, bringing one crutch up, then the next, steadying himself, launching awkwardly toward Jack. Claire stood to help, but

Jack had already positioned himself beside Charlie's broken arm, was laughing as he helped him along. Claire moved to the front door, held it open for the duo as they slowly made their way forward, then looked to Jack's truck in the driveway. There, in its bed, was Charlie's bicycle.

"MY BIKE!" squealed Charlie, jumping, then letting out a pained yelp.

"Easy, easy." Jack laughed as Claire tensed, but Charlie showed no signs of lasting damage.

"Charlie, please be careful." She smiled as she said it because there was no containing the boy's joy. Jack looked to her questioningly, and she took his place propping Charlie up while he ran to the truck, popped the tailgate down, and easily pulled the BMX to the ground.

"MY BIKE MY BIKE MY BIKE!"

"It's good as new, with two key improvements," said Jack, all business, rolling it forward. "This license plate lets everyone know you're a serious rider, and this red seat has magical protective powers—especially in combination with the blue and silver paint."

"Like Captain America," said Charlie, equally serious, and Claire felt such love for both of them then that she could have wept. She'd almost lost him. No, she'd almost killed him.

"Mom, don't worry. The chances of getting hit by another car are statistically unlikely. I Googled it," said Charlie, and Claire struggled to hold back tears. "The best thing I can do for myself is get back on my bike. I'm not scared."

Claire nodded, choking down a tumbleweed in her throat.

"I hope this is okay," said Jack, turning to her. "I hope I haven't overstepped."

"No, no, Jack, you're wonderful," she said, wiping at her mouth and eyes. "This is so kind and generous of you. I honestly don't know what we'd do without you."

"Can we bring it inside?" asked Charlie. "Can we park it in my room?"

"Why not?" said Claire, but Jack was already maneuvering the bike through the door. She prepared to brace Charlie, but he was ahead of her too, crutching forward, already smoother with the movement.

"Kinda hurts my pits." He grinned, and Claire laughed, following them to Charlie's room and watching as they settled themselves in. Claire checked her watch, 12:41 p.m.

"So, I thought I'd go for a run," she said carefully once Charlie was back in his bed, Jack at his side, the BMX propped against the windowsill. "Get some air. It's a beautiful fall day."

"That sounds like a great idea," said Jack. "You know we're just fine here."

"Thank you," said Claire, kissing the top of Charlie's head. He had yet to look away from his bike.

"Where'd you find the red seat?" said Charlie.

"Bye, kiddo," said Claire, pivoting down the hall and out the front door.

She started out at a light jog, automatically pressing the button on her watch, then quickly pushing it off again. What was she thinking? This was the last trek she'd ever want tracked.

Her adrenaline more than made up for her lack of conditioning. After she rounded the first corner on her block, she picked up the pace, racing through Jack's neighborhood and out to the edge of town, retracing her steps down the county road where they'd driven that godawful night, turning the corner onto one of the side lanes she remembered. The pavement jarred her, and so she ran along the narrow shoulder, letting the crushed gravel cushion her gait. The sludge of last night's alcohol slurped through her veins, weighing her down, adding drag. Her breath, sharp and steady, sounded like a metronome with a voice, every other footfall the word *no*, every intake of air, *oh. Oh no, oh no, oh no, oh no, oh no, oh no, oh no.* She pushed it harder, trying to drown out her own breathless mantra. She was at a full sprint now, pain barking at her shins, when she crested the last hill and saw the bridge down below. The little blue truck was waiting there already, pulled over in the same spot they'd parked his rental car all those weeks ago. Claire suddenly wanted to turn back, but gravity pulled her down the hill, and she flew, reckless, to the bottom. Slammed into Matt's truck and bent over her knees, gulping for air.

"You're early," said Matt, who was leaning against the hood, smoking. The toxic cloud caught her lungs just wrong and she began to hack, coughing and spitting into the ditch. Then she vomited again. Fucking hangover.

"Jesus," she heard him say as she crouched there, coughing. When it felt safe again, Claire settled gingerly onto the gravel shoulder, hugging her knees. She couldn't bring herself to look at him.

"What do you want, Matt?" she said finally. "What are we doing here?"

"Well, I missed you too!" he chortled, blowing smoke out his nose, coughing a little himself.

"Don't be ridiculous," she said, pushing up to stand, then thinking better of it. If someone happened to drive by, they were less likely to spot her sitting down here on the edge of the ditch behind the truck. "I don't have long. Whatever you thought was happening between us, wasn't. It was all a huge mistake."

"Sure," he said.

"And what the hell was that at dinner last night?" she hissed, finally turning to stare him down. "Poking at everyone? Asking Charlie if he wanted you to 'beat up' whoever did this to him? Are you trying to get us caught?"

Matt laughed softly. "That's a good question," he said.

"What the fuck is that supposed to mean?"

Matt dropped the cigarette, ground it out with a quick twist of his boot, then walked over to sit down next to Claire. She stiffened and pushed herself away.

"Relax, I'm not gonna touch you," he said, and Claire actually tried, for a moment, to remember the attraction. But there was nothing there, no hint of the gripping magnetism that had pulled her to the brink in the first place. *What the actual fuck, Claire?* What had she been thinking?

"Look, I still can't believe it was your kid that we—I can't believe it was Charlie. I had no idea, and when I found out, I wanted to die. At the very least, I wanted to find you right away and tell you how sorry I was. I mean, what are the fucking odds? I'll tell you what the fucking odds are, they're Matt Marlow odds."

Rage gripped her. "We are not gonna talk about your shit luck," she said, trembling. "Not another word."

"Jesus," Matt said again. "Fine. I'm still sorry. Take it or leave it. I'm not a monster. What are the police saying?"

"Nothing," she said, incredulous. "That's the thing: they've got nothing. They've told us they don't think they'll catch the driver, that there was no evidence at the scene. They've talked to Charlie three times, and he didn't see it. Didn't see us," she amended. "He doesn't even know the color of the car or anything. Jack even got his bike back somehow, so, I don't know. It feels like it's over. I'm afraid to believe it, but I think . . . I think it's over."

"Wow," said Matt.

"Which is why I can't understand why you behaved so recklessly last night at dinner! And meeting like this is an absurd risk. Where is the car?"

"I was trying to gauge how much he knew. I've been completely in the dark, don't forget," he said. "The car is hidden."

"Hidden where? Not at the hotel, still?"

"No. It's my car—it was Dad's, actually, it came to me when he died—but I told my mom it was a rental and that I had to return it. She's letting me use her truck, but I don't know."

"What don't you know?" she said, dread creeping up the back of her neck.

"Well, for one, I don't know what will happen if anyone *does* find it. I can say I hit a deer, but I don't know if they'd buy it."

"And for another?"

"Well," he said, digging into the ground with his boot heel. "I don't know if it's the right thing to do."

"The right thing to do?" Claire spluttered. "What do you mean the right thing to do, Matt?"

"Look," he said. "No matter what happens, nobody has to know you were with me. If you want to lie about this for the rest of your life, you can. I'll never tell about you. You have my word."

"Your word?" Claire shrieked, then lowered her voice. "Your word? Can you hear yourself? If you get caught for this, it will only be a matter of time before I'm caught too. It will destroy my family."

"Not if I confess," he said. "Not if I say it was me, that I was alone."

"And why would you do that? Can't you hear me? They don't have anything! What is going on with you? What don't I know?"

Matt shook his head, rested his chin against his drawn-up knee.

"Claire," he said. "It's not like you know me at all, actually."

Claire felt as if she might be sick again. She wondered how she'd get the strength to run home, how she'd pull herself together before she got back. It was true; she didn't know him at all. And that was terrifying.

"What about Lib and Jack? Have you thought about them?" she asked. Jack had hinted at some discord, though he hadn't said much. But certainly Lib's son showing up in their lives had to cause some wrinkles. "It's a big deal, you know, you coming here. Don't you want to build a relationship with them? Confessing would destroy any chance of that. And you're driving Lib's truck, for Christ's sake! She could be . . . booked as an accessory or something!"

Matt smiled. "You watch a lot of TV," he said.

"Why are you so calm about this? What is wrong with you? You obviously aren't thinking clearly. And you're going to destroy us both!"

"I'm thinking clearly," said Matt. "Look, I don't know what I'm going to do yet, so just relax. And I don't expect you to get it, but . . . I'm sober for the first time in my life. I know I told you I was before, but all I can say is I didn't really get it either. Now I do. And as far as I can tell, if I want to have any chance of staying this way—which I think in my case actually means staying alive—then I have to be rigorously honest."

Claire would have laughed if she wasn't so furious. So a few weeks of supposed sobriety, and apparently he was a saint? She dropped her head back in disbelief, saw the clouds spin past, and grew dizzy, put her head back down between her knees. She didn't want him to build a relationship with Lib and Jack. She wanted him to leave town and disappear from their lives altogether.

"There are a lot of different ways to be honest, Matt," she said, and he laughed.

"I can't imagine living the rest of my life carrying this secret around, Claire," he said softly. "Looking over my shoulder. Worrying I'll slip up. I'm gonna be forty next year. Maybe it's time to grow up."

"You'll go to jail," she said.

"Maybe. But I'm honestly not sure how different it would feel at this point than living with this secret, lying my teeth off in meetings, waiting for more shit to go sideways like I have all my life."

Claire couldn't think how to respond to that. She pawed around at the ground, trying to find just the right rock, just the right words to pick up and hurl at him. Came up empty.

"Matt, I'm afraid to say it out loud, but I'm almost certain we're free of this. You're free."

"That's the thing, Claire," he said. "I'm not."

Chapter 18

The morning after her strange conversation with Matt in her bedroom, Lib waited in bed for hours until after she heard him leave. He took his sweet time readying himself for work, as always, and if he was worried about her late rising—or even noticed it—there was no sign of it. Her bladder felt about to blow, pressing painfully against her pelvis, but she couldn't risk a single squeak of the floorboards. Even after the truck pulled away, she lingered a few extra minutes just to be sure.

Then Lib rocketed from bed and headed straight for the bathroom. Once relieved, she could think a little straighter. She didn't want to put words to what she feared, couldn't have anyway if she tried. Her anxiety felt alive but vague, like yet another ghost trailing her. The one thing she knew for sure was that she needed to be alone and think.

She skipped breakfast, hopping down the front steps and out into the fall morning, still cool. The grass was too wet to cut, though it badly needed mowing. When was the last time she'd run the tractor through? Just more evidence she was out of rhythm, not that she needed any more. Problem was, she'd lost her will to care.

"Always been alone; gonna die alone," she grumbled, heading out toward the back shed and the prairie bed. Even as she said it, she could hear how ridiculous she sounded. How she loathed self-pity, the bosom buddy of arrogance, each sucking the oxygen from the room in equal measure. Lib knew she was going to be fine, whatever happened. She just needed some time with the dirt. It would do her good, just as it always had every time she couldn't remember how to take care of herself. She'd come around. Very few things could be counted on in this lifetime, but the way the earth kept regenerating itself was one of them.

But instead of lying down among the prairie flowers as planned, Lib swerved toward the old granary shed where she'd kept the Toyota before Matt had borrowed it. What she suspected nibbled gnatlike at her eyes, annoying, persistent, uncomfortable. She couldn't put off finding out any longer. She'd spent all of last night obsessing, putting two and two together and coming up with six and nine and forty-three, and she needed to start canceling out possible equations. She stood a long time contemplating the heavy slider door, weather-worn and imposing. Took a deep breath, squared her hands against the side rim, and pulled.

A car, where an empty space should have been. Four wheels squatting there on the dirt floor, headlights peeking from beneath the tarp that usually covered Lib's pickup. Slowly, she lifted the corner, understood the impact before she even laid eyes on the damage.

"Oh," she breathed. "Oh, Matt."

Lib backed slowly out of the garage. She hadn't expected to solve it so quickly. To confirm the worst of it without some sort of confrontation or long drawn-out hunt. She moved to pull the door shut again, then stopped. Stood there, waiting, listening for directions from inside herself. She had a choice to make.

Which type of liar are you? Jack's voice reverberated inside her skull. She thought about nature versus nurture and all the things she'd never had the chance to impart to Matt. But everybody knew DNA was a powerful thing. She thought of a documentary she and Jack had once watched about twins separated at birth, raised thousands of miles apart, who ended up with identical handwriting, the same unique limp. Had her big lie been unavoidable all this time, something embedded in her cellular makeup? Just as she might have passed on Mama's alcoholism, had she passed her own inability to tell the truth down to her only son?

Now that it's out, do you wish you could go back? Matt had asked her.

Lib brushed her hair back from her face, then carefully braided it into a strong, thick cord, all the while staring at those guilty tires in the dirt, the treasonous door of the shed a mouth gaping as if it had had no idea. *Better close this door, Libby.* She fixed the bottom of the braid with a tie from her wrist. She pressed her palms to her chest. Waited for the heat.

And when it came, she knew.

She would go to Jack, and she would tell him about Matt. And, this time, she would say the rest, she would use the word—*I was raped, that's why*—and it would hurt like hell, but it would be okay.

But only if she stopped this madness right here, if she made the right decision now.

The open shed door waited.

"No," she said, turning back toward the house, leaving it yawning open for the world to see what it had been hiding. Come what may, Lib had no intention of hiding or running away from anything ever again.

~

Jack spent the morning catching up in his shop. There'd been a small logjam of projects, folks waiting on one thing or another, but he'd put his own life on the back burner since Charlie's accident. Now something about the big shake-up with Lib had loosened his insides—not to mention the relief of finally getting his hands on the boy's bicycle—and when he'd woken this morning, he'd felt more like himself again. What was stuck had come unstuck.

Larry Ripon's ATV was dead, and the man had been to the library Googling again, and he wanted Jack to look at the electric starter before he caved and took it into Ritchie's Small Implement. Nan across town liked to blow her leaves the first sign of them, and she already was having trouble with the thing, probably a simple spark plug issue. Jack figured he'd head out to Larry's to take a quick look, pop over and pick up Nan's blower, then swing by Mike's for the plug on the way home. It felt good to realign himself on his familiar grooves, and Jack even found himself whistling again.

Things went as expected at Larry's: they hovered and clucked; Jack made suggestions; Larry fought him on every one. In the end, Jack suggested Ritchie's was the man's best bet and left him to it. Nan had the blower propped against her mailbox so that was easy enough to pick up. He was just pulling up to the hardware store when he saw Mike outside—with Lib's son, of all people. Like the universe had caught wind that he was feeling better and decided to mess with him a bit more.

Jack let the truck idle, watching. The two of them looked as if they were having an argument of sorts, which was unusual; Mike was one of the calmest, easiest-going fellas Jack knew. Was that what Matt did? Went around making things harder for folks? Screw it. Last thing he needed. This was not his problem to solve, and the pleasant high from making actual progress on his own issues still lingered. Jack pulled back out and headed for home. The spark plugs could wait, and it was about time to go to Charlie's anyhow.

"Jack's here!" yelled Charlie from the front stoop as Jack pulled up in the truck. Apparently he was out practicing on his crutches. Jack grinned at him. Claire appeared behind him, dressed again in her running clothes. Good for her. She'd been looking pretty rough lately, especially at dinner the other night. He didn't know much about alcohol problems. Never had a taste for the stuff himself. But he'd lived in Wisconsin all his life—drinking capital of the country—and there was just a certain energy about certain people, and he could feel it with Claire. If she was struggling with more than this accident, then picking up running again might be just what she needed. Who knows, maybe they were all getting back on some kind of track.

"Charlie wants to practice using his crutches outside today," said Claire as he approached. "Please don't let him do anything crazy. I agreed to fresh air, not a marathon."

"I have never cared about running in my life," said Charlie, teetering as he kicked up a walnut with one of his crutches, and Jack laughed.

"Charlie, you and I can sit a spell. Let's leave the running to your mother."

"It's good for my head," said Claire. "I won't be long."

"You go. We're fine here," said Jack. Claire blew them each a kiss and loped away.

"I thought that woman would never leave," Jack said, grinning over at Charlie—but Charlie had one crutch held high over his head, and he flung it in the direction his mother had run. Then he took the other and started banging on the sidewalk, in the process tipping himself to the ground.

"Hey, hey, hey." Jack rushed to him, gathering the boy more safely into the grass, taking the crutch away. "I didn't mean to offend you. It was a joke. *Your* joke, in fact."

"She's a joke," Charlie choked, and then the boy was full-on crying.

Shocked, Jack fussed there beside him, alternating between mopping at his face with his handkerchief and squeezing his shoulder. "What on earth is going on? Did something happen?" he asked, but Charlie only cried harder. Jack wondered if he should take off after Claire, wondered how to handle whatever this was.

Then, as quickly as it had come on, the crying jag ended. Afraid to make a sound, Jack returned both crutches to the boy, helped him to his feet. Watched as he paced back and forth in the driveway, back to practicing. Jack didn't know what had specifically vexed the boy so, but he felt it in his own old body: a bone-weary sadness. This had to be some kind of delayed response, maybe even a more natural one, to the trauma the child had endured. Of course he'd thought about how strange it was that Charlie seemed almost unperturbed about what had happened to him—clearly, there was more going on beneath the surface. In a way, it was a relief.

"Charlie, you've been through a lot," Jack said, but Charlie was silent, save for the occasional hiccup and the click-clack, click-clack of his crutches against the sidewalk. Jack watched the little boy's back, shoulder blades working hard like baby bird wings. Then, without stopping, he spoke.

"So, now that you actually have a kid, are you gonna move in with Lib?"

Jack blew out his breath. He'd been expecting something else, something more to do with Claire.

"Well, I wouldn't really call him . . . he isn't exactly my kid. He's not even a kid at all," Jack stammered.

"Do you like him?" Charlie asked.

"I don't really know yet," Jack said honestly.

"Well, I don't," Charlie said in a harsh tone Jack had never heard him use before.

"I guess I didn't realize you'd spent any time with him," Jack said, certain that Charlie couldn't have, in fact. When would that have happened? Jack had been with him every day. The boy was housebound, for Christ's sake. Was he jealous?

"It's just a feeling," Charlie muttered, wedging the padded tops of the crutches beneath his armpits as he stopped to adjust his glasses. "Anyway, it's so cool that you got me my bike, but I can't even ride it." At this his little voice rose again, and Jack rose too, sidled over and put his arms around the boy. Charlie began shaking against Jack's embrace, and he felt his own eyes well in response; for the boy, for himself.

"Charlie, I know it doesn't feel like it right now, but this awfulness will pass," Jack tried.

"I'm sorry I said that about my mom," Charlie blurted into his chest. "She's not a joke."

"Oh, I know that, son. We all get mad. Especially, I think, at the people we love the most."

"You don't," Charlie said.

"Well, now that's not true at all," Jack said, returning to the ground, encouraging the boy to join him, but Charlie went back to pacing, click-clack.

"You want to know a secret?" Jack said. "Something I haven't told anyone else in the world?"

Charlie nodded, wiped his nose into his armpit.

"I'm mad as hell at Lib."

Charlie stopped, his eyes widened.

"Madder than I've ever been at anyone in my whole life."

"At your own wife?"

"At my own wife. Imagine how terrible that feels."

"What'd she do?"

"Well, she didn't tell me about Matt. I had no idea he existed."

"You asked her and she lied?"

"Well, no." Jack frowned. "I never thought to ask her. What would I have asked her? 'Hey, woman, do you have a secret son you're not telling me about?'"

"Excuse me, ma'am," Charlie said, using that voice of Jack's again, doing a little swoop with his hip that apparently implicated a courting man. "You seem like a nice lady. Wanna get married? By the way, have you murdered anyone?"

Jack chuckled. Charlie crutched over, maneuvered to the ground with Jack's help. Jack nudged into the boy; he nudged back.

"Well, that settles that thesis, then," Charlie said.

"How's that?"

"A lie is still a lie even if you never said it out loud."

"Oho," Jack said, letting that sit.

"So, are you getting divorced?"

"No! I mean, I don't think so." Maybe it was a symptom of an unconventional marriage, but the word *divorce* had never occurred to him. It was a label for other folks, not them.

"Are you mad at Matt too?"

"No, of course not."

"Is Matt mad at Lib?"

"Well, I don't really know that either," said Jack, considering. He hadn't thought too much about what this had been like between Lib and Matt, he realized, and he felt a little ashamed. Pretty tricky, he supposed. Of course it was. *Oh, Lib*, he thought, despite himself.

"Maybe he should just be happy he's got his mom back," said Charlie. "And also that he got another dad out of it. Usually divorce means you can't see one of your parents ever again."

"Is that so, you think?" asked Jack, frowning.

"For sure," said Charlie.

"I don't think that's quite right. I think plenty of folks get divorced these days, unfortunately, but they share the kids. The court makes it so."

"Do you know any?"

"Well, sure."

"Who?"

Jack couldn't think of a single example just then, but he grew gravely worried. Were Claire and Dan discussing divorce? Were they arguing when Jack wasn't there? Was Charlie hearing things? How much more could the boy take right now?

"Charlie, listen. I've got a game," Jack said, thinking fast, remembering a conversation he'd had once with Lyle, of all people, after Jack's dog had died, before he'd taken in Tinker. God, he'd been miserable over that sweet old soul, loved him like a person—a depth of feeling he'd confessed only to Lib, who'd been sympathetic but hadn't quite understood, and Lyle, who'd surprised him in a way that actually helped. "Let's rewind to before this terrible thing and pretend it never happened. Tell me everything that's good about your life. Name something you love."

"Science," he said, slapping at his cast.

"Good," Jack said, slapping his own thigh back. "What else?"

"My bike, of course," Charlie said.

"Absolutely," Jack said. "Science, your bike, what else?"

"I love my mom," Charlie said, clearly still feeling guilty. "And I love my dad."

"Excellent choices," Jack said. "What else?"

"Frogs. Bridges. The Opera House. Climbing high. Dreams when I get to fly. Hot chocolate and whipped cream," Charlie said, smiling now, sounding like his old self.

"Good! Anything else?"

"Well, you," Charlie said, a little sheepishly, sending him a small smile. Jack closed his eyes, nodded.

"Absolutely. Now, are you ready? Get this—everything you just said? Accident or no accident, it's all still true."

Charlie wrinkled his little nose, and Jack waited, a little shyly, hoping it struck the boy the way it had him when Lyle had accidentally astonished him in precisely this way all those years ago. He didn't know if Lyle had meant the idea to be so profound, but it was. This was too: Charlie's broken bones would heal; his young age would work in his favor and time would work its magic; and all the things that were good in his life would still be there for him to enjoy. Not bad, Lyle. Not bad, Jack Hanson.

"I don't get it," Charlie said.

"What don't you get, son?"

"I don't get why that's a game."

"Well," Jack said, then couldn't think what else to add.

"Can we go in and play Pass the Pen now? Charlie asked, but he was noticeably light again, dimpled and glowing with sweat and late-afternoon sun. Jack nodded, not really hurt. He'd clearly helped the boy. And he was making sense to himself too. He'd made himself feel better.

Inside, settled in next to Charlie in front of the TV, he imagined Lyle sitting there with them. *Let's pretend none of this ever happened*, ghost-Lyle said. *Tell me everything that's good about your life.*

Except, instead of *life*, Jack heard *wife*.

He thought about Lib, before. Everything he'd believed about her, before all this. That she was the most beautiful woman he'd ever laid eyes on. That her hair contained so many nuanced shades of silver that it honest-to-God glittered in the moonlight. That she was somehow both the strongest and the softest—and most definitely the smartest—woman he'd ever known. That she'd been through a lot, but she wasn't mad or resentful. He liked helping her, because she never asked. She was curious about the same things he was. They had their adventures, and he always liked having her along better than being alone. She let him have his puzzles. She didn't make a big deal out of every little thing. She made things grow. She took an entire house and rebuilt it from scratch. She laughed easily. She brought him treasures, always surprised him—even when the surprise was a terrible one, he allowed. Even now.

Well, Jack, ghost-Lyle said as Charlie stared at the TV, unhearing. *Isn't that all still true?*

~

Claire had meant it when she said to Jack that running was good for her head, though she hadn't been thinking of it that way until she said it out loud. Dan was driving her crazy, either pressuring her to spend her days making sure the police were doing their jobs (then criticizing her for doing it differently than he would have) or ignoring her entirely, off to yet another late meeting or lost in his phone. And yesterday's run to meet with Matt had been disastrous, but today she just wanted to be free, and if she couldn't find that feeling in alcohol, maybe she could find it on the road. Being outside, especially without headphones or her cell phone, gave her the sense that time was on pause, that she was invisible, and that's what she needed more than anything right now. She wasn't delusional; she knew the walls were closing in. Tomorrow was a train barreling toward her down the tracks, but today she was still alive. Today, they still didn't know who she really was or what was going to hit them. Today, she could still pretend she was a good person, that she still had time to become someone better.

There could be no more outrunning the truth: she had said she wouldn't drink and then she did. She'd failed the simplest test, despite the highest stakes, and she couldn't make sense of it, and she didn't want to anymore. She was exhausted just from thinking about alcohol, hungover or not. She'd grown so weary of her constant deliberations, her own rhetorical questions. Yes, she could stop at two drinks (one of her remaining litmus tests), but the unspoken rest of that answer was this: she'd spend the rest of the night pissed off about it, passing time until the next day when it was time to try only two drinks again.

She'd made up so many little games over the years—*I will only drink on weekends, I will only drink if everyone else is, I will only drink if I work out first*—and she'd lost every one of them, and nobody else even knew she was playing. Maybe she hadn't gotten into the same sorts of trouble as Matt, maybe she wasn't dancing on bars or falling drunk off her barstool, maybe she didn't drive with Charlie in the car—did she?—but she absolutely thought about alcohol all the time, and that was the crux of it. She loved her booze like a person, like a friend. Like the best friend she'd ever had.

Just barely at the border of town, Claire spotted a power walker coming toward her in the distance. Lib, she realized, even though her hair was pulled back. She recognized her purposeful stride, the inherent power in the swing of those arms. Could Claire ever make it on her own like that? Could she live alone, with no one to reflect herself against? *Not in a million years*, she thought. Who was she, if not theirs?

Faking what she felt had always worked for her in the past. That was the thing about marriage or any prolonged stretch of time with another person: if you just waited out whatever you were feeling, the natural ebb and flow of life took over. One day you absolutely loathed the person you had married, fantasized about murder as you watched him chew his Cheerios open-mouthed. Other days you caught him side-eyeing you as your kid did some amazing thing or another, and it hit you that no one else on the planet felt precisely the same way you two did about the child you'd made together—a connection so strong it had to be love.

But the other awful truth was that things were not going well with Dan, despite her best, most frantic efforts. After that godawful sex the night before last, she'd silently cried herself to sleep beside her snoring husband and woken paralyzed with disgust. It wasn't just the unplanned hangover or the distance between them—this out-of-sync living wasn't new. What was new, different, was that she was feeling it so acutely now, her loss of self, her loss of control. The growing fear, his growing disdain. And she'd been so worried about how unfair it was to Dan that she didn't love him the way she should, the way he deserved; now she was starting to realize it was unfair to her too. At the very least, unsustainable.

Now she admitted it: She played a role in their unhappiness. In the numbing out she'd experienced maybe even as far back as giving birth to Charlie, spending her days changing diapers instead of red-inked copy. She probably had put an unreachable distance between them when she'd refused to have a second child, despite their original plans for three or four kids, the dreams they'd discussed from that sunken mattress in their second apartment, back in Wrigleyville. She probably had been living in a bubble of her own making, fortified by the vodka and wine that provided just enough protection from everyone's expectations and judgments. The question was, even if she could manage not to blame Dan for her misery moving forward, how could she possibly undo all the damage now?

She watched the stronger woman approach, her mind filled with shameful questions she'd never dare to breathe. *Do you think it's possible to love your child but hate being a parent? Which is worse, a broken home or a broken mother? Now that Matt found you, do you think you'll just know how to be a mom?* Claire was the one who needed the therapist, not Charlie. Maybe when she talked to the insurance company again, she'd check into it for both of them.

And though she could no longer comprehend what she'd ever seen in Matt, there was no denying that she missed the way she'd seen herself when she was with him. *That's all I want*, Claire thought, slowing her pace as Lib neared. *To be seen.* And how was that possible, wanting so badly both to be seen and to be invisible? How did Lib handle all her alone time? How did she know for sure how much she mattered to Jack? How did she know who she was at all?

"Hello," said Claire, and Lib came to a stop before her, as if they'd planned it. As though the two of them had set out to meet each other at a designated time and place, though of course they hadn't. Lib crossed her arms, and Claire felt herself do the same.

"Were you coming to see me? Or Matt?" Lib asked, and Claire was so taken aback by the question that she felt her mouth drop open, her arms slip back to her sides.

"No, just . . . out for a run. If you're looking for Jack, he's back at my place with Charlie," she said, and Lib nodded.

"I need to talk to you about something anyway," said Lib. "It's bad."

Claire felt her blood stop its flow, freeze in place in her veins. *He fucking told her after all.*

"I'm just gonna say this. I think Matt was involved in Charlie's accident. I can't say for sure, but I believe it's so. And I want you to know I am going to help you, whatever's next. I feel responsible. I'm sorry, Claire. I didn't know. I'll go to the police right now with you if you want. I shouldn't have hidden him, but it was never my intention to aid and abet an actual crime."

Claire blinked back at the woman. She was so self-assured, so matter-of-fact. And only half-right.

"I don't . . . I don't understand. Did . . . did Matt tell you this?"

"No, but he's said a few things that gave me pause, and then this morning I found his car."

"His car," Claire repeated.

"Under a tarp in the shed where I usually keep the truck he's been driving. He told me it was a rental and that he'd returned it. Now, why would he lie about that?"

For the first time, Claire detected a tremor in the older woman's voice. That's where he'd hidden the car? On his own mother's property? Was he trying to get caught?

"I don't understand," she whispered again. Her mouth felt dry, tasted salty.

"Of course you don't. I'm sorry. I shouldn't have just blurted it out like this to you," said Lib. "I don't know what's gotten into me. I'm not much for drama. I was on my way to find Jack. I know we don't know each other like that. I shouldn't have just laid this on you, especially when I don't know for sure what's going on. My son has . . . alcohol problems. Certain struggles. I just don't know if . . ."

The two women stood facing each other, neither moving. Claire wanted to run but there was nowhere to go.

"I don't know what to do," said Lib. "That's the truth. I don't know what to do, and I need Jack's help. I need . . . Jack."

This is her son, Claire realized. Lib was turning on her own son. Could she ever imagine doing the same to Charlie? No, she'd protect him at all costs.

"But how do I protect him now?" said Claire, aloud, before realizing she'd done so.

"Protect him? You want to protect Matt, after knowing all this?"

"No, I meant . . . No. I don't know."

"It's probably just shock," said Lib. "I've shocked you. Let's . . . let's just walk together to your house. Is that okay?"

Claire felt Lib place a hand on her lower back, the way Dan used to, and something in her melted on the spot. She let the older woman turn her around, and Lib kept her hand there as they walked together. It was such a tender intimacy. Claire felt an avalanche start to release inside her. Everything she'd been holding onto, everything she'd been trying to direct and drive, it all fell apart.

"Wait," she said, crumbling, crumbling. "Lib, wait."

The two women stopped again, and Claire felt the question burble up from an unexamined place.

"How much does Matt drink? I mean, have you seen it? How many drinks does he have? When does he do it?"

Lib frowned back at her, searching her face, as if deciding something.

"Well, the way he's explained it to me, it's not really about how many drinks he has or how often. He says it's about the first drink. He says, 'One drink and my brain lights up like a pinball machine.'"

Claire's legs gave out, and she slid slowly to the ground. She felt Lib's hand run up her upper back, brush the back of her neck and up the crown of her head as she slipped out of the woman's grip. Lib squatted down beside her, then settled back onto her butt, cross-legged. They sat there in the road, facing each other, knees touching.

"I was in the car," Claire blurted out.

"What?"

"You're right about Matt, but he wasn't alone. I was with him. We were drunk. I was drunk. I hit my own baby. I ran away. I mean, I didn't know it was him when we left—I never would have left if I'd known it was him. I made a huge mistake, but it's over, and he's okay, but now Matt is gonna tell, or you are, and if you do, I'm gonna lose Charlie and Dan forever and probably Jack too, and the whole town will hate me, and we'll probably go to jail, and I have no idea how to get out of this, and I'm terrified, Lib. I'm scared to death." She was sobbing now, big, choking, slobbery hiccups, so hysterical that she couldn't have said the next part out loud, even if she'd wanted to: *And me too. My brain lights up like that too.*

"My God," said Lib. "Oh my God."

"I don't even care about any of it anymore, I swear. I'd go to jail if I thought it would make a difference, let Dan divorce me, all of that is survivable. But the thing I cannot live with is Charlie knowing. He can't know, Lib. He can't know. He can't know."

Lib breathed out, long and slow, rubbing her hands all over her own body, clutching at her thighs and arms.

"Please help me, Lib," said Claire, and Lib stopped. She looked a long moment at Claire, so long that Claire thought she might have actually disappeared. That all those years of tiptoeing and starving and secret drinking and shrinking into herself in the dark and negotiating pieces of herself away might have finally added up to some sort of cosmic smiting and poof: she was invisible, at last.

Then Lib reached out and put her hands on Claire's shoulders. She began to swoop down in long strokes, rubbing Claire's arms, then her bent legs, then her hair, her face. Claire closed her eyes against the woman's hands, silently weeping as she worked. She had never been touched in quite this way before, and there was only one other thing that had ever made her feel so safe, so loved, so seen, and she knew it was her wine, and she knew she'd have to give it up for good this time. And she had absolutely no idea how she would replace it, or survive the loss. Nor did she have any idea how to describe what was happening beneath Lib's touch, but she would have given anything, in that moment, for this feeling to never, ever stop.

Lib did stop, then, and Claire thought it was over—but the older woman took Claire's hands in her own, brought them to her mouth, and breathed hot air into them. She watched, as though in a trance, as Lib pressed Claire's own hands to Claire's own sweaty stomach. Lib placed her hands on top of Claire's and held them there, closing her eyes.

Claire closed hers, too, and waited as the warmth spread.

~

Jack and Charlie were still watching TV in Charlie's bedroom when they looked up to see Claire and Lib standing together in the doorway. When he first saw his wife, even with all their nonsense right now, Jack felt that same tingly flash he always did when he laid eyes on her unexpectedly. But then he registered the strangeness of her being in this house she'd never set foot in before, saw how her face was drawn down over her high cheekbones and tugged into a tight frown, and a prickling chill dulled the heat he felt. He looked to Claire next to her, and she'd obviously been crying pretty hard, her pretty face all puffy, her pale skin blotchy. *Oh God.*

"What's going on?" asked Jack, standing. "What is it? Are you hurt?"

Lib opened her mouth as if to speak, then shut it again. Her scowl deepened, and she turned to Claire beside her. Claire looked from Jack to Lib, and then the two women stared at each other for a long moment. Jack tried to read what was happening but couldn't.

"Hells bells, ladies, what is it?"

Claire finally broke her gaze with Lib, looked down to her feet, and nodded, once.

Lib cleared her throat.

"Jack, let's talk outside," she said. He moved aside for Claire to take his seat, but she climbed into Charlie's bed beside him instead.

"Aw, Mom, come on!" Jack heard Charlie say as he followed Lib out the front door.

"What are you doing here? Is Claire okay?" said Jack, grabbing Lib's arm. He felt a static shock, and at his touch she pressed herself into his arms, and he didn't fight her, he just held her there, and they stayed that way for a long time, swaying. It was their first embrace in God knows how long. Her hair smelled of flowers and sweat, good old sweet Lib. *What are we even doing*, he thought, an expression he'd picked up from Charlie, who added the word *even* to most of his directives and opinions. *I'm tired of all this. I just want you.*

"I was on my way to tell you something when I ran into Claire, and the whole thing got worse," said Lib into his shoulder. "But what I really want you to know is that I was coming here already to find you. To tell you a truth."

"A truth," he repeated, nuzzling her crown.

"I know you love my independence most, but the truth is I need you," she said. "I need you, and I know you don't like that, and it's embarrassing, and I'm sorry."

"Jesus, Lib," he said, pulling away. "What does that even mean?"

"It turns out I'm not as independent as I thought," she said, swiping at her nose.

"Lib, you're supposed to need me. Independence isn't about need. It's about not holding anyone else responsible for your shit. It's about not making your happiness my job. You're right, you've never done that with me, and I love that in you. I wouldn't say I love it most, but it's right up there."

Lib nodded, sort of slow and dumb, and he wondered if it was possible they'd had a thirty-three-year misunderstanding.

"What's wrong with Claire?" he repeated.

"I was coming to find you and tell you something about me, and I'm going to, but first I need to tell you something about Matt," said Lib, pulling Jack down beside her to sit on the front step. "I found his rental car in my garage this morning, under a tarp. He told me he'd returned it."

"Huh," said Jack.

"But I don't know, it was kind of like a final straw or something. He's been acting strange, he's said a few things, and then . . . well, I thought he might be the one who hit Charlie. With the car."

"What?" said Jack, feeling his gut roll low and menacing.

"I thought he did it, and I wanted to tell you the truth and ask what to do."

"Wait, wait, wait," said Jack, his head a complete scramble. Matt hit Charlie? And covered it up? And had the audacity to sit through dinner with the boy, ask him impolite questions? Had the audacity to keep this secret while Charlie struggled to recover and Jack nearly died himself from the outrage and frustration of it all? It was about more than he could take.

"And you told Claire? That's what upset her? Is she in there telling Charlie now?" he said, rising, unsure if he was headed to protect Charlie, or kill Matt, or both.

"Wait, Jack, there's more," said Lib, pulling him back down. "I thought you might want to go to the police. And I'm willing to do that, even though it means my son will likely go to jail."

Jack looked at her then. Even after everything, he still kept forgetting that Matt was her boy. That maybe they'd had a lifetime of distance, but he was still hers, and she, his. *Still*, thought Jack, picturing Charlie in there with his mom, bearing this terrible news without him. *Still.*

"Jack. I ran into Claire on my way here, and I probably shouldn't have, but I told her. I told her, Jack. And . . ."

"And what?" he said, impatient now. What could be worse? Why was she dragging this out?

"She knew."

"What?"

"She knew, Jack. She was in the car. It's all true, and she was with him."

Jack clutched at his chest, where his heart seemed hell bent to bust. Flashed to the parking lot, Claire and Matt and the beer. My God, could he have stopped this somehow? If he hadn't been absorbed in his own drama with Lib? He stood up, staggered, and Lib flew up beside him.

"No, wait, Jack. I get it. I feel the same way, but think this through. Think what it would do to Charlie to know this. What it would do to him to have his mom in that kind of trouble, maybe even in jail."

Jack sank back down to the stoop. She was right. He imagined Charlie's little brokenhearted face. How much he was already struggling over a couple of broken bones. How could he possibly recover from something like that?

"This is insane," he breathed.

"If Claire decides to tell the truth, I'll help her," said Lib, her voice shaking. "I told her as much. Even if it means losing Matt. My son for hers. I'll do it."

Jack was panting, his flannel brushing rhythmically against his wife's long-sleeved T-shirt.

"If Charlie finds out his mom did this and that she lied about it, it'll wreck him," said Jack.

"I don't see how it wouldn't," Lib agreed.

"But at the same time, he deserves to know the truth," he said, looking over at his wife. "He deserves it."

"I agree with that too."

"Oh, Lib," he said, deflating, putting his arms around her again, feeling sorry for all of them, for her too. "What a thing."

He felt her stiffen, then soften, and then they were both finally crying. He kissed the top of her head over and over, sifting back through everything she'd just said. Each time coming up empty-handed in a different way, slippery grains of truth sliding right through his fingers.

"So," he said, pulling out his handkerchief, blowing. *One thing at a time.* "You came here to tell me you need me and to tell me the truth about Matt, even though it meant losing him."

"I don't want to lose either of you. But you were right, that stuff you said about taking the choice away from you. I never saw it that way, and you're right. I don't want to make choices without you, Jack. I'm tired of all this, and I just want to be with you, however that looks, whatever that takes. And I don't think this choice is mine alone to make."

"Not mine either, I suppose," said Jack, again picturing Charlie inside with Claire. He thought again of the conversation they'd just had, Charlie's latest thesis: *A lie is still a lie even if you never said it out loud.* The boy had no idea how prescient he'd been.

"You know the worst part?" said Lib, sounding small, just barely on this side of keeping it together. "I ruined Matt's life once, and now I'm set to ruin it all over again."

"Naw, naw, I don't think that's so," said Jack, putting his arm around his wife. "You didn't do this, Lib."

He knew that much, at least. At some point, a person's life was entirely his or her own.

"Jack," she said, taking his hands into hers. He couldn't help but notice how hot they burned. "There's one more thing. Something I should have told you a long time ago."

~

"Do you want to play our game? Make stuff up about people?" said Charlie, and Claire blinked at the ceiling, half-numb, still shaken. Jack and Lib had disappeared out the front door—God knows what they were deciding out there—and she'd climbed into Charlie's bed with him, as she'd taken to doing lately. He hadn't asked to play this game in ages, and she was as out of practice as she was out of sorts. Completely wrung out, barely able to put two thoughts together, let alone tap into her imagination. But his little voice was so earnest and sweet, cutting right through the messy rest into the core of her. This was the kind of moment that had always scared her, she realized. That this person she loved and admired more than anyone in the world might see right through her one day. That he would know she was not enough, that she had no idea what she was doing. But she would have done anything for him just then, anything at all, and so she took a deep, shaky breath.

"Okay," she said, muting the TV with the remote. She described the girl on the screen: "She's an orphan who has just been adopted, but she hates, absolutely hates, her new parents."

"Not because they're mean," Charlie said, "but because they have a terrible, terrible smell. Like, putrid."

Charlie giggled and shivered, snuggling into her, and her breath caught. He was making his voice smaller today, a little babyish, the way he did sometimes. She knew he could sense her sadness and that it brought out a kind of childishness in him, and she wanted to do better, as much as she secretly enjoyed it. She felt raw with love, exposed and vulnerable, as if every layer of her skin had been peeled back and pinned down, like those diagrams in his favorite field guide.

Charlie changed the channel.

"This guy has seven girlfriends, and he thinks they all love him soooooo much," Charlie said, making his voice high and airy. "But really he doesn't know they all formed a secret club, and they're about to vote him out."

She laughed, took the remote he offered, suddenly imagining the teenager he'd be in just a few short years. Would he lose his silliness? His sweetness? Did kids like this stay good, or was there a particular sort of goodness that was doomed in this world?

"Are you sad, Mom?" Charlie asked.

"I am," she admitted.

"I know another game," he said. "Jack taught it to me. It's for when you're sad."

"Maybe after a nap," she said, yawning. "Are you tired?"

Charlie yawned back reflexively, inhaling a bit of spit that turned into a snort, triggering a fresh round of giggles that caught her too. She indulged the laughter for a bit, then closed her eyes, pretending to sleep.

Would this ever come easier? Would Dan have bailed so quickly on this game, or would he have refused to take any moment with Charlie for granted? She worried that it wasn't in her, sober or not. That, especially as Charlie grew up, his disappointment in her would grow too. That it would become harder to pretend that she knew what was best for him, that she knew what she was doing, that she could be relied on not only for fun but for critical guidance. Most terrifying of all, that he would find out what she'd done to him.

She could never, ever survive losing him. That much she knew.

But then she felt his little fingers tickle hers, his small hot hand push into her own.

And so they lay that way, side by side, for an eternity. It might have been minutes; it might have been hours. Time sweetly suspended, afternoon sun slanting through Charlie's window, blanketing them both in buttery gold. Charlie fell asleep, snoring softly like a little squirrel, and Claire dozed too. She wandered in and out of wakefulness, exploring on her own time a world that somehow seemed less threatening, slower, more expansive. Every now and then, her body jerked her back to reality, then released her again, the sun like a sedative she'd swallowed, slowly churning through her, warming her from within. With the exception of Lib's hands on her earlier, she couldn't recall the last time she'd felt this relaxed while sober.

She was in a house. A different house, but hers. A fire burned in the belly of a brightly painted ceramic wood stove in the corner, a light haze of smoke curling up to a lofted ceiling. The front door and windows were framed in crisp white trim to match the snow that had just started falling outside, fat flakes already sticking to autumn's bones like a long-awaited meal. She felt clear-headed, clean. That she had everything she needed to guard against the elements. Charlie was in his bedroom, a different room with the same bed, and he was talking to someone, she wasn't sure who. She only knew it was not Dan.

Then she was outside, though she hadn't crossed through the doorway, and although all the houses and buildings looked unfamiliar, she knew it was still Anthem. Her senses sang. She could hear the exquisite groan of tires on freshly packed snow, smell the ice crystals prickling her nose from the inside out, shut her eyes against the vivid dazzle of a sky so blue and boundless it defied reality.

"You're free, Claire," she heard—Matt's voice?—and she felt it to be true, though she couldn't see who said it. She was completely alone as she ran, the slippery crunch beneath her shoes, so satisfying; the frigid air seizing her lungs, so alive. She turned corner after corner, each street decorated for a different season. She ran past jack-o-lanterns glowing from within, past stalks of corn bound to front porch pillars; she kicked through an avalanche of gourds spilling out onto the sidewalk. Rounding an avenue she'd never seen before, she ran right through Christmas. Thick green garlands drooped beneath the wet weight of snow, and a windsock Santa flailed in front of a cream brick house. Claire stopped, mesmerized by his boneless holiday waltz. She trudged across the front yard, frosty ice stinging her calves and ankles, her legs and feet suddenly bare. There, through the front picture window, she watched as Charlie squatted before a festooned tree, picking through piles of presents. He was safe and happy. But she could not go inside. This was Dan's house, it dawned on her, just as she tripped the alarm. "You, there!" said the same voice—Santa. "I see you."

Claire startled awake.

Charlie still slept, snuggled into her armpit, his sweaty hair plastered against one side of his flushed little face. Claire gently rolled him off her numb arm, pushing through her mind's cobwebs, grappling for the peace she'd found in the dream. What exactly had she been free of? Somewhere, the alarm still sounded.

It was her phone, she realized, ringing from the pocket of the belt she wore when she ran. She pulled it out, not to answer but to make it stop—then saw the restricted number and changed her mind.

"Hello?" she whispered, careful not to disturb her sleeping boy.

"Claire, it's Officer Nick," said the now familiar voice at the other end, giddy in a way she'd never heard it. "I've got some good news. There's been a break in your son's case."

Chapter 19

The snow fell earlier than Lib remembered it ever having come, covering the sleeping garden beds with a soft white coating that stuck, though it was only November. Lib stood at the kitchen sink, finishing up the last of the dishes she'd let lie from breakfast and lunch. Luckily, she'd gotten most of the winterizing done; the shrub roses and black-eyed Susans cut back. Extra mulch laid, hoses brought in, prairie burned.

The snow was light enough that she could use a broom to sweep the porch clear, which she'd done just before dishes, in anticipation of Jack's arrival. It was Wednesday night, and she was looking forward to spending an ordinary hour at the café. Simply sitting and sharing a made-from-scratch meal with her husband and a handful of people she now considered family. The only one who actually shared her DNA would be missing, of course, but that was temporary; a single season in a lifetime of seasons.

Matt had confessed. She still could hardly believe it, and for several mornings afterward, those were the first two words she'd think upon waking: *Matt confessed*. In doing so, he'd taken away from her the agonizing choice of whether to turn him in. And in a further twist that both comforted and confused Lib, he'd left Claire Taylor's name out of it entirely. He'd done it, he told the police, case closed.

After that, events moved with a dizzying swiftness uncharacteristic of the Anthem Lib knew. Matt did not even have a trial, as he'd been quick to make a plea bargain and take his lumps straight-up. Because of his past struggles with addiction, no other evidence beyond the car, and because the Taylors had written a victim's impact statement that called for mercy—something that still didn't sit quite right with Lib, relieved as she was—Matt was routed into a deferred prosecution path aimed at rehabilitation and minimal jail time. He was serving six months in county, and if he stayed clean for a full year after his release, his charge would be downgraded to a misdemeanor. It seemed remarkable, but Jack said the officer had told them that 98 percent of cases never make it to trial and that six months in jail for a nonfatal accident was considered a victory. Lib could hardly believe that, but what did she know?

"I'm actually looking forward to doing the time," Matt had told her, smiling across the visitor's table on her first trip to county. He was different somehow. Calmer. His face less bloated, his skin clearer, the whites of his eyes unmistakably brighter. He said it was the longest he'd ever been sober—"like, truly sober, not just dry." Said his sponsor had been pushing him pretty hard to confess, and Matt had started to think the man might even go to the police himself. "So much for anonymity," Matt had laughed, and Lib had listened for the old spite and sarcasm but found no trace of it. "Mike says anonymity isn't about privacy, it's about ego. And he says amends aren't about being sorry, they're about being different. And for the first time in my life, I feel like I finally know what all that means," he'd said, and she'd shaken her head back at him, still more skeptical of his recovery process than she cared to admit. But she was trying.

In private, Matt's confession was still a stone Lib turned over and over, though she was growing used to its smoothness and edges, its unique weight in her hands. She was hardly one to throw a stone anyway, glass houses and all. Copping to what he'd done was probably the right way, maybe even the only way, but she still couldn't say for sure that she would have chosen it for him or done the same in his shoes. Hadn't she decided on a different path entirely, all those years ago? Then again, her own reluctant, more recent confession had brought a lightness to her body she'd never felt before, and she would be hard-pressed to relinquish it at any price. So who was to say if she'd do it all differently now?

She'd finally told Jack everything. At the time, he seemed to have taken it in stride; said all the right things, insisted it didn't change how he saw her. Said if anything, it made him admire her more. That he just wanted things to go back to the way they were—but she still didn't know if they really could, on his part.

She'd catch him looking at her sometimes, maybe with pity on his face, or something darker. The heat between them hadn't cooled, but it had changed. There was a new tenderness to their lovemaking—but there was also something that sometimes felt to her like withholding. Was he imagining things he didn't want to see, things she'd never wanted to tell him about in the first place? Or was it still about the lying? Had her deceit really been that big to him that he'd never be able to get past it?

All these questions and observations were in her head, her gut. There were tiny dustups, such as the way he'd resisted when she'd told him she might like to volunteer with a rape crisis center—the idea had been Matt's, of all people—working the hotlines, being that voice at the other end. The training process would take four weeks. *Just to answer the phone?* Jack had said, which for some reason had wounded her deeply. He'd later apologized, encouraged her, even—not that she needed his permission; she'd already enrolled. First he tried telling her he'd been worried about losing that much time with her, which she just hadn't bought. Later he'd admitted he didn't think it was helpful for either of them to keep revisiting something so awful.

He'd been wrong. She loved the job; it made her feel better. In those calls she heard her own story told in different ways, over and over again, and she felt almost foolish now, that the fear of telling Jack had held so much power over her. That deep down she'd honestly believed herself ruined and hadn't even known she thought so, all these years later. As a result, she felt younger. At the beginning of something instead of at the end.

She didn't know if Jack would ever get it, nor how much it mattered to her whether he did.

At county, the waiting rooms were filled with families split into puzzle pieces, and Lib couldn't always correctly guess how they fit until the pictures formed in front of her. Her whole life, she'd thought of family as a father, a mother, and a set of kids. Even as an only child, she knew she'd never really be a part of anyone's family tree. Not even after she'd technically gained an extended family through marrying Jack—one he didn't feel a part of anyway—or attaching herself to Carolina and her girls. It was just something she understood about herself; her twisted, wayward roots, her missing branches.

But something about seeing all those families waiting on a loved one in jail, all the different ways people came together and stayed together despite the rending, had her viewing her own life through softer eyes. She was Lib, wife of Jack. Mother of Matt. Auntie of Frannie and Kit. Grandmother, even, of Charlie? Jack had certainly grown into a grandfather, almost as if he'd been one all along. Charlie seemed a part of her husband in ways no paperwork could ever define or annul. Maybe that was what made a family—what the right person brought out in you. Who you became with each other that you weren't, or couldn't be, alone.

Maybe the strangest responsibility of this new season was to carry a fresh secret that wasn't hers. To be part of something terrible with someone else, instead of by herself. Only she, Jack, Claire, and Matt knew the truth of what had happened that awful night, of Claire's unspeakable involvement in the accident. It wasn't as if they'd made a collective pact not to tell. A tacit agreement had materialized between them that each was free to do what he or she needed to do—which made Lib nervous, unsettled. Matt had obviously made his decision, and, for now, Lib was following Jack's lead. He'd concluded there were no immediate gains to be had in sharing this particular truth, and its certain casualties would be Claire and Charlie. And as far as Lib was concerned, they'd been through enough.

Then again, who could say how Charlie himself would change as he grew? He might even come to resent Matt, which would most certainly cause a rift between him and Lib, if not Jack. Lib worried that Claire had pressured the family into not pressing charges out of self-preservation or even some misplaced sense of loyalty to Lib. Or that

Charlie ultimately hadn't wanted to press charges because he was protecting Jack by protecting Lib, Matt's mother. That was childish logic—and Charlie wouldn't be a child forever.

Further muddling things, there was something going on at the Taylor house these last months. Rumors down at the café as to Claire and Dan's marriage and a third party, someone at the school where Dan worked. Not that Claire was some innocent, and whether she worked herself out wasn't really Lib's business. But she had felt the woman's missing heat with her own callused hands that day they'd met in the road. That sort of unsteadiness, that certain emptiness wasn't the sort of thing that went away on its own. The young woman had a tough path ahead of her, whichever way she decided to go. She seemed as though she could use a friend, but Lib was not that woman. She needed someone her own age. She needed a Carolina.

Lib hugged herself with hot wet soapy hands. The girls, at least Kit, seemed interested enough in pursuing a friendship with Claire. Maybe that would be enough. Truth was, it wasn't about Lib and Claire's age difference so much as the unfair responsibility Lib sometimes felt when she caught that look in Claire's eyes. The haunted questioning. Wondering if she'd gotten away with something, wondering if she really even wanted to. She'd have recognized that look anywhere, and it made her wildly uncomfortable. It depended, she supposed, on her mood. Some days she'd give of herself freely. Some days she'd need Claire to go it alone. Besides, she had her hands full with Jack's guilt. Not telling Charlie the truth still didn't sit with him, and every time she thought it was settled, he made some comment that made her worry otherwise. All of it left Lib in a tenuous position, giving what she could on a given day, but no more.

Last week, while Dan was at work, the four of them had gone together to the clinic for Charlie to get his cast off. He'd asked for Jack and only Jack to accompany him into the exam room, and so Lib and Claire had sat in the waiting room, side by side.

"I hate being back here," Claire finally said. Then, "I don't know if I can do this." And Lib had watched the woman's leg shaking. Sighing,

Lib reached for her hand. She placed Claire's hand on Claire's thigh, held hers on top just so, and Claire's leg stilled. Then the younger woman's stomach gave a long, low growl.

"You know, Claire," Lib had said, "maybe it's time to eat." What she didn't say, but thought, in Carolina's voice: *Maybe it's time to take up your space in this world without apology.* And Claire had doubled over anyway as though she'd heard it, just bent herself right in half in the vinyl armchair, whether in pain or relief or guilt or some other invisible assault, Lib couldn't say. Claire didn't speak again the rest of the appointment, but Lib kept her hand right there on Claire's hand, on Claire's leg, until Jack emerged with a triumphant Charlie, his own leg a ghostly shriveled prune, exposed but strong.

Lib dried her hands with the dish towel and plucked her wedding band from the new bowl on her sill. She'd placed the pink and blue swirled treasure here, a match to the one she'd given Jack this summer. His was perfect for the sugar, hers for the ring. When he'd given her the bowl last month, she'd known instinctively what it meant, even before she read the folded note he'd set inside, two words scrawled in his careful, familiar hand: *STILL TRUE.* It meant they were moving forward, just as they were. That she was his and he was hers, even if it didn't look like what other people had, even if there was no guarantee. For now they'd admitted they needed each other—more to the point, they'd admitted that it was okay to need each other. Everything between them had still happened, along with everything that had happened before they knew each other and everything still to come. His note had meant that Lib was still Lib, and Jack was still Jack. That he would probably keep choosing her. That she would probably keep choosing him. That they could use their matching treasures for different purposes, in separate spaces, together.

She slipped the band onto her finger. Even her house felt different to her now, yet again. Maybe she could add on, she thought, pulling on her barn coat and lacing up her boots. Maybe she'd extend its shelter to Matt, if he decided to stay in Anthem when he got out. Maybe even Jack, if he ever wanted that. She imagined the talk around town if they ever finally gave shacking up a try.

Or maybe she'd just continue to care for the house on her own; she the lone architect of its rooms, the sole keeper of its stories.

~

The truck sat idling at the base of Lib's driveway, exhaling puffs of sputtering heat, its occupants bent ever so slightly into each other's warmth. Jack watched the snow piling softly in front of the headlights, covering the tracks of everyone and everything that had come before. Next to him, Charlie breathed against the passenger window, drawing *C* after *C* into the fog. They had a surprise in store for Lib—Charlie's idea—and they were waiting at the bottom of Lib's driveway for Claire, who'd asked to meet them there on foot, multitasking by getting her run in.

"She should be here soon," Jack said.

"Yeah. Running clears her head," Charlie said.

"Mm-hmm," said Jack.

"Like biking does for you and me."

"Mm-hmm," Jack repeated, smiling.

"Better than drinking," Charlie said, and Jack held very still. Charlie had never said a word about this before.

"Well, I certainly agree with that," Jack said.

"She got a coin last night, she showed me. It says thirty days, but it isn't money. All of her friends rubbed it and blew on it and gave it good wishes, and then she put it in my hands and did the same thing."

"Well. That sounds nice."

"Sounds germy to me," Charlie said. "Did you know there are up to three thousand different bacterias on money at any time? Also why did they make a coin you can't spend?"

Jack felt himself mist up, and so he moved quickly to cover for himself, leaning in to tug on the paisley handkerchief he'd finally remembered to give him, the boy's very own to match Jack's. He wouldn't be needing one anymore this year, now that it had grown so cold, the fence finished and no real opportunities to work up a sweat. He wasn't sure if Charlie would use it anyway, but the boy had immediately tied it around his neck the way Jack did sometimes. Such a tiny neck, so fragile; Jack pushed the thought away, just as he had to too often these days when he couldn't stop thinking about how close he'd come to losing him. Jack couldn't help it, sometimes he drove himself crazy, either with images of Charlie in distress—lying in the ditch or any number of future disasters, such as falling from the Anthem water tower—or the resentment that burned like gut rot over the idea of the injustice the boy didn't even know he'd endured. Jack hated lying, knowing this thing about Claire that the boy didn't. But he'd finally found the one thing he hated more: seeing Charlie in pain.

Jack felt the truck jostle as Charlie leaned down to scratch his leg again, as he had incessantly since the cast had come off. After Charlie's big surprise for the ladies, they'd all be heading to family dinner at the café. Maybe it was the unexpected shift in season, maybe it was that Matt was serving his time and Charlie's casts were off, but—his private fits on the boy's behalf notwithstanding—tonight he was just happy to be sitting here next to this healing and excited little boy, on their way to a good meal with family. The night felt hopeful, full of possibility.

"Jack?" Charlie said, slowing his itch. "I have to make a big confession."

"Oh yeah?" Jack said, squinting through the flakes to watch for Claire.

"I lied. I saw Matt hit me with the car."

All at once, the air left the cab of the truck.

"I decided I had to tell you so you know I'm not a liar. Or not a liar anymore, after this one. But I don't want you to tell my mom. I want it to be just between us. I don't want them to take her away."

"Charlie," Jack wheezed, barely a whisper. "What do you mean, take her away? Charlie, what exactly did you see?"

"Please don't be mad that I lied," Charlie pleaded, and a shame as thick as the snowfall settled over Jack. He was the one who'd lied. He'd denied Charlie the dignity of the truth to protect him, and now Charlie was confessing the same?

"Charlie, I am not mad that you lied. Why did you, though?" Jack said, dreading the answer he already knew.

"My mom was with him," Charlie whispered. "Please don't be mad at her. Please."

"You're saying you saw her too?"

The little boy nodded, swallowed. Smeared the *C*s from the window with a tiny hand with bitten fingernails.

"In the road. I saw her streaky hair leaning out the side of the car, and I already knew she talked to him by that car all the time, because I watched them sometimes at the Save Rite from up in the Opera House. I told the ambulance guy that my glasses flew off, but they didn't. Can you believe they didn't? Centrifugal force is my current thesis. I threw them in the weeds before the ambulance got there. Is that a separate lie? I think no, I think it counts with this one."

"Oh, Charlie," Jack said. "Charlie, Charlie, Charlie. I can't believe you've been living with this and haven't told any of us. I can't believe you felt you couldn't. I don't know what to say."

"I knew I could tell you when I wanted to." Charlie shrugged. "I just wanted to wait until my mom was safe. And I didn't want to make you feel sad either."

Jack had probably never felt sadder. And safe? What a completely inadequate, indefinable word. Who among us was ever safe, no matter how many ways we sold ourselves out to believe we were?

"So you're not going to tell, right?" Charlie continued. "I know you don't believe in lying and you don't believe in secrets, but in this case if I kept the secret, I was lying, so now at least I'm not lying, and all you have to do is keep the secret with me."

"Charlie." *I can't promise you that*, he wanted to say. "Can I ask you something first? Do you think you'll ever tell? Are we just keeping the secret for now?"

"I don't know." He shrugged again. "I don't really want to talk about it."

Jack nodded, swallowed.

"Jack?"

"Yes, boy?"

"Are you sad?"

"I am." Jack swallowed, tugging at that handkerchief again. "But it's not your fault."

"How about we play a game?" Charlie said, pulling Jack's flannel shirt from the seat between them and covering himself with it like a blanket. "Tell me everything good about my life."

Jack let out the breath he didn't know he'd been holding, unclenched his teeth. Unbelievably, he laughed.

"You've got science," Jack croaked. "Your cast is off. Your bike is fixed. I bet there's hot chocolate and whipped cream at the café tonight. You've got a new bandana and my favorite shirt for a new blanket. Your mom loves you. Your dad loves you. I love you."

At this, Charlie grinned.

"I get the game now," Charlie said. "It's a good game, Jack."

Jack took another breath, then another; clenched and unclenched the wheel. He couldn't imagine not telling Lib this thing, or Claire, or even Matt for that matter. Carrying this secret was just as unfathomable as keeping the truth from Charlie had been. And yet, he was just now realizing that he'd never really been in control of that either. All of his decisions had been based on protecting Charlie, but Charlie had known all along.

"There she is!" hissed Charlie, pointing at the shadow of Claire running toward them in the dusk. Jack flickered his headlights and pulled his own handkerchief from his pocket, gave his nose one of the big honking blows that always sent Charlie into a fit of giggles—including now. So he blew it again, then again, letting Charlie laugh as Claire approached in the headlights.

"You sure you got it all?" Charlie teased, and though Jack had nothing left to expel, he took a deep breath in again and blew, anyway, for the boy.

First, they surprised Lib. Jack knew she'd been expecting only him and his truck, not this motley trio rounding the crest of the driveway; Claire jogging on foot, Charlie, impossibly, on his bicycle. "Lib!" Charlie hollered in Jack's deep voice, slipping and skidding up the snow-covered gravel. Lib let out a schoolgirlish giggle as she pushed through the front door, pulling it tightly shut behind her.

"Look at you on that bicycle, like the casts never happened! In the snow, no less!" she said, staring in wonder at the boy, and Jack knew exactly what she was thinking, because he was thinking it too: *Oh, the healing powers of youth and time.*

"Last week!" said Charlie, apparently forgetting that Lib had been there at the clinic with them, turning the bike again to ride down the driveway. "Look, I'm doing it! I'm doing it!"

"Careful, son," Jack cautioned, watching as Charlie came to a slow-motion skidding stop midway down. He couldn't tell if the boy's joy was an act—it seemed so genuine. Could both things be true? Could he really be okay? Would he always?

"We said he could try to ride from your place to the café if we followed behind in the truck," Claire explained, giving Lib a cold, sweaty hug in greeting. "It's probably a terrible idea, but you try telling him that."

"Quit worrying, you guys. What's the worst that could happen?" Charlie hollered, giggling maniacally as he rode off.

"Lord have mercy," Claire whispered, running after him. "Wait until Jack and Lib are in the truck, please!"

"Are you ready?" said Jack, reaching out a gloved hand to Lib.

"Ready as I've ever been," she said, taking it, then wrapping herself around the puffy thickness of his parka-covered arm, letting him hold her steady as he led the way down the driveway and into the warm puttering truck. At the bottom, they buckled themselves in and waited as Charlie wobbled into view ahead of them, the boy slowing every now and then to let Claire catch up as she ran. Jack put the truck in gear, and they slowly crept forward, beginning their long, slow parade to the café, the windshield wipers flapping at the gently falling flakes.

He considered his wife beside him. Her new lightness. She seemed younger to him in a way she'd never quite been, not even back when they'd first met. She was visiting Matt at the county jail three days a week, plus working that hotline, and that meant she wasn't as available to him as she'd once been. Or maybe that wasn't quite so. She was stingier with her schedule but freer with her spirit. Some of the solitary pursuits she'd protected throughout their marriage were open to him now; she didn't mind if he joined her for quiet reading time in her living room or weed pulling in her gardens. She laughed easily, and she hung on tighter when he held her, as if she'd been holding back ever so slightly all these years, just enough that he hadn't noticed until it all changed. Most of the time he was happy for her. She was "finally fully herself," she'd explained one night. But he hated what that meant about all those years they'd already shared: that he hadn't been enough for her to feel the way she did now.

He was still angry all the time—angry with Matt, angry in general, in a way he'd never struggled through before, but in a way that he trusted he would likely do something about. And he was no longer angry with Lib—at least, he didn't think so. How could he be, once she'd told him the whole truth? What her mother had let happen to her, what she thought she'd found in Jon Marlow. Why Matt hadn't been a blessing but evidence. But it still stung that she felt like she had to keep it all from him. That he'd somehow think less of her. That's what hurt the most, even still.

Then again, he supposed, he was about to keep something big from her too.

He was trying. Maybe the old Jack would have stayed frustrated and stubborn, focused too hard on the components that didn't quite fit, the mechanics of it all, but if he practiced paying attention to how she felt instead of obsessing over how she worked, they seemed to get along even better than they had before. Maybe this was what grace felt like. Maybe the very best things were too big and good to be understood. Maybe what was holy, by definition, couldn't be truly comprehended by mortal man. Maybe that was what he'd always sensed in the two of them, and in everything they held dear: that together they were so much bigger than the sum of their respective working parts.

Maybe he could do the same for Charlie—give a little more credence to how the boy felt than to what was right. And if the boy changed his mind, well, Jack could change his. Maybe there *were* varying degrees of lying. Maybe only the things that really mattered would ever stay true.

"Is he wearing your bandana?" said Lib, leaning forward to squint at the boy as he pedaled down the hill.

"My flannel and my wool cap too," Jack replied, clocking the flannel over the backpack atop Charlie's coat, the hat's oversized flaps winglike at Charlie's ears, the gifted bandana fluttering in the wind. Behind him in his blustery wake, Jack's oversized flannel billowed out like a cape.

"He really is something," Lib said.

As they drove, neither one could take their eyes off this extraordinary, ordinary boy.

He looked almost as if he were flying.

Acknowledgments

A gratitude list, in no particular order and not nearly effusive enough: Kathy Steffen, for her stack of worksheets that taught me it was possible. Eva Schutz, for that first plot party and indulging me all those bedtime readings of the day's new pages. Grace Schutz, who refused to read a book I'd written unless it was completed with an actual cover—more motivational than you know. Erin Celello (there really are no words) and Ann Garvin for The 5th Semester, for doula-ing this first draft and delivering countless pep talks. The incomparable Marly Rusoff, who fell in love, believed, tried. Peggy Payne and Michelle Wildgen, for convincing me it could be better and showing me how. The generous authors who read the manuscript and offered enthusiastic blurbs before they even knew whether it would be published: Susan Gloss and Nickolas Butler. Anna Schaal, for her nursing expertise. Those early close readers: Sarah Miller, Sara Nelson, Eliza Fournier, Sue Schutz, Jenn Ebbott, Helen McLaughlin, Carolyn Dingman, Jason Voelker—and especially my parents, Marc and Peg Ginsberg, who read every draft at least once and tell everyone they know that this is *the best book they've ever read*. Pence Revington, for teaching me it was all still true. Luis Alberto Urrea, for listening and looking me in the eye before scribbling, "Keep writing. Never stop. Wear the bastards down." Dennis Lloyd, Janie Chan, Sheila McMahon, Alison Shay, and the rest of the team at the University of Wisconsin Press, for all their hard work, seen and unseen, that finally made my first book real. Heidi Bell for forcing that last polish.

And Andy Q, my truest still. I don't think I'd have tried at all if you hadn't been so fiercely, insistently, unflappably sure—and that goes for more than just this book. See you at "home."